——————— ℘CR ———————

"Griffin has quilted together a wonderful, heartwarming story that will convince you of the power of love."

    -New York Times bestselling author Janet Chapman

"Griffin's lyrical and moving debut marks her as a most talented newcomer to the romance genre."

    -*Publishers Weekly* starred review

"A fun hop to scenic Scotland for the price of a paperback."

    -*Kirkus Reviews*

"Start this heartwarming, romance series!"

    -Woman's World magazine

"With the backdrop of a beautiful town in Scotland, Griffin's story is charming and heartwarming. The characters are quirky and wonderful and easy to feel an instant attachment and affection for. Be forewarned: You're likely to shed happy tears."

    -RT Reviews

"Ahhh, this series is my own little vacation to a land I love, even if the land in this series is a fictional Scottish fishing village where the men are braw, kilt-wearing, and have full respect for women."

    -Gourmonde Girl

"The best thing about this series is the way that it touches you as a reader. The characters are deeply written, with flawed characteristics that make them seem familiar – like real people that you know and see every day."

    -Ever After Book Reviews

"I dearly loved this romance, and I dearly love this series."

    -Book Chill

"Patience Griffin gets love, loss, and laughter like no other writer of contemporary romance."
-Grace Burrowes, New York Times bestselling author of the Lonely Lords series and the Windham series

"Patience Griffin, through her writing, draws the reader into life in small town Scotland. Her use of language and descriptive setting had me feel like I was part of the cast."
-Open Book Society

"Griffin has a knack for creating characters that I find engaging from the opening page. I love the Kilts and Quilts series."
-The Romance Dish

"I love Patience Griffin!! These Kilts and Quilts books are among my favorites EVER!!!"
-Margie's Must Reads

"Ms. Griffin paints a vivid picture of Gandiegow with the ever meddling members of the Kilts and Quilts. Fans of LuAnn McLane and Fiona Lowe will enjoy The Accidental Scot."
-Harlequin Junkie

(About *The Laird and I*) "I have read it. I'm reading it again. *laughing* It is like putting on your softest nightgown and slippers."
-Becky, a reader

"This author has a way of choking me up in parts and that does not happen a lot to me. If you are looking for a great series to fall in love with then I suggest you give this one a try."
-www.AHollandReads.com

""Patience Griffin seamlessly pieces compelling characters, a spectacular setting, and a poignant romance into a story as warm and beautiful as an heirloom quilt."
-Diane Kelly, author of the Tara Holloway series

————————— ෨෬ —————————

BOOKS by
PATIENCE GRIFFIN

———— ෨ඥ ————

KILTS AND QUILTS SERIES:
ROMANTIC WOMEN'S FICTION

———— ෨ඥ ————

From the author of It Happened in Scotland

Blame it on Scotland

A
Kilts and Quilts™
Novel

Patience Griffin

Kilts & Quilts
PUBLISHING

COPYRIGHT

ISBN 978-1-7320684-0-7

This is a work of fiction. Names, character, places, an incidents are either the product of the author's imagination or are used fictitiously, and any resemblance to actual person, living or dead, business establishments, events, or locale is entirely coincidental.

Published by Kilts & Quilts™ Publishing

For Kathleen Baldwin...
Writing is more fun with friends! Especially a wonderful friend like you!

For Sue, Carin, and all my Clan...
Your devotion to the Kilts and Quilts novels makes writing these books a joy. Thank you for being my book groupies!

PRONUNCIATION GUIDE OF NAMES

Aileen (AY-leen)
Ailsa (AIL-sa)
Bethia (BEE-thee-a)
Buchanan (byoo-KAN-uhn)
Cait (KATE)
Deydie (DI-dee)
Ki (KI)
Lios (lis)
Lyel (LI-el)
Moira (MOY-ra)
Ryn (ren)

DEFINITIONS

bampot—crazy person
biscuits—cookies
céilidh (KAY-lee)—a party/dance
chuffed (chuhft)—very pleased
dreich—gray dreary weather
fash—to trouble, worry, or vex over
fat quarter— a one-fourth yard cut of fabric, usually measuring 18" x 22"
Gandiegow—squall
horseshite—manure
nappy—diaper
Postie—postman
rad—radiator
shite—(shite) expletive

1

A LONG THE DARK ROADS of the Highlands, Tuck MacBride sped toward the small fishing village of Gandiegow, cutting it close...again. It wasn't as if he was doing it on purpose. His luck was, as such, he found himself in these predicaments more often than he liked.

He'd left the pub in Inverness with plenty of time to get back, catch a nap, and still help John Armstrong on his fishing boat today. But when Tuck had climbed into his auto to leave, he'd closed his eyes for only a moment before the long drive back to the village. He'd woke with a start with barely enough time to make it to Gandiegow.

He checked his watch again. *Oh crap!* He pressed down harder on the accelerator.

Inverness should've been fun, a diversion, but turned out to be just as boring as the last time, and the time before that. In moments like these—alone and in the dead of night—Tuck had to admit he had no real purpose to latch on to. Everyone mistakenly assumed he moved from place to place and from job to job because he was bored. They thought he longed for adventure, that he was one of those guys who enjoyed pulling up stakes to satisfy his wanderlust. They were wrong. He'd been running away for so long that it felt more natural *to go* than to stay.

His brother Andrew, Gandiegow's Episcopal priest, had an inkling of what drove Tuck to do the things he did—possibly the only one in the world who understood. Time and time again, Andrew urged Tuck to *be still* long enough for God to fill the void.

Horseshite. What did Andrew know? Life had always been easy for him. Aye, he was a good person and Tuck didn't begrudge him for that. It just wasn't easy for Tuck to be the older brother—though only by a year. At thirty-two, Tuck should be settled by now, like Andrew. But Tuck was different than his brother. Andrew hadn't suffered with dyslexia for his whole life. Trouble hadn't chased him as it did Tuck, despite Tuck trying to do the right thing. *St. Andrew*—Tuck had dubbed him that when they were kids—was perfect. The perfect child for their schoolteacher parents. The perfect Episcopal priest to tend his parishioners in Gandiegow. And most recently, Andrew had married the perfect wife, Moira. Andrew was the good sheep, and well, Tuck was the opposite. Though he didn't like it, he had no choice but to accept his darker role amongst the branches of the MacBride family tree.

If it wasn't for Andrew, Tuck would've picked up and been long gone from Gandiegow by now. Gandiegow might be the perfect place for some people to while away their life, but the village was too small to hold Tuck's interest. He'd tried, really tried to make a go of it and stay on the northeast coast of Scotland...*for Andrew's sake*. But from the start, it had felt as if the cards were stacked against Tuck.

Seven months ago, when he'd arrived in Gandiegow, Tuck had been ostracized for missing Andrew and Moira's wedding. Yeah, he'd cut it close then, too, and unfortunately missed the ferry off the

Isle of Lewis. Some might say he'd done it on purpose. And maybe he should've caught the next one to at least make an attempt. But he hated weddings. Wasn't it enough for everyone that he'd been willing to sacrifice his principles for Andrew and at least make an effort to attend his nuptials?

Tuck glanced in the rearview mirror as if seeing into the past and scoffed. Those sacred vows and the wedding registry weren't worth the paper they were written on. At one time, he'd believed in marriage—the binding of two souls. But that was before his heart had been betrayed and stomped on. Witnessing two people standing up in front of the kirk—willingly chaining themselves to each other—wasn't Tuck's idea of a good time. But out of deference for Andrew and his bride, Tuck had gone to the pub that night in Stornoway and raised a glass to Andrew and Moira. And instead of rushing to Gandiegow, Tuck had taken a short-term fishing job. Hindsight was a taunting bitch. If he'd known the consequence of not going right away, he may have done things differently. He didn't want to admit it, but deep down, he knew he'd crossed a line by not standing up with Andrew at his wedding. But eventually Tuck *had come* to Gandiegow and then stayed way beyond what was comfortable for him. Especially since everything had been bollixed from the start.

Being late this morning would only confirm Gandiegow's opinion of Tuck. He took the next bend in the road too fast, skidded a little, but the Almighty must've been rooting for him. He came out of the curve just fine.

Never in a million years did Tuck imagine Gandiegow would make such a stink about him missing the wedding. To them it was a capital crime. The townsfolk let him know from the start that he was lower than the mud on their work boots. And since then, Tuck had been accused of a lot of things—filching pies, stealing wellies from the General Store, and making off with the virtue of more than one woman in the village.

Okay, the part about the women might be somewhat true. But every lass he'd bedded had been willing. And he'd made it clear with each one, too, he would never come close to proposing marriage again. Sometimes, when he lay awake at night, he wondered at Andrew and Moira. Those two made marriage look easy. *And fun.* But Tuck wasn't kidding himself. He would never marry. His past had proved marriage wasn't in the cards for him.

"Good for Andrew and Moira," he said to no one as he rounded the top of a hill.

On autopilot, it barely registered there was a car sitting cockeyed in the middle of the deserted road, until he had to throw on the brakes. "Holy crap!"

Adrenaline flooded his system. He barely missed the stationary vehicle. His own auto slid sideways, nearly tumbling into the gulley before coming to a complete stop. For a full minute, Tuck couldn't pry his hands from the steering wheel as his headlights illuminated a field of spring barley. Finally, he looked over at the other vehicle.

He jumped out ready to give the driver a piece of his mind. But two steps from his vehicle, he saw a figure slumped over the steering wheel. He ran the rest of the way and yanked the door open.

"Thank heaven," said the man weakly as he lifted his hand. With his other hand, he clutched his chest and labored to breathe.

Heart attack—was Tuck's first thought. "Hold on there. I'll ring for help." He pulled out his mobile but had no signal. He cranked his head toward the road ahead and behind. No one was out. "Let's get you to the hospital." Tuck slipped his arm around the man's waist and eased him from the car, then supported him, rushing as fast as he could back to his own vehicle. After settling the man in the backseat, Tuck dug around in the glove box, found the first aid kit, and pulled out an aspirin. "Here."

The man opened his mouth and Tuck dropped the pill inside.

"Chew." Tuck wished he could sprout wings and fly over the curvy, hilly byways of the Highlands. "What's yere name?"

"Raymond."

"Okay, Raymond, I'll get ye there as fast as I can." Tuck U-turned in the middle of the road and tore off the way he'd come, heading back to Inverness, his worries of ten minutes ago now gone.

It seemed to take forever, but finally they made it to Inverness and arrived at the emergency room. The medical staff came to the rescue, maneuvering a gurney to the auto and hoisting the patient on it with practiced choreography. The man didn't look great, but there was gratitude in his eyes as he gave a weak wave to Tuck as he was wheeled away.

Tuck stood at his car, watching the emergency crew enter the hospital and then the doors closing behind them. He said a quick prayer—acting as if he was St. Andrew or something—that the man would be all right. As Tuck closed the car's back door, he noticed something lying on the floor. He reached in and pulled out a wallet, knowing it must've fallen from Raymond's pocket while removing him from the car.

Tuck trotted into the hospital and spoke with the nurse behind the reception desk. "Can ye tell me how Raymond is doing? The one they just wheeled in here with a heart attack?"

"Are ye family?"

"Nay. But I found him while driving back to Gandiegow."

"Sorry," the nurse replied. "I can't. Privacy laws."

"Here." Tuck handed over Raymond's wallet. "Can ye make sure that he gets this?" Tuck gave his own name and information, ex-plained again which patient, and watched as the nurse wrote everything down.

Mentioning Gandiegow to the nurse reminded him of his com-mitment to be on John's boat. As he walked from the hospital, Tuck pulled out his phone and called John's number. No answer, which meant John had already pulled anchor and was out to sea. Next, Tuck tried the satellite phone on the boat, but John didn't pick up then either. *He's probably pulling a net.* Tuck pocketed his phone, slid into the driver's side, and started the engine.

As he put the car into gear, the adrenaline rush began to fade. He'd never know whether Raymond lived or died.

Tuck took his time driving back—*no need to hurry now.* He'd catch the afternoon run with John on the boat and everything would be fine. John was thirty-seven, five years older than Tuck, but the age difference seemed much greater. John was married with his own fishing business, and Tuck was unconstrained, no responsibilities, not a care in the world…footloose and fancy free. And that was the way he liked it.

He made a detour into Lios to treat himself to a fresh cup of coffee and a pastry at the little bakery on the corner. He sat at his table, congratulating himself that he'd done a good thing in the wee hours of the morning, maybe even saving Raymond's life. He picked up the discarded newspaper lying on the table beside him and ordered another coffee. By the time he drove down the road leading into Gandiegow and parked, it was almost noon. Once John returned from the morning run, Tuck would explain everything. Then he'd join him on the boat this afternoon to make up for his absence this morning.

In the meantime, Tuck headed to Andrew's to squeeze in a nap.

He whistled as he strolled away from the car and made his way through town. As Mrs. Bruce was stepping into the General Store, he said *hallo*, but she only gave him a disgusted look.

What was that about? But he wasn't going to let her ruin his good mood. Besides, her attitude was nothing new. Gandiegow took every opportunity to blame Tuck for every infraction, real or imagined.

Upon entering the parsonage, an ominous feeling enveloped him. Things were too quiet—a deathly silence—before the clamor of Andrew rushing into the hallway. The grave expression on his brother's face looked as if he'd recently given last rites. "Where have ye been?" Normally, Andrew would have asked after Tuck's welfare first, but this time his greeting, tone, and demeanor were strained. St. Andrew seemed to struggle with remaining neutral. And he was losing the fight as accusation had bled through his words.

"What's wrong?" Tuck asked, unable to tamp down the panic.

Andrew nodded toward the room from where he'd come. "Not here. We'll go in the parlor and sit."

Just tell me! But Tuck held it together and followed him down the hall and into the room.

Doc MacGregor stood at the window, his back stiff and straight. Desperate panic flooded Tuck and he had a hard time catching his breath. "Is Moira all right?" But at that moment, she walked in with a tray, her features drawn and tight as well.

Tuck nodded to Doc and then took his place at the end of the sofa.

Moira poured him a cup. "Here."

Andrew stayed by the fireplace. "Tuck, we have some bad news. I wanted to be the one to tell ye. John Armstrong had an accident on the boat this morning."

"What?" Tuck nearly toppled his tea.

Doc walked over and stood next to Andrew. "He got his arm caught in the winch drum. Lucky he hadn't gone too far from town when it happened."

"By the grace of God he made it back," Andrew added.

The coffee and pastry from Tuck's celebratory breakfast threatened to resurface. Winch drum accidents could be fatal...especially if the fisherman was alone when it occurred. Tuck jumped up. "Where is he? Is he going to be okay?"

Andrew stepped forward and laid a hand on Tuck's shoulder, his brother having only compassion in his voice now and pity in his eyes. "He's at the hospital."

Doc nodded. "Half the town has gone to Inverness to be there with him and Maggie."

"His arm?" Tuck asked. "Can they save it and sew it back on?" Television dramas did that sort of thing all the time.

Doc shook his head with finality. "Gone. There wasn't anything left to save."

"Oh, God." Tuck collapsed back on the sofa and Moira wrapped a quilt around his shoulders. He hadn't realized he was shaking. He looked up at Doc again. "Is he going to make it?"

Doc's lips pursed together as hesitation flickered in his eyes. He seemed to be searching for the right words. "The next seventy-two hours are critical."

"We'll take ye to the hospital," Andrew offered.

"No," Tuck nearly yelled. Mrs. Bruce's look of disgust now made perfect sense. "I need to lie down." He caught each one of their looks of astonishment. Tuck didn't explain that he was going to be sick. He rushed from the parlor, barely making it to the toilet before losing his breakfast. Afterward, he slunk into his room and slipped into bed.

Thoughts kept dive-bombing him, keeping him from sleep. "Good Friday, my arse," he muttered. He'd never felt so terrible in his life and didn't know how to fix it.

A while later, a light tap sounded at the door. "Tuck? I left a sandwich for ye in the refrigerator." Moira's voice held concern.

"Thanks," Tuck said, but he couldn't eat. He listened as Moira and Andrew talked quietly as they walked down the hallway, and then the cottage door shut behind them. Tuck rose, more restless than ever and left the cottage, too.

The village of sixty-five homes felt deserted as he plodded across town to the pub. No one would be there this time of day. If the door was open, as doors were usually unlocked here in Gandiegow, he'd help himself to a drink and leave his money by the cash register.

"Hold up," Brodie hollered.

Tuck turned to see the tall, dark-headed fisherman stepping from his boat and taking long strides toward him.

Tuck had worked a lot for Brodie over the last several months. The two of them, though they'd gotten off to a rocky start, had built a strong friendship in the days that followed Brodie's wedding to Rachel.

Brodie caught up to him. "I heard what happened." He pointed back at John's boat, and Tuck couldn't believe he hadn't noticed it was already docked when he'd arrived back in Gandiegow. "How are ye doing?"

Tuck exhaled and shook his head. "As expected. John's life is ruined and I feel like hell! The tar and feathering will begin as soon as the others return home from the hospital." He swept his hand through the air to encompass all of Gandiegow.

Brodie nodded. "I get that. What are ye going to do now?"

Tuck glanced heavenward—not delivering a prayer this time, as he'd done out on the deserted road with Raymond clutching his chest—but looking up to heaven in frustration. The Almighty didn't give a rat's ass as to what was happening here and now. "Leaving town seems like the best idea, don't ye think? At least until everything calms down."

"Aye." Brodie's expression conveyed his understanding. He knew exactly the hell that Gandiegow had put Tuck through. He shrugged. "Ye could always come back later. Like I did." Brodie had left for several years, returning recently to take over his grandfather's fishing business.

"Where did ye go? France? Italy?"

"Nay. I stayed in Scotland, working for Ewan McGillivray. Have ye heard of Here Again Farm?"

Tuck shook his head.

"It's a huge operation. Maybe he has an opening for you." Brodie pulled out his cellphone. "I'll give you his number."

"Sure." Tuck retrieved his mobile and punched in the number for later. "I really appreciate this."

Brodie clamped a strong hand on his shoulder, as if to steady Tuck. "This is all going to work out, ye hear?"

"Thanks." But Tuck wasn't nearly as optimistic. His gut churned, making it feel like rough seas had taken control of his insides. But where good weather could fix rough waters, nothing could undo the fact that John was maimed. Or worse! What if he died?

Aye, Tuck's excuse was valid for not showing up on time, but he'd made excuses before. It didn't feel right to try and defend himself against what had happened. Besides, Gandiegow would never listen and believe him anyway.

As soon as Brodie walked away, he dialed Ewan. Tuck asked after work, but left out the part of why employment elsewhere was necessary—*to escape the dirty looks and forego the cold shoulder treatment from the Gandiegowans until the end of time!*

The guy on the phone said all the jobs were filled for the upcoming shearing season. Tuck's stomach sank. There would be no escape to Here Again Farm. He went mute.

Ewan cleared his throat, breaking the silence. "Do ye have any tinkering experience?"

"Aye. I filled in for Gandiegow's tinker, when he was sick this past winter."

"Excellent. My cousin Hugh just asked if I knew of anyone who could babysit the weaving machines at his wool mill. He's owner of the mill and Laird there in Whussendale."

"Can I get his number?" Tuck jotted it down on his hand, thanked Ewan, then hung up.

As Tuck dialed Hugh, Andrew came out of the kirk and noticed him. "Crud." Then Andrew walked in his direction. "Double crud."

Tuck shut down the call before he finished dialing. He probably wouldn't get the job anyway.

"Any word on John?" Tuck asked.

Andrew shook his head. "Not yet. But I wanted to talk to you. *Alone.*"

Tuck sighed. "A sermon?"

"Of sorts."

"Great." No one could beat Tuck up more than he was already thrashing himself. Wasn't his brother smart enough to know that?

"It's not what ye think," Andrew said. "I just want to say, if ye're thinking of leaving, *don't.* Stay, and see this through. Moira and I will be by your side the whole way."

"I know that." But Tuck worried what his brother and Moira would suffer if they supported him in this disaster. They would surely be ostracized, too!

Andrew's expression said he was reading Tuck's mind. His words confirmed it. "The people here are good, hardworking folks. Give Gandiegow a chance to show ye they can be reasonable."

But the townsfolk hadn't been reasonable with Tuck from the moment he stepped into the village. Tuck wasn't a perfect man like his brother. He was flawed, seriously flawed. And now John had to pay for Tuck's mistakes.

"I've never asked anything from ye," Andrew said. "Stay. Please. For me?"

Tuck was so conflicted, but he found himself answering anyway. "Aye. I'll stay."

"Thank you." Andrew gave Tuck the validation he could never find within himself. "You could help me get ready for this evening's service."

"It's probably best if I don't attend."

"Nonsense. Good Friday is all about mistakes and the promise of redemption. Ye have to be there."

But Tuck didn't go to the service at the kirk after all. Instead, he headed to John's boat, the Indwaller, intending to handle the nets alone. It was a gutsy move, as none of the Armstrong brothers would thank him for taking out their fishing boat and catching their catch for them. But Tuck owed John, and the least he could do was to look after their family fishing business, when they couldn't.

As Tuck stood on the dock, it wasn't lost on him that what he planned to do was dangerous—go out fishing alone—the reason John had lost an arm to the sea today. Tuck shuddered. He should've been there to prevent John's accident. For all he knew, Raymond had died from his heart attack, and John's arm being lost would've been for nothing.

Tuck stepped aboard the boat, his hand automatically reaching up to make contact with the cross hanging on the mast—an Armstrong tradition. He pulled away, as if the wooden talisman might burn. John Armstrong and his brothers lay stock in the power of the cross, especially when it came to fishing, and Tuck had always abided the ritual. But today…he couldn't touch the cross. Not today. Maybe not ever again.

Tuck had been so consumed in his own thoughts that he hadn't noticed the blood covering the deck. *Crimson. Enough to be deadly.* Again, he felt sickened at how he'd failed John. He really did want to run. Far away. Instead, he threw the roped bucket overboard and hauled up water to clean the deck. And the winch drum. With everything he had, he began scrubbing each plank.

God! If only his own sins could be washed away this easily.

2

TUCK PULLED UP TO THE fishing grounds and dropped anchor by the first buoy. The sea breeze caressed his face and water stretched out in all directions for as far as he could see. It felt good to be beyond the disapproving faces of the villagers of Gandiegow. The only problem was that his own guilt followed him, an unwelcome stowaway.

As he pulled out the logbook, an idea came to him. Since John couldn't do it, Tuck would take his place on the boat. Not as captain, of course, but as an extra body to help out. At least until John could return to fishing.

But Tuck needed to do more! With John out of commission for a while, how would the Armstrongs survive? Tuck had done all kinds of odd jobs around Gandiegow. Surely he could land something steadier so he could funnel money to help John, Maggie, and the kids. *Aye*, it was a good plan, and he felt better.

By the time he rounded the bend and headed into the harbor, the sun had gone down on Good Friday. Services were over. He couldn't help but feel that he'd both dodged the bullet and let his brother down by not being in his pew at the kirk. Gandiegow looked deserted, and Tuck guessed Andrew's words of redemption fell on few ears.

It didn't matter. Redemption was a pipe dream anyway, only reserved for the lucky and the good.

Seeing the town empty caused a cold chill to run down his spine. John must really be in trouble with so many Gandiegowans keeping vigil with Maggie, John's wife, at the hospital tonight.

He pulled the Indwaller up to her post and tied her off. Instead of heading to the parsonage to eat and rest, he decided to find that extra job first. Spalding Farm was only a few miles out of town and would be a good place to start. He went to the General Store—thank goodness no one was there—and he checked out a car for the evening by writing his name down on the clipboard, which hung on the wall. Gandiegow had a small fleet of *shared* vehicles. No sense in owning one when there were no roads within the village, only walking paths There seemed to always be a spare available if the need for a car arose…like now.

He hurried to the car park on the edge of town and got into his reserved vehicle. He felt relieved he hadn't been spotted. But as he closed the door, he heard Andrew yell.

"Tuck! Wait."

Not in the mood for more of St. Andrew's wisdom, Tuck put the car in gear and drove off to Spalding Farm. Working at the farm would allow Tuck to keep his promise to Andrew—*to stay in Gandiegow and see this through*—and help the Armstrongs at the same time. Until now, Tuck was content to float from job to job, wherever he was needed in Gandiegow, tinkering or fishing mostly. Before yesterday, he liked keeping his options open. But things were different now.

When he pulled up to Colin Spalding's sizeable cottage, he found the young gentleman farmer on the doorstep, ready to go in for the night.

"Hey, Tuck. What brings ye here?" His brows came together. "I heard about John."

"From Ramsay?" Ramsay was the youngest of the Armstrong brothers and Colin's closest mate.

"Aye," Colin said with no blame in his voice.

"Can we talk for a minute?"

"Only if ye'll stay for supper. Soup's in the slow cooker."

Tuck's stomach rumbled as if it remembered just then that he'd missed a couple of meals today. "Aye. Food sounds good."

They walked in together, straight to the large kitchen, and took turns washing their hands in the farmer's sink. As Colin ladled their dinner into soup bowls, Tuck got right to it. "I'm after additional employment. Do you have any extra work that I can do?"

Colin shook his head. "Sorry. Robert is starting on Monday after school."

Bollocks. The Almighty was definitely out to get Tuck. Robert was just a kid. A stupid teenager. What was he going to do with his money? *Waste it.* But Tuck shouldn't judge, because that's exactly what he'd done when he was Robert's age.

"Eat," Colin said.

Tuck had lost his appetite, but had to stay, forcing himself to clean his bowl, before pushing away from the table. "I have to get back. Early morning."

By the time Tuck returned to Gandiegow, more lights were on in the cottages than when he left. But the pub wasn't open and no one was out.

He made his way to the parsonage and slipped in quietly, hurrying to his room. He felt like a kid again, sneaking in after hours. He just didn't want to talk to anyone right now. Especially his brother.

Saturday morning, he successfully avoided Andrew and Moira before leaving for John's boat. He arrived early to ready everything for the trip to the fishing grounds. As he went to undo the lines to leave, Ross and Ramsay, John's brothers, stepped aboard.

Crap! I really don't want to have this confrontation now.

"What are ye doing here?" Ramsay asked. But there was more puzzlement in his question than accusation, which was baffling.

Tuck answered him honestly. "I thought I'd lay the nets for you two, while ye tend to yere brother."

"We wanted to clean up the boat first, before we go to the hospital." Ross glanced around, looking mystified, probably due to the sparkling deck.

"John is sure to be asking after the Indwaller when he wakes," Ramsay said.

Tuck was embarrassed, wishing he was anywhere but here. "I took care of it yesterday." He'd overstepped then—*being on the boat without the Armstrongs knowing*—as he'd overstepped this morning. He knew they'd probably want to kick his arse for taking the Indwaller out without their consent.

"Well..." Ross said. "It seems ye've got it under control." He turned to his brother. "Let's head to the hospital."

"Aye." But as soon as Ramsay stepped back on the dock, he stopped and spoke to Tuck. "Ye'll be careful?"

Tuck nodded and the brothers walked away. He was relieved Ross and Ramsay hadn't punched him, but still wondered why they hadn't, for he'd been responsible for what had happened to John. Tuck threw the lines and pulled away from the dock. The short trip to lay the nets went off without a hitch and soon he was returning back to town.

He hurriedly cleaned up at Andrew's cottage then drove to the North Sea Valve Company, which sat on the outskirts of town. He wasted no time in finding the owners of NSV, Pippa and Max, and asking them about any openings.

"Sorry, mate," Max said.

Pippa looked truly conflicted. "Alan Drummond just took on the last position as line mechanic. We'll let you know if anything comes up though."

The new company was only just getting rolling and Tuck understood they had to watch their finances closely, if they were to keep the doors open. In a village the size of Gandiegow, jobs were scarce.

As he left the factory, he got a text. The number looked familiar, but he couldn't place it until he read the message.

Hugh McGillivray here. Ewan says you're looking for work. I need a tinker immediately. Call me.

It was the first break Tuck had gotten since he'd arrived in this village. But it wasn't the break he needed! He couldn't very well stay in Gandiegow, plus work at the wool mill in Whussendale, which was more than an hour away. He closed the screen without replying, and tried desperately to come up with his next move.

Back at home, after the afternoon run, he found a note on the counter from Andrew.

Moira and I have gone to the hospital. A plate for you is in the oven.

Tuck breathed a sigh of relief, glad he wouldn't have to interact with Andrew tonight. Tomorrow, though—Easter—would be another story. One of Andrew's old sermons came to mind: *Let tomorrow take care of itself.* For tonight, Tuck would eat and be in his room before Andrew and Moira got back from the hospital.

Tuck rose early, planning to sail under the radar again, but God had other plans. Just as he put out the first net, dark threatening clouds appeared on the horizon, and by the looks of it, the storm would be a doozy. He couldn't bide his time out in the North Sea until Easter was over and risk John's boat to the storm. Instead, Tuck made a run for Gandiegow and had only just tied off when the first gale force wind hit and the sky let loose with all its fury.

Tuck sneered at the cross on the Indwaller before dashing up the pier. The Almighty was having his way with him—scolding him with the storm, and kicking his arse until he made it to the kirk on time for Easter service.

Andrew was waiting for Tuck in the hallway when he arrived home.

"Ye're coming with us to the kirk." Andrew's steady voice had the power of the Lord behind him.

"Aye." What choice did Tuck have with both Andrew and God hounding him?

Tuck was going for Andrew's sake alone, not the Almighty's. For when John had needed Him most, God had forsaken the faith-filled fisherman.

Tuck, though, never lost sight of the truth. God wasn't the only one who could be implicated in John's accident…Tuck had blood on his hands, too. He could've dropped off Raymond at a nearby farm, let someone else deal with him, but Raymond probably would've died for sure then. What was the Almighty playing at to put Tuck into such an impossible situation?

Andrew stood there, watching, his gaze never wavering, as if waiting to make sure Tuck wasn't going to make a run for it.

"I'll get ready to go," Tuck finally said.

"We'll wait for you." Andrew's words were firm and his expression spoke loud and clear: *You'll not miss out on this Holiest of days.*

"I won't be long." Tuck went down the hall to clean up. When he came out of his room, seven-year-old Glenna, who was Moira's cousin, waited for him. She looked sweet in her Easter bonnet and pink plaid dress that Moira had made for her.

Glenna took Tuck's hand. "Happy Easter, Uncle Tuck."

It was enough to make his heart melt. He loved this little girl. He picked her up and gave her a hug. She didn't judge. She didn't point out all his faults. She was a little ray of sunshine in this dark world.

From the start, he and Glenna had a special bond. Maybe it was due to the fact that they both were a little lost. Tuck, because of his rocky past, and Glenna, because she lost her parents in a car accident a few years ago. If he planned to ever have a family—which he didn't, not since Elspeth, his ex, had cured him of such an affliction—he'd want to have a sweet little girl like Glenna.

Andrew with his cleric's collar and Moira in her plum-colored dress appeared in the hallway and the four of them left for the kirk. As the people started to arrive at the church, Moira and Andrew took up their posts beside Tuck. Whenever anyone sent an accusing glance his way, Andrew would smile at them, as a reminder there would be no condemnation in God's house.

Andrew gave Tuck a reassuring nod, before leaving to put on his robe. Tuck was left with the females.

Moira smiled over at him. "Glenna and I are going to run to the restroom. We'll see you in the Sanctuary."

Tuck nodded. He should've gone in and sat at their pew, but like an idiot, he hesitated.

A second later, the kirk door opened again, and the Narthex became deathly quiet. Maggie, John's wife, walked in, looking pale and fragile. For the first time ever, her long black braid over her shoulder wasn't neat and tidy. But being a strong Scottish lass, she had her I'll-get-through-this expression pulled tight across her face. Gads, the women of Gandiegow were stronger than any man. Baby Irene was asleep on Maggie's shoulder and her seven-year-old son, Dand, was beside her. His eyes were swollen and red, as if he'd been crying.

The kids! John wasn't the only one wounded. The rest of the family was hurting, too. Tuck's heart ached and he felt like crying, too.

Gandiegow's quilters descended upon Maggie. Deydie, the head quilter, the oldest and most crotchety of the bunch, gently took Irene and handed her off to her dearest friend Bethia. Two other quilters strategically maneuvered Dand away to where the men lingered off at the side. Tuck stepped farther away, too, to avoid Maggie's piercing blue eyes. He should've walked nonchalantly into the Sanctuary, but he stayed glued to the spot, as apparently, he wasn't done torturing himself.

Deydie, short and squat, had unusual concern in her cataracted eyes. "How are ye holding up, Maggie?'

Maggie, though she momentarily chewed her lip, nodded stoically.

"And John?" Bethia asked, as she gently rocked baby Irene.

"He's...he's..." Maggie—sturdier than the largest boulder above the village—broke down, sobbing.

Overcome by witnessing her emotion, Tuck inhaled sharply. Maggie's tears made John's predicament more real than the blood on the Indwaller's deck.

"There, there," Bethia cooed. All the other women, too, made comforting shushing noises at Maggie, as they reached out to touch her.

The men of the village put their heads down and hurried for the safety of the Sanctuary.

But Tuck couldn't stop watching.

"He'll never fish again!" Maggie cried in declaration. "You know how scared I've been for him lately. Fishing is too dangerous of a job. And I've gotten the doctor to agree with me that John is to quit, now that he only has one arm!" She shuddered at her words. "It's just as well, but how are we to survive? John will never live on the dole."

None of them would. Gandiegowans were a proud people.

Deydie got up in Maggie's face. Her fierce eyes glowed as she took Maggie's arm and shook it lightly, until Maggie looked at her. "Don't you worry about it none, lass. We take care of our own. I have an idea."

Och, but an *idea* wouldn't feed the bairns—Dand and baby Irene—and the look on Maggie's face agreed with Tuck's assessment.

He shoved his hands in his pockets and moved farther out of sight. But Rachel, Brodie's wife and one of the few people Tuck could call *friend*, zeroed in on him. Discreetly, she made her way over and pulled Tuck away into the deserted hall and out of earshot.

"What are you doing?" She had a way of cutting through the bull, one of the many reasons Tuck respected her.

She stared at him hard, because he hadn't answered. "Don't you dare run away. That would only make things worse. Moira said Andrew asked you to stay. Besides, you live here. This is your home."

Tuck couldn't call what he'd been doing *living*, especially when compared to his brother. Andrew belonged to this village, was completely invested here, whereas Tuck hadn't had real roots since wearing short pants.

"I'm not running." But guilt kept pummeling Tuck. Was there any way to make things right? He wanted to help out the Armstrongs, but all the strikeouts he'd encountered only showed him that the tide was against him. He had no extra money. No savings. If only he hadn't wasted his coin on clothes, the pub, and wooing women over the years. Now, he wished he had every pence back.

"Brodie and I are worried about you." Rachel's pinched eyebrows magnified her concern. "Working the boat for John is a nice thing to do. Stay and help out. Ross will be back to take over and you can be his first-mate."

It's not enough! Tuck wanted to yell. In that moment, a thought lightninged across his mind. Maybe he could have it both ways. He'd talk to Hugh. He could work for both the wool mill, plus continue to take John's place on the boat. Hard work would atone for Tuck's sin. It wouldn't make up for what he'd done to John, Maggie, and the kids, but it would be a start. Tuck could commute between the two jobs, be a part-time resident at both Gandiegow and Whussendale. As an added bonus, he'd keep his promise to Andrew...in a way.

But not today.

"Listen, Rachel, if Andrew asks, tell him that I couldn't stay." He didn't want to share his plan with anyone just yet. He had to make sure it would all work out first.

Rachel opened her mouth to argue, but music started playing in the Sanctuary. The quilters and Maggie moved forward, coming into view, as they led Maggie into the service.

Brodie, along with Rachel's daughter Hannah, stepped into the hallway near them. "Are ye ready, luv?" He offered his hand to his wife as he nodded to Tuck in greeting.

Rachel's eyes delivered the message before her words. "Don't go." But she didn't stick around to find out what Tuck was going to do. She must've seen the determination on his face.

Across the Narthex, Andrew appeared, robed in his Episcopal priest garb, positioning himself at the doorway to the Sanctuary. There was nothing Tuck could do now. He'd have to explain it all to Andrew later.

As soon as Andrew marched in and up to the pulpit, Tuck left the kirk and headed to the parking lot, ready to plead his case to Hugh, and explain in person the strange work arrangements he'd need. As Tuck drove up the hill and away from Gandiegow, he kept telling himself that everything was going to be okay. He wasn't running away. He was heading toward a solution. But no matter how hard he tried, Tuck couldn't shake the feeling that once again, though he was trying to do the right thing, it still would go all to shite.

3

KATHRYN BRECKENRIDGE, Ryn[1] for short, waited in line at Edinburgh airport's Border Control, hugging her dead mother's patchwork tote with the swan appliquéd on the side. Ryn's nerves were shot. It didn't help a bit that there was a baby right behind her with her young mother holding her. Maybe her anxiety had nothing to do with the baby. Since Mom's death last month, Ryn hadn't been right. Her stomach ached most of the time and she had moments where she was sure she had a low-grade fever.

The baby cooed again and Ryn jumped as if gunfire had gone off. She closed her eyes, hoping the torment would be over soon. But that's what she'd been saying to herself for the last eight hours, during the final leg of the horrible trip from Minneapolis to Edinburgh.

It had all been too much with the trip feeling more like nursery time with a half-dozen diaper-wearing passengers onboard. The

---

[1] Pronounced (ren)

flight could've been a time for Ryn to unwind and a chance to process what had happened these last several months. God knew she needed some peace and quiet to figure out what she was going to do next. But the babies screwed up that plan—the squealing and crying, sometimes in stereo—making it impossible for Ryn to think.

But it's more than that, the little voice inside reminded her. Her issues with babies went deeper than a few wails. But as always, Ryn tamped down the old hurt, hoping this time would be the last time, and the pain would never rise to the surface again.

"First time in Scotland?" asked the young mother from over Ryn's shoulder in her lilting Scottish accent.

Ryn turned around to see the drooling blond-headed baby latch onto her mother's braid and pull it to her mouth.

She jerked her gaze away and focused on the mother instead. She was probably close to Ryn's age, twenty-eight. "Yes. First time." Ryn's birthday had been three weeks ago. She'd spent the day packing up Mom's things into boxes for Salvation Army. She'd only kept a few items—the pearl-handle embroidery scissors, a jar of her mother's buttons, and a small stack of fabric fat quarters—all packed away in Ryn's checked bag.

"Are ye here on business?" The mother smiled and nodded toward Ryn's attire.

Ryn glanced down at her belted, black pantsuit paired with her sturdy Mary Jane heels. The same clothes she'd worn to her mom's funeral. "No, not business." Ryn was more comfortable in jeans and a printed tee, but it was important to make the right impression when she met her Scottish cousin for the first time.

Behind the mother, a sharp-dressed guy in a herring bone sports jacket leaned closer and eyed Ryn as if he was interested. Instantly, her stomach hurt worse, and she made a point of dismissing his come-on. For the past two years, she'd deliberately taken a hiatus from all men, especially wary of the good-looking ones. Her past relationships had been with extremely handsome men, every last one of them oozing with charm. Charm—perfected and honed—but their honeyed words were only a means to get her into bed.

Ryn was done making the mistake that *Charm equaled moral character*. One cheater too many had cured her of her propensity toward handsome males. Moving forward—*if and when* she ever dated again—she'd take a kind-hearted, pasty dumpling over *good-looking* any day.

The Border Control officer called out, "Next?" He waved Ryn over.

Ryn stepped up to the counter and presented her passport.

"Name?" the officer asked, as he flipped it open and peered at the document.

"Ryn Breckenridge."

His head popped up and he raised an eyebrow. "The bird, *wren*?"

"Sorry. Long flight. I'm *Kathryn* Breckenridge. The tenth *Kathryn Iona* in a row. My mother Kathy and my grandmother Kay came up with my name, *Ryn*." She was talking way too much!

The officer nodded kindly as if he didn't mind her babbling. "What's yere reason for traveling to Scotland?"

Ryn kept it short. "I'm looking for my family." But her voice cracked when she said *family*. In truth, after losing her mother, she had no family left in the U.S., as Granny Kay had passed a year ago.

He tilted his head to the side. God, she hoped he wasn't getting the wrong idea, worried she wasn't stable enough to enter the country.

For a moment, Ryn chewed the inside of her cheek, but then told him a more detailed truth. "Mom and her cousin, Maggie, made a quilt when they were girls—*the Goodbye quilt*. Last month, before Mom died, she asked me to return the quilt to Maggie here in Scotland." Ryn squeezed her tote to let him know that Exhibit A lay inside…and to reassure herself the quilt was safe.

The officer's eyes narrowed, but then he declared, "Ye're on holiday." He stamped her book and slid it toward her. "Next?"

For rattling on, Ryn gave him an apologetic smile while retrieving her passport.

As she followed the Baggage Reclaim sign, she muttered to herself, "This trip could be a wild goose chase." The notion nagged her so often she murmured, "I should put music to it and turn it into a country song. What in the world was I thinking?"

She'd been rash. Or maybe it was the grief. She should've found someplace temporary to stay. Instead, she'd pared down what she owned, put the rest in storage, and used the last of her savings to buy a ticket. "I made a promise," she repeated to herself, though speaking it aloud didn't have the reassuring effect she'd hoped.

In fact, Ryn was scared to death. Feeling queasy. And praying to God that she'd find Maggie and deliver the quilt before her money ran out. If she didn't, what would she do then? When Mom got sick, Ryn pretty much burnt all bridges with her graphic arts customers. She was too distraught to give them an explanation of why she couldn't complete their orders. She was in shock. She couldn't bear to repeat the horrible truth to her clients over and over again: *My mom's dying and I just can't talk about it.* She had some strong, definitive feelings about pancreatic cancer…it sucked!

Ryn stood by the baggage carousel and waited. Yeah, she'd done a lot of waiting over the last three months, which had been pure hell. Mom's diagnosis, the hospital stays, the funeral. Now, she waited here in Scotland, needing to fulfill an errand. *Her mother's last request.*

There had been no closure at the end. Just sorrow. The relationship with her mom had been complicated, right up until her mother's final breath. Her mom was no jewel, but she was all she'd ever had, and Ryn loved her. But her mother had kept too much hidden and left too soon, still not answering the questions which weighed heaviest on Ryn. Like *Who is my father?*

The last time she'd asked, and gotten no answer, had been when Ryn was fifteen. If only she could go back to before the fatal diagnosis. Ryn would've asked again and waited her mother out, and not backed down when Mom pursed her lips and changed the subject. Now, Ryn would never know…

Her blue roller bag appeared on the conveyor belt. Ryn set her tote between her feet, the fullness of the bag making her feel comforted that the Goodbye quilt would soon be safe and sound with Maggie. She tugged her roller bag from the carousel, securely positioned the tote back on her shoulder, and walked through the sliding doors which led to the rest of Scotland.

Surprisingly, the sun was shining and her spirits lifted. But as she pulled her phone from her pocket to connect with Maggie, adrenaline clashed with her nerves and she experienced an internal earthquake. Her hand shook as she pulled out the two pieces of paper she'd printed off from the internet. One was how to make an international phone call with her cell phone, and the other piece of paper held Maggie's number, which she'd found from a Google search.

Ryn should've called her while back in Minneapolis, but she'd kept putting it off, trying to get through one minute at a time. There'd been so much to do, so many calls, that she couldn't add in one more. And now she was kicking herself for not making that initial contact. It just made this moment that much more nervewracking. Ryn read through the directions one more time and then dialed.

A man answered, "Ross Armstrong."

"Oh, hi. I'm Ryn Breckenridge and I'm looking for Maggie."

Ross sighed. "Maggie's not here. She's fixing to go to Whussendale—"

"Whussendale?" But at that moment, Ryn's phone died.

"Dammit!" Buying a new cellphone battery was just another thing she shouldn't have put off! Ever since her mother's death, Ryn hadn't been herself. She'd always been the responsible one, always on task, always the grownup. But losing Mom had Ryn acting and doing things so unlike her. *Like coming to Scotland so unprepared!*

Ryn glanced up and read the sign. "Tram." As a plan came together, her despair dissipated. She'd go into the city center and find a battery. Then head to Whussendale, wherever the heck that was. "One problem at a time."

She looked around her surroundings, which felt foreign and unfamiliar. She found the ticket machine, bought a ticket, and waited. When she boarded, she was concerned whether she'd be able to catch her stop as the conductor's burr was strong and hard to understand.

She shouldn't have worried. The woman next to her on the tram took pity, giving her an idea of where to look for a new battery for her *mobile,* and alerting her when they arrived at the appropriate stop. Ryn thanked the woman and stepped off. She pulled out her map, but when she glanced up to see the name of the next cross street, she couldn't believe what she saw in the charity shop window, only four feet away.

An old-fashioned black Singer Featherweight sewing machine!

And the sign propped against the treasure read twenty pounds. *Twenty pounds!*

Not believing her eyes, she couldn't stop herself from going inside to inquire if the price was correct and if so, did the machine really work? She'd always dreamed of owning a Featherweight. They were made of all metal parts and known for their durability and straight stitches—perfect for a serious quilter. Her brain raced and she began rationalizing. She could put a Featherweight to good use while she was here in Scotland. Though she wasn't the best hand-piecer, that's exactly how she'd planned to piece her True

Colors quilt. The cut fabric lay folded neatly in her roller bag ready to be sewn together. But instead of hand-stitching, wouldn't the quilt come together much faster, and more accurately, with her very own Featherweight sewing machine?

At Ryn's request, the shop owner retrieved the machine from the window, plugged it in, and it whirled to life. Before the clerk could change the price, Ryn paid the woman and left.

About ten yards from the shop, Ryn leaned against a stone building and questioned her rashness, as the sewing machine, in its cute black case, felt like dead weight, pulling her left arm from its socket. *Just another example of something I should've considered before blindly taking action!*

Ryn shook her head and wryly laughed. "This Featherweight should've been named *heavyweight*."

She balanced the machine on top of her roller bag and precariously pulled it along, giving her left arm a break.

Down the next block, she found exactly what she needed—a store which sold cellphones. The only problem was that they didn't have a battery that would work with her model. After negotiating with the salesman, she walked away with a used cellphone and new battery, her pockets now considerably lighter. But at least she could communicate with the outside world again, once she charged the phone.

As she exited the store, a bagpipe began to play. Ryn stepped out to see a piper dressed in a regal uniform of a red kilt, sporran, knee socks, tartan sash, and a tall black feather bonnet atop his head. This wasn't the sort of thing she'd see in front of a shop in Minneapolis. Tourists gathered around, some taking selfies and then dropping money in his case at his feet. Ryn, too, left a pound for the performer, before walking on.

Her rush of adrenaline was waning and giving way to jet lag. She pulled her heavy luggage into a pub for a place to sit and for some sustenance.

After ordering soda and a half sandwich, Ryn prodded the middle-aged waitress for answers before she got away. "I need to get to Whussendale. Do you know the best way to get there from here?"

The waitress screwed up her face in concentration. "Aye. I know where it 'tis, but there's no bus or train to the village. Let me call my brother." She pulled out her phone.

"Your brother?"

"He owns a shuttle service. Maybe he's available. Either he or one of his drivers could possibly get ye to Whussendale."

At the mention of a shuttle, Ryn felt her wallet emptying further. But without the bus or train, it seemed her only option.

The waitress smiled at her as she put her phone to her ear. As she spoke, Ryn only picked up a few words because her burr was so thick. While the waitress listened, she smiled at Ryn and nodded her head. "Aye. She'll be waiting for ye here at the pub."

"The cost?" Ryn asked before she hung up.

The waitress nodded. "How much is it?" She listened before conveying the answer. "Hundred and fifty pounds."

"A hundred and fifty?" The amount seemed astronomical, especially since Ryn was so short on cash. Again, she kicked herself for not being more prepared.

Her dismay must've shown on her face because the waitress nodded in understanding and then spoke again with her brother on the other end of the line. "Och, but Peter, 'tis on yere way home. What's the family rate?" The waitress' frown transformed into a wide grin. "Aye. Twenty pounds." She looked at Ryn expectantly.

Ryn returned her grin. "Yes. Absolutely. That would be great." The waitress hung up and Ryn couldn't stop smiling. "You saved me."

"'Tis no problem. Us, lassies, have to stick together. Besides, I can see ye're not some rich golfer come for holiday. Ye seem like a lass on a mission."

Ryn glanced over at her overfull tote which held the quilt. "Something like that. I really can't thank you enough."

The waitress nodded. "Not to worry. Now I'll get yere food and drink."

Forty minutes later, the waitress' brother arrived. He waved to his sister, grabbed Ryn's suitcase and sewing machine, and they were off to Whussendale with Ryn tucked in the backseat.

Her driver introduced himself as Peter, but he wasn't nearly as chatty as his sister. That was fine with Ryn, as she wanted to take in the scenery. But the warmth of the sun on the window and the gentle rocking of the car lulled Ryn to sleep.

She woke to find them on a road not much wider than her compact computer desk, which she'd sold before leaving home. "Where are we?"

"Not five minutes from Whussendale."

There were woods on either side of the road, reminding her of a state park in Minnesota. Which was weird since they were in Scotland. Around the next bend, a very small town came into view. It was nothing more than a row of cottages, a couple of businesses, plus a church surrounded by a stone fence, which enclosed a cemetery.

Peter looked back at her again. "There's more, lassie." He pointed to the left. "The wool mill is in that direction. Look through the trees. 'Tis famous. The best wool in all the Highlands comes from that mill, and of course, from the sheep at Here Again Farm and others in the area."

That was the most her driver had said. Ryn looked and saw what he was talking about. The wool mill looked larger than the village itself. And it wasn't like anything she'd seen in the States. It didn't resemble a normal factory but was a group of architecturally interesting buildings—some wood, some stone. "What's behind the mill?"

"The cottages for the employees." He brought the car to a rolling stop. "Where do I drop ye?"

Ryn had no idea where to find Maggie. She glanced at her watch and then out the window. The wool mill seemed much more alive than the sleepy village. "Can you take me to the mill?"

"Aye." Peter turned left and drove toward the group of buildings.

Now, Ryn could see the layout more clearly. A little walking bridge was over the small river to the right. And straight ahead she could see the waterwheel in front of one of the larger buildings.

"The waterwheel still produces electricity to this day. She's a testament to simpler times." His voice held nostalgia. "My auntie is from Whussendale and used to work in the kiltmaker's shop." He pulled the car in front of a small building which read Gift Shop and Tearoom above the doorway. "Will this do?"

A fresh case of nerves overcame Ryn. "Yes. This is fine." She didn't know for certain, if she would be fine or not, but she was here now and had no choice but to stay.

She slipped out of the car and dug around in her tote. From her wallet, she pulled two twenty pound notes and handed them to Peter, who had already retrieved her suitcase and sewing machine from the back. "Here."

He frowned at her outstretched hand. "Och, lass, 'twas twenty we agreed upon."

She grinned. "The rest is for giving me the *family rate*."

He smiled at her knowingly, as if he wouldn't want to take charity either, and pocketed the money graciously. She waved to him as he pulled away. She worried his face would be the last friendly one she'd see in Scotland, but other worries bombarded her, too. What if Maggie wasn't really here in Whussendale? What then? Where would Ryn stay? It occurred to her that maybe she should've asked Peter for a card, in case she needed a ride back to Edinburgh.

She positioned her tote and then pulled her suitcase-sewing machine bundle into the cafe. When she looked up and took in the new surroundings, she was taken off-guard and became a little breathless at what she saw.

Not six feet away, a man with blond hair conversed with a young woman, standing behind the café counter. He wasn't just any guy. He was kind of perfect. He wore a black polo embroidered with the Whussendale Wool logo, and sported a red, blue, and green kilt with an accent of purple running through it. Lower still, he showed off his manly legs in thick, knee-high cream-colored socks, finishing off the look with army boots. Clearly it was a uniform, of sorts, as the female clerk wore a similar polo and her skirt was made of the same tartan, too.

What took Ryn off-guard was how Tall Blond and *Kilted* affected her. Sure, he was handsome, but she'd easily blown off the good-looking sports-jacket-guy at the airport.

The colorful kilt he wore couldn't be the lure either. She'd seen several kilts in Edinburgh, including the bagpiper outside the cell-phone store in all his regalia.

Ryn scrutinized *Kilted* more closely. His hammer and screwdriver, hanging from his belt, told a story: He wasn't wearing a manly skirt to draw a touristy crowd, like the piper. *Kilted* was on a break from doing manual labor...*real work*. And dang it! Ryn hated how appealing that was to her. She'd sworn off men, especially the good-looking ones.

She tamped down her curiosity about *Kilted*. And got down to business. Now she just had to get the flirtatious clerk's attention and stop her from twirling her hair and gazing upon her kilted customer unabashedly.

Both of them turned to Ryn. *Kilted* smiled. The clerk didn't.

Ryn took a step forward, reminding herself, *I'm not in Scotland to date or to hook up.* Those days were over. She was smarter now. More enlightened, with the past laid to rest. Ryn's job, for the next couple of days was clear. She was here to fulfill her dead mother's last request. And that was all.

The clerk's attention went back to *Kilted,* though he still stared at Ryn. The clerk, *poor girl*, regarded him as if she was making wedding plans…or perhaps the clerk had him in mind for her afternoon dessert. Either way, she devoured him with her eyes. Ryn might've, too, but seriously, she'd had enough heartache from men like him.

"Hallo," *Kilted* said smoothly, as if he liked what he saw. His deep baritone didn't surprise Ryn, but honestly, why couldn't he have spoken in a falsetto or with a lisp?

Ryn nodded and remained quiet while she sized him up. Six-three? Early thirties? Dang his dimpled smile! Ryn had gone out with a slew of men like *Kilted* for practically all of her post-puberty life. After *the incident* in high school, her mother made Ryn return to dating right away. Mom's voice still rang clear in her memory…one of the few times Mom acted like a mom. "Don't let Joey Naut define who you are, or who you will become."

And yet, in some ways, that's exactly what Ryn had done. Ever since that fateful night in the pool house, she'd chosen the same type—*good-looking men who were used to getting exactly what they wanted*—as if her younger self wanted another chance to go back and do things differently, but most importantly, to not be so naïve again.

The same week she'd turned fifteen, Joey Naut singled her out at his graduation party, and took her to the pool house to make-out. At the time, she thought she was so cool, the luckiest girl in the world, until he took her virginity without her permission. He'd kissed her slowly at first and then more passionately, so she barely noticed when he'd pushed her hem up and her underwear down. She vaguely only realized something pressed against her *down there*, but honestly didn't know that it was *it,* until he forced his way in and there was pain. He'd finished almost as soon as he started, and laughed when she ran out. She ran away from him, the party, and what had happened. When she got home, she slipped upstairs, making sure her mother didn't see her. No amount of showering could wash away Joey Naut. She had no intention of ever telling her mother or anyone. But luck wasn't on her side. When Ryn missed her period, she had no choice. It was the hardest thing in the world to confess to Mom what Joey had done and that she was pregnant.

Ryn had finally learned it was best to keep the sordid details of her past close and use it to douse her proclivity for men like the one who stood at the counter now. Silently, she bolstered herself up as if building an impenetrable wall between them.

Over the last two years, she'd worked hard to break the cycle. Some might say she'd gone about it all wrong—going cold turkey and isolating herself with absolutely no dating. Lonely, yes. But the silver lining? There'd been no need to refill her birth control pill prescription. And lately, she'd been feeling resilient. Until this moment, she'd thought her *Joey-esque* days were a thing of the past. Ryn glanced at *Kilted* again and reminded herself to remain vigilant.

"Here, Tuck." The clerk shoved a bagged pastry at the kilted man, who now had a name. Next, she gave Ryn a sideways nod and a frown. "Can I help ye with something?" Her words lacked conviction, except sounding somewhat annoyed.

"Are ye lost?" Tuck asked. Probably because Ryn stood there like an out-of-place pillar for way too long.

Ryn straightened. "I'm looking for my cousin."

"Who might that be?" The woman's head pivoted from Ryn to Tuck, as if weighing his million dollar smile against Ryn's relatively simple attributes.

"Lass?" he said. "Who is it ye're looking for?"

Ryn tightened a grip on her bag, which held the Goodbye quilt. "I'm looking for Maggie Armstrong."

Tuck's easy smile evaporated, his perfect face turning grim, and his mouth becoming a stubborn line pulled across his lips. "Why would ye be looking for her here?" His voice wasn't sweet honey now.

If she was in her element—*and in her own country*—she would've been more bold and chucked his attitude back at him with a *What's your problem?* Someone needed to cut his six-foot-three down to four-ten. Instead, she controlled herself. "Earlier, I spoke with Ross Armstrong on the phone. He said Maggie was headed to Whussendale."

The blood drained from Tuck's face. "Why?"

Ryn shrugged. "I don't know. My phone died before I could get any details."

Tuck turned into a feral mountain lion. Ryn didn't even know if mountain lions existed in Scotland or not. Regardless, Tuck spun around, leaving his bagged pastry on the counter as he and his kilt marched toward the door.

"Tuck?" called the young woman from behind the counter.

But Tuck soldiered out, slamming the café door behind him.

Ryn and the young woman stared at the door, but for completely different reasons: Ryn was confused, and the clerk was disappointed.

"What was that all about?" Ryn asked.

But the young woman turned and flounced through the saloon doors to the kitchen, as if Ryn hadn't spoken at all.

Perfect! Was this a preview of how it was going to be in Whussendale? This trip was going swimmingly so far!

So what am I going to do now? Ryn could search for someone else to ask. But what if they snubbed her, too? And where was she going to stay tonight? The village was too small for a hotel. And if Maggie wasn't here, where did that leave Ryn?

4

D AMMIT! TUCK STOPPED just outside the door and exhaled. Gandiegow had caught up to him.

Ten days had passed since Easter. Ten days of driving back and forth. Ten days avoiding the people of Gandiegow. Ten days to start feeling like himself again. Why did the American lass have to go and ruin it? He stomped across the wool mill grounds toward the weaver's shop.

One word from her and Whussendale no longer felt like a reprieve. Hugh had been thrilled to have Tuck in town, was fine with the odd-hour work arrangement, and even offered one of his petrol-friendly cars for the drive back and forth to Gandiegow. Tuck liked the young Laird immediately, especially since he hadn't asked a lot of questions as to why Tuck had come here.

He wasn't fooling himself. Gandiegow and Whussendale had close ties and surely everyone knew the circumstances as to why he was here.

In Whussendale, Tuck had been able to breathe, deep breaths

even, without it hurting so much. Now though, the Yankee lass brought back the crushing guilt which made him feel like shite.

He had a lot of questions, but he didn't care a whit why the American was here in Whussendale looking for Maggie. The less he knew about Maggie and her goings-on the better. But why had the American come to *this* small village to find her?

He turned back around and wished he hadn't. The blasted Yank was hurrying toward him, dragging her roller bag over the yard. He'd never met her before, but he recognized her, which was ridiculous. Maybe he identified with the bone-weary tiredness resting behind her blue-gray eyes…the same weariness that plagued him. If she hadn't mentioned Maggie, he might have thought she was cute, as she rushed toward him with her tote looped over her shoulder, the bulk of it bouncing up and down as she hurried along.

She wasn't a classic black-haired beauty or a blond bombshell. This cinnamon-colored ginger with her long locks and smattering of freckles across her nose was just an average everyday lass of medium height. But it was her wholesome quality that pulled him in. She wore the-girl-next-door thing well. And she looked familiar. Really, really familiar. How strange…

"Excuse me?" She was a little out of breath.

"What's yere name?" He sounded abrupt, but he had no patience today.

The question brought her to a halt a few feet away. Her eyebrows squeezed together in caution. "Ryn Breckenridge."

"Why are ye looking for Maggie?"

Normally, he didn't interrogate people. It was none of his damn business what others were up to. But in this instance, he wasn't particularly feeling, or acting *normal*.

"Like I said—Maggie's my cousin. Actually, she's *my mother's* first cousin."

"You didn't answer my question." He could tell this lass was different from regular birds. Perhaps it was her wary stance, or the stubborn set of her jaw, or that she didn't give two pence about his looks or charm. *Not in the least.* Tuck's ego took a hit, because most women fell over themselves to get his attention.

Ryn's frown conveyed her frustration, so he wasn't surprised when her tone matched her expression. "I have something for Maggie."

Aye. The bouncing tote. The lass held onto it for dear life. "What's in the bag?"

"It's a quilt. I was sent here to bring it to Maggie."

There's that name again. This *Ryn* brandished Maggie's name as if she didn't know she wielded a weapon. A dagger. And each time she uttered *the-woman-who-must-not-be-named*, it cut deep, carving chunks out of his well-being and patience. Did she do it deliberately?

He towered over her. "Why didn't ye just put the quilt in the post? It would've been cheaper. Less trouble." The post would've saved him, too, from this moment. "Why did ye come all the way to Scotland?" And to the wrong town *ta boot.*

As she shifted to the side, her focus changed to something beyond his shoulder, perhaps to a movie playing out in her head. She was quiet for so long, he wondered if she might have gone mute.

"You wouldn't understand," she finally said quietly. A moment later, she faced him head-on and stared him square in the eyes, as if to say she wasn't backing down or stepping away from her purpose. "I couldn't trust the mail with the Goodbye quilt."

When she said *goodbye,* her voice hitched a little and her eyes changed to a dark faraway hue. The indignation of a minute ago transformed into pain, and hell, he didn't like that he'd caused the mist to come into her eyes.

A flashback hit him from nowhere, hard and fast. He was seventeen again—another time, another place...a different lass. He was studying for exams to enter college when Elspeth's tears had him proposing, anything to fix what he'd done. *Or what I thought I'd done.*

It'd been the worst time of his life. Until now. John. Maggie. The guilt.

Tuck shook it off, not sure where that stray thought had come from. He hadn't thought about Elspeth in years.

But then a wave of relief hit him. *Elspeth.* That name was also the cook's name at the wool mill's café. Lara, the clerk, had introduced him. That's what brought on this treacherous and terrible walk down memory lane.

He fixated on the present and regarded Ryn, forcing himself to put her near-tears from his mind. It may be cruel, but for his own self-preservation, he chose to be a jack-ass and dig deeper. "What the hell's a Goodbye quilt?" He didn't like being an insensitive jerk, but it was his best defense against female waterworks.

At that moment, a van pulled into the driveway leading to the wool mill. He recognized the vehicle—one of Gandiegow's. The instant the driver came into view, Tuck's blood ran cold. *Maggie.* He hadn't seen her since Easter morn, nor heard her name since leaving Gandiegow. *Until the American lass said it today.*

The van pulled in front of the third building—the Laird's office— and stopped. Tuck had only been in Hugh's office once, when he'd taken the job.

Maggie slipped out of the van, not shutting the door right away. She leaned in and spoke with the others in the vehicle.

"Who is that?" Ryn asked. "Is that Maggie?"

"Aye."

Ryn smiled and took a step forward as if she was an arrow aimed at her target.

Automatically, Tuck reached out to stop her, but thankfully paused before going through with it. "Stay," he commanded instead.

He shoved his hand in his pocket, knowing he'd crossed a line.

The American lass thought so, too. With fire in her eyes, she glared at him. "I'm not a dog."

"What I mean is, now's not the time." He turned back to the van to watch.

In the passenger seat, Rowena, Maggie's sister, was speaking and gesturing animatedly. He couldn't hear what they were saying, which made him wonder all the more why Maggie was here. Tuck should've taken that moment to escape, instead he stayed frozen to the spot and lost his chance. When Maggie turned around, he wasn't prepared for her haggard expression. Fatigue and loss hung on her like widow's garb.

John's not dead, Tuck reassured himself. Andrew would've contacted him if John had passed.

Maggie's eyes drifted in Tuck's direction and like lightning, recognition hit. Her spine straightened and her haggardness turned to disgust. Aye, seeing him invigorated her, but not in a good way. She now looked ready for battle and on the verge of the mother of all tirades. And Tuck would've deserved it. Maggie had more to hold against him than John's injury, or working John's fishing boat without permission. *Sinnie.* Tuck had chatted up Maggie's youngest sister, and Maggie had been very much against Tuck and his bad reputation taking Sinnie on a date. They'd had a dram at the pub together, that's all, except a chaste kiss afterward. They hadn't gone out again, but that didn't stop everyone from assuming things had gone farther than they had.

Maggie slammed her door and took a determined step toward Tuck. He braced himself. But through the van's closed windows and doors, baby Irene saved him when she let go with a muffled cry. Maggie about-faced, gave a worried glance at the van, and then hurried into Hugh's office.

Tuck realized then, Maggie's errand wasn't to drop off something to Hugh and leave. She took nothing in with her!

A minute later, she came out, looking headstrong. And the way she held herself, and the fact she kept her eyes straight ahead, let Tuck know he wasn't worth her effort. She repositioned herself behind the wheel of the van.

Hugh came out, too, with his phone to his ear. He motioned to Tuck. "Do you have a minute?"

"Aye. Only just." Tuck was watching the van.

Hugh slipped his phone in his shirt pocket. "Come with me to Kilheath."

Kilheath Castle. Hugh and Sophie's home.

Already to his auto, Hugh raised his hand. "Are ye coming?"

Tuck shoved both hands in his pockets now and stalked over to the Laird's Smart Car, leaving the American lass to her own company. Cramming oneself into such a small vehicle wasn't easy, but the Laird was determined to reduce his carbon footprint. According to Hugh, squeezing in like a sardine on the few days he drove to the mill was a small price to pay.

Tuck folded himself into the passenger's side, but unfortunately, glanced up at the wrong moment. He wished like hell he hadn't caught the lost look on Ryn's face as he shut his door.

Hugh nodded toward the American lass as he started the car. "Tourist? Should I get someone to show her around?"

Ryn was digging in her bag now, probably looking for her phone or something.

"Not a tourist. She's come to see Maggie, her cousin." The cramped space and Tuck's bad mood left little room or patience for discussing Maggie's cousin. Especially since Maggie drove the vehicle only a few meters ahead.

Hugh put on the brakes. "Go tell the lass to come with us."

Tuck cranked his head around as if Hugh had miraculously expanded the interior of the car. "Where do ye expect me to put her?

On my lap?"

Hugh grinned, but had the courtesy to keep whatever smart comment he'd thought of to himself. "After we get done, come back and deliver the lass to Maggie."

Tuck didn't want to, but he kept quiet, his mind racing. *Why is Maggie here in Whussendale?* He must've been pretty caught up in his thoughts, only just realizing the Laird was telling a story.

Hugh gave him a quick glance before putting his eyes back on the road. "Are ye listening? It's a capital idea. And Sophie is excited about the prospect. She's been scheming ever since Deydie suggested it. I have my own ideas, too. We aren't just going to focus on quilting. After we get one under our belts, we'll expand the retreat to other crafts, too."

Not really interested, Tuck only nodded while keeping an eye on Maggie's back wheels.

They pulled up to Kilheath Castle's front entrance as Sophie rushed through the massive mahogany double doors. Maggie disembarked, along with her seven-year-old son, Dand. Rowena stepped out and tried to grab the lad's hand, but she missed, as he stomped off to the side of the road, kicking rocks here and there as he went.

"Don't go far," Maggie called after him.

Tuck felt sorry for the kid. With his da in the hospital, it'd probably been no picnic at home for him.

Sinnie, the youngest sister, slipped out of the van, holding baby Irene who was bigger than a mite now, over a year old. The bairn was red-eyed and sniveling. When Irene saw Maggie, the babe reached out, whining until her mother took her.

Tuck felt sorry for Maggie, too. She looked as if she had nothing left to give.

Dand picked up a small branch and whacked it against the side of the Laird's car.

"Stop that," Maggie scolded.

Tuck examined the door, but there was no damage. The Laird hadn't seen what had gone on as he was behind the van.

Hands fisted around the branch and Dand as red-faced as Irene had been, the boy shook, his anger clear. His eyes welled, but his pride was working hard not to let him cry. "I don't want to live here!" He dropped the stick and ran into the forest.

Live here? Tuck had trouble drawing a breath. He'd been walloped with something bigger than Dand's stick.

Maggie sighed and turned to her sister. "Rowena, can you look after him?"

"I'll go." Sinnie hurried after the boy.

"Tuck?" Hugh held out a box from the back of the van. "We need to get these to the east wing."

Tuck was rooted to the spot. *Maggie is moving here? Why?*

Sophie led Maggie, along with the baby, into the castle.

Rowena headed toward the woods, too. She probably understood it would take both she and Sinnie to coax the headstrong Dand back to the castle.

"Come," Hugh said quietly. "If ye were listening earlier, ye'd not look so shocked. We'll talk as we get these in the house."

Tuck didn't have to ask any questions. Hugh waited until they were inside and upstairs alone in the master bedroom in the east wing.

"Whussendale is closer to the hospital, which will make it easier on Maggie to see John," Hugh began. "But it's more than that. Deydie has been making plans with Sophie to have a quilt retreat here in Whussendale."

But Tuck didn't see the connection between the retreat and Maggie moving to this village. "I don't get it."

"Maggie will be the one in charge of our retreats," Hugh said.

No! Tuck wished he could shove the five ton anchor off his chest.

Oh, hell. He grasped the big picture. Deydie had put this in play to make Maggie the *breadwinner*, and John certainly wouldn't thank Tuck for it.

Hugh went on. "Rowena and Sinnie are staying temporarily to help get the kids settled. We're lining up babysitters as Maggie will be busy pulling the retreat together."

Tuck couldn't stop thinking on how devastating this would be for John. A lost hand. A lost profession. God, it would surely feel as if his manhood had been cut off, too.

Hugh pounded Tuck on the back. "Quit looking as if it's the end of the world. It will all work out. Ye'll see. Now, let's get the rest of their things from the vehicle."

Three trips later, they had the Armstrongs's possessions stowed in their rooms.

Back outside, Tuck looked at his watch. "I better get to Gandiegow."

"Aye. But first—" Hugh nodded to something beyond Tuck's shoulder "—ye better take the car and bring the lassie the rest of the way to Kilheath."

Tuck whipped around, and sure enough, at the bottom of the hill in the bend of the road, the American was clumsily wheeling her bag toward them.

He didn't want to help her. Not for any selfish reason either, but because he was feeling like Maggie. He'd reached his limit today of what he could handle, too.

Obediently, Tuck took the keys from Hugh. "Her name is Ryn Breckenridge."

Hugh nodded. "Perhaps she'll be a blessing for the Armstrongs."

Tuck believed she would be a nuisance, but kept his opinion to himself. He drove down the hill and pulled up beside the American. She was looking a little worn around the edges, and he regretted thinking ill of her.

"Jet lag?" he asked, idling beside her.

She swiped her red hair out of her face. "Yes. I've hit a brick wall."

"Get in. The Laird wants ye up at the castle." Tuck put the car in park and hopped out. He reached for her tote, but she shied away.

"I've got it," she said.

He took the sewing machine case and the roller bag, carrying them both to the boot of the car.

"They'll never fit," she said.

"I'll make them." Tuck wedged in her possessions, but had to leave the lid open.

Ryn settled herself into the passenger seat with the tote on her lap. She cradled it to her chest as if protecting a precious child.

"I've got to tell ye something before we get back up the hill." It made no sense why Tuck felt obligated. Why did *he,* of all people, have to be the one to tell Ryn about John and the accident? "There's something ye need to know."

She turned toward him, and without warning, it hit him again that Ryn Breckenridge seemed so familiar.

Tuck faced forward, placing his hands on the wheel, but not putting the car in gear just yet. "It's about Maggie."

"What about her?"

Tuck glanced out the window, stalling.

"Tell me," Ryn said quietly. It sounded more like a soothing nudge.

Tuck cleared his throat. "Her father died recently…and John, Maggie's husband, had an…an accident the next day, on Good Friday."

"A car accident?"

Tuck didn't want to go into the details and he didn't want to admit the part he'd played in John losing his arm. "No. John had a boating accident."

"Is he going to be okay?" Ryn asked.

No! Tuck wanted to yell. *John will never be the same again.* "I don't know."

Ryn looked ready to ask more.

He put his hand up, inhaling deeply, but the breath he so desperately needed evaded him. "I'm just telling you this so you won't bug Maggie." It was clear Maggie couldn't take on anything more.

"Oh." Ryn hugged the tote tighter.

He put the car in gear.

"Then why are you taking me to her?" Ryn asked in a small voice.

"The Laird said to deliver ye to the castle, and we always do what the Laird says."

Ryn nodded and looked out the window. She said something to herself, or maybe it was to him. He wanted to ignore it, but his damned curiosity won out.

"What did ye say?" Tuck glanced over at her.

She turned her eyes on him, more pleading than inquiring. "Will you hang around until I know what I'm doing?"

Then she did the damnedest thing—she bit her lip and waited.

Her request made him uneasy. He wished she would quit looking at him that way. He glanced at his watch, remembering his *out.* And for the first time, Gandiegow didn't feel like a prison sentence, but an escape.

Besides, Ryn should know straight up that he wasn't the rescuing kind. He was no hero. No matter how the lass looked at him. He was the villain. Didn't she know?

"Och, lass, no, I can't wait around with ye. I'm needed back in Gandiegow."

5

R YN STARED OUT THE WINDOW, her eyes burning. She should be used to abandonment by now. Her father. Her mother's aloofness. And death leaving her without anyone. But why did this stranger, Tuck, affect her this way? She shouldn't have asked for his help in the first place. She was definitely off kilter. But heck, she was after all, in a foreign country all by herself. No one to lean on. No one to confide in.

The loch, gray with mist surrounding the edges, caught her attention. Or more accurately, the pristine white swan, gliding gracefully on the water, had her wondering: *Is Mom here?* Ryn knew she was being irrational, but since her mother had died, she'd seen swans over and over again.

Mom loved swans. On the day of Mom's passing, a trumpeter swan had been swimming on the pond outside of the hospital. The next day, Ryn had seen one flying overhead while leaving her mother's condo. And everywhere, Ryn had seen swans plastered on billboards. It felt like a swan invasion. Each time, Ryn couldn't shake the feeling that the swan was a sign, her mother letting her know she was right there with her.

She turned to Tuck. "Has that swan always been here?"

"Dunno know. I've never seen it here before today."

A moment later, the castle came into view, a three story, sprawling estate that could've been seen in any BBC production. Tuck looked determined to be rid of her and she wondered if he expected her to hop out while he drove by. When the car came to a complete stop in front of the castle and Tuck turned off the key, Ryn was surprised. And hopeful. Maybe he'd changed his mind and was going to hang around to help her adjust to the situation before he abandoned her.

"I'll walk you inside," he said begrudgingly before getting out.

"Thanks." She slipped from the car with the tote in her arms.

Tuck carried her luggage and sewing machine to the door, but then left them outside. "Stay here." He went in, leaving her gawking after him.

Was he warning the residents of Kilheath Castle that she was crashing the party?

A second later, he opened the door and she noticed he held the collars of two humungous dogs. They weren't barking at her, but they were definitely eager to make her acquaintance by the way they were panting and trying to break free.

Tuck nodded to his charges. "This is the Wallace and the Bruce, Scottish Deerhounds." He cocked his head, gesturing to her. "Come in. I believe the Laird is upstairs."

Ryn reached out a hand to each dog, let them sniff her, and then she scratched them behind the ears. She laughed, wishing the rest of Scotland was this welcoming.

The entryway could've been in a magazine for Scottish architecture, all rich dark wood. The walls sported stately portraits, intricate tapestries, and a substantial coat of arms. The windows were adorned with heavy draperies, being held back with regal pull ties. The crowning glory of the entryway was the dual staircases with the newel posts caps carved into horses' heads and thick balusters lathed perfectly in the Baroque style. Ryn ran a hand over one of the horse heads, as if she was giving the horse a *good boy* rub, but really, she just needed to make sure she wasn't imagining all of this.

An older woman, wearing an apron over her dress, rushed in with a bone in each hand. "Come here, boys."

Tuck let go and the dogs bounded after the woman. "Mrs. McNabb, Kilheath Castle's cook," he explained.

He gestured to the stairs, allowing Ryn to go first with him following behind. They found the group in a large, floral decorated bedroom with massive windows.

"Laird, I did as you asked." Tuck didn't wait around to introduce her, but backed out of the room without glancing her way.

The man Tuck nodded to was the same one who'd whisked Tuck away in the Smart Car. He must be the Laird.

The Laird and the young woman beside him both offered Ryn a welcoming smile. But the person she'd come to Scotland to see didn't acknowledge her existence. Maggie was bouncing a fussy wispy-curly-red-headed baby in her arms while gazing out the window.

The sight made Ryn's heart clinch. *All the babies on the plane and now this.* Why did Maggie have to have a baby, too? God must enjoy throwing curveballs at Ryn.

In high school, after *the incident*, she'd stopped babysitting. She'd done a pretty good job since then of keeping her distance from small children. Occasionally, when she saw babies in the grocery store, Ryn would quickly maneuver her cart away before they got too close. She looked side to side now, but saw no way to escape to a safe distance.

The young woman beside the Laird smiled and stepped forward, offering her hand. "I'm Sophie McGillivray." Her tone put a question mark on the end as if to say "And you are?"

"I'm Ryn Breckenridge." Ryn hesitated. "Maggie's cousin."

Maggie glanced her way at the mention of her name, but she seemed too distracted to absorb what Ryn had said.

She had been so anxious to meet Maggie and give her the Goodbye quilt. Now Ryn was anxious for another reason. And after what Tuck told her, now wasn't the time to blurt out that Ryn's mother—and Maggie's childhood friend—was dead.

"You caught us at an awkward time," Sophie said.

Ryn fit right in as she felt awkward, too. "I'm sorry for barging in like this."

"Nonsense."

At that moment, there was a ruckus and whoever caused it was coming up the stairs and their way. Two women appeared with a boy between them. The taller one had the boy by the collar, and he was struggling to get away.

"I don't know what ye're going to do with him," the taller one said.

The boy ran to Maggie—she must be his mother—and wrapped his arms around her waist, though he had to work at getting his hug by shifting the baby's legs. The little girl squawked in protest.

Maggie cocked her head at the shorter woman. "Sinnie, take Irene." And she handed off the baby.

Maggie knelt down and put her arms around the boy while she gave him eye contact. The distant woman of a moment ago was present for her son. Her pinched eyebrow relaxed and a softer side of Ryn's cousin became clear. "Dand, I know this is a big change."

"I don't want to be here," he cried.

Maggie smoothed back his dark hair. "This isn't easy for any of us. I need ye to be a big boy for me and for yere da. Ye'll have to be the man of the house until Da gets back and on his feet."

It was the perfect thing to say. The boy's expression went from pitying himself to determination. He stood taller and nodded at his mother.

"Thank ye." She kissed him on the head and hugged him tight.

Ryn felt really uncomfortable now. She was an outsider, standing in the middle of an intimate family moment.

"How about we give Maggie a minute alone before she has to leave?" Sophie said. "We've biscuits and tea in the kitchen."

Dand perked up, wiggled out of his mother's arms, and was the first one out the door.

None of this was the way Ryn had imagined. She had expected the storybook version of her coming to Scotland, where she'd be accepted into the family fold with a jolly family dinner with hugs and laughter all around. She likely would've heard stories about her mother and the antics the two cousins had gotten up to. Before coming, there was no doubt in Ryn's mind that she and Maggie would've had an instantaneous bond. But the truth was Maggie was eight years older and seemed to have little in common with Ryn, besides sharing the same family tree.

Maggie was a wife and mother, and at a totally different place in her life. Ryn, though, would never be a mother…a decision that had grown over time and one that had nothing to do with terminating her pregnancy. And everything to do with how she'd grown up.

Ryn knew her mother loved her, but Mom never embraced parenting. Mom, though, always held motherhood at arm's length and treated Ryn more like a younger sister than a daughter. Kind of like the Gilmore Girls, but without the warm-fuzzies. Early on, Ryn understood she was a lot of work for her mother—on bad days a nuisance and on good days a tolerable roommate. At times, Ryn felt cheated, like when she visited her friends' homes and their mothers acted *motherly*.

Despite her mother's shortcomings, Ryn loved her mother. When

Ryn was little, she used to think it was her fault her mother was always on edge. But she'd come to realize that Mom was doing the best she could in a bad situation. Mom had been only eighteen when she'd given birth to Ryn, and nurturing just wasn't Mom's thing.

And getting married isn't my thing. Ryn's track record with men was dreadful. She'd come to the conclusion that good men weren't only *hard to find*...they just didn't exist! Besides, she'd done fine on her own these last two years, and only lonely some of the time.

Suddenly Ryn's mood plunged, making her feel more cut off than before, and it didn't help that Maggie continued to ignore her. Sure, it had nothing to do with her and everything to do with the circumstances surrounding Maggie's husband's accident. But knowing that didn't make it hurt any less.

"Come." Sophie stood at the door with pinched eyebrows, her concerned gaze fixed on Ryn.

Ryn gave Maggie one more glance, held her tote tight, then followed Sophie out the door.

"Are ye hungry?" Sophie said.

Ryn nodded, still a little shell-shocked.

"We'll get ye something more substantial than biscuits, then I'll find a place for ye to stay. I believe the potter's cottage is ready."

"The potter's cottage?" Ryn asked.

"Hugh has plans to turn Whussendale and the woolen mill into a tourist hotspot. He wants to bring in artisans to round out the village, offering more than just woolen products."

Ryn followed Sophie down the stairs into the kitchen, which was a huge open room, big enough to house a full kitchen staff. Near the open hearth was a simple long dining table made of oak. There Dand sat, scarfing down a stack of cookies.

Sophie turned to Ryn. "I should introduce you to yere other cousins."

"Other cousins?" Surely she meant the boy, Dand.

The taller woman took the baby from Sinnie. "I'm Rowena, Maggie's sister. And this is Sinnie, the other sister—the baby of the family."

Sinnie rolled her eyes at her sister.

Once again, Ryn felt discombobulated, and it wasn't just because the baby in the room stared at Ryn with pure curiosity. Why hadn't Mom said something about the sisters? She'd only talked of her *wee cousin Maggie*.

Rowena peered at her, as if she understood Ryn's confusion. "Sinnie and I are *after thoughts*. We came along much later. I expect that we're closer to yere age. I'm twenty-six and Sinnie is twenty-two."

"Almost twenty-three," Sinnie piped in.

Ryn nodded. "I'm twenty-eight. Three weeks ago." She'd spent her birthday alone, packing up her mother's things.

Sinnie smiled at her. "I'm sure we'll be fast friends."

Those were the most comforting words Ryn had heard since she'd set foot in Scotland.

Dand stood and wiped crumbs from his clothes. "I'm going to the loch."

Rowena set Irene to her feet, and like a newborn colt, the little one wobbled toward her brother. "We'll go to the loch together."

"I don't need ye to go with me," Dand whined. "I'm not a baby."

At that, Irene began fussing. Sinnie gave her a cookie and the red-haired angel smiled.

"Aye, ye're not a babe, Dand," Rowena said. "But I'm going with you anyway."

Dand complained all the way out the door, but Rowena stubbornly stayed close, as if bound to the boy with invisible thread.

Sophie turned to Sinnie. "I'm taking Ryn to the potter's cottage. Do you and Irene want to come along?" She glanced upward as if thinking of Maggie in the rooms above.

Sinnie picked up Irene and adjusted her on her hip, kissing the top of her head. "What do you think, little bug. Would a nice walk put ye to sleep?"

They all returned to the front door and retrieved Ryn's luggage. Outside, the sky was gray and the air thick with humidity.

"It's *dreich* today," Sophie said. "Dreary weather."

They hadn't taken four steps from the castle before Sinnie began her interrogation. "So, Cousin Ryn, where do ye hail from in America?"

"Dallas, Texas, these last five years." Ryn had been transferred there with her big corporate job. When they'd downsized, she'd gone on her own and had made a decent living until Mom needed her. "But five months ago, I moved in with my mother in Minneapolis." The winter had been hell—both the weather and watching her mother die.

"What brings ye to Scotland?"

That was a loaded question. But Ryn answered anyway. "Did you know about my mom? She and Maggie were close at one time."

Sinnie frowned. "No. I knew we had relations in the States but nothing more."

Since Ryn was a young girl, she'd dreamed of meeting her family in Scotland. But apparently, her Scottish clan hadn't given a thought to her or her mother. Ryn felt embarrassed and kept facing forward so they wouldn't see her disappointment. Maybe this trip was for naught. A fool's errand.

Sinnie touched her arm. "Hold up. I have to tell you something about Maggie. She doesn't share things easily. Because of our age difference, she tends to act more like a mum to me and Rowena, instead of a sister."

That did appease Ryn's bruised feelings.

The crunch of gravel from behind, had them stepping to the side of the road as Maggie in the white van passed.

"Maggie's off to see John," Sinnie said. Irene had indeed drifted off to sleep on her aunt's shoulder. "He had an accident and is in the hospital."

"Tuck told me. I'm so sorry."

Nothing else was said as they walked the rest of the way to the wool mill compound. Ryn took a moment to glance along the row of buildings. Some had signs out front—like Dye Shed, Mill, and Weaving Shed—while other buildings remained unnamed. Sophie led them to a path that wound behind the complex.

"So how is my cousin..." Sinnie paused as if searching for a name.

"My mom's name is Kathy," Ryn provided. This was the time to say something about her mother's death, but the whole ordeal felt too raw just to say, 'she died.' Since losing Mom, Ryn couldn't count on keeping her composure, as her tears had a mind of their own, streaming from her eyes at the most inopportune times.

"Are ye all right?" Sinnie asked, touching her arm.

Ryn didn't realize that she'd stopped in the middle of the path. "Yes. I'm fine. It's just—" she took a deep breath "—my mother passed away last month." Repeating those words felt surreal and she'd never get used to saying it. She'd been by her mother's side when she'd taken her last breath, she'd picked out a casket, and surprisingly Ryn didn't completely lose it when she stood over her mother's grave. But still, every cell in Ryn's body proclaimed it was only a bad dream. How could it be possible her mom was gone?

"Oh, no." Sinnie moved closer, reaching out a hand and gently touching Ryn's arm. "I'm so sorry."

As if closing ranks, Sophie sidled up to Ryn's other side, patting her back.

Just then, it occurred to Ryn what Sinnie and Rowena were suffering through also. She touched Sinnie's arm. "I'm so sorry to hear about your father. Tuck told me."

"Thank you," Sinnie said, looking stoic instead of sad. "We're okay. He wasn't an easy man."

Ryn understood firsthand how parent-child relationships could be complicated.

"Come now," Sophie said. "Let's get ye to the cottage."

The three of them went silent. What little comraderie between them was now riddled with sadness and thoughts of the ones they'd lost. Ryn had ruined it with her announcement, and it hadn't helped that her words were choppy while doing it, and her voice hitched here and there. Even if she wanted to, she couldn't glance over and catch either one of their eyes right now, as she felt way too self-conscious for being an emotional mess.

Sophie led them to the first cottage on the left side of the little horseshoe of homes. Oddly, the potter's cottage sported two doors, sitting close together—the left one red, the right one blue. Sophie took them to the red door, but pointed to the blue. "The blue one's Tuck's cottage. For now."

Ryn wondered what she meant by *for now,* but didn't ask. As she glanced down the row, she realized several of these duplex cottages existed amongst detached ones, but each door had been painted a different bright color.

Sophie pulled out the key and unlocked the door. "The inside has been refurbished and the electrical updated." She pointed to Ryn's sewing machine. "I'm sure ye'll put the electrical to good use." She held the door wide.

Ryn stepped in first and stopped. Light flooded in through the windows, highlighting the cheery interior, speaking to her girly side. "It's perfect." Each window had been covered with different fun plaid fabrics, set on the diagonal. Someone had wanted to instill a bit of whimsy in this one-room cottage and the room wore it well. A bed sat at the far wall, a kitchenette on the right side of the cottage, and a loveseat was placed in front of an empty hearth.

"So ye like it?" Sophie beamed at her, knowing full well that Ryn did. She held out the key. "It's all yeres."

"What about the potter?" Ryn asked, though she was looking a gift horse in the mouth.

"We haven't found him or her yet. You enjoy it for as long as ye're here."

Baby Irene sighed in her sleep.

"Why don't ye lay her on the bed?" Sophie said to Sinnie.

Sinnie strode over and carefully laid the child down. Next, she stacked pillows around her, as if building a protective wall. When she was done, she turned to Ryn and put her hands on her hips, smiling.

"Now, Cousin Ryn…tell us why ye're clutching yere bag the way that ye do."

&⊃⊂&

John was sick to death of lying in this hospital bed. "Day twelve," he muttered to himself. He looked out the window. The damned nurse had pulled the curtains for him to see the rain beat against the glass, punishing it, exactly as he was being punished.

He glanced down at his upper arm, where half of it was missing, and then down to the empty space where his right hand used to be. The doctors said he was lucky, but he sure as hell didn't feel lucky. "More like cursed."

He'd worked hard at being a good man all his life. He'd become a fisherman, following in his da's footsteps. John had watched out for his brothers when Da had died suddenly of a heart attack, four-plus years ago. John had been a faithful man to both his wife and the Almighty. He hadn't missed a Sunday service in years. Yet, here he laid, less than a whole man. He looked up at the ceiling, searching for heaven. What had he done to deserve this?

The rain came down even harder, making him think of rough

days at sea on the family fishing boat. "It was better than this." Anything was better than being trapped in this net of an *effing* hospital. He couldn't get anyone to tell him when he could leave this damn place…or when he could go back to work. Every time he asked, the doctor would sidestep. Then afterward, he'd hear Maggie and the doctor whispering in the hallway. Something about a possible second surgery. Even whispering more about fishing. Surely, they wouldn't keep John from doing the work he loved. The work he was born and bred to do.

A knock sounded on the frame of his open door. "Come in." He didn't look to see who it was. He was tired of the villagers giving him pitying glances when they thought he wasn't looking.

Father Andrew, in his blasted white cleric's collar, strolled into his peripheral vision. The young Episcopal priest took up his post directly in front of John, blocking his view of the storm outside. "How are ye today?"

John wasn't in the mood for niceties. "How do ye think I am?" He sounded bitter, and why shouldn't he? The Almighty's representative had both of his appendages and didn't need help steadying his left hand as he brought his shaky spoon up for a bit of broth. John glared over at the tray with the cold bowl and offending spoon, which waited to be taken away.

Andrew clasped his hands in front of him, relaxed as a calm sea. "What can I do for ye?"

Gawd, how did the priest look so composed all the time? "I want nothing." *Except what the Almighty has taken from me.*

Andrew nodded and walked away. John was shocked and relieved that Andrew would give up so easily and leave him to fester alone in his misery. Except he didn't go.

A chair scraped against the floor as the interfering pastor pulled it near. Once again, Andrew had proven to be as tenacious as any salty fisherman.

John glanced over as the priest took his seat, positioned so he too could look out at the storm.

"I don't feel up to praying, Father, if that's what ye have in mind." John closed his eyes in frustration, wanting solitude.

"Nay. We're just going to sit and enjoy the view."

John scoffed. The city beyond his room wasn't the right view. It wasn't the North Sea and its fury lashing against the wheelhouse window.

Andrew seemed at peace in his silence. And why shouldn't he? He was a man who hadn't suffered loss. He had his limbs. He had his family. He could preach on Sunday instead of being stuck in a hospital.

A bad taste formed in John's mouth as Tuck crept into his mind. "I hear yere brother has been working *my boat*." Ross and Ramsay had broken the news. It irked that they didn't badmouth Tuck for their eldest brother losing his hand, and part of his arm!

"Aye," Andrew answered, still staring out the window. The priest was enacting some new game. He'd badgered John into talking about the accident as soon as he woke, but now he didn't even have a few comforting words, and was as silent as the grave.

"Ross said Tuck hasn't missed a day." Which tasted bitter in John's mouth. It was Ross who'd found the envelope in the wheelhouse where Tuck had sold the catch from the day of the accident. What was the good-for-nothing playing at? Assuaging his guilt? Did he think he could be forgiven with the payment of selling a few fish?

"He's a hard worker."

"Ha," John hissed. "Of course, ye'd take his side." He hadn't planned to ever utter that thought aloud. Andrew and Moira had been conscientious visitors, showing unflagging support for him.

"I don't take sides," Andrew said calmly. "I pray for something good to come out of all of this."

John lifted his amputated arm and shook it at Andrew.

"Something good?" But there was a price to pay for roaring at the priest—his arm hurt like a son-of-a-bitch.

Incensed beyond reason, John's head felt near to bursting. Aye, yelling at the vicar was surely a sin, but how could the Almighty—if He was *just*—not understand?

"Get out," John said coolly, nodding at Andrew. "I've nothing more to say."

"What's going on?" Maggie's voice was frail and it stabbed at John's heart. His fierce wife was defeated, surely as he was.

"I heard ye yell." She came to stand by his side, but he didn't look up at her.

"'Twas nothing," Andrew said.

But John didn't need him fighting his battles for him. *It's my job to protect my wife.* But he didn't say it. Instead, he mustered up a bogus smile before turning to her. "The priest was just leaving."

"Aye," Andrew concurred. "I'll come by later in the week. Moira will want to come, too."

In other words, John better watch himself.

As soon as Andrew exited, Maggie turned her worried and concerned eyes on John and ran a hand through his hair. "Are ye in pain? Yere brow is furrowed."

Yes, he was in pain. But the phantom throbbing from his nonexistent hand was nothing…when compared to the pain in his heart.

"Do ye want me to get something from the nurse to take the edge off?"

"Nay." He didn't know what else to say to her. He couldn't tell her the trouble he felt brewing in him. He couldn't burden her more. Maggie was too fragile. *And I'm the one who did this to her.*

Maggie glided to the other side of the bed. "Mum called. She's having a hard time of it with Da gone."

John closed his eyes. *We're all having a hard time of it.* "Coira is a strong woman. She'll be fine." His relationship with his mother-in-law was contentious at best, but he never wished ill-will toward her.

"Scoot over." Maggie moved his IV and crawled in beside him. She situated herself under his good arm so she was cradled up against his shoulder. She sighed as if he'd been the one to take her worries away. But he'd been the one to cause them. The accident had disrupted all their lives. *I don't deserve her anymore.* But instead of making her go, John held her close and breathed in the scent of her hair.

6

R YN STOOD IN THE MIDDLE of the cottage, biting her
lower lip, staring from Sophie to Sinnie. How did Sinnie know
her tote bag held the special quilt?

"Och, Sinnie, let Ryn get her things in the door first." But
Sophie's reproach didn't hold even a morsel of reprimand.

Sinnie beamed at Ryn. "Her things are in the door."

Sophie grabbed the tea kettle and went to the sink, looking like
she might be settling in for a while. "Ye know what they say about
the curiosity and the cat."

Sinnie's eyes danced with merriment. "That the cat got the scoop
before anyone else?" She pulled the roller bag to the armoire near
the bed, then expectantly looked over her shoulder at Ryn. "Tis a
good time to spill the beans. The babe is asleep, and Sophie and I
are great listeners."

For a second, Ryn felt a kinship with Sinnie—the two of them
sharing the curiosity gene. It felt good, knowing she had family ties,
but they were distant ties at best. *Distant* and *distance* played off of
one another in her mind. When Ryn returned home to Minnesota or

Dallas or wherever she landed, her cousins might as well be on Mars for as much as she'd see them.

I better make the most of this trip, then.

Ryn set her tote on the table as Sophie and Sinnie drew near. She'd hoped to reveal the quilt with Maggie present, but Maggie had more on her mind than show-and-tell. As Ryn pulled out the bundle, Sophie and Sinnie each took a corner and spread out the quilt.

"'Tis gorgeous," Sophie exclaimed.

"I recognize the fabric used for the Flying Geese blocks," Sinnie said. "Mum put that in my Around the World quilt, which is back home in Gandiegow. Ye'll have to come visit, so ye can see all my quilts."

Ryn smiled at her, knowing that was one of the magical things about quilting: Fabric could connect two distant cousins, even though they hadn't met before this day. And also, fabric could bring back memories as easily as thumbing through an old box of photographs. "This quilt hung in our living room above the couch for as long as I can remember. I dubbed it the Family Tree quilt, but my mother insisted it was the Goodbye quilt."

Sophie nodded at the spread-out patchwork. "It makes sense why ye would call it the Family Tree quilt."

The modified Sampler quilt was only twenty-eight inches wide and thirty-six inches tall, consisting of twelve blocks—a Nine Patch, a Rail Fence, a Thistle block, and others. Appliquéd over the assortment of blocks was a tree, stretching from the top of the quilt to the bottom.

"Why is it called the Goodbye quilt?" Sinnie asked. "Did yere mum and Maggie think they'd never see each other again?"

"No. Mom said it was only meant to be *goodbye* until the next summer. The idea was to transfer the quilt between them every year, but Mom never made it back to Scotland. She had to get a job that year to help Granny Kay pay the bills." Granny was a single mother, just as Ryn's mom had been.

Ryn never met grandfather, just like she'd never met her father. There were ten consecutive Kathryn Iona's nestled away on their family tree. How many of them had raised their baby girls without a man by her side? Ryn could've been one of them, if she hadn't gotten an abortion.

She stared over at the little body of Irene—face relaxed, eyes closed, her cheeks that of a cherub. What would've happened if she'd kept the baby her mother insisted she *take care of*? The little boy or girl would've been thirteen, nearly the age when Ryn had gotten pregnant. Her heart squeezed. With each breath Irene took, Ryn's became shallower.

But Mom had been right. If Ryn had gone full-term, her life would've been completely different. She would've been forced to drop out of high school. College and a degree in graphic arts would've only been a dream. There was no way she could've supported a baby on her own. Diapers. Daycare on a minimum wage job. Sleepless nights. All things Mom mentioned that she'd known all too well.

You're just a child yourself, she'd said. *Ryn, you don't have a clue what it takes to be an adult.*

It would be years before Ryn would comprehend why her mother had been so adamant. Adult finances weren't for the faint of heart.

Mom was right about something else, too. She'd been in no position to help raise another baby. And she needn't drive the point home. Ryn knew what her mother was capable of. She'd already reached her limit with barely enough bandwidth to raise her own teenage daughter.

Irene shifted, tucking her legs underneath her, making Ryn look away. At fifteen, she couldn't have kept the baby, but that didn't stop the sense of loss that snuck up on her right now. Her vulnerability made perfect sense, considering she lost her grandmother last year and now Mom a month ago.

Ryn had made peace with the truth—she was predestined to go it alone. No nuclear family. No husband, not now or ever, because she could no longer afford to make any more mistakes on Mr. Wrong, or Mr. Right Now. She'd accepted the fact she would be the last Kathryn Iona in her family tree.

Sadness drove her to reach out to the Goodbye quilt. Her fingers automatically traced the tree, from the trunk up to the branches at the top. As she pulled her hand away, she gently tucked her grief away, too, as if turning under the raw edges of an appliqué piece before stitching it down.

Ryn became aware of the silence she'd brought down on the cottage. Dwelling on the past only exposed her pain to others, which in turn made them uncomfortable. Yeah, she was stupid sometimes, letting her emotions get the best of her. She should know by now that wishing her life was different was only a waste of time.

Ryn's gaze met Sinnie's sad smile. Her cousin studied her as if trying to make out the source of her pain. But then she nodded and looked back at the quilt, as if deliberately not prying into why Ryn was in such a funk. "Is there a reason the tree doesn't have any leaves?"

Ryn shrugged. "I don't know." She'd planned to ask. But in light of what Maggie and her family were going through, the question seemed small and insignificant. Irene sighed contentedly as she stretched her limbs and rolled over. The sleeping baby didn't seem to have the worries of her parents or her brother.

Ryn took the ends of the quilt from Sophie and Sinnie. "I'll put this away."

"Why don't you hang it up?" Sophie pointed to the long skinny shelf above where Irene slept. "It would look lovely over the bed."

Ryn stared at Sophie incredulously. Didn't she know Ryn was to hand off the quilt to Maggie?

Sinnie was reading her mind again. "Hang it for now. Ye can give it to Maggie later."

But hanging the Goodbye quilt smacked too close to making this cozy cottage Ryn's own. "I'm not sure that I should."

Apparently, Sophie was. She took the quilt from Ryn. "Sinnie, grab those six canning jars from the rack in the kitchen."

Ryn watched as Sinnie went to the open shelf. The jars were filled with dried beans, macaroni, and other items you might find in a stocked pantry. One of the jars, though, was filled with buttons.

"There's only five," Sinnie said as she picked up two and carried them over to Sophie.

"Another jar should be under the sink with nails, nuts, and bolts," Sophie said. "Ryn, take the other end and we'll get this quilt up."

Obediently, Ryn grabbed the quilt, holding it high, making sure not to drop her end on the sleeping baby. Within a few minutes, the quilt was hung without hammering a nail, and looking as if it was ready for a photo shoot for *Shabby Chic Magazine*.

"There. Now that should make you feel like ye're at home," Sophie said.

But Ryn didn't have a home right now. As a modern day Scarlett O'Hara, she'd been procrastinating about where her next address might be.

Sinnie strolled over and stood next to Ryn to look at the quilt, too. "When Maggie is back from seeing John, we'll show her the quilt."

But it didn't sit well with Ryn. What if Maggie didn't approve of Ryn acting like the quilt was her own—hanging it wherever she pleased, putting it up in her cottage like she meant to keep it forever?

Her cottage. How strange it sounded, but for now this was home. If only for the night.

Sinnie nudged her, acting as if they were old friends. "I bet the quilt will inspire Maggie. She's done nothing to prepare for the retreat she's supposed to head up. When Deydie finds out, she's sure to take her broom after my sister's backside."

A flurry of thoughts and questions hit Ryn, but she didn't open her mouth quick enough.

"Whussendale's first retreat is coming up fast." Sinnie went to the bed and gently sat next to Irene.

Sophie pulled down three mugs from the shelf. "Two days," she muttered, as if it wasn't nearly enough time.

"Wait a second." Ryn had a few question. "First, what kind of retreat? And secondly, what's a Deydie?"

Sophie laughed good-naturedly and all the tension and sadness lifted from the room. "Deydie McCracken is the head quilter in Gandiegow."

"She's old," Sinnie said matter-of-factly. "And bossy—"

"But kind in her own way," Sophie interjected, as the kettle on the stove whistled. She poured the steaming water into the red teapot. "The retreat was Deydie's idea. Now that John can't fish, Maggie is supposed to run the retreats here in Whussendale so she can earn a living."

"Why can't someone else do the retreat until things calm down for Maggie?" Ryn asked. That seemed much more reasonable.

Sinnie picked at a string on the quilt. "Deydie insists it's Maggie's job. When Rowena and I tried to jump in and do it for her, we were told to mind our own business." She shook her head. "As if our own sister isn't our business."

Sophie bobbed her head. "Deydie gave me the same lecture."

"Let me see if I have this straight," Ryn said. "Maggie's husband just had a serious fishing accident and Deydie wants Maggie to start up and run a retreat center here?"

"Aye. All retreats will be up at the castle until a retreat center can be built," Sophie added.

"Fine," Ryn said, but she still had a point to make. "Can't *this*

Deydie see Maggie isn't in any shape to run anything—except to the hospital, and take care of her children?" She'd like to give this Deydie a piece of her mind.

Sophie and Sinnie gawked at her in surprise.

"Och," Sophie said. "Isn't *our* Ryn a feisty one?"

Our Ryn? Sophie's words made Ryn feel as if a flannel quilt had been wrapped around her shoulders.

"Aye, our Ryn's feisty," Sinnie agreed, grinning. "But she hasn't met the likes of Deydie yet."

Sophie handed Ryn a mug. "Come sit at the table. Deydie isn't as bad as we're making her out to be."

Sinnie made a throaty muffled 'hah' while walking over to the small kitchen table to join them.

"Be nice," Sophie chided, but then turned to Ryn. "It's true. Deydie has wanted to have retreats in Whussendale for some time now to take advantage of our wool products. But I've been too busy to get the wagon rolling as I'm the kiltmaker's apprentice."

Sinnie took Sophie's hand and squeezed it. "And too busy with yere new husband."

Sophie blushed. She used a sip of tea to hide the secret smile, which rested on her lips.

Sinnie set her forearms on the table and leaned forward. "Here's the deal. Deydie may be ancient, but she's still as sharp as a new needle. She saw a way to get what she wanted and at the same time to help Maggie out."

Ryn cradled her hands around the warm mug, shaking her head. "How is burdening Maggie *helping her out?*"

"Old Deydie must believe that working on the retreat will take Maggie's mind off all her troubles. Now, let's drink our tea before it gets cold," Sophie seemed to smile at a non sequitur thought. "Maggie's the best wool quilter in Gandiegow."

"True," Sinnie smiled proudly. "Maggie should be chuffed at the spectacular wool quilts she's designed. She's won three first-place ribbons at the Scottish Quilt Championships."

Sophie nodded to acknowledge the accomplishment. "Also, Whussendale is much closer to the hospital for Maggie to visit John. I tried to tell Deydie that adding the retreat now would be too much for Maggie."

Baby Irene cooed from her side of the room. Ryn looked over to see the child roll over, sit up, and stare at them.

Sinnie went to her. "What are you doing, little bug?"

Sophie laughed. "I think she was only pretending to sleep until I mentioned her mum's name."

Sinnie picked up Irene. "We'll head back. She's ready for a nappy change."

"Ryn and I will stay and finish our tea. I'll be home in a bit," Sophie said.

There was a plunk on the ceiling. Then another and another.

Sophie nodded at Ryn's luggage. "I hope ye've got a good raincoat with yere things."

Ryn glanced down at her jacket. "This is all I brought." Which didn't compare with the oilskin dusters they both wore.

"I'll dig out an extra for you when I get back to Kilheath. Maybe it'll ease up before we head back." Sophie smiled warmly and then took another sip of tea.

Sinnie opened her coat and wrapped Irene inside. The baby cuddled to her as if she'd been cocooned against the weather many times before. "I'll meet ye back at the castle." She dashed out.

Sophie popped up and went to the kitchen cabinet. "There has to be some biscuits in here. Mrs. McNabb just stocked the place." She produced some McVities Digestives and came back to the table, ripping open the sleeve. "Here."

Ryn took one of the cookies.

Sophie sighed, grinning. "Hugh has big plans for Whussendale.

At the prospect of holding retreats here, his wheels have been turning. He thinks we should build the retreat center between the green grocer and the church. And because supplies will be needed for the retreat center, he'd like to add a haberdashery to Whussendale with quilt fabrics, wool for knitting, and paper crafting supplies for those who scrapbook. What vision he has!" She laughed. "Big plans for such a small village."

Ryn's wheels were spinning now, too, but not about turning Whussendale into a crafting hotspot and filling the town with artisans. She was thinking about Maggie. Surely there was some way she could help her cousin so she wouldn't have to be in charge of the upcoming retreat. Ryn didn't think it was enough to offer to help...Maggie needed more assistance than that. In fact, Ryn thought Maggie needed it off her plate completely.

She turned to Sophie, who was taking a second cookie. "I have an idea."

Sophie put the cookie down. "You do?"

This was pretty bold, even for a woman who'd hopped a plane and flew all the way to Scotland by herself. Maybe Ryn should mull it over for a day, but there wasn't time. The quilt retreat was in two days! "What if I take Maggie's place and head up the quilt retreat for her?"

Sophie's look of surprise was nearly comical at first, but then she gave Ryn a worried shake of her head. "Deydie expects Maggie to not only oversee the retreat, but to teach as well."

Ryn nibbled a little on her cookie before answering the implied question. "I can teach. But I don't have any experience with making wool quilts. Do you think the retreat goers would be opposed to switching? Let's say to making a Modern quilt?" She had, after all, brought her True Colors quilt with her to work on while she was in Scotland. "I can give you a list of the fabric they would need." But then remembered how remote Whussendale was. "This is short notice. Will finding fabric be a problem?"

Sophie broke into a smile. "Getting fabric won't be an issue." But she sobered in the next second. "It's Deydie ye'll have to worry *aboot*."

Ryn looked side to side, as if looking for a phantom Deydie. "How will she know? She's not here."

"True." Mischief danced in Sophie's eyes and a maniacal grin came to her lips. "It's not often, *or ever*, one of us can pull one over on that old quilter."

Ryn touched her arm, trying to bring Sophie back to what was important. "I'm not trying to fool anyone. I just think Maggie can't handle doing this retreat."

"True."

"Then let's *not* tell Deydie what we plan to do. Deal?" Ryn asked.

"Aye. At dinner tonight, we'll break the good news to Maggie."

Ryn put her hand up to throw on the brakes. "Let's not say anything to Maggie just yet." There were a lot of ducks to get in a row.

"I understand," Sophie said. "When do I get to see the quilt that you're going to teach?"

"It's in my luggage. I'll show you after I unpack." Ryn stifled a yawn and ignored the growing effects of the long flight and her crazy day. "I better get that fabric list together for you."

"There's paper and pens in the basket on the counter." Sophie rose. "I'll leave you to it. I have to speak with Mrs. McNabb. Dinner is at six. Hugh and I expect you to be there. "

"Okay." As her new friend left, Ryn glanced over at the Goodbye quilt and felt comforted. "Just like home."

What a strange day and a strange turn of events. At least for the next few days, she knew what she would be doing and where she was going to stay.

She rolled her suitcase to the bed and laid it on top, covering the spot where the baby had lain. She pulled out the True Colors pieces and took them to the table. For the next few hours, she holed up in *her* cottage, writing up the list of fabric for Sophie and the instructions for the quilt. She worked until she could no longer ignore her aching head. The clock on the wall alerted her that she'd been up nearly thirty hours. *No wonder I feel like I hit a brick wall!* She slid her suitcase to the floor and stretched out on the bed.

She woke to the sound of tapping at the door. Discombobulated and feeling unsure of where she was, she crawled out of bed and made her way across the cottage. When she opened the door, she had to blink a couple of times, waiting until the faces of Sinnie, Rowena, and the boy Dand fully registered.

Dand, wearing a kilt, stepped inside authoritatively. "The Laird said for ye to come to dinner."

Rowena pulled him back by the shoulder. "We're here to fetch ye."

"But only if you want to come," Sinnie added. She held out a heavy raincoat and Wellies to her. "Sophie asked me to bring these along."

Ryn's stomach had been trying to wake her for the last hour. "Thanks." She took the items from Sinnie and slipped on the Wellies and the coat, making sure to grab the list for Sophie before she left.

The four of them walked back to the castle together while Dand told how he'd like to go fishing on the loch.

"The Laird said I could use the dinghy," he said cheerfully.

"But only if an adult is with ye," Rowena said firmly.

Dand stomped his foot. "He didn't say that." The two argued the rest of the way.

Instead of using the front entrance, Sinnie and Rowena guided them around to the side. "Sophie said that since we're family, we should use the kitchen entrance."

"Oh." Ryn didn't know about *family* but Sophie had been very welcoming.

As they walked through the door, wagging tails and whining met them. The Wallace and the Bruce, not inconspicuously in the least, kept glancing to their leashes on the hook, as if the newcomers were to take them for a walk.

"Boys, get away from there," Sophie said laughing. She wore a blue plaid dress with a thin belt at the middle, tights, and a pair of flats. The dogs ran to her, plopped their rumps down on the tile, assuming their place by her side like sentinels. She handed them both bone-shaped treats.

When Rowena and Sinnie slipped off their coats, Ryn noticed they, too, were wearing casual dresses. Ryn looked down, grimacing at her now crumpled black pantsuit. She groaned, inwardly. If she'd known she should dress nicely for dinner, she would've worn one of the cute outfits in her suitcase.

Sophie came to her and slipped an arm around Ryn's shoulder. "You're fine. Don't worry about it. We should've told you we were dressing for dinner." She shrugged. "It's Hugh's idea. He's trying to revive the old traditions of Kilheath Castle."

Ryn stuffed her embarrassment away as she pulled the list of fabrics for Sophie from her pocket. "Here's a sketch of the True Colors quilt for the retreat and the fabric needed."

Sophie gazed at the picture first. "This is grand. When the Whussendale ladies see this, they'll have no problem switching from doing a wool quilt to a Modern. I know I'll enjoy making such a bold quilt." She scanned the list of fabrics. "And this looks doable. Between all of us here, we should have enough fabric to make your quilt. If not, there's always the quilt shop in Inverness." Her eyes twinkled and her smile was so genuine, Ryn was beginning to believe it was all going to work out fine.

Hugh, wearing a kilt and looking his part as Lord of the Manor, strolled into the room, smiling at the group. Nonchalantly, he nabbed a piece of bread from the counter.

Sophie swatted at him, but he got away. "Mrs. McNabb said she left you yere favorite—haggis potato apple tarts—but I'll not tell ye where they are if ye don't stop with the filching."

He laughed, scanning the kitchen. "Where did ye hide them this time, wife?"

Sinnie and Rowena went to the counter and retrieved the plates and silverware.

"Come, Dand," Rowena said. "Ye'll help with setting the table."

"Do I have to?" But Dand was already picking up the napkins before following them to the door.

"Make room for one more," the Laird called to them, but they were gone.

Sophie pulled the roast from the oven. "Who else is coming to dinner, Hugh?"

Hugh patted the Wallace's head. "I invited Tuck to dine with us."

Involuntarily, Ryn's libido bounded to life. *Kilted's coming to dinner?*

Hugh smiled at Ryn as if he knew what she was thinking and was one step ahead of her. "I thought Tuck could keep our American guest company."

A second later, a knock came at the kitchen door. Ryn couldn't help but compare the tapping on her door with this more forceful one. And she was much more aware of her surroundings. And her body!

"Enter," Hugh hollered.

The dogs hurried to the door with their wagging and whining renewed.

Tuck appeared...as handsome as before, but was wearing a blue and green kilt this time. It suited him and she nearly ran to his side like one of the dogs.

This is so confusing! She'd done well these past two years and had easily stifled any stray longings for the occasional good-looking male.

But Tuck had her rethinking her position on keeping a healthy distance from him. She hadn't known until this moment that she hadn't really been tested until now, and resisting all the others had been a frigging ride in the proverbial park!

She felt swayed a little as she gazed at his legs under the hem of his kilt.

Staring at him in all his prettiness made her want to throw in the towel…hell, maybe the whole laundry basket! That boy-crazy young woman of her youth wanted to bust free and see where *Kilted* might take her. For the rest of her life maybe. For some crazy reason, she couldn't recall any of the past pain.

The only coherent thought she could conjure up rang through her like a bell, as if being called to the dinner table. She felt ready to run in its direction, pull up a chair, and have her fill.

This time will be different.
This time will be different.
This time will be different.

7

TUCK LINGERED INSIDE the kitchen doorway and catalogued the scene: Sophie putting on oven mitts, Ryn looking uncomfortable and as guarded as before, and Hugh with a stupid grin on his face.

Yeah, Tuck caught the Laird's gaze flitting from him to Ryn, as if his glances back and forth were two hummingbirds playing tennis.

The Laird better not be playing matchmaker. Tuck wasn't in the mood!

Rowena and Sinnie bustled into the room and both stopped short. Rowena glowered in silence. Sinnie smiled and pulled a kitchen towel from the rack. "Hello, Tuck."

The little sister was much more civil than the older ones.

He meant to greet her back, but his 'hello' came out as a grunt.

God, he wished he'd bailed on dinner. But Hugh had been firm in his request.

Sinnie picked up the hot casserole dish. "Why are ye back so soon?" She stopped and waited for his response with the dish held waist-high.

"Magnus called and needed me to fix the weaving machine." Tuck left off the part about how the seas had become too choppy anyway to be out alone, which forced him back to Gandiegow.

Magnus's mandate to return to Whussendale had turned out to be a blessing, saving Tuck from the town meeting Deydie had called. The village, both men and women, usually met before an upcoming quilt retreat to make sure that everything went off like clockwork. All the fishermen were included, as their muscles were necessary to move the out-of-town quilters' luggage from the coach to Quilting Central and back again. Or…whatever task Deydie demanded the fishermen do.

Sophie gestured to the counter. "Everyone grab something and take it into the dining room."

Ryn picked up the bread basket and a stack of serving spoons. She held back, which made perfect sense, as the lass wouldn't know which direction to go.

Hugh took the salmon and Tuck grabbed the tatties and mashed turnips.

Like single-file soldiers, they made their way to the dining room, which held a long table capable of handling at least thirty. Only one end tonight was set, making the gathering cozier.

As Tuck scanned the room, he breathed a sigh of relief. Not until that moment did he realize he'd been holding his breath. Dand was there, taking his seat, but more importantly, Maggie wasn't. *She must be visiting John at the hospital.*

Maybe dinner this evening at Kilheath Castle wouldn't be as torturous as Tuck had imagined.

Hugh motioned for Tuck to sit next to Ryn. Once again, Tuck got the feeling the Laird was messing in his business again when he shouldn't be.

As Dand reached for the bread, Rowena's hand shot out and stopped him.

"Aunt Wena, I'm hungry."

"Ye'll wait for grace."

Automatically, the Scots offered their hands to one another. He noticed Ryn seemed momentarily confused. Finally, she slipped her hand in his, applying no more pressure than if her fingers had the force of a butterfly. And Tuck wasn't having it. He not only gripped her hand, he squeezed also, for good measure. He glanced over and saw a red tint fill her cheeks.

She may not like him, but at least he hadn't lost his charm. Ryn stared straight ahead as if she was pretending that he didn't exist. Strange, the warmth of her cheeks must've spread into her hand and straight into his chest. The feeling was foreign, and at the same time, he remembered that feeling and the rush of betrayal that came with it. He loosened his grip, but didn't let go.

Tuck couldn't meet her eyes right now, either. But as he lowered his head to pray, the side door to the dining room opened.

"Wait," Hugh said. "Maggie's here."

Tuck's mood plummeted as Maggie came through the door. She seemed distracted, cradling baby Irene as if the child was her life preserver. Which was weird as Tuck was the one who was drowning. In guilt. In uncomfortable awareness. And feeling claustrophobic in the twenty by fifty foot room. It certainly didn't help when Maggie's eyes fell on him and an unquestionable disdain washed over her.

Sinnie scooted back her chair, hurrying to her oldest sister. "I'll take the little bug."

Dand popped up, too, talking while he did, "Hurry, Mum." He surprised everyone by pulling out the chair for his mother. "I'm hungry." Irene leaned over from Sinnie's lap and tried to grab his hair as he sat back down. "I'll say the grace, if ye want." *Another surprise*. But then the boy rushed through the Selkirk grace as if he was on fire and a bucket of water waited at the end of the words.

"Some Folk hae meat that canna eat,

And some can eat that want it.

But we hae meat, and we can eat,

So let the Lord be Thanket!"

"Well done," Hugh said, smiling. Rowena, though, looked at Dand as if she wanted to correct the boy's haste for which he'd addressed the Almighty.

Ryn slipped her hand from Tuck's, a moment before he realized he was still holding her. Instantly, he missed the softness of her fingers as he went sort of empty inside. Maybe he was only missing the warmth of her hand. Both sentiments were ridiculous. He'd only just met the lass.

Hugh picked up the salmon and passed it to Maggie. "So, Ryn, tell us about yereself. Sinnie says ye're from Dallas."

"And Minnesota."

"Two completely different climates, I believe," Hugh remarked as he passed the tatties around.

"Yes," Ryn said. "After growing up in Minnesota, I never really got used to the heat in Texas."

"I'm sorry to hear about yere mother," Hugh said.

Ryn nodded then stared at her plate. At the same time, Sophie reached over and took her husband's hand. It was no secret Hugh's family was all gone—his sister, mother, and father. The only relative he had left was his Aunt Davinia. Tuck was surprised Hugh's pushy, but well-meaning aunt, hadn't come for dinner to see Ryn Brecken-ridge for herself. It occurred to him that Hugh's butting-in-nature probably came to him honestly through his aunt.

"Do ye have any brothers or sisters?" Rowena asked, getting into the spirit of things.

"None. I'm an only child." Ryn glanced at Maggie as if she wanted her attention.

"And yere father—" Hugh asked, "—where does he live?"

Ryn bit her lip. "I don't have one."

Tuck felt sorry for her. But wasn't it refreshing to have someone else at the dinner table under the spotlight, instead of him?

Sophie patted Hugh's hand. "Let our guest eat. Ye can interrogate her after the apple tarts."

Hugh smiled. "Aye. Sorry, Ryn, for being such a boor."

Next, Hugh engaged Dand with all the adventures he could get up to on Kilheath's estate.

"And I promise I'll show ye the cabin out in the woods," Hugh said at the end.

"Tonight?" Dand asked excitedly.

"Nay. Ye and I will trek out to see it in the morn." The Wallace nudged Hugh's elbow and he laughed. "We'll bring the dogs along with us."

At that, he turned to Tuck. "Will ye take the van back to Gandiegow in the morning for Maggie?"

Tuck's first reaction was to stare at Maggie, but then he wondered why the Laird would want him to commute in a petrol-guzzler such as the van, to Gandiegow and back.

Before Tuck could say anything, Hugh addressed the issue. "Brodie called and said Rachel needs the van to pick up new furniture for Partridge House." *Rachel's nearly completed B & B.* "You drive the van, and—" Hugh paused for a moment, smiling at the American lass, "—Ryn, if ye could follow Tuck to Gandiegow with his car, it would surely help us out." He nodded toward Dand. "I have a very important appointment in the morning."

"What if she doesn't know how to drive?" Tuck asked.

Ryn sat up straight, looking indignant. "I have a driver's license."

"Make sure to take yere passport with ye, too," Hugh said.

Tuck believed the Laird wasn't thinking clearly. "But the lass won't be able to get up that early in the morning."

"I'm happy to do it," Ryn said. "Anything to help out."

Tuck frowned at the Laird. "What will she do while I'm fishing?"

Ryn rolled her eyes. "*She'll be fine.*"

Hugh chuckled. He must've thought the pretty Yank was endearing or something. "Sophie said you brought yere sewing machine with ye."

Ryn's attitude melted away and a smile took its place. "I found it at a charity shop after I landed."

"Ye can sew at Quilting Central until Tuck is done. It'll give you a chance to meet the quilters of Gandiegow."

"But—" Tuck tried again.

Hugh's raised eyebrow ended Tuck's argument.

Aye. Tuck got it. He was in Whussendale and the Laird's word was law.

Hugh turned his attention to Ryn. "We're happy to have ye here in our wool community. If ye need anything for yere cottage, Tuck's yere man. He's agreed to deal with the cottage repairs in his spare time."

Ha! Spare time? The long list of repairs Hugh had given him was gathering dust. Holding down two jobs, in two villages with a drive in between, had kept Tuck plenty occupied. But he wasn't complaining. Keeping his hands busy, kept Tuck's mind from wandering into the dark corners.

Guiding the American lass to Gandiegow was just another of his chores. He glanced over at her and assured himself she was just a temporary inconvenience. *A verra tempting, good-looking, appealing inconvenience.* But an inconvenience all the same. Her being here only added more to his long list of responsibilities.

Suck it up, Tuck old boy. This is just more of yere penance.

Tuck kept his head down and ate the rest of his meal in silence. When dinner and dessert were over, he excused himself. "I've an early morn." He didn't glance in Maggie's direction or look to see if Ryn was ready to go. *Let her stay here late...hell, all night!* It was none of his business if she had trouble dragging her arse out from under her warm quilt in the wee hours of the morning. He stalked toward the door and his escape.

"Walk Ryn back," Hugh said.

Tuck halted, and exhaled, getting his emotions locked down tight before turning back to the Laird. "Sure. Where's she staying?"

Hugh grinned. "In the cottage attached to yeres."

⊱⊰

Ryn stepped from the castle into the misting night air, which had been rain only an hour ago. *But a lot could happen in an hour.* During dinner, she'd centered herself once more and now her attraction to the kilted Scot beside her was gone. Or so she thought. As Tuck—sulky and put out— took his place beside her for the walk back to their cottages, Ryn's nonsensical insides warmed and her emotions turned jittery with excitement.

What was wrong with her? This walk wasn't a date. A shallow, good-looking man was the last thing she needed. She'd scratched men like him—the *bang-and-go* type—from her list.

Besides, Tuck didn't want her any more than she wanted him. He saw her as a nuisance and an obligation.

The jitters fled and her emotions sagged as a familiar feeling crept over her. She'd grown up a burden to her mother. A tag-a-long. Extra work. Never one to be fully cherished. Now once again, Ryn slipped into her role, a burden to someone new, and in Scotland no less.

Man, this sucked.

When they were no longer in earshot distance of the castle, she got up her nerve. "You know, you can drop the act."

He glanced over, not impressed.

"Tell the truth," she said more bravely then she felt. "You're tickled pink to have me along for company."

He grunted in reply.

She lobbed right back, "You certainly have a way with words." His behavior was doing a nice job of helping her to tamp down her attraction to him. Or at least that's the story she told herself.

Yeah, I'm a big fat liar. Her weakness for good-looking men was legendary…her Achilles' heel. Hell, maybe her whole foot and body, too! And at this moment, Tuck really shouldn't be all that *desirable* anyway. Automatically, her head turned to examine his face. She didn't need a sixty-watt bulb to make out *his landscape* in the partially clouded moonlight. Yes, he was still as handsome as before, and she hoped the added *heaping-helping-of-grump* would mar his perfect features…but it didn't.

Air huffed from her lungs, taking the wind out of her sails. She better tell him how it was going to be, this time without the sarcasm. But when she touched his arm to get his attention, he jolted to a stop, looking stunned. She pulled her hand back. "I'll do my best to stay out of your way. Believe me, you're the last person I need to be around."

He recoiled as if her honesty had burned. Now, because of her bluntness, she was stuck either explaining her past and all the times gorgeous men had wronged her, or let Tuck believe this was personal. Which it wasn't. This was more about her than him. How did she always dig herself into these holes?

"Listen," she started, "allowing me to help return the van—*as in doing this favor for Hugh and Sophie*—is a small price to pay for letting me stay in their cottage." Without their generosity, she'd be *shit out of luck*—no roof over her head and walking back to Edinburgh, whatever direction that might be.

Tuck gave another grunt, but this one sounded less aggravated, and possibly could've been an *aye*…if run through a Klingon-to-Scottish translator first.

Embarrassed and feeling awkward, she trudged away, leaving

Tuck behind. To keep the ever-increasing mist out of her eyes, she pulled her hood tighter around her face. Protection against the weather. That's what she told herself.

After a moment, she heard something. Was he talking to her? She slung back her hood. "What did you say?"

Never stopping his stride, he put his hands in his pocket and walked straight to her, maintaining eye contact. "'Twasn't anything to do with ye," he said quietly.

"Then you'll be happy to have my company?" She knew she was pressing her luck, but couldn't help but push his buttons.

He shrugged as if admitting nothing. "Do you know how to drive a manual transmission? Do ye have a map? Ye'll have to drive to Gandiegow on yere own, ye know."

"I'll be fine. I'll use my GPS." But first, she'd have to remember to charge her phone.

"Ye'll have to remember which side to drive on, too. Ye're used to driving on the *wrong* side of the road." He'd said it as if that was the reason why he was against her going.

"I look forward to the challenge."

He sighed. Not in an *I'm-so-glad* exhale. Instead, he sounded defeated. "Then I guess I'll appreciate your company on the trip back to Whussendale." His voice held no convincing tones, only resignation.

For a second she thought to dig deeper to see what was going on with him, but was afraid she already knew the answer—*incredibly superficial*. She'd bet her last dollar that he'd run out of his favorite hair gel, and Whussendale wasn't exactly a stone's throw away from a drugstore with his particular brand.

The downpour from earlier returned. She was surprised he didn't cover his head and make a run for it. She certainly wanted to. But instead she matched his pace, deciding to show him she was a badass, too. They trudged up the hill toward the wool mill and the cottages beyond.

When they reached her door, Tuck nodded a goodnight and then walked the few paces next door to his half of the duplex...if she could call it that.

Suddenly she was cold.

ℬↃↂℬ

Tuck went into his cottage, shrugged out of his raincoat, and hug it on the hook by the door. He was grateful for the boot mat underneath which served as a drip pan. In the square mirror adjacent to the door, he caught his reflection and didn't recognize himself. Not just how his hair looked a mess, but the pinch between his eyebrows made him look like a man who gave a damn. Which he didn't.

God, he was never surly. Or if he was, he never let it show—a lesson he'd learned in his youth. Surely his bad temper had to do with Maggie and the announcement of her moving to Whussendale. She'd put him off his game. *Aye*, there'd always been a chance of running into Maggie in Gandiegow, but only between the walk from the parking lot to the boat. But now, her close proximity would keep him ever mindful of what he'd done to their family.

He took a seat at the table and couldn't help but dwell on the lass next door. He wasn't exactly upset with how things turned out tonight. He just didn't need the problem of spending time with a bird like her. Ryn came with complications. *Like being Maggie's cousin.*

In spite of himself, he grinned. The fact she cut through his bullshit was overwhelmingly attractive. Unusual, too. Hell, he liked that part of her so much, that if he was giving her a score, he'd have to give her high marks for her straight talk and not tripping over herself to get his attention.

His phone vibrated. He pulled it out and answered. "MacBride here."

"It's Willoughby." The wool mill's ancient kiltmaker. "There's no way I can sleep with the sink dripping as it is."

Willoughby went silent, and it wasn't because he had nothing to say. Just the opposite. Tuck had been here long enough to know what the old man was about. To ask a favor from Tuck would be a sign of weakness. But tonight, Tuck was too tired—both physically and emotionally—to play tactical moves with the old guy.

"I'll be right there," Tuck said.

"Really? Ye usually whine a bit first that ye're too busy." Willoughby didn't wait for a response but hung up.

Tuck pocketed his phone, slipped on his coat, and picked up his toolbox by the door. If the old man had called after Tuck had removed his wellies and was settled in for the night, he might have argued with him first, a little. But really, Tuck didn't mind spending time with Willoughby. He figured one day he'd be the old bachelor. And he hoped, if he got a little lonely, someone might be kind enough to share his company…even if it was over a dripping sink.

Tuck walked out into the rain and the night gathered in around him, feeling as if not another soul was alive. Even the lights on in the various cabins just pointed out the truth. Tuck was a lone wolf. In the past, when he had suffered bouts of loneliness, they were purely self-inflicted. He was a roamer, a wayfarer, always restless, better at saying *goodbye* than sticking in one place for too long. He wasn't raised to be this way, nor was he like this before he was seventeen. When Elspeth tore his heart out, it was like a switch had been flipped and he had turned into a person who was constantly trying to outrun the life that everyone expected him to settle into. *A wife. A family.* Nay, those ideals were given up long ago.

Willoughby's detached cottage sat on the far side of the horseshoe of dwellings, next to Magnus's cottage, Willoughby's brother. The walk was short, but gave Tuck time to anticipate the fine whisky that would surely be waiting, as he knew the old man would've poured it while calling. After the initial blustering, while

Tuck fixed his sink, he and Willoughby would have a nice visit, something that had been happening every few days since Tuck had arrived.

Willoughby opened the door at the first knock. "What took ye so long?"

Tuck strolled in and handed his wet coat to the old man. "Here."

Willoughby motioned at the hook. "Don't be cheeky. Hang it up yereself."

Sure enough, the dram sat on the table. Tuck could also see the tap was indeed leaking. "Do ye mind if I have a taste before the work is started?"

The old man waved at him as if he couldn't be bothered with such questions, all part of the act, but something seemed different about him tonight.

Tuck sat his toolbox on the table, took a sip of the whisky, which warmed his insides, and then got busy fixing the faucet.

Willoughby shuffled over and peered over Tuck's shoulder while he worked. "Do ye have plans to ever marry?"

Tuck twisted around and grinned at the old man. "I hope ye're not asking for yereself. I like the lassies."

Willoughby swatted the air with an *I'm-wasting-my-time-on-you* manner. "So much cheek."

Tuck set his wrench down and grabbed a new washer to replace the old one. He didn't meet the old man's eyes. "I have no plans to ever marry."

"Why not? I see how the females of Whussendale are fawning over ye."

"*Doesna* mean a thing. Fresh meat is all I am," Tuck answered, hoping this line of questioning was over.

"The Laird seems happy with Sophie." Willoughby went back to his chair and sat. "That Sophie is gifted when it comes to making kilts." He sighed a ragged breath. "But she's busy these days."

"Aye. I understand a quilting retreat is coming to Whussendale soon."

"A retreat," Willoughby said absently. "What about ye? I only loved one woman."

Aye. The old man was in a mood tonight, but Tuck wouldn't judge. "I hate to ask, but was that one woman *yere mother?*"

Willoughby actually chuckled. "If I wasn't so comfortable, I might come over there and kick yere arse." He sighed again. "Nay. Beatrice was her name. We were young and in love. I never got around to making her mine. I was apprenticing with the kiltmaker at the time and I let that be more important than having a family of my own."

"Do you know what happened to her?"

"She married another." Willoughby paused, making Tuck look over his shoulder to check on him. The old man gazed off into the distance with a sad, almost heartbreaking faraway look. "I heard she died yesterday in Inverness." His words embodied regret.

As thought-provoking silence filled the room, Tuck finished tightening down the tap.

"What about ye?" Willoughby finally said. "Have ye ever come close to marrying?"

The old man had been honest with Tuck, so he told him the truth. "Once." He put his tools away, concentrating on getting them in the correct spot, and not meeting Willoughby's eye. It was one thing to tell the truth, but it was quite another thing to show your face while doing it.

"She left me at the altar," Tuck confessed. The single worst thing that had happened to him...*until John's accident.*

"Why did she leave ye?" Willoughby asked.

Tuck closed the lid to the toolbox. "I need to get to bed. Early morn." He downed the rest of the whisky. "I'll see ye tomorrow."

With great effort, Willoughby pushed himself out of the chair.

"Right. Tomorrow. Sleep well."

The old man was at the sink, checking the tap as Tuck let himself out.

It rained steadily now, a peaceful rain. The same kind of rain, fifteen years ago, on the day of his wedding. Tuck and Andrew stood at the altar for an hour, waiting on Elspeth. Then another hour pacing while phone calls were made by her parents and his parents, looking for the lass. The memory filled Tuck with humiliation and emptiness, the first of many dreadful emotions that day. There'd been fear she'd had an accident, but when no such word came, Tuck thought she might've run off and that he'd never see her again, never know why she hadn't come. Out of desperation, that night, he'd gone to Elspeth's house, hoping to find her, but knowing it would only turn into an evening of commiserating with her parents. Tuck was shocked when her mother, drawn and sullen, had said Elspeth could be found upstairs in her room. Relief had Tuck tearing up the steps. He found her crying in her bed, but he was so happy she was okay. But then she told him the baby was gone. As she sobbed he held her, trying to comfort both her and him. Starting a family at seventeen wasn't ideal, but he'd accepted his responsibility and was actually looking forward to being a father. But then the truth came out.

She'd gotten rid of the baby...on their wedding day. A baby, she admitted, that wasn't Tuck's. She'd slept with her best friend's brother while holidaying in France. Up until then, Tuck hadn't allowed himself to question the timing that he'd known in his heart was off. He'd believed her when she'd said it was *their baby*.

He straightened his shoulders as if shaking off the past and trudged back to his cottage. He didn't regret any of it. Betrayal and living a lie had made him into the man he was today. Not in the least bitter, as he was able to enjoy the company of women to its fullest. Actually, he'd become grateful that he'd learned an important lesson at such a young age. It wasn't a bad thing to relive the past. Re-membering it all, only shored-up his resolve to never take women and relationships serious again.

His cottage lay ahead and he frowned when he saw someone standing on the porch, pounding on his door. The darkness hid her identity until he drew nearer and heard her whispered yell.

"Tuck, wake up! It's me, Ryn."

8

"WHAT ARE YE doing out here, woman?"

Ryn shivered violently, knowing she must look terrible. "I knocked on the wall and you didn't answer." The only thing she wanted in the whole world was to go to sleep and stay like that forever. She shivered again. "The roof." Her teeth chattered. "It's leaking. Right over the bed."

"Oh, shite. The materials to do yere roof is coming next week." Tuck turned the knob. "Just so ye know, I don't keep my door locked. I wish ye would've just gone on in. Standing out here, ye'll catch yere death of cold." He went straight to the hearth, struck a match, and lit the readied stack of tender and logs. "Stand over here." Next, he went to the rad and turned the knob to heat the room.

She'd put on Sophie's raincoat, but her pajama bottoms from the knees down were soaked. Her tennis shoes were beyond water-logged.

Tuck's eyes followed to where she looked and he put out his hand. "Give me yere wet jacket." Instead of waiting for it, he went to the armoire and pulled out a robe. "Take off those wet pants while

I check on yere roof."

She shivered again, feeling too cold to actually respond. It wasn't just the wet clothes and the cold temperature. She was one of those people who got cold when extremely tired.

He handed off the robe as he took her jacket. "I'll be back." He hesitated at the door. "Before I come in, I'll knock first. To make sure ye're decent."

"Okay."

As soon as he was out the door, she slipped off her shoes, wet socks, and pants. She wiggled into his robe and tightened the sash. The robe smelled of laundry detergent, a hint of smoke from the fireplace, and something irresistible. She inhaled deeply to take it in.

But crushing on Tuck wasn't productive. She decided to focus on her cold feet next. Her choices for warmth were digging through his armoire drawers for socks or putting her tootsies under his covers to get them off the cold stone floor.

Hesitantly, she went to his bed. She stood at the side, chewing her bottom lip, until she decided on a plan. The second she heard Tuck's warning knock, she'd jump out of bed, and pretend to be examining the quilt lying on top—the quilt, a combination of evergreens, bear paw patches, and appliquéd bears. She pulled back the blanket and climbed inside. She snuggled down, drawing the quilt up to her chin as she rubbed her icicled feet together.

Tuck's scent surrounded her. She closed her eyes and soaked him in. She wouldn't allow exhaustion from this super long day and her current drowsiness to pull her into sleep, though. She'd stay alert, she'd listen for his knock, and in the meantime, she'd get warm.

A moment later, she dropped off into the abyss of perfect slumber.

∞⌘∞

Tuck assessed the state of Ryn's bed—a big wet spot had formed in the middle. No wonder she had been pounding on his door. He looked up at the ceiling, wishing the supplies for her roof had come a week ago. This could have been Willoughby's home. Tuck certainly didn't want his old friend to be in this predicament. Also, Tuck needed to find a way to carve out more time for home repairs, or else, the Whussedalians and the Laird would have his hide.

He just wasn't sure where that time was going to come from. At some point, something would have to give.

Sighing, he pulled the bed over to the side and out of the way of the leak. From under the sink, he retrieved a bucket to capture the constant drip from the ceiling. As he pulled the quilt from the bed, the hanging on the wall caught his attention. This quilt was different with a tree seeming to grow out of the bottom blocks as if reaching up for the sky. For a moment, he wondered if this was the Goodbye quilt that Ryn had mentioned.

He draped the wet quilt over two dining chairs to dry. When he went to take the sheets off, there lay a piece a jewelry. A charm? He picked it up, examining the silver swan. He shoved it in his pocket to give it back to Ryn. As he stripped the sheet, he wondered what he'd do with Ryn for the night. Maybe he could walk her back up to Kilheath and have her stay there. But the prospect of running into Maggie had him digging for other options.

He arranged several other items in the room so they wouldn't get wet. Finally, he turned out the light and went next door to his cottage. Keeping his word, he tapped lightly. He didn't hear an answer. He knocked a little harder. When she didn't call out, he cracked the door open and peeked inside.

At first, he thought she'd left, but then he saw his quilt move. He stepped in, smiling...the lass had surprised him again. When he drew near, he saw she slept.

Oh hell. It did something to him to see her like that. An innocent angel. Peaceful. And he wanted nothing more than to crawl in beside her and pull her close.

Instead, he hung his coat by the door, retrieved a pair of sweatpants from the drawer, and took an extra quilt from the armoire. He checked to make sure her eyes were closed before slipping off his dungarees and donning the sweatpants. Once again, the temptation to crawl in beside her flooded him, as if he was a dinghy engulfed by a rogue wave. And maybe if she'd been some other type of lass, he would have slipped in next to her and kissed her awake.

He carried a chair over to where she slept and quietly sat, propping his feet up on the end of the bed. He noticed her shoes rested haphazardly under the frame and he bent down to straighten them for her. For a few more moments, he watched her sleep, then closed his eyes. Morning would be here soon.

Tuck woke suddenly with the acute awareness of being watched. Darkness filled the window panes, but the hearth's embers gave the room a soft glow. He tilted his head to look at Ryn, which caused a pain to shoot through his neck. *Large men shouldn't sleep in small chairs.*

While he rubbed his neck, he stared at the lass. Aye, the lassie was staring back. Not with sultry eyes, but wide-eyed as if a deer frozen by the sight of a gun barrel.

Shite. With his feet propped the way they were, she surely felt blocked in. "Sorry." He dropped them to the floor and scooted his chair away from the bed, giving her plenty of space.

She sat up, rigid as a plank. "I'm the one who should be sorry." She glanced from side to side. "I didn't mean to fall asleep."

When she bit her lip like that, he wanted to kiss away her apology. "Don't fash yereself."

She swung her legs over the side, talking fast. "I was looking at your quilt—"

"And decided to take it for a test drive?" He laughed, trying to put her at ease.

She stopped and stared at him once again. "I never meant to take your bed. I can go back to my cottage now."

He shook his head. "Stay put. Yere bed is waterlogged."

She glanced at the space on either side of her, as if his bed might swallow her whole. "But I can't stay. This is *your* bed."

"I'm fine where I am." He kept the crick in his neck to himself. A funny thought hit him and he said it just to get a rise out of her. "Unless ye're willing to share." He'd seen fire in the lass earlier and he was keen to see it again.

But once again, she surprised him. She scooted over and patted the mattress in invitation.

∞∞

Ryn never saw a man move so fast, as Tuck knocked over his chair trying to get away. It looked comical, enough to laugh, but actually, she was more insulted than entertained.

Horrified, Tuck stared at her. "What's wrong with ye? Inviting a stranger into yere bed!"

As smooth as he was with the young woman at the café when Ryn had arrived, she was surprised by his reaction. She was certain he'd been offered into many women's beds and at a much shorter acquaintance, too.

Humiliated and embarrassed, Ryn frowned at his gorgeous face. "It's not what you think. I figured if you were going to paw me, you would've tried something when you found me sleeping in your bed." She being *Goldilocks-to-his-big-bad-wolf*...or something like that.

She started to slide out again, this time on the opposite side of the mattress. The big Scot looked as if he wanted to bolt for the door.

She put her hand up to make him stay. "Listen, I'll just go back to my cottage and sleep in the chair like you've been doing. We're going to have to get up soon anyway."

He stared at her as if contemplating the universe, remaining as silent as the chair lying sideways on the floor.

She rolled her eyes and stood, but was quickly reminded of the cold stone floor. She scanned the room for her shoes.

"They're over here." He leaned down and retrieved them from under the bed. But he didn't give them back. His mouth fell into a frown as if it was ready to say something he didn't quite approve of. "Stay. We can both share the bed."

The way he was looking at her, she figured he intended to stack the pillows between them as a barrier.

The only explanation she could come up with, as she automatically climbed back into bed, was she'd never been this tired before. He took his place on the other side. She was buzzing with curiosity, wanting to catalogue his every move, though she shouldn't. He was a big man, moving smoothly like the king lion of the pride. Her mind went all kinds of naughty places as curiosity hummed through her. What if he reached out and pulled her to him? As sleep deprived as she was, she didn't have the willpower to stop what her inner hussy wanted.

I better pretend he isn't here. Which wasn't easy! All her nerve endings tingled with hopeful anticipation.

She wanted to turn and face him, to pretend they were cozy in this bed, sharing secrets. And share other things the dark of night brought on.

"Goodnight, lass," he rumbled.

His voice made her tremble.

"Are ye cold?" He shifted and she could tell he was pulling the covers off himself.

She squeezed her eyes shut, as her eyes might give her yearning away. And dammit, if he did one more nice thing and decided to tuck the quilt in around her snuggly, her resolve to not be attracted to him would crumble. She might shamelessly throw herself at him and live with the embarrassment of being a complete tart later.

But Tuck didn't tuck the quilt around her. Hell, he barely got near her. He gently laid the quilt on top, as if she was as breakable as the wisps of hand-blown glass.

She wanted to yell at him she wasn't delicate. She was sturdy, dammit. And a woman! She turned to him, ready to make a declaration to let him know she could hold her own. But he was back on his side of the bed, hands stacked behind his head with his eyes closed shut.

No quilt covered him. She let her gaze freely run the length of him. Halfway down, she saw the one thing that could appease her bruised feelings.

Tuck is attracted to me, too.

Relief spread through her, though she shouldn't care. History had a way of repeating itself, especially when it came to her and her affinity toward gorgeous men. Every bad relationship. Every heartache. Every letdown. All of it should've had her running for the hills.

But instead, the only *running* that came to mind was the running of her hands over him. All over!

"Damn little hussy," she murmured to her impulsive inner self.

"What?" Tuck said sleepily.

Oh, God. She wanted to pull the quilt over her head and hide. "Umm—I said I'm feeling a little *fussy*."

"Right," Tuck chuckled, as if he had her number.

At least he had the decency to not open his eyes and see for himself that she was in a bad way.

He sighed deeply. "Get some sleep."

Easier said than done. She shut her eyes, feeling frustrated with herself—for she hadn't had any intimate contact with anyone in the last two years. A girl could get lonely. Strange how she hadn't been tempted once, since she'd made her mind up to not get mixed up with men like him again. As she drifted off, she imagined she bravely travelled to his side of the bed and cuddled up to him, as he wrapped a protective arm around her shoulder.

Sometime later, she woke, feeling warm and safe, listening to her own heart beat in her ear. Slowly, she realized it wasn't hers. *But his!* And she was draped over Tuck's chest! She sat up quickly and his arm fell away from her shoulder. The action caused his hand to land on her hip. As she twisted to see his sleeping face, his fingers spontaneously enveloped her and squeezed, as if trying to pull her closer.

She broke free and scooted off the end of the bed. Turning back around to check on him, she found him awake now.

"Sorry," he said, his voice full of gravel.

She opened her mouth to say he didn't look sorry in the least, but clamped her lips down tight.

He looked relaxed, not in a hurry to get to the fishing grounds like he had yesterday. "Ye never told me what a Goodbye quilt is." He gestured to the adjoining cottage as if it was here in the room with them. "The one hanging above the bed, is that it? That quilt wasn't there before."

It made her feel ridiculously warm that Tuck had been paying attention to what she'd said. Usually, when men were this gorgeous, their hair gel blocked their capacity for caring about anything else beyond what they saw in the mirror.

"Yes. That's the Goodbye quilt." Heat rose into her face. Why did she feel so self-conscious with Tuck?

Maybe because I was cuddled up to him like he was a teddy bear. A very good-looking, sexy teddy bear!

"It wasn't me who wanted to hang the quilt there." She sounded defensive, though his tone hadn't been judgmental or condemning. She didn't owe him an explanation, but she couldn't stop her mouth from running out of control. "Sophie wanted it hung above the bed. I'm worried Maggie will think I was keeping it from her. But Sinnie said Maggie won't mind."

Tuck's eyebrows pinched together. "Sinnie's right. Maggie has more pressing matters."

At least he didn't seem as mad and upset as yesterday when Ryn had mentioned Maggie's name.

He sat up and scrubbed his beautiful face with his hands. "We should get ready to go." He stared at her, waiting.

Ryn realized she was staring at him as if he was the Greek god of gorgeousness. "Yes." She scrambled for her shoes and slipped them on. "Do I have time to grab a quick shower?"

He grinned, looking devilish, as if he might ask to join her. "Sure. Coffee or tea? I'll make us something for the road."

She shook her head. "Neither. I'm more of a hot chocolate kind of girl."

Tuck grinned, as if she'd given him the right answer. "Ye'll have to wait until we get to Gandiegow for hot chocolate. Quilting Central will have it. It's fully stocked."

Ryn wanted to ask what Quilting Central was, but she was on the clock. "I'll be quick." She grabbed her coat and went next door. With her face hot from blushing, she barely noticed the cool bite of the April morning air. She hurried through her shower, experiencing the mother lode of all butterflies. She couldn't help but feel excited for having slept in his arms. Her brain knew she was being ridiculous, but of course, her inner floozy wanted to keep reliving, over and over, the feeling of her body pressed against his.

Though she seldom wore make-up, she quickly applied some from her small stash. She spent more time with her hair than usual, too. She knew what she did—primped for him, and she hated herself for it. She'd sworn off the old pattern, yet she couldn't stop herself from ramping up into the silly-boy-crazy-girl she'd once been.

Twenty minutes later, she was back at his door, knocking. When he opened it, her stomach tightened. *Oh, good grief!*

He handed her a piece of paper and she had to stop herself from grinning stupidly. *It's not a love note.* This same kind of giddy craziness was what had gotten her in over her head and in trouble in the past. Thank goodness, he didn't notice.

"I know ye have yere GPS," he said. "But I've drawn ye a map, in case it doesn't work."

The map was more detailed than she expected, since she hadn't been gone that long. "This is amazing. You're a gifted artist." Along the route, he'd drawn a landmark for where she should make each turn—a castle ruins, a sheep field guarded by a rock wall, a distillery.

He ignored her *gifted artist* comment. "I've written my mobile number on the bottom. Go ahead and type it in. Call me, so I'll have yeres also. The Laird wouldn't like it much if I lost ye since he put me in charge of ye today."

She pulled out her phone and did as he requested. His phone bleeped, and with a mischievous grin on his face, he typed something in before saving her as a contact.

She leaned over, trying to glance at his screen, but he pulled it away.

"What did you type in there for me?"

"Never ye mind. We better go. I've fish to catch." He handed her a set of keys. "I'll take the van. You take the car. Oh, before I forget." He dug in his pocket and pulled out something. "Here. I found this in your bed. I assume it's yours."

She took the charm. "Yes. It's my swan." Actually it was her mother's. Ryn looked down at her bracelet and saw the empty loop, where the swan should be. She'd have to fix it later. She weakly smiled up at him. "Thanks." And slipped the swan into the side pocket of her bag, zipping it up securely.

"Ready?" He put his hand on her back to guide her out.

Because she had the self-control of a randy monkey, she leaned back into his light touch. Maybe she should join a twelve-step program, like AA. Did they have Gorgeous Men Anonymous? She definitely needed it as she certainly had developed a crush on him.

It was early morning, yet it felt like the middle of the night. Everything glistened from last night's rain, though nothing fell from the star-studded sky now. Ryn was caught up in her own thoughts, trying to rationalize why she was behaving like she was. Especially since she'd done so well the last couple of years. She glanced over at Tuck and once again an overwhelming whoosh of attraction hit her. She was glad for the silence. And gladder still, when they made it back to Kilheath Castle where both of the vehicles sat.

Tuck went to the white van, but stopped before getting in. "Are ye sure ye'll be all right on yere own?"

"Aye," she said, using her best Scottish burr, trying to lighten her own frame of mind.

But her Scottish play-acting only made him frown, as if an old memory tried to burrow its way into his temple. "Stay alert and be ready for anything—coos on the highway, water over the road…anything."

"You worry too much," she said with her plain-Jane Midwest accent. But she couldn't help but think he was thoughtful for worrying about her. As Tuck nodded and got into his vehicle, she searched her own memories. Had any of her past gorgeous men been as considerate as Tuck?

It took several miles before she got comfortable with driving on the opposite side of the road. It helped to have Tuck directly in front of her. He seemed to be taking it slow to make sure she didn't lose sight of him.

Ryn knew they were close to their destination, when Tuck slowed as they went down a very steep hill. She rode the brakes and hoped like crazy those suckers held so she wouldn't land up in the ocean. Relief swept over her as she pulled into a parking lot, where she positioned her car next to the white van in the still dark morning.

She turned off the engine and got out of the car. Tuck did the same, but then leaned over and gazed down the walkway which bordered the sea. He seemed conflicted. "I'm not sure what to do with ye. The lights are off at Quilting Central."

Ryn felt awkward. "I guess I could take a nap in the car." She wasn't sure why the Laird wanted her to come to Gandiegow, if she had nowhere to go. And Tuck wasn't offering for her to tag-along on the fishing boat with him.

"Come with me," he said. "I have an idea."

9

T UCK USHERED RYN ALONG QUICKLY, hoping another solution would present itself. The only cottage with lights on—that didn't belong to an early morning fisherman— didn't feel like an option at all. But, unfortunately, Deydie seemed to be the only person awake in Gandiegow.

God, he hated that he had to do this...for himself and for the American lass, too. Why hadn't he considered this when the Laird had directed Ryn to help bring back the van so early in the morn?

Tuck knew why. Since the moment he saw Ryn, he'd been preoccupied. Thinking with his *pants*, instead of his *noggin*. Well, look what it had gotten him.

No matter the tongue-lashing or the glares he certainly would get from Deydie, Tuck slogged on toward the head quilter's lighted cottage at the far end of the village. Would the Almighty never let up with the trials and tribulations? *Probably not.* Heaven knew Tuck deserved each and every pothole or roadblock the good Lord set in his path.

He glanced down at Ryn, and surprisingly, his tightened chest eased a little. But then he saw the worried look on her face. "What's the matter?"

"My new sewing machine." She stopped short and stared up at him. "I didn't even check to see if it got wet when the roof was leaking."

"Och, lass, stop yere fashing. Last night I put yere machine out of harm's way on top of the table. There'll not be a drop on it when ye return."

She exhaled deeply and laid a hand on his arm. "Thank you."

He wasn't used to playing the hero and was surprised he enjoyed being one in her eyes.

She relaxed then, and like a kid at the fair, she cranked her head, this way and that, as if her eyes couldn't soak up the picturesque village fast enough. This lass was a curious one.

"How many people live here?" Ryn asked.

"Dunno. At last count, there are sixty-five houses—if ye add in Rachel's new B & B and the cottage Casper MacGregor is having built for himself and his new wife Grace."

"The town seems really special. It would be amazing to live in a place like this. Don't you agree?"

"Looks can be deceiving."

Ryn spun toward him with her brow furrowed and her eyes wary. She acted as if he'd pissed in her porridge. "Don't tell me how looks can be deceiving. I'm an expert on the subject."

He could see she'd been wounded. Her eyes were clouded with the bruises of past disappointments. But if they were old memories, why was she including him? Where was the hero-worship of a moment ago?

He aimed his next words at her, and at the same time, he spoke of the village which surrounded them. "Gandiegow passes judgement quickly and holds grudges. I don't believe it's right or fair." His failure to sway the townsfolk in his favor these last four months still stung.

"But the town looks idyllic."

"One might think so." Stupidly, Tuck had listened to his brother, who'd begged him to stay. Andrew spoke of how uplifting a loving community could be. About how having supportive people surrounding him could make a man feel the power of the Almighty. Sure, it sounded good on paper, but for Tuck, Gandiegow had only offered up criticism and accusation.

He sighed.

"What's wrong?" she asked.

He could've asked her the same thing. Why had she looked at him with distrust a few minutes ago? She didn't know him.

But he couldn't expect her to open up, when he had no intention of telling her about his own frustration, which had taken root in him. He grimaced at the houses then, for he missed this place. *It makes no sense!* How in blazes could he be homesick for this God-forsaken village? In Whussendale, he'd been able to breathe without constant judgement being passed. But still, Tuck missed Gandiegow. The pub. The constancy of the North Sea crashing against the walkway. And dammit, he missed his brother. Even more frustrating, he missed the *effing* people of Gandiegow as well. Tuck never imagined that would happen, not in a million years.

"We should hurry," he said through gritted teeth. This conversation had slowed down the inevitable encounter with Deydie.

But in the next second, he felt bad for his clipped tone. Maybe later, after the morning run, he'd give Ryn a proper tour. He could show her the kirk and take her by the parsonage to meet Andrew, Moira, and Glenna. Tuck could show Ryn the progress on Partridge House, Rachel's B & B. He could introduce her to everyone in the village. But that thought died. He wasn't in good standing with the townsfolk, and if anyone thought Ryn was connected to him in any way, they'd snub her, too. At that moment, the two of them passed the kirk and Tuck had to revise his thought. Andrew and Moira would never treat Ryn with anything less than complete acceptance, like they'd done for Tuck.

As they approached Deydie's cottage, Tuck worried it might be in vain. Deydie was known to make the steep climb up the bluff in the wee hours of the morn to the big house at the top, where her granddaughter Cait lived with her famous husband, Graham.

"This is it." Tuck drew in a fortifying breath and knocked. He barely had a chance to glance down at Ryn before the door swung open.

Deydie's look of surprise turned to a glower, probably when her brain caught up to her eyesight. "What're ye doing here?" Her old rheumy eyes drifted down to Ryn. "Who's this?"

Tuck had a moment of belligerence and spouted off to the old woman, something he'd never done before. "I brought ye a stray."

Ryn cranked her head around. Now he had two women glaring at him!

"My name is Ryn Breckenridge."

"She's Maggie's cousin," he added.

Deydie bobbed her head. "Aye. Ross said ye were looking for Maggie."

Tuck noticed then that Deydie's table was covered with fabric. On top lay a rotary cutter and a mat. All tools of the old woman's trade—quilting.

"Get yere arses in here," Deydie growled. "April's cold weather is enough to make me think old man winter has a hankering to stay in Gandiegow."

Tuck hesitated, but didn't protest, though he needed to get to the boat. He crossed over the threshold obediently, as if he was a lad the size of Dand, instead of a headstrong man. But *aye*, he meant to save his backside from Deydie's weapon of choice—her broom—as it was always in arm's reach.

Deydie waddled over to the stove and turned on the heat under the tea kettle. "We'll have us something hot to drink."

Tuck shoved his hands in his pockets. "We returned the van, as the Laird requested." He made sure he stressed *Laird* so Deydie knew Tuck was only following orders. "I didn't want to drop the lass off at Quilting Central without yere permission." The arse-kissing was over-the-top, but necessary. "Might Ryn stay here with you? After I pull the morning nets, I'll take her back to Whussendale with me."

Deydie stopped and examined him, as if he were a fish she planned to gut. A moment later, she pulled down a teacup...*instead of a fillet knife*. When she turned back around, she glared even harder at him. "Why are ye still here? Be gone with yereself. I'll watch the lass."

Ryn turned panicked eyes on him and the message was clear—*Don't abandon me again!*

"I'll return." Tuck hated leaving the baby seal alone with the killer whale. He had no choice though. He stalked to the door.

"Take this with ye." Deydie yanked a paper sack off the counter and shuffled toward him.

At first, he thought she was offering him a meal for the boat, and was both surprised and pleased with her kind gesture. But his nose soon figured out the truth. This was no sack lunch she offered, and smoothing things over with this ole she-badger—*or Gandiegow*—was a lost cause. Deydie shot him that horrible grin of hers as she cracked open the bag. Was she making sure he got a good whiff of how she felt about him? Aye, he took her meaning. He ranked lower in her mind than her smelly, week old garbage.

Tuck left without another glance in Ryn's direction, knowing he *couldna* worry anymore for the lass. His own problems heaped way too high for him to care a whit about the comings and goings of another.

He trudged to the burn barrel at the back of Deydie's cottage and tossed in the sack. From the metal milk box, he pulled out a waterproof match. When he struck the matchstick, the flame took hold and he dropped it into the barrel. From the horizon, the boats leaving the harbor caught his attention and he cringed at how late he was.

And he'd sworn to never be late again.

The fire came to life with a crackle and a spark, burning bright, illuminating the back of Deydie's home. He wished for a fleeting moment the fire could help him glean what was happening inside the cottage. But only for a moment.

The fire died down quickly so he laid the lid on the barrel to stifle the rest of the flames. When he was satisfied the fire was out, he rushed back through town.

For the last few weeks, Tuck worked hard to avoid the people of Gandiegow, trying to slip in and out without being seen. But his efforts had been in vain. Each day, no matter the maneuvers he made, he ended up face to face with one or another of them. Today, dammit, was no exception. Mrs. Bruce stood in front of her cottage, sipping a mug. Why was she up so early? He knew the answer. She was enjoying some peace and quiet before her houseful of bairns awoke. Tuck had no choice but to pass by her to get to the boat.

In situations like these, he never knew whether to say *hallo*, or whether to keep his trap shut. Should he make eye contact or pass without saying a thing? Most of the time, he ended up somewhere in between—making a noncommittal grunt while keeping his head down. But this morning, he had a crazy idea. For the hell of it, he'd pretend the people of Gandiegow cherished him, like they did his brother Andrew. It was a blasted fairytale from an *effing* grown man.

He gathered his courage, trying not to feel as if he was walking the plank. When he got close enough, he nodded to Mrs. Bruce and gave her a smile as if he meant it. "Hallo. Fine morn for a hot cup of brew."

Mrs. Bruce, looking startled, fumbled with her mug, nearly dropping it, as "G'morn," came automatically from her lips. She seemed as surprised as him! Then her brow furrowed and her mouth fell open awkwardly, as if her glare and pursed lips had nowhere to go.

Tuck nodded again and kept moving toward the boat. Without warning, a genuine smile grew inside and warmed him against the cool morning.

Hmm. He wished he'd known sooner that giving Gandiegow a wide berth had been the wrong approach, and that facing the adversarial townsfolk head-on, could be a bit of fun.

He hadn't felt this light in a while. Not since before John's accident.

∞∞

John drifted in and out of sleep, feeling warm and wonderful. With Maggie cuddled next to him, he felt whole, right.

Instantly, he came awake, the truth grabbing him as surely as the winch drum had done on the boat. He broke out in a cold sweat. *I'm not whole. Not anymore.*

He stared down to see if his wife was really there or if she was a phantom, too, like his gone-arm, when it pained him so. But Maggie wasn't a dream, as she was, indeed, nestled up to his disfigured body. "What are ye doing here?"

Maggie burrowed deeper into his side. "I can't sleep without ye."

Shame and anger built inside John. What kind of man couldn't shake off his problems for his grieving wife? *Either now... or then.* If only he'd done what Maggie had asked, the morning of the accident. She had begged him to stay—*please don't go on the morning run.* She'd never made such a request...though since Irene's birth, Maggie had seemed fearful and made grumblings of him finding a safer job. He'd chalked her irrational trepidation up to hormones, hoping sooner or later, she'd realize her worries were unfounded. Though his lost arm proved they were real.

The night before John's accident, Maggie had lost her da, Lyel, in a car crash near Aberdeen. The news had crushed her. The two of them weren't close, but John supposed that made losing her da all the harder. Maggie's sobs that awful night had sounded more like a wounded animal than the strong woman John knew her to be. And it shook him to his foundation.

God, if only he'd done as his wife had asked, he wouldn't be lying in this hospital bed. He'd be a whole man. And Maggie wouldn't have suffered the one-two punch of losing both of her men—*in a sense*—within hours of each other.

John cursed himself, for he'd always been too focused, too driven his whole life. Making a living and providing for his family had been everything. That morning, he'd been too dead set on getting to the fishing grounds early, too busy to take the time to comfort his wife. He'd thought he would comfort her later that evening.

But if he was being honest with himself, drive and ambition wasn't the only reason he'd left her that morning. He wasn't comfortable with grief. With hers, with his own, or with anyone else's. He'd wanted to get away from Maggie, out on the water, where her tears couldn't reach him. But then…

He glanced down at where his arm should be.

A man should be able to put aside his own problems now to help his wife. John certainly had enough time on his hands now. But dammit, he only had enough energy to ponder on all the things he could no longer do. He was weak and as vulnerable as a caught fish heading for the processing plant.

A knock came at the door and the doctor entered.

Maggie shot up and scooted off the bed, taking the vinyl chair. John instantly missed her next to him.

"Let's talk about you going home," the doctor said.

Home? John didn't have one anymore.

Because he'd been trying to get away from his wife and her grief that morning, he'd lost everything. His home. His village. And his community. He felt sick all over again. And angry. He couldn't look at Maggie.

But he shouldn't blame her. This was Deydie's doing. The decision had been made while he was in his second surgery. In the recovery room, she'd told him what Deydie wanted—for them to move to Whussendale—but he'd been near out of his mind with pain. He had no right to argue with Maggie about it now. He'd given his word he wouldn't fish again. *For her.*

He'd been captain of the boat. Head of the family. Now baby Irene was of more use to the family than he was. He was now a man completely robbed of power in the prime of his life. Defeated. It made him physically ill *his wife* was forced to be the breadwinner, all because he hadn't been man enough to withstand her grief and hold her in her hour of need.

Maggie cleared her throat. "When can John come home?"

The doctor gave him an encouraging nod. "If he continues to improve as he has, he'll be headed home at the end of the week."

John didn't feel encouraged.

Maggie, smiling, took John's hand and squeezed. "The nurse said something about physical therapy?"

"And occupational therapy, too," the doctor started.

Ha! What occupation!

As the two of them discussed it, John stared out at the bleak spring morning. Tall buildings stood in his line of sight. He should get used to having a different view. Everyone kept mentioning his *new normal.* As if the *effing* words fixed everything! To hell with the *new normal!* He wanted his *old* normal back!

John hadn't prayed since the Almighty saw fit to rip his arm from him, but he offered up to Him the same questions he'd been asking himself since he woke up in this nightmare.

Lord, why me? He'd done everything he was supposed to do. When John's own da died nearly four years ago, he didn't question, but took up his father's mantle.

Why take my living from me, when ye know I love the sea? And to make me live in a godforsaken landlocked village? What are ye thinking, Lord? Am I such an awful man?

And this was the hardest question of all: *Is this my punishment for leaving Maggie alone when she needed me most?*

John waited a heartbeat, then two, but no answer came.

What could he expect? Not only had the Almighty taken his right arm, he had turned a deaf ear to him, too.

10

R YN LOOKED ACROSS the short expanse of the postage-
stamp-sized cottage. Deydie was frowning at her and Ryn
frowned back. It wasn't her idea to be dropped here with an
ancient reluctant babysitter. And Deydie certainly hadn't been kind
to Tuck. Later, Ryn would have to ask him how he'd managed to get
on the wrong side of the old woman.

Though Ryn wasn't thrilled about being here, something about
Deydie reminded her of Granny Kay, making her miss her
grandmother terribly. In some ways, Granny Kay had been more of
a mother than Mom. She'd taught Ryn how to cook and sew. She'd
made her soup when she was sick. Losing her last year had been
devastating. Sometimes Ryn's chest ached from loneliness and
emptiness. She belonged to no one now and no one belonged to her.
She felt adrift and wanted nothing more than to have a family, a
home, to feel settled. She'd had such high hopes of finding her
family here in Scotland. However, she'd set her sights too high, and
now, was trapped here with Deydie. who was acting as if it was her
fault she was here. Ryn wished she'd done what Tuck had

suggested—put the Goodbye quilt into the post for Maggie and skipped the trip to Scotland altogether.

Deydie gestured toward the table. "Do ye quilt?"

"Yes," Ryn said.

"Then ye know how to use a rotary cutter?"

Ryn stared at the green mat on the table. "Yes."

The kettle whistled and Deydie hurried toward it. "I need a collection of one-and-a-half inch strips and two inch strips. Make them super scrappy."

Ryn eased over to the ironing board where tartan remnants lay flat in a pile, fully pressed. She picked them up and took them to the table, positioning them on the mat. She grabbed the rotary cutter and began slicing the fabric into carefully measured out pieces.

Deydie filled two teacups. They were prettily painted and dainty, not at all fitting with what Ryn had seen of Deydie and her demeanor. A utility stein or perhaps a witch's caldron seemed more fitting.

"We're all making Gandiegow Crossing Path quilts," Deydie said. "Here's yere tea." She didn't hand it to Ryn, but set it in the windowsill. "I put milk in it...as is proper. Do ye like scrappy quilts?"

No, Ryn thought, wishing she could pull off one of Tuck's non-committal grunts. She liked her fabric planned and perfectly contrasted in advance. A modern-look—clean and organized. Just one of the reasons she was a diehard Modern quilter. But Deydie didn't seem to be the kind of woman who would *agree to disagree.*

If only this old woman was her Granny Kay, Ryn could've answered playfully. *Sure, I like scrappy quilts. As long as the fabrics are all solid, placed in a particular order, and the quilt looked Modern in the end, I could go for a scrappy quilt.*

"It depends," Ryn finally said.

Deydie's frown deepened as she put her hands on her hips.

"Depends on what?"

Ryn paused for a second to form her answer. The cottage was filled with scrappy quilts. Two slung over each of the rockers by the fireplace. One pulled neatly over the bed. Even the kitchen curtains were sewn together with scrappy strips. And Deydie herself wore an apron of patchwork scraps. It was plain to see this woman represented the scrappy quilt movement, using what she had to make something both beautiful and functional. Also, truth be told, Deydie was ancient and didn't seem the type who would be into *modern anything*.

Choosing her words carefully, Ryn gave her a sliver of truth. "Scrappy quilts are fine by me, but it depends on the design, I guess. Everyone likes different things. Don't you think?"

Deydie harrumphed as she pulled off her apron and waddled to the door. "Go on and cut that blue tartan. It's good shirting fabric and will look nice along the borders." She grabbed her jacket from the hook. "I have to run up to the Big House. Me granddaughter, Caitie, is pregnant and I like to get the breakfast started for her. Help yereself to the Kilts and Quilts Poppy Seed Bread under the foil on the counter. It's damn good. I'll return shortly." The door slammed behind her.

Ryn wished she could go back and amend her answer…befriending the old woman would make the morning go so much smoother. The wiser thing would've been to ask to see a picture of the finished Gandiegow Crossing Paths quilt first, or at the very least, inquire about the other quilts Deydie had made.

Involuntarily, Ryn shuddered. Deydie was frightening. And unapproachable. Ryn should've heeded Sophie and Sinnie's warning.

She took a sip of tea and was surprised she didn't mind the added milk as much as she thought she would. She glanced toward the door and then went to see the bread under the foil. She grabbed a slice and ate it over the sink—like a kid sneaking candy before supper. She downed it quickly, not wanting Deydie to catch her taking a break. The old woman was right. It was good! She washed her hands and got back to work.

Ten minutes later, when the old quilter returned, Ryn was pressing more fabric.

"It's time to go to Quilting Central. The ladies are coming early today. We all have so much to do."

Together, Deydie and Ryn packed up the cut fabric into the wagon outside the front door. Ryn couldn't help but gaze over to the ocean, wondering when Tuck would come back and rescue her.

The early morning air was crisp and filled with moisture as they walked along the same path as she'd come with Tuck. But where Tuck had been quiet, Deydie pointed out the highlights.

She motioned to a small, tired-looking cottage. "And there's where the Bruces live. The cottage is busting at the seams. She's got five bairns and another on the way. I've tried to tell her where those babes come from, but she seems deaf in that quarter."

Ryn opened her mouth, but didn't get to ask about the next building.

"This is St. Henry's Episcopal Church. *No Church of Scotland here*. Which surprises everyone, except us Gandiegowans." Deydie chuckled as if a joke was woven amongst her words. "Father Andrew is our pastor. He married our Moira, and because she's happy with him, then the Episcopal priest is fine by me." Deydie looked over at her. "Tuck and Andrew are brothers."

"Oh." Ryn was surprised Tuck had a priest for a brother.

As if Deydie read her thoughts, she added the rest. "Those brothers couldn't be any more different. Tuck's a scoundrel. He absconded with many hearts from the young lassies of the village. And a few of the older hearts, who should've known better."

Deydie's words confirmed Ryn's initial impression of Tuck. But in her heart, she was having doubts about judging Tuck so quickly. Maybe she and Deydie were wrong about him. He'd been nothing but a gentleman with Ryn. But then again, *love-'em-and-leave-'em* men could be tricky that way, and sly. All wolves in sheep clothing.

Deydie stopped in front of a building, handing off her bundle to Ryn. "This is Quilting Central." She didn't need to make an announcement as a patchwork sign above the door clearly marked it.

Deydie went inside and flipped on the light switch. "Put yere things over there."

The room was spacious and filled with tools and equipment quilters needed and loved. Tables and sewing machines took up the center of the room. Cutting mats and rulers were organized to one side, along with ironing boards and irons. Two longarm quilting machines rested at the back of the room near a small kitchen area. A comfy sofa was located near a reading nook with shelves of books. The walls had been turned into design walls with quilts in various stages of completeness. Many of the walls displayed the same quilt design made with different fabrics.

Deydie joined Ryn as she examined the design. "That's the Gandiegow Crossing Paths quilt."

"I can't believe how many different ways it's being done." One of the scrappy quilts was designed as a Colorwash with the fabric patches at the bottom done in dark fabric, but gradually faded to nearly white by the time it reached the top.

"This one's Maggie's," Deydie said. "She's finished the blocks and arranged them on the wall, not knowing her da would be dead by nightfall. Then the next day, John had his accident." Deydie glowered at the door. "'Twas no accident. If he hadn't been alone…"

What was that about? But Ryn knew better than to ask, especially since there was such vehemence in the old woman's voice.

Deydie turned back to the design wall and carefully straightened one of the blocks. "We'll piece Maggie's quilt for her as she'll be busy with the Kilts and Quilts Retreat in Whussendale now." Deydie peered over at Ryn. "Ye said ye're a quilter, eh?"

Ryn nodded, then looked at the other quilt designs. Another of the Gandiegow Crossing Paths quilt was made with Christmas fabrics. Another—bright Batiks.

Her gaze went around the room to all the quilts. Every one was made in a traditional style, from the Log Cabin quilt over the arm of the overstuffed sofa to the two scrappy Pinwheel quilt tops stretched out on the long arm quilting machines.

Ryn was in love with this space, but there was one problem…there wasn't a Modern quilt in sight. How would Deydie react if she found out the first Kilts and Quilts Retreat in Whussendale would feature a Modern quilt? And with Ryn as the teacher? *She won't take it well. Not well at all.*

Deydie cleared her throat. "Bring in the things from the wagon. Then I'm going to see if ye really have any quilting skills."

In this one area, Ryn didn't worry, feeling confident she could pretty much pass any test the old quilter threw at her. Granny Kay had Ryn on a stack of phone books in front of a small sewing machine at the ripe age of four, making pillows for her stuffed animals. Mom showed Ryn how to mend and hem, not long after. Though back then, Ryn's stitches weren't nearly as even as they were now. But when Granny Kay and Mom took her along to a quilt guild meeting, Ryn was hooked. She begged Mom to make a quilt of her own…a blue jean quilt. Granny Kay gave Ryn a stack of jeans from a garage sale and one month later, Ryn had a new comforter for her twin bed. She loved every aspect of quilting. Except perhaps the initial pressing and cutting of the fabric.

As ordered, Ryn brought in the rest of the items from the wagon. Deydie barked out orders, pointing to where she should put things away. As she was bringing in the last item, another old woman showed up. This elderly woman was Deydie's opposite—tall, slender, with her white hair bobbed short.

Deydie took a hold of the woman's arm and dragged her over. "Ryn Breckenridge, this is Bethia. Ryn is Maggie's cousin from America." It wasn't the most elegant of introductions, but it got the job done.

Bethia smiled. "I'm Deydie's oldest and dearest friend. No one loves the old girl like I do."

Which said a lot about Bethia and her capacity to befriend the growling dog.

Deydie harrumphed again, but underneath the gruffness, she seemed pleased with Bethia's declaration.

Deydie picked up two pieces of fabric, grabbed Ryn's hand, and thrust them into her palm. The woman certainly knew how to switch gears. "Time to show us if ye can sew a quarter-inch seam. Use that machine." Near the designated sewing machine sat a roll top desk, piled so high with fabric, there was no way for which to pull down the lid.

Out of the corner of her eye, as Ryn walked away, she saw Deydie and Bethia put their heads together. Bethia listened, nodding, while glancing at the design wall next to where Ryn took her seat.

Ryn looked, too—*Maggie's unfinished quilt top*—and she was getting a clue as to why the two women looked as if they were scheming.

Ryn switched on the machine, changed out the current presser foot with a quarter-inch one, and easily stitched the two pieces together. She snipped the thread and stood. Deydie and Bethia lumbered over to her.

Deydie, the judge, put out her hand. "Let me see." She pushed her glasses up and brought the fabric close to her rheumy eyes. "'Tis good." She sounded shocked.

Ryn knew her quarter-inch seams were spot-on. "I've been sewing my whole life."

Bethia patted her gently on the back. "Lassie, yere *whole life* isn't that long. Not when ye compare yereself to Deydie and me."

Deydie nodded. "Ye're just getting started. A pup. Nothing but a wee babe."

"I'm twenty-eight." Ryn gestured to Maggie's quilt. "Can I get to work now, piecing Maggie's quilt for her?"

Bethia's chuckle sounded like wind chimes in the breeze. "She may be a pup, but she's quick, isn't she?"

"Aye, but cheeky" Deydie said. "Get to work now."

Ryn pulled a few of Maggie's blocks from the design wall and began stitching them together. She felt a little guilty, because this was the second time she was interfering in Maggie's life, when not asked by Maggie herself. The first was to volunteer to run the retreat. The second was now, stitching Maggie's quilt together. And the third interference would be when Ryn taught the True Colors quilt at the upcoming retreat, instead of Maggie's prize-winning wool quilt design.

As the sun rose, the building filled with women and Quilting Central came to life. Bethia brought Ailsa and Aileen, two matronly quilters with matching plaid dresses, to meet Ryn. Next, she brought a younger woman, Amy, who had a tight grip on the hand of a rambunctious little boy. Each time there was an introduction, Ryn would stop and listen closely, making sure she could put names to faces later. The Scottish quilters hovered over her, asking questions about herself and what it was like to live in the States. Ryn didn't mind the attention, because it made her feel included.

Deydie spoke with a thirtysomething-maternity-topped woman. Ryn knew they were talking about her because Deydie kept pointing in her direction. Ryn's stomach churned. She always felt uncomfortable around pregnant women, but she had to squelch those feelings quickly now, because they were headed straight for her.

"Ryn," Deydie called out. "This is me granddaughter, Caitie MacLeod."

"Cait Buchanan," the pregnant woman corrected. "I just wanted to welcome you to Gandiegow." Her Scottish burr wasn't as strong as the other women Ryn had met. Fortunately for her, Cait's sincere smile put her at ease.

"Thanks for the welcome," Ryn replied. "Everyone has been so nice."

Deydie harrumphed at something going on at the next table. "I need to help Bonnie with her half-square triangles."

Cait smiled fondly as Deydie toddled away. "That's my gran. Always bossy. Always in charge." She took the seat next to Ryn and looked more serious than before. "I wanted to tell you something about small towns." She scanned the room. "News travels fast, especially personal information."

That sinking feeling came over Ryn. Surely, Cait hadn't heard that Ryn had slept in Tuck's bed last night!

"Bethia talked to Sophie, and told me yere mother died recently. I knew I had to meet you." Cait picked up a quilt block and spread it out on the table. "My mother died from cancer when I was thirteen so I'm aware of what losing a mother feels like. I also heard from Deydie that the only family you have left is Maggie, Rowena, and Sinnie."

Ryn nodded, not completely sure what Cait was getting at.

Cait touched her arm. "It's hard to come to Scotland alone and feel like you don't have anyone in the world. That's exactly how I felt." So it was understanding which Cait offered, not pity. "It's not easy. But I can guarantee things will get better. I'm here to offer my friendship. Now tell me what Deydie has you working on so I can help."

Ryn was glad Cait had switched the subject from her mother's illness and death to quilting. Talking about quilting didn't hurt nearly as much. "I'm piecing Maggie's quilt together for her. And yes, your help would be appreciated."

For the next hour, she and Cait worked on the quilt, while Cait entertained her with stories about herself and the other quilters of Gandiegow. Ryn worked hard to keep her eyes anywhere but on Cait's six-months-along belly. She kept telling herself that focusing on having a friend in the small fishing village was so much better than being freaked-out over Ryn's short-termed pregnancy of long ago.

At 10:30, the door chimed and everyone turned to look, including Ryn. Tuck stood in the doorway, scanning the room. His cheeks shone red from the wind, and his hair was disheveled. Ryn was surprised when he didn't stop to primp in the mirror as he passed to put his rich blond locks back in place.

As Tuck headed toward Ryn, the crowd's mood shifted, from the cheery conversation before he arrived, to hushed dark whispers. Like an indoor tennis match, their heads glanced from Tuck to her, then back to Tuck. Ryn didn't understand their frowns and shuttered hostility. Yes, it was aimed at him, but it was also being lobbed her way as well. Where were the welcoming quilters from earlier?

"Are ye ready to go?" he said quietly. "I'm needed back in Whussendale."

"Sure. Let me shut everything down first."

The door opened again, and at first, Ryn was taken aback because the man wearing the cleric collar looked so much like Tuck. Maybe not as smooth and put together, but he had an undeniable angelic quality. She liked him right away. Beside him was a woman near Ryn's age who wore a plum-colored dress.

"That's Andrew, my brother," Tuck said for her benefit. "And with him is his wife, Moira."

From across the room, Andrew smiled at Tuck. He took Moira's arm, and the two walked their way. But when Andrew's eyes drifted over and landed on Ryn, he stopped suddenly in the middle of the room. His angelic face drained, turning as white as his cleric's collar, as if he was in the presence of Beelzebub himself. A moment later, his bewilderment at seeing her turned into…hate?

Ryn sucked in a breath. The pastor's attire made his evaluation of her official, as if it had been issued by God himself.

Moira turned to Andrew with a questioning look. He said something Ryn couldn't make out before the two of them moved closer. The priest acted as if he was at war with himself and the battle had to do with Ryn.

She looked up at Tuck to see if he knew why his brother disliked her so, but his brows were pulled together, as if he was as confused as she was. Ryn didn't have time to ask what was up before Andrew and Moira were upon them.

Andrew had wiped his face clean of all surprise and anger. But his smile ended up appearing rigid and phony—as fake as the wood dresser in her last apartment.

The priest pulled at his collar. "Hallo, Tuck." He peeked over at Ryn again.

Ryn caught the downturn of Tuck's mouth and he was acting wary as hell.

"Andrew." Tuck turned to the woman. "Moira. This is Ryn Breckenridge." Tuck's mouth was a hard straight line, all of it aimed at his brother. "Ryn is Maggie's cousin from America."

Andrew stared hard at Ryn, his face screwed up in deep concentration, as if he was trying to rearrange her features.

Tuck shoved his hands in his pockets. "What the hell is wrong with you, Andrew? Why are ye acting so weird?" He didn't wait for an answer but tilted his head to the side and spoke to her. "My idiot brother isn't usually so rude."

Moira laid a hand on Andrew's arm and the priest seemed to

come out of whatever trance he was under and smiled sheepishly at all of them. He gave Ryn a contrite nod. "Sorry. I didn't mean to stare." His eyes shifted to Tuck. "It's just that ye look like someone *we* used to know."

Tuck certainly didn't seem to understand Andrew's pointed words or meaningful gaze. He looked as clueless as Ryn felt.

"It's nice to meet ye," Moira's eyes didn't meet Ryn's. But then again, Andrew was staring enough for the both of them.

"We'll see you later. We have to get back to Whussendale." Tuck put his hand on the small of Ryn's back and guided her toward the door.

Tuck's strong hand felt like protection against whatever the priest was thinking, and to how the rest of the room had turned on her. And she may have even leaned into Tuck's hand. She couldn't be sure.

With all eyes on them, Tuck ushered her out. As the door closed behind them, the murmur of the quilters buzzed like a swarm of bees. She recognized the sound—*gossip*.

She looked up at Tuck. "What was that about?"

"I have no idea." But something seemed off. Tuck may not have understood what was up with Andrew, but Ryn would've laid money on the fact Tuck knew why the quilters were up in arms and whispering about him.

Ryn wished she could be like him—not intimidated. But she wasn't built like that. Besides, she was a foreigner in a strange land, who had to depend on the kindness of said-strangers. She was, also, someone who longed for acceptance. Longed for people to love and care for her again. But she was a woman without a family or community. For a while this morning, she felt at home amongst the quilters. But now, she couldn't help but worry about the change of events: *Did I commit some forbidden Scottish faux pas?* Because she certainly didn't feel at home in Gandiegow any longer.

11

TUCK DROPPED HIS HAND from Ryn's back and kicked a rock from the path into the water. A nice metaphor for what the townsfolk would clearly like to do to him. "I should've warned ye."

"You think?" Ryn's voice was pitched higher than usual. "That was so awkward. What did I do for them to turn against me?"

"Ye were seen with me, 'tis all." He was used to Gandiegow's snub, but Ryn wasn't.

"I guess you did warn me a little. You said Gandiegow passes judgement quickly and holds grudges. But they were very nice to me earlier. Even Deydie. In her own way. Until, well, you know…"

"You should consider yereself lucky. Not me. I screw up once—" more like ten times and then some "—and now I'm lower than a…" He stopped there. "Let's just say I'm not Gandiegow's favorite person."

"What about your brother? Does he feel that way about you, too?" She frowned. "Or is it just me he doesn't like?"

"Honestly, I don't know what his problem is. I haven't a clue why he acted the way he did with you. He's the nice one in the family. And to answer your first question…Andrew and Moira have stood by me, always believing the best of me." Though no one else did.

Ryn was looking at him. Not the look she gave him this morning when they were talking about how *looks could be deceiving*. She gazed at him now as if seeing the real him for the first time.

When they got to the parking lot, he opened the car door for her. She seemed surprised and it kind of ticked him off—he had manners, dammit! He waited until she strapped herself in before shutting the door for her.

He looked back one more time at Gandiegow before going to his side of the car. Tuck had left the envelope with all he'd earned the past couple of weeks at the parish house, feeling certain he hadn't been seen. No one would think it strange if he went into Andrew's house, as half of Tuck's things were still there. The directions for Andrew on the outside of the envelope were clear: *Money for John and Maggie Armstrong.* Tuck had used his left hand to write the note so no hint of whom it had come from would be left behind. He was proud of his perfect plan to funnel money to the Armstrongs. Andrew could be trusted to make sure John got the money, and more than likely, Andrew would do it in a way where John wouldn't be offended. Tuck knew John's feelings on charity. Charity was for the weak and for those poor unlucky bastards who couldn't fend for themselves.

But Tuck felt haunted—both by John's accident and by how Andrew had acted at Quilting Central. If Andrew's strange behavior wasn't due to the envelope lying in his open Bible, then what was it?

Tuck shook off the feeling he'd missed something important and climbed into the car, ready to take Ryn back to Whussendale.

As soon as he started the engine, Ryn turned to him and said, "How was the morning catch? The weather seemed good."

Her interest in his morning warmed him. "Better than usual," he answered. "Both the weather and the catch." He wondered if he should offer to take her out on the boat sometime.

No! What a dumb idea. She was only here for a short visit. She meant to spend her time with Maggie, then be on her way. Crazily, that thought depressed him, so he put it from his mind.

"How was yere morn? Was it hard to suffer through with Deydie?" he asked.

"Once I got used to her, it was okay. She and Bethia put me in charge of working on a quilt Maggie had started."

Surprisingly, this time Tuck only had the slightest twinge when Maggie's name was mentioned. Maybe it was because Ryn put him at ease.

He turned the conversation to his adventures on the Isle of Lewis and his tales of Stornoway for the rest of the trip. She laughed at the predicaments he found himself in and he couldn't help but think Ryn Breckenridge was the easiest lass he'd ever talked with. The time flew by. When Tuck pulled up to the wool mill and parked the car, he turned off the engine, shifted toward her, wanting to know more. "So tell me what is it ye do for a living?"

"I own a graphic arts business." She frowned. "I was doing pretty well, until..." she trailed off.

"Ye know, only yesterday, Hugh mentioned he needed the wool mill's logo updated. Ye should talk to him. See if ye could help him out."

Ryn looked up at him with grateful eyes. "That might be a better way to pay back his kindness, and Sophie's, for letting me sleep in the potter's cottage."

Tuck watched as Ryn's gratitude reached her lips in the form of a smile. He had the strong urge to lean down and see how her lips fit against his.

If he played this right, he might get a chance.

He reached over and rested his hand over hers and unexpectedly his heart kicked up. Man, it was tapping out a rhythm he hadn't felt before. "I'm concerned ye've developed a condition."

She didn't move her hand away, but stared at his hand covering hers. "What condition?"

He grinned at her. "Amnesia."

"What?" Her gaze drifted up to his face.

He raised an eyebrow at her. "Did ye forget that ye slept in *my cottage*? And in *my bed.*"

She looked away, but her hand was still under his.

Because he had balls of steel—and he couldn't help himself—he allowed his thumb to caress her palm. "Ye know, I'm not Hugh and Sophie."

"Hmmm?" she said distractedly.

He'd bet next week's wages at the wool mill she was feeling as heated up as he was. "Hugh and Sophie expect nothing in return for their kindness," he said quietly. "But I expect repayment."

She turned to him then, her eyebrows pulled together, perplexed in her girl-next-door innocence. "What kind of payment?" Next she glanced at her bag as if she might pull out a fiver and hand it over. Caution grew on her face then, and he couldn't help but smile internally. He could watch her forever as her emotions played out.

She shrugged. "I guess you could sleep in my cottage, since I slept in yours?"

What an excellent idea. But Tuck's line of thinking included more benefits than a roof over his head and a quilt to spread over him. He imagined Ryn lying on her pillow with her hair fanned out. Automatically, Tuck reached over and touched her cinnamon-colored hair and was rewarded with how silky it felt. "Ah, lass, thank ye for the offer, but I have a more immediate way for ye to pay me back." He poured it on thick, but what use was his vast experience with women if he couldn't use what he'd learned?

She shot him a stern teacher's frown to his bad boy behavior. "Forget it. I'm not having sex with you."

He pretended to be shocked, but truthfully, he liked how she gave him hell—straightforward attitude, no wavering. "Nay, not sex." Though the idea was tantalizing. "I was thinking of only a small token. A kiss."

He cupped her neck and leaned in, pulling her closer. She complied, and he should've gone in without hesitation. Instead, he stopped inches away, searching her eyes, wanting her permission first. This wasn't normal for him. But nothing was normal about how he felt around the American lass. As a rule, women were lined up outside his door, poised and ready for kissing. But not Ryn. She was different. *And different felt good.*

Their fate hung in the balance while he waited, both of them gazing into each other's eyes. He'd never been so exposed. And a funny thought hit him. By leaving his soul this wide open, she could see into his deepest self. He was like a pair of red-hearted skivvies hanging on the line, out for all the world to see. He could've stopped this madness by kissing her. He also could've pulled away and not found out how she tasted. He was in new territory, though, unwilling to end the magic, which had filled the interior of the car.

Her eyes took in every detail of his—once, twice, and then a third time—before she finally nodded. "Okay."

Okay what? He'd forgotten the question. He'd gone from feeling vulnerable to sinking into a sort of contentment he hadn't known existed.

She closed her eyes and leaned in, reminding him of the *permission* he'd needed, and she kissed him first.

God, the feel of her lips against his was heaven and she smelled great, too. *Hallelujah* broke out within the car, the angels singing, but the melody was probably only in his head. Warmth and gratification spread through him. He was alive, everything wonderful and right. Then, without breaking the kiss, she upped the game by scooting closer. One arm snaked around his neck and the other wrapped around his waist. Hell, he could break out into song now, too. The kiss was hot and sweet, long, and filled with the freshness of a first time. He could see the promise of things to come. He lost himself in it and didn't care that he'd gone as sentimental as a cheesy Hallmark card.

Normally, in this situation and at this point, Tuck would be working out how to get the woman into bed. But she was different. Unfamiliar calculations began firing upstairs: *What is it about this lass?* Crazy, hot sensations roiled through him. Kissing Ryn was leap years ahead of everyone else. No one made him feel this way. True, he'd been in a dating drought since John's accident. That ill-fated morning had changed Tuck. He was different now. Perhaps, kissing from here on out would be different, too.

Finally, she pulled away a little, keeping her eyes down, looking shy, but with a secretive smile lining her mouth. He held onto her, not letting her move any farther away. With nothing to lose, he lifted a lock of her hair to his nose and was rewarded with the scent of flowers from her shampoo.

"Lilac?" He smiled, knowing the scent well—outside his bedroom window when he was a wee lad at his parents' home. Later on as a teenager, the aroma of lilac had clung to him as he'd climbed out the window for late-night merry-making or a forbidden rendez-vous.

At the present, lilacs not only hung in the air, the scent tugged at Tuck, threatening to recall a buried memory. He wouldn't dig. Especially, not now. He was too busy savoring how wonderful Ryn felt in his arms.

"Yes, lilac," she whispered, as if she was afraid the spell might break, too.

But in that moment, things changed for Tuck, and he slightly pulled away from the smell of her hair.

But the fragrance of lilac had liberated that niggling memory, and try as he may, he could no longer ignore it.

Raw emotion knocked him from his mooring. His insides teetered. His senses went off-balance. Three unrelated things bounced around in his head, trying to piece themselves together to solve the puzzle—*Ryn, lilacs, and timing.*

It was too early in the season for lilacs…the timing was off. With his life unsettled and in turmoil, the timing was off, too, especially to meet a lass like Ryn. *Aye, that's what's bugging me.* Now was the time for him to stay focused with his only objective to make money…so as to make amends to John and his family. The last thing Tuck needed was to take on a new lass—one who would demand his time and energy. He had to stop things between them *right now.* Timing was everything, but the timing was off.

No, that's not it. He sat back, staring at Ryn, becoming more aware that something bigger loomed, which warned him to keep his distance from her.

Old treacherous feelings welled up inside. *Loathing. Betrayal. Embarrassment.* He'd been trying to outrun those feelings for what seemed like his whole life. But as he stared at Ryn, those deadweight emotions piled on, washing over him again and again, relentless crashing waves, not letting him catch his breath.

Suddenly, it hit him, and Tuck understood what Andrew was about.

The resemblance was uncanny! It was almost scary how one human being could look so much like another.

Hell, why hadn't he realized it before? Ryn had looked so familiar at first glance. Tuck shook his head, trying to un-see the similarities. And heaven help him, he wanted to get the smell of lilacs out of his nose, too. Lilacs smelled of betrayal.

He was seventeen again with Elspeth crying, her hair smelling of lilacs. He'd done the right thing. But taking responsibility had only made his parents and everyone think less of him when he'd told them he'd gotten Elspeth pregnant. A week later, Elspeth had been a no show. He'd been left at the altar, holding a red rose. No news until later that night of what had happened. *What she did, and the truth about what she'd allowed me to believe.*

"What's wrong?" Ryn's eyes were no longer gleaming and glistening like before. Now her face was filled with concern and worry for him.

He wanted Ryn to stop. *Just stop!*

He blinked. God, he couldn't believe his eyes! He reached blindly for the door handle, trying to un-see the truth, but that little *mother-effer* came skidding and crashing through his mind, wreaking havoc like a hundred car pile-up.

How could he not have noticed before? The resemblance was uncanny...and cruel. A feral growl tore his insides as he turned away. Ryn didn't just look like his ex- fiancée.

Ryn is Elspeth's dead ringer!

12

R YN CLUTCHED TUCK'S HAND, hoping to reverse
the sudden shift in his mood. But the second his eyes—which
were filled with loathing and animosity—fell on her, she
dropped her grip. She scooted back and waited for Tuck to tell her
what was wrong. Instead, he exited the car, slamming the door behind him, making her wince.

"What just happened?" she asked the universe. She fell back
against the seat with a heavy sigh, watching through the semi-
fogged-up window as Tuck stomped away.

Not again. "I'm such an idiot."

She and Tuck had just shared the most amazing kiss—powerful,
mind-blowing. She felt certain his world had been rocked, too. But
the whole debacle was a repeat of every relationship she'd ever had.
She'd let herself be sucked in by his charm and good looks. And
what did it get her? Nothing. Except he glared at her as if she'd
sprouted horns and mauled him.

Ryn felt paralyzed, her ego mowed down, and she stared into the
nothingness of her lonely existence. Finally, she got out of the car

and dragged herself toward her cozy cottage.

Before going in, though, she hesitated outside, wanting to go to Tuck's door and ask him, *What the hell was that all about?*

But she couldn't knock. She'd awoken an awful beast within him. Whoever said women were moody didn't have a clue. Tuck had just proven that men's moods could shift without warning—doing a one-eighty in a heartbeat.

The pure vehemence in his gaze haunted Ryn. She opened her door to escape inside. The moment still felt shockingly fresh. And honestly, she didn't want to see him. Not now. She could only withstand so much rejection in one night.

She left her things by the door and made a beeline for the wall—the one she shared with Tuck. She laid her hand on it as if searching for signs of life. Was he lounging right now in the bed she'd slept in last night? Was he laughing at her for being such a fool?

Her head fell against the wall and she whispered to herself, "Kathryn Iona Breckenridge, you were right about him. He's exactly the same as all the other *lying-cheating-good-looking-good-for-nothing bastards* that you've dated."

Yes, the friendly, easy-going wolf had lured her in, but then like all the other *bastardly* wolves, Tuck had revealed his *bastardly* true colors. Exactly the reason she'd come up with her True Colors quilt. The design was meant to remind Ryn of her past relationships. From bright to dark. Deadly and unexpected as a lightning bolt. The quilt also represented how she was to stay alert, centered as the circles on the quilt, with her only objective to remain true to herself.

Her heart ached. *No more!*

She wouldn't be suckered again. She'd remain diligent. Her attraction to him had masked the truth about the man. Yes, she was programmed for the likes of Tuck, but she was long past due to switch the channel. Time to come up with a healthier way to live. Mom always told her candy would rot her teeth. If only Ryn had been warned that eye-candy could break her heart.

She scanned the room, only now noticing how things had changed. The waterlogged mattress had been removed and in its place was a new one, wrapped in plastic. Clean sheets and a new pillow sat on the table. She glanced up and the ceiling had been fixed as well.

She pushed away from the wall and picked up her things by the door. Time to put any notions she had about Tuck away for good. No matter the kiss had been phenomenal. "I mean it," she said firmly to the room, but it wasn't a convincing performance. She tried again. "I have too much to worry about with the retreat to keep thinking about Tuck." Or any of the rest of the bastards who'd toyed with her heart.

There was a knock on the door. In unison, her breath caught and her heart jumped. Adrenaline and endorphins flooded her system as she rushed to the door. *He's come to apologize!* She was acting way too eager, but dammit, she just couldn't help herself.

She flung open the door and a smiling Sophie stood there, holding a folded patchwork quilt. As Ryn's brain processed the information, her soaring heart turned belly-up and dropped to the floor, shot down cold with the arrow of disappointment.

Sophie's smile fell away and concern filled her face. "May I come in?"

Ryn didn't trust herself to speak just yet, but stepped to the side to let Sophie enter.

Sophie laid the quilt on the table, then turned around and studied her face. "I can plainly see ye're not okay." She touched her arm. "Tell me what's wrong."

Mortified, Ryn felt tears spring to her eyes and she had to work hard at not spilling the beans about how *love-em-and-leave-em* Tuck had treated her.

"It's nothing." Ryn looked away, focusing hard on the quilt Sophie had brought. The way the quilt was sprawled on the table, gave her a good look at the design. "My mother had a pineapple quilt once. But Mom's quilt wasn't made with flannel plaids and a thistle medallion in the center."

It was the right thing to say to throw Sophie off the scent. Her expression turned to one of understanding. She wrapped an arm around Ryn's shoulders. "I can't imagine what ye've been through, losing yere mother so recently."

Ryn felt guilty using her mom to deflect Sophie from the awful truth—being upset over a man. *Again!*

Sophie led her to a chair. "You look a little flushed."

Mark that up to Tuck, too. Ryn automatically touched a finger to her freshly kissed lips.

"I'll make ye some herbal tea, then I'll get the bed made up." Sophie retrieved the kettle from the stove and took it to the sink. "We need for ye to have a good night's sleep for the retreat tomorrow. I'm sorry about the roof. We've been keeping Tuck so busy with the wool mill that there's been no time to really work on the cottages." She paused, as if thinking. "Hugh should really contract out the remodeling to someone else. Tuck has enough on his plate."

Though Sophie had placed Ryn in a chair, the talk of Tuck had her jumping up. She went to the shelf and retrieved two teacups.

Sophie smiled at her. "Are ye nervous about tomorrow?"

No, I'm nervous about the man next door, the one who kissed me silly and then stomped on my fragile heart. Not something Ryn could say aloud. But she could tell Sophie a different truth. "I think I'm ready. I would like to set up early, though, if I may."

Sophie laughed and dug around in the pocket of her wool dress. "I'm glad you said something." She handed her a skeleton key. "It's to Kilheath. Come and go as ye wish, day or night. Think of the castle as yere own. The key's to the kitchen entrance."

Ryn pocketed the key. "Thank you."

Sophie made the tea, while Ryn stripped the plastic off the new mattress. They sipped a little at their teacups, but then got busy putting the room to rights. While the two of them made up the bed, Sophie filled her in on the various village quilters. When they were done, she didn't stay, but gave Ryn one more squeeze and left with a wave.

Sophie's companionship had raised Ryn's spirits, but now alone, they fell a little. She went to the old-fashioned refrigerator and saw it had been stocked with yogurt, milk, and a casserole dish marked Shepard's Pie. Ryn couldn't get over the kindness she'd met, since coming to Whussendale, but invariably her mood was tainted by the man next door. She wished she could put him behind her as easily as he'd slammed the door on her after the kiss.

Her stomach felt queasy so she left the food for tomorrow and slunk off to bed, completely exhausted. But once she was under the Pineapple Thistle quilt, sleep eluded her. For a long time, she lay listening—wondering what her duplex-mate was up to. But the only sounds she heard were from the night. Suddenly a phone rang from the other side of the wall. Because she'd been concentrating on every noise—so as not to think of Tuck's lips on hers—the phone startled her.

The wall may have muffled Tuck's words, but Ryn made out every one. "Hallo." A silent pause followed and then, "Aye." Pause. "I'll be right there." Footsteps sounded and then Tuck's door opened and shut.

Ryn jumped up, ran to her window, and looked out. Tuck walked away from their connected cottages and crossed to the other side of the horseshoe of homes.

I can't believe it: Booty call! That's what it had to be…and the flirty café clerk came to mind.

Ryn plunked herself down in her chair, wishing she had duct tape to lash herself to it. She wanted so badly to chase after him to find out where he'd gone. For the next forty-five minutes, she stared at the thistle clock hanging above the sink, as every scenario of Tuck kissing and touching another woman cruelly played out in her mind.

Finally, she stood and went to her suitcase, resolutely.

No, she wouldn't go knocking door to door to find Tuck.

No, she wouldn't go next door and insinuate herself into Tuck's bed, a replay of last night, but this time make herself more seductive than the drooling fool she'd been in her sleep.

And no, she wouldn't drag a chair and camp outside, tapping her foot on Tuck's stone porch until he returned home.

With skeleton key in hand, she grabbed her notebook, determined to go to the castle without giving Tuck another thought.

Outside, the night was dark, no moon in sight. For a brief second, every scary movie—where the heroine stupidly heads out into the dark alone—made a chill run up her spine.

"You're being ridiculous," Ryn whispered as she tried to lock her door with her trembling hands. "Whussendale is as safe, as safe can be."

"Aye. Ye are being ridiculous," said a deep familiar voice.

She jumped in surprise, but immediately spun around, feeling pure relief when she saw Tuck. He leaned against a tree, not ten feet away from her cottage's window.

She crossed her arms over her chest, because she wanted nothing more than to run into his arms. "What are you doing? Spying on me? Peeping Tom? Peeping Tuck?" She piled on loads of attitude to cover up how warm he made her feel, and for how silly she must've sounded talking to herself. But really she was grateful. It was hard being all alone in the world. If something did happen to her tonight, between the cottage and the castle, at least one person had seen her set out.

He pushed away from the tree, pointing to the top of her cottage.

"I was just trying to get a look at yere roof. Willoughby said Declan patched it while I was away."

"Oh." The moon made an appearance, making Tuck's features easier to make out.

He came nearer and her stomach squeezed in anticipation.

"Who's Willoughby?" she asked nervously.

"The master kiltmaker. That's where I've been. Willoughby needed me to check the damper in his fireplace." He stopped in front of her. "The more important question is what are ye doing out here alone, with it being so late?" His head tilted down and she knew he looked at the items in her arms. He reached out, not taking her notebook, but the key to her cottage. Then he finished locking the door for her. "If ye were running away, I'd think ye'd bring more than some paper and a stack of fabric."

"I'm not running away."

His face turned a bit hard as if she'd answered him wrong. She knew he wanted her to *get the hell out of Scotland!*

Ryn set her feet as if she wasn't going anywhere…just to spite him. "I'm sure you've heard already. I'm taking Maggie's place and teaching at the quilt retreat tomorrow."

"Aye. I heard something about it."

"I guess I'm a little nervous about tomorrow, because I can't sleep. I decided to get a head start on setting up."

"A dram of whisky usually works for me."

"For nerves?"

"For dousing insomnia," he said, as if he wasn't scared of anything. He came closer. "I should walk ye to the castle then."

His offer didn't sound like an offer at all. It sounded as if he'd been charged with an unpleasant obligation.

"Don't *fash* yourself," she said, emphasizing what he'd said to her last night while she lay in his bed. Though she was trying to be tough, the thought of him watching over her again, involuntarily soothed the rocky feelings he'd caused when he'd stomped away from the car.

But she couldn't trust him. Good sense made a go at returning. *He's only trying to get into your pants. Just like all the rest of the gorgeous men you've known.* But the lecture barely registered because he stood near. Her raging hormones had turned her resolve into the firmness of warm pudding.

Tuck touched her arm to point her in the right direction. It should've been innocent enough, but dammit, the contact felt as if firecrackers had been set off on her insides. Her stomach fluttered wildly and her legs became as reliable as stacked marshmallows. Abruptly, she pulled away, wanting to yell, *No! Not this time!* She'd let him kiss her earlier, which had been clearly a mistake. She couldn't allow him to keep reeling her in and then tossing her back. But that was exactly what this gorgeous fisherman was doing.

She took a steadying breath. "Thank you. I'm fine on my own." She took off at a clip. "It's not a long walk."

And damn, if his large stride didn't make it easy to catch up to her. "'Tis my duty, lass. The Laird said to watch out for you."

She was so unbelievably conflicted. On one hand, she wanted him to take her to the castle like in some fairytale. *Prince Charming waking Sleeping Beauty with a kiss.* But this princess wanted His Charmness to want to be with her *for her*, and not out of a sense of obligation. And at the same time, she knew better. She knew better than to want him at all!

They walked along in silence for a while, but then Tuck spoke.

"I'm sorry about earlier."

Sorry? "Yeah? Well, that makes me feel better. That you're sorry you kissed me. I'm not used to men apologizing afterward," she said sarcastically.

"That's not what I'm sorry about," he said.

"Sorry you met me then?"

Tuck gave a mock laugh. "The truth?"

The truth could hurt, and for a moment, she wasn't sure she wanted to know. But deep down, she had to know more about Tuck MacBride. "Yes. The truth." She braced herself, waiting for the blow.

"It's not what ye think," Tuck said quietly. "After we kissed, I realized why ye look so familiar to me. And it might explain why my normally hospitable brother wasn't as warm and friendly as he's known to be."

"Who do I look like? An old flame? A ballbuster?" Ryn couldn't believe she was being so crass. But she was tired, on edge, alone in the world, and had left her filter beside her mother's grave.

By the look on Tuck's face, she'd nailed it.

"Ye've no idea," he finally said.

He went silent again for another long moment. This time she saw he wasn't at war with telling her the truth, but with the ghost from his past.

"I don't get it." And she really didn't. "You can't blame me for taking it personally that you turned into a jerk after kissing me. You have to admit we've spent a lot of time together since I arrived. Why didn't you say something sooner? It's not like I suddenly trans-formed into…into… What's the ballbuster's name?"

"Elspeth."

"Yes, Elspeth. You should've said something." But relief swept through Ryn. Her imagination hadn't run rampant. *He was interested in me from the start.*

But the actuality hit Ryn. His interest hadn't been in *her*. It was his residual feelings for his old flame, sputtering about, that had burnt Ryn in the crossfire.

She didn't wait for him to tell her why he hadn't said anything. The pain of rejection returned and she stomped off.

He caught up to her once again. "Hold up."

The sincerity in his voice had her turning toward him.

He reached out and lightly ran his hand down her arm. "I don't know why I didn't see the similarity at first."

"So it took kissing me to see that I look like your ex?"

His eyebrows crashed together and she knew she'd struck a nerve.

"The point is," he started, "I'm sorry for how I behaved when I figured it out. Ye should know I really enjoyed the kiss we shared."

"I enjoyed it, too." She couldn't believe she'd admitted it. But the kiss had been hot. Surreal. The best kiss she'd ever had, except *best* didn't come close to describing what they'd shared.

His fingers encircled her arm and he gently tugged her closer. As his gaze fell to her lips, Ryn became defenseless to what happened next.

Like a woman with no restraint—*whatsoever!*—she went up on tippy-toes and kissed him, even wrapping her arms around his neck to anchor him to her. At first he didn't move, proving she'd surprised him. Hell, she'd surprised herself. But then he kissed her back, tenderly. The kiss felt like a cool drink on a hot day. Or the warmth of fleece around her shoulders during a winter storm. Or just that feeling of coming home, after being gone so long.

Her brain attempted to keep her steady, begged her to not succumb. *Plant your feet on firm ground! This isn't real!* Sure, somewhere deep inside, Ryn understood this kiss was nothing more than an extension of the apology he'd given. And possibly, Tuck was only kissing her, looking for some skewed closure with his old girlfriend. But the truth was Ryn just didn't care. It felt too good. Too right. And with each second, her inner voice faded and the spell of his kiss swallowed her up as the magic—of him, of her, of them together—weaved a cocoon around them. A dangerous web. But she kept kissing him back.

Slowly, Tuck pulled away, acting as if he didn't want to. "I better get ye to the castle."

Ryn was super self-conscious, feeling as if she should apologize to him now. But then the enormity of it hit her. This must be what alcoholics suffered when they fell off the wagon. And it didn't feel good. She'd betrayed herself. She'd taken one look at Tuck and all the hard work from the last two years was washed away. "Oh, crap."

"Are ye okay?"

"Yes. I just have a lot on my mind."

"Do you want to talk about it?"

"No." *Hell no!* "I'm fine." She hated it even more, that with every moment she spent with him—his kisses aside—she was seeing he was more than *good looks and hard muscle*. He had *depth*! Showing he cared about her and the other little things he kept doing, was deceiving her into going down the wrong path with no way to get back.

At Kilheath, she used the skeleton key to let herself in.

"Thanks for walking me here." She tried to slip in and shut the door, feeling both anxious to be rid of him, and at the same time, she didn't want him to go.

Tuck stopped the door with a strong hand. "Nay, lass. I'll see ye in."

It was a good thing he did—he knew where the light switches were. And the direction of the ballroom.

When he turned on the light of where the retreat was to be held, Ryn saw Sophie had been busy, probably with the help of Sinnie and Rowena. The room had been set up with six long tables, extension cords running to each one. Design walls—made with flannel-covered plywood—were leaning against the wall behind each table. At the front, three design walls stood, clearly there for Ryn's use while she taught.

She looked up at Tuck. "This looks great."

He shrugged. "If you say so. Reminds me of a scaled-down

Quilting Central."

"It's perfect."

At that moment, the Wallace and the Bruce wandered in, tails wagging. They automatically scurried to Tuck's side, as if he had treats in his pocket.

Tuck dropped down on one knee to scratch them both simultaneously behind the ears. "Awww, ye are worthless guard dogs."

Ryn's insides couldn't help but glow, for how he showed his affection for the dogs.

Tuck turned his attention back to her. "Do you want me to hang around until you're done?"

"No. I'll be fine."

He stood. "Promise to call me when ye're ready to go. I'll come walk ye back up to the cottage."

She shook her head. "I appreciate the offer, but don't you have an early appointment to go fishing?"

He nodded, but the look on his face said he was standing firm. "Call me."

He stared her down until she nodded.

"All right then." He patted the dogs one more time and then left.

The dogs trotted over to her then, looking forlorn. As she ran a hand over each of their furry heads, the dogs gazed sadly at the doorway Tuck had gone through.

"I know how you feel. But enough, already. Let's get to work."

First she pinned her quilt blocks to the design wall. Then she went to the stack of solids on the ironing board and began pressing them. She lay out and arranged the quilt fabrics on a table as if assembling a smorgasbord for the retreat goers, making it easy to take what they needed for their quilts. If she'd had more time, she would've made up kits for each of them, but decided it was more important to draw a picture of the True Colors quilt, using the poster board and markers Sophie had left. Ryn sat at the table and began sketching.

About halfway through the drawing, she yawned uncontrollably and her eyes watered. She wouldn't quit though. It was important to have a mock up for the quilters to see.

Ryn woke to a warm hand on her shoulder, gently shaking her. "Lass, wake up."

She knew that voice and smiled without opening her eyes. *If I play possum, will Tuck kiss me awake?*

He must've squatted down beside her, because she felt his solid arm go around her waist. Her insides shivered as he softly spoke into her ear. "Hen, ye need to get back to the cottage. Ye'll have to be up in a few hours for the retreat."

"Hmmm?" she said, smiling as he held her tighter.

The dogs whined as one nuzzled into her hand. The other one burrowed his way in and nuzzled her, too.

"Come now," Tuck said soothingly. "I brought yere sewing machine down to the castle for ye. Am I to carry ye back to the cottage like a wee babe?"

Reluctantly, she opened her eyes. "I'm awake." Though the thought of him carrying her off, as if he was a Scottish Rhett Butler, had Ryn smiling even more.

He stood, offered his hand, and she took it. When he pulled her to her feet, they were awfully close. Close enough for her to lean into him, or go up on tippy-toes again and steal another kiss.

Tuck cleared his throat, breaking the moment. "Let's get ye back to the cottage."

Outside, the car waited with the heater blowing hot air. *How considerate,* she thought. She added it to the other times when he'd surprised her.

He drove her back down the hill, around the corner, and then up to the wool mill and the cottages beyond.

"Hey!" Ryn turned to him. "How were you able to retrieve my sewing machine? You locked my cottage." She felt for the key.

"I have keys to all the cottages. When I knocked and ye didn't answer, I knew you must've fallen asleep at the castle." He gave her a look that said *you should've called for me to come get you sooner*. "While I was in your cottage, I took the liberty of setting your alarm for eight o'clock. Does that work for ye?"

"The retreat starts at nine, so yes, I guess that's fine."

He was not only considerate, but thoughtful, too.

He left her off at the door and waited until she was inside before she heard him pull away in the car.

Ryn fell onto her mattress, grateful for the bed being made up. Before she drifted off, Tuck waltzed across her mind. Thank goodness he'd set her alarm, because there was no way she was crawling out of bed now to take care of it.

She slept soundly until her alarm went off. And with the alarm, the butterflies in her stomach woke up, too. Not the kind of warm and delicious butterflies Tuck set off whenever he was near—or whenever she thought of him. But she had the kind of butterflies that came from real nerves. *Why did I volunteer to run this retreat?* Nothing in the world qualified her to be a quilting instructor, except her love of fabric and a passion for designing and making quilts.

As she hurried to get ready, she wished she'd gotten up an hour earlier, but she couldn't begrudge the extra sleep. Something told her it was going to be a very long day.

She practically ran to Kilheath and was relieved to see Sophie, Sinnie, and Rowena in the kitchen, preparing trays.

"Sorry I'm late," Ryn said.

Sophie gave her a warm smile. "Och, it's only eight-thirty. No one will arrive for another hour.

Ryn opened her mouth, but Sophie put her hand up.

"I told everyone to come at 9:30 this first day. I figured we could all use the extra half hour to get things ready."

All three of them carried the coffeemaker and breakfast goodies into the ballroom.

"I'm glad you found the drawing materials I left for you."

"Thanks for everything." Ryn looked at all three of them. "I really appreciate all you did."

At that moment, Maggie, carrying Irene, walked into the ballroom. Unlike before, Maggie seemed to wake up to where she was and take in the whole room. She set Irene to her feet and the little one ran to her Aunt Sinnie who held out a cream pastry. As Maggie made a beeline for her, Ryn's nerves kicked up another notch.

"Ryn, was it?" Maggie glanced back at her sisters who were watching them. "Rowena and Sinnie say I have *you* to thank for getting me out of running this retreat."

Irene squealed as Dand came into the room.

"Mum? I can't find my Wellies."

"Why do you need them?" Maggie asked.

Irene slammed into her brother with a *whoomf.*

"Mum! Tell her to stop hitting my nuts!"

Sinnie grabbed Irene. "We'll help ye find yere Wellies after we have a cuppa." Rowena corralled Dand and they headed out the door. Sophie went with them, too, leaving Ryn alone with the one person she'd come to Scotland to see.

Maggie turned her attention back to Ryn, but her eyes kept glancing up at the Modern quilt pieces pinned to the design wall. "I'm headed off to the hospital. John, my husband, called early this morn. I'm afraid he had a rough night again." She looked anxious to leave. "I hope we get a chance to talk while ye're here." Her voice sounded sincere, but not hopeful. "Thank you again."

Maggie revolved toward the door and hurried off. That's when Ryn realized she hadn't had a chance to say a word. Not about the Modern quilt. Not about her mother. Not about the Goodbye quilt she was supposed to deliver.

Sophie returned, laying copies of Ryn's pattern in each of the quilter's spots. "I printed these off." She glanced her way and stopped. "Are ye all right?"

"Yes." But Ryn didn't feel very well. The persistent stomach ache—she'd been nursing for a while—returned, and she was certain of the cause. She hated letting her mother down by not fulfilling her last request.

Ryn walked to the front and reviewed her notes once again. Before she knew it, the room was filling with women and their sewing machines. While they set up, they chatted merrily amongst themselves. Ryn watched as they stole glances at the True Colors quilt up on the design wall. Some whispered to each other after taking a look, but mostly they smiled at her, which boosted Ryn's confidence that perhaps this day wouldn't be the disaster she'd envisioned.

Sophie grabbed the bell from the small round table at the front and rang it. "Does everyone have their cup of tea and snack so we can get started?"

The women hurried with their morning snacks to sit down.

Sophie went back to the front and the room became quiet. "I want to introduce ye to Ryn Breckenridge who is Maggie, Rowena, and Sinnie's cousin. Ryn's from America and has graciously agreed to teach us her True Colors quilt for the first Kilts and Quilts Retreat of Whussendale." None of this was a surprise to the village women, but Ryn was glad Sophie's voice was firm, as if to say, *Be nice. The American lass has been through so much already.* She turned to Ryn. "Ye're up."

Ryn smiled sheepishly and walked to the front. "Thank you, Sophie. Everyone should have a True Colors quilt pattern at their station. Your fabric is lined up on the side table." Ryn told them how to start the quilt and then helped the women gather their solid fabrics. Just as she was beginning her speech on the value of negative space in a Modern quilt, Tuck appeared in the doorway and she stumbled over her words. All thoughts, pertaining to quilting, were gone.

She was trying to wrap her brain around why Tuck carried a basket of wool scraps looped over his arm. Even stranger, when their eyes met, he acted as if he was giving her fair warning that a major storm was coming. *A hurricane? A typhoon?*

Sophie looked beyond Tuck and then she looked worried, too. She took off in his direction.

What was going on?

But Sophie didn't make it all the way to the doorway, before Deydie appeared with her wrinkled face lit with excitement. But that quickly faded. Her rheumy gaze fell on the True Colors quilt and she looked puzzled and confused.

Ryn wanted to make a run for it as she watched Deydie's frown grow while she worked out the truth.

Ryn was the one standing at the front.

Ryn was the one pointing to the True Colors quilt.

Ryn was the one who was going to be skewered.

Deydie waddled down the middle aisle and yelled at Ryn. "What in damnation is going on here?"

13

TUCK HATED THE WAY Ryn was glaring at him from the front of the ballroom. He knew she felt betrayed and he wanted to explain.

He set down the basket Deydie insisted he carry, and walked toward Ryn, taking the clear path along the side wall. Sophie and Deydie blocked the middle aisle.

If only he'd had a chance to warn Ryn the old quilter was coming, but there'd been no way to give the American lass the heads up. Deydie had waylaid him as he'd started the vehicle to make the trek back to Whussendale.

Ryn, hands on her hips, met him halfway. As she leaned close, he inhaled, but she wasn't coming near for his pleasure. She was ready to give him hell.

"Why did you have to bring *her*?" Ryn hissed.

"'Tis not my fault. Ye've met the woman. Do ye really think I had a choice?" Deydie was the one person for which Tuck kowtowed.

"Couldn't you have at least prepped her? Told her I was taking over the retreat for Maggie?"

"Honestly, I couldn't get a word in edgewise," he said. "For a good part of the trip, she lectured me on my past transgressions. I was quite relieved when her mobile rang in mid-rant." He paused, looking to see if Ryn believed him. "That poor soul on the other end. Deydie barked out orders as if a Royal Army captain had possessed her. I think it 'twas Moira who bore the brunt of the tongue-lashing."

Tuck cringed when he saw Deydie break away from Sophie. She waddled toward him and Ryn, the old woman grimacing ferociously as every last wrinkle participated in her pudgy face.

She shook a stubby finger at Ryn and there wasn't a damn thing he could do about it. "Why didn't ye tell me ye were running the retreat? We spent enough time together the other morn. 'Tis lying, in my book, omitting something like that."

"I didn't want to rock the boat." Ryn glanced at Sinnie and Sophie sideways. For a moment, he wondered if Ryn might throw her new friends into Deydie's path. But she surprised him, by taking the high ground. "I'm sorry. I should've said something."

Deydie pointed to Ryn's blocks on the design wall. "Where's the wool quilt Maggie was to teach?"

Ryn bit her lip. "I don't know enough about wool quilts to teach a class on it."

"And those quilt blocks hanging there? *Doesna* look anything like what my quilting ladies do."

Ryn shrugged, looking embarrassed. "It's my own design. I call it the True Colors quilt."

The lass seemed to be holding her breath while Deydie peered hard at the quilt for a full two minutes.

"Where did ye learn to make a quilt like that?" Deydie asked.

"The style is called Modern quilting."

When one of the local Whussendale quilters approached,

Deydie's hand shot up like a roadblock. "The American lass is busy just now. Ye can speak with her when I'm done."

Mrs. Bates heeded Deydie and slunk back to her spot.

Tuck felt bad for her, *and bad for Ryn, too.* He wished he'd driven on when Deydie had called out to him back in Gandiegow. He would gladly have suffered Deydie's broom to keep Ryn from having to deal with the old woman now.

Deydie nodded at Ryn. "Ye'll be done here tomorrow, aye?"

"Yes," Ryn said.

Tuck saw the gleam in the old woman's eyes. He'd seen it before. Deydie was up to something.

"Then ye'll come to us the next day and set up."

"Set up for what?" Ryn asked, looking confused.

Deydie pounded her on the back, giving her a most frightening smile. "The workshop. I never thought I'd say this, but it's high time we expanded our quilting repertoire."

First, it sounded ridiculous for Deydie to say *repertoire.* She was too *Caledonian beef and potatoes* to say something so French. Secondly, Tuck felt that sinking feeling coming on. Deydie was a bull, unpredictable, and Ryn had no idea of what she was getting herself into. But it was too late. Deydie's stubborn face said she'd have her way. Tuck felt it in his gut. *This'll only end in disaster.*

Deydie shot the American lass that awful maniacal grin of hers. "Ryn Breckenridge, ye're coming to Gandiegow to turn us into a bunch of Modern quilters."

☙❧

"You want me to do what?" Ryn couldn't believe it. *Deydie isn't upset that I'm teaching a Modern quilt?*

"Lass?" Tuck's look of concern disarmed Ryn.

But Deydie wasn't done issuing orders. "Tuck will bring ye to Gandiegow. Sophie's agreed ye can come to us next, when ye're done with the Whussendale quilters."

Ryn spun on Sophie, and her response was a sheepish shrug.

Deydie tapped Ryn on the arm, hard. "Ye'll stay in the room over the pub. Our Kilts and Quilts hospitality manager, Rachel, says the quilting dorms are off limits while we repaint the walls before the next retreat. The smoke from the fireplaces, ye see, has the walls taking on a dark cast. Now, if Rachel's bed and breakfast were done being built..." Deydie waved her hands in the air as if dispersing the B & B's image. "Did ye hear me, Tuck? Bring the lass and she'll teach us her Modern quilt."

The old woman was being heavy-handed and issuing out orders as if Ryn herself didn't have a say in the matter.

What if she was due back in the States? What if she had a life to get back to? Of course, she didn't have either, but Deydie didn't know that and should've at least assumed she did.

Unless, I look like the lost soul that I am.

Ryn automatically turned to Tuck to see if he saw the real her, and dammit, he seemed to thinking along the same lines. His gaze was filled with concern and some other emotion she couldn't nail down.

Ryn swept that thought aside. His strange expression had to do with Deydie bossing him around, too. Ryn opened her mouth to stick up for herself and Tuck.

But the old quilter plodded ahead as if Ryn had agreed to everything. "Aye. Right. I need to call Bethia to let her know of the change in plans and the quilting workshop ye're going to do." She stared at Ryn. "Go on now and get back to yere teaching." Without another word, Deydie waddled over to Sophie and Rowena, leaving Ryn alone with Tuck.

Ryn had things she wanted to say to him, but then Sinnie appeared with two steaming mugs. "Cocoa for the both of ye. I expect you need it after getting bushwhacked by Deydie." The monitor at Sinnie's belt gave a toddler gurgle. *"Somebody's* up. I better run and get Irene before she gets into trouble."

Ryn didn't even have time to thank her for the hot cocoa before she rushed off.

Tuck turned to Ryn with genuine concern and interest in his eyes. "Are you okay, lass?"

"Other than the near heart attack that Deydie gave me just now?"

He reached out a hand as if to steady her, but pulled back at the last moment. "Ye'll survive. We all do."

But Ryn wasn't sure she was going to survive his deep baritone burr and his *make-her-fall-for-him-again* look of concern.

She turned away, focusing on the Whussendale women who were quilting. "Yes, I'm fine." The morning class had gone well, better than she could've hoped for.

Ryn realized Tuck was scanning the length of her, as if looking for bumps and bruises. His gaze was probably meant to be brotherly, but dang it, if he didn't give Ryn goosebumps just the same.

"What are you wearing?" he asked.

"This old thing?" she answered, smoothing down the front. "You've might have heard of it. It's called a dress."

He chuckled. "A dress, huh? I like it."

Unwittingly, her stomach did a flip-flop, reliving the kiss...okay, the two kisses they'd shared before.

She watched him closely. And if she wasn't mistaken, his benign gaze turned meaningful—a gaze filled with promise. Her little black dress had been holding out on her in the past. The snug sheath had never caused this kind of reaction before.

"I'm glad you like my dress," she heard herself saying and was immediately mortified. A heated blush flooded her face and she spun away from him. "I better get back up there."

"I'll pick you up early Monday morning," he said.

She didn't look back as she walked to the front, but waved an arm behind her. "Fine. Sounds good." *Oh, dear!*

That's when she noticed all eyes were on her. Sophie, Rowena, the cook Elspeth, Lara, and all the rest of the room. They looked ready to ask her a thousand questions about her and Tuck.

Deydie saved Ryn, though, as the old woman came shuffling back into the room. "I'd like to say something to the group before ye get back to teachin'." With some effort, she huffed herself to the front. "Most of ye know me. I'm Deydie McCracken of Gandiegow, and me granddaughter came up with the Kilts and Quilts Retreat. Sophie, Sinnie, and Rowena—" Deydie's eyes skimmed the room and landed on Ryn with a frown "—and the American lass have done their part to bring the first Kilts and Quilts Retreat to Whussendale. Enjoy it, for this is the last of easy street ye'll see. In the future, the burden shouldn't land on these young women alone. I expect ye all will help. Aye?"

Aye went up around the room, as if Deydie's reputation had preceded her.

Deydie nodded. "Good. Now, get back to sewing."

Ryn took that as her cue and hurried to take Deydie's place.

Surprisingly, Deydie didn't leave the ballroom, but took a seat next to her basket. She pulled out an embroidery hoop and began stitching while Ryn self-consciously gave the next instruction. It was unnerving to have the old quilter there, watching her every move, but Ryn pushed through her uneasiness for the sake of the quilters…and for the sake of Maggie.

An hour later, two tall, good-looking men showed up in the doorway.

Sophie appeared at Ryn's side and answered her question before she could ask. "Those are my cousins, Ross and Ramsay. They're here to retrieve Deydie. They're on their way to the hospital to visit my cousin John. Come. I'll introduce you."

As introductions were made, Deydie gathered her things, and

finally Ryn could teach the Whussendale ladies without being scrutinized.

Without any more incidents, Ryn taught the rest of the day and didn't see Tuck again. She wondered about him, though, several times…and she shouldn't have. When she returned to her cottage in the evening and saw that his light wasn't on, she wondered if he'd stayed the night in Gandiegow. Exhausted down to the toes of her tights, Ryn fell into bed and dreamed of him.

The next morning, she either heard him leave his cottage or she dreamed it, but was too tired to fully wake to find out. Besides, she shouldn't care what he was doing. She was self-aware enough to know she was acting like a boy-crazy fool. Which always got her into trouble.

Later when she woke, she kept her thoughts to *getting ready* and then hurried to the castle. But as she walked, she couldn't stop thinking about Tuck. She didn't understand her hang-up on him. And though she knew it was wrong, she looked for him everywhere. It was as if her DNA was searching for him.

The morning session went well as all of the quilters had finished the appliquéd circle blocks. Slowly, Ryn was learning the names of the village women. Sophie started a list of what they would need for future retreats and laid it on the table besides Ryn's teaching notes—nametags were on top of the list.

After lunch, while Ryn gave the instructions for how to cut the angle correctly for the lightning bolt pieces, Tuck came strolling into the ballroom. He hitched his head at her as if they needed to speak.

Ryn wanted to run to him—*an old habit*—but instead, she finished what she was saying before going to the doorway, walking slowly, though she wanted to sprint.

When they stood nearly toe to toe, he spoke.

"Lass, I wanted to remind ye that we're leaving earlier in the morning than we did before. I hope that's okay with you."

"Sure." She liked her sleep, but Deydie's command still felt fresh.

"Good." He looked around at the quilters and then discreetly slipped a note into her hand. "Read it later," he said quietly. And then he was gone.

Ryn went back to the front of the room while the note burned a hole in her hand. Her mind raced with questions. What could it mean? A love note? Did he want to meet for a romantic rendezvous?

"I'll be right back," she said to the room. "Bathroom break." She was barely out the door before she opened the note in her hand.

Knock on my door, when you get back to the cottage.

Tuck

She leaned against the wall. "Well, now I'm more confused than ever." Her imagination ran wild. *She'd knock. He'd pull her into his cottage and pin her against the door with a kiss. A romantic movie would have nothing on them.*

Heated up, Ryn fanned herself with his note. Finally, she went back into the ballroom and tried to stay calm the rest of the afternoon. But it was hard to do with Tuck's impending kiss and make-out session on her mind.

For the quilters' sake, Ryn did her best to cool her jets. She put Tuck on the back burner so she could keep her focus on quilting instead of whatever Tuck had planned for them this evening.

When Ryn completed her final lesson of the day, and of the retreat, she didn't have to worry about cleanup. All the Whussendale quilters pitched in and put Kilheath's ballroom back to normal.

Sophie handed Ryn her bag. "Ye did a fine job. Mrs. McNabb is making sea bass for supper. Would you like to come to dinner this evening?"

Ryn should be starving and sea bass sounded great, but...

"Thank you for the offer," she said. "But I'm tired." And anxious to see Tuck. Also, Ryn's stomach still bothered her. The abdominal pain was so constant now she was starting to believe it would last forever.

"All right then." Sophie hugged her. "I can't thank you enough for stepping in for Maggie. I know she appreciates it."

"Oh." Ryn felt guilty for not thinking of Maggie once today.

"When ye're done in Gandiegow, yere cottage here in Whussendale will be waiting for you."

"Thank you." But the thought threw her off even more. Ryn had no idea where her future lay. But tonight, she knew what she was doing. She hurried off to Tuck.

She rushed back to the horseshoe row of cottages, but didn't knock on Tuck's door right away. Instead, she opted for a quick shower, and afterward, she applied fresh makeup. Nervously, she went to Tuck's and quietly rapped on the heavy oak door.

When the door opened, he didn't pull her inside. He didn't kiss her. What he did give her was a regretful expression, as if he'd poured her a bowl of cereal, but then didn't have sugar to sprinkle on top, or any milk to go with it, either.

Ridiculously, Ryn felt too emotional for words. She'd built this up in her mind and had no one to blame but herself. All her expectations deteriorated. Crumbled. And scattered all over the floor.

"Sit down," he said. "Over there." He pointed to a chair in front of the hearth.

She slipped off her coat and he took it from her like a perfect gentleman. Except, deep inside—her brazened side—she didn't want him to be a gentleman right now. She wanted him to kiss her passionately, like he'd done before.

She sat in her designated chair. Tuck, though, pulled his seat farther away, but then sat, too.

He leaned forward and rested his arms on his knees, staring at the crackling fire. "I thought we should get things straight before we leave in the morning." He paused, as if checking with the fire first, before going on. "It's like this, Ryn. I think ye're a nice lass and all…"

She couldn't believe her dashed expectations could've fallen even further. But they did. Like a huge boulder plunging into a lake and quickly sinking to the bottom.

He frowned. "It's best for you if I keep a distance."

How can it be best for me? That sinking feeling drowned her. She was completely off her rocker. Had she seriously been thinking they were going to have some kind of relationship or something?

She consoled herself that it was loneliness' fault. Loneliness had caused her to be irrational. Extremely irrational!

Mustering up what little self-respect she had left, she stood, putting her hands on her hips. "Fine by me! But let's be clear about this. What you're really trying to say is that you want *me* to keep my distance *from you*!"

ഇ⊙യ

Damn, if she wasn't smart! Ryn had nailed it. And it was good Tuck had made her mad. *Aye*, she needed to keep her distance from him, because he, sure as hell, wasn't strong enough to stay away from her. The truth—his crazy attraction to Ryn was nothing more than his subconscious remembering his puppy love for Elspeth. But it didn't exactly explain the intensity of how he felt for Ryn or how strongly he wanted to be near her. *Day and night.*

This whole debacle was his fault alone and Ryn didn't deserve any of it. She was a decent lass and he shouldn't have kissed her. But he couldn't bring himself to wish it had never happened. He just couldn't.

He hung his head, knowing he had to drive the knife deeper. "As I said before, ye're nice and all, but ye're not my type."

Her eyes snapped to him as if he'd thrown cold water on her. But his American lass had might and strength. Her eyes were on fire, ready to burn him to a crisp, and she'd never been more alluring. A woman like this could definitely hold his attention for more than a moment. Maybe a lifetime.

"You keep saying I'm not you're type," she huffed. "But I don't believe it. I think I'm exactly your type and this is why you're doing this." Determinedly, she walked to her coat on the hook by the door. As she reached for it, she turned back to him. "Who were you thinking about when you kissed me? Was it me or your old flame?" She shook her head. "It doesn't matter." She stared him down as if he was the bastard, he and everyone else knew him to be. "I'm exactly your type, Tuck MacBride. And that's what scares you."

He held his breath and waited for the rest of it. For surely, there was more.

She raised an eyebrow and then speared him right through the gut. "There's something you ought to consider, Tuck. I might be your type, but you're just not mine."

14

R YN SHOVED HER ARMS into her coat. "Are we done? I
have a lesson plan to tweak for the quilters of Gandiegow."

"Aye. We're done." He sounded final. And at the same
time, he sounded sad, and she wondered if he wanted to take it all
back. But she revised that thought. He couldn't be sad. He was a
love 'em and leave 'em jerk!

Ryn held it together—*barely*—as she turned the doorknob. She
couldn't help but look back at him.

Tuck stood, as if there was one more thing he had to say.. But he
remained silent. She pulled open the door and went outside, proud of
herself for taking the high road by not slamming the door behind
her. That might show him she cared.

And pathetically, she wanted him to run after her. But he didn't.
Just as well. He might have seen she was on the verge of tears.

Damn him.

She was a dumbass for repeating her past. But even more of a dumbass for ever seeing good in Tuck.

I told you he'd break your heart. Which was a stupid thought. Her heart wasn't broken, not even close. He'd bruised her ego, was all. She'd be fine. She was in Scotland for one reason only—to fulfill her mom's last request. But with Maggie gone most of the time, and Ryn set to teach the True Colors quilt to the women of Gandiegow, the transfer of the Goodbye quilt would have to wait.

Tuck had certainly shown his *true colors* tonight.

She stomped inside her cottage, more mad at herself than him. "I wonder if Uber comes this far out and would be willing to take me to Gandiegow." For she wasn't looking forward to another car ride with *Mr. Love-'em-and-Leave-'em* to the fishing village.

She changed into her sweats and climbed into bed. Though she was exhausted, she couldn't sleep. She could've blamed her stomach hurting. But more than likely, feeling crappy had to do with her own self-abuse of wanting another gorgeous bastard like Tuck. Over and over, she replayed her argument with him, wishing things had turned out differently. But it was futile and a waste of time. There was nothing she could do to change the outcome. The only thing to do was to brace herself for the morning and seeing Tuck again.

She closed her eyes and the next thing she heard was Tuck's alarm clock going off in the cottage next door. She heard him get up. She heard his shower. She wished more than anything she could beg off today and stay in bed…for the rest of her life!

Instead she crawled out and put herself together—for the women of Gandiegow, and not for Tuck.

With her bag in hand, filled with the True Colors quilt fabric, and her sewing machine in the other, Ryn walked stoically out of her cottage. Tuck stood there, as she knew he would be. He reached out to take her sewing machine, but she jerked away.

"I have it." She stalked to the car and set her things in the backseat.

While Tuck got behind the wheel, Ryn took her place on the passenger's side. They left the radio controls untouched as he started the car and drove away.

The silence was crushing. She couldn't help but think of the last time they'd rode in the car together. This car ride to Gandiegow wasn't filled with the congenial conversation as before. *Before they'd kissed*, Ryn reminded herself, making a note that kissing gorgeous men ruined everything.

The awkward silence grew along with her underlying hostility. She'd be damned if she was going to speak first and fix what had happened last night. It was his fault, after all. She didn't look over again to see his set jaw and his dark eyes facing forward. She could feel the stubbornness roiling off of him. Well, Tuck was getting what he deserved—the silent treatment. And she was giving him exactly what he asked for—*distance*. She needed distance, too, wishing now she'd been the one to suggest it first. Also, wishing she'd handled things differently from the first moment she'd seen him.

When they got to Gandiegow, Tuck was out of the car and had her sewing machine in hand before she could say *I've-got-it* again.

He started walking and she hurried to catch up.

Without looking at her, he began talking. "I'll take yere machine to Quilting Central and then I'll walk ye to Deydie's." He gazed in her direction. "And I'll take no argument from you this morning."

"I don't want to bother Deydie. I'll just stay at Quilting Central."

"Ye'll go to Deydie's. I'll feel better if ye do."

Ryn grabbed his arm to bring him to a stop. "Do I really care how you feel?"

Suddenly, pain seared through her abdomen, so much so, she gripped his arm for support to keep from doubling over.

Tuck set down the machine and laid a hand on her back. "What's wrong? Are ye all right?"

She straightened up. "Nothing's wrong. I'm just hungry. Or more likely, you bossing me around is making my stomach hurt."

"Ye're going to Deydie's. No argument." He picked up the sewing machine and her bag, leaving her nothing to carry as he motioned for her to go ahead of him.

"I don't like being told what to do." But she was grateful he was carrying her things. She promised herself she'd do a better job of taking care of herself...more sleep and eat better. That's what she needed to fix her stomach issue.

"I can tell you don't like being bossed around."

"And yet, you insist on taking me to Deydie's."

"Och, I feel terrible about that." He grinned and the tension broke a little. The light from the lamp post caught the laughter in his eyes and the dimples on his cheeks.

And damn, if she didn't feel drawn in again. "I can see you're all broke up over it."

When Deydie opened her cottage door, her rheumy eyes took in everything. Ryn wished she could've stopped Tuck from putting his hand on her back and guiding her in.

When they were all the way inside, Tuck must've realized what he'd done, because he shoved the offending hand in his pocket. "The lass isn't feeling well. Can ye feed her?" Tuck looked at Ryn with real concern.

She stepped away from him. "I'm fine. I just had a little cramp on the way over here. Probably because I got up so early." She felt proud of her excuse.

Tuck didn't argue, but said his goodbyes and disappeared out the door.

"Hot tea is in the pot. Porridge is warm on the stove." Deydie shuffled to the fabric on the table. "If ye want eggs and bangers, ye can make them for the both of us."

The thought of food made Ryn more nauseous. "I'll just have

some tea."

Deydie eyed her. "I know yere problem. *Lovesick.* Ye need to be careful with that lad. I saw how he was looking at ye. And ye at him. Ye better stop the shenanigans with that one right now. Cow-eyes have gotten more than one maid with child."

Ryn had been pregnant once and would never be again. "There are no shenanigans or cow-eyes." But that wasn't exactly the truth. She had to keep reminding herself that Tuck had flat out rejected her last night. "Believe me. Nothing is going on." With her hand shaking, she poured herself a cup of tea.

"I'm going up to the Big House. Go lie down on the bed over there until I get back. If ye argue about it, my broom will find yere backside."

The lone bed with the blue and brown Flying Geese quilt on top looked inviting. "Well, if you're going to force me, I will."

Deydie grabbed her basket by the door, flipped off the light switch, and exited. Ryn appreciated the glowing embers in the hearth, a welcome nightlight. She hung her coat up and with some trepidation, slid under the quilt. It was so cozy she instantly fell fast asleep.

An hour later, Ryn woke as Deydie made her way through the door. Ryn scooted off the bed and righted the quilt, feeling embarrassed to have slept so soundly in the old woman's bed. The good news was she did feel a little better.

"All rested?" Deydie asked. "Ye better be. 'Tis time to go to Quilting Central."

Ryn gathered her things and followed Deydie out. As they walked to Quilting Central, Ryn realized she knew nothing about the group she would be teaching today, or Deydie's expectations. "How many are attending the class?"

"*Retreat,*" Deydie corrected. "I expect there will be fifteen or so. My ladies have been working hard, taking care of other retreat goers. I thought they were due a retreat of their own."

"Will I be doing a short *retreat*, like in Whussendale?"

"Depends," Deydie said.

Did that mean the old woman might kick her out at the end of the day? "I was just wondering since I only brought clothes for just a couple of days."

In response, Deydie only grunted as she opened the door to Quilting Central. "Give me yere pattern and I'll make copies while ye get yere quilt up on the front wall."

Ryn dug out the pattern and went to the front to do as she was told. Her nerves were running high, which made her stomachache return.

And it didn't help that Deydie was wrong about the number of women who were coming today. As the quilters began filing in at 8:30, Ryn started counting. She was already up to thirty-one and not everyone was in the door yet.

Bethia sidled up to Ryn and laid a gentle hand on her arm. "Don't worry, lass. Everyone is a mite curious. We have more than Gandiegow here. I see a van-full has come from Spalding Farm to see the Modern quilter."

Ryn's stomach churned and she thought she might vomit.

Deydie made her way up on the stage. "Take yere places everyone." She scanned the room and frowned. "For those of ye that didn't sign up beforehand, make sure to add yere lunch order to the paper on the counter over there. Also, remember to pay Moira. Moira raise yere hand."

Andrew's wife shyly raised her hand as all heads turned to look at her.

"Before I get Ryn up here, for those that need it, Amy has all the solid fabric kits to make Ryn's True Colors quilt. Make sure to pay Moira for that, too."

A few women got up and went over to the table, but the majority stayed in their chairs.

"Ryn, get up here and explain what a Modern quilt is."

As she walked up, several women nodded and she recognized a few of them from her first visit to Gandiegow. But mostly, the crowd was new and did indeed seem curious.

At that moment, the bell above the door jingled as Cait entered. Surprisingly, her belly had grown bigger in just a few days! She waved to the room. "Sorry I'm late." She seemed to make a point of smiling at Ryn as well.

Ryn's fears eased at seeing her new friend. She started the retreat, giving them the same spiel about Modern quilting she'd given to the Whussendale group. After that, she moved straight to the initial directions and everyone got to work. But as the blocks went up on the wall, they weren't the solid fabrics which were in Deydie's kits or the ones displayed in Ryn's quilt. Yes, there were a few solid background fabrics, but the majority of the blocks were filled with tartan fabrics!

Deydie must've noticed it at the same time and she shuffled over to Ryn, grinning. She pounded her on the back. "Me quilters have put their own touch on yere True Colors quilt. Some of them think it ain't quilting unless there's tartan in it."

The quilts coming together on the design wall were beautiful. Ryn couldn't believe how making a fabric change could change the character of the quilt. In some quilts, the solid grey pieces had been switched to a gray print, giving the quilts a subtle dimension. But mostly, the tartan was added to the circles and made each quilt pop with its own personality.

"I like what they've done," Ryn said.

"It just goes to show that my quilters have a lot of ingenuity." Deydie smiled proudly. "Some old dogs don't mind learning new tricks, as long as they get to do it their way." She turned to Ryn. "Ye're looking peaked. Go get something to eat. Claire brought croissants and scrambled eggs."

The morning was going well, but Ryn still didn't have much of an appetite. But she went to the kitchen area and put some food on her plate, though only nibbling at the food a bit. She was grateful to abandon her breakfast, when a group of quilters had questions about cutting the lightning bolt strips for their quilts. She returned to the front and went back to teaching.

At the next break, Cait brought Ryn a cup of tea, along with a worried look. "How are you doing? Are you feeling okay?"

"I'm fine. I've been a little queasy that's all." Ryn wasn't about to burden her new friend with how bad she really felt.

Cait pointed to Ryn's phone lying by the sewing machine. "May I?"

"Yes." But Ryn wasn't sure what Cait wanted with her phone.

"I'm giving you my number. That way ye'll have a way to get a hold of me, if you need someone to talk to. Okay?"

Ryn couldn't believe the generosity of Cait. "Thank you. I might take you up on it."

"I mean it. Call me. Women have to stick together. It's the only way to get through life's complications…by leaning on one another."

The first day ended with Deydie and Cait treating the group to a lasagna dinner at the restaurant. Ryn wasn't trying to be rude as her plate sat nearly untouched in front of her. If she felt better, she would've gladly eaten the delicious-looking food and would've enjoyed the fellowship of the quilters more. They'd been attentive throughout the day and seemed to have forgiven her for whatever she'd done the last time she was in Gandiegow.

Ryn looked down at her plate again. She just wanted the dinner to be over so she could go to bed.

At that moment, the door opened and a beautiful, long brown-haired woman with a great figure came in…followed by Tuck!

Jealousy whirled to life in Ryn, as the two of them chose a table in her line of sight. The woman and Tuck were close, talking and laughing, and Ryn didn't like it one bit.

Bethia laid a hand over Ryn's tight fist. "That's Rachel, our hospitality manager. Tuck helped out today to paint one of the quilting dorms."

Ryn looked closer and saw the paint splatters on both of them.

The door opened again and a little girl tore in, gripping a small quilt under her arm. "Mommy! I caught two fish. Brodie helped!"

A tall, dark-haired, good-looking Scot sauntered in after the girl, grinning. He held a small bucket with a lid on it. This man gave Tuck a run for his money in the *gorgeous* department.

Bethia leaned closer to Ryn. "That's Brodie, Rachel's husband. And the lassie is Rachel's daughter, Hannah."

Brodie headed straight to Rachel and planted a kiss on her lips. The tight coil inside of Ryn eased a little. She glanced at Tuck and he was staring back at her.

Brodie held out the bucket to Hannah. "Ask Dominic nicely if he'll fry them up for ye."

Smiling, Rachel rescued the quilt before Hannah took the bucket from Brodie. "I thought we decided her fish quilt couldn't go out on the boat anymore."

Brodie shrugged, beaming. "The lass insisted her quilt missed going out to sea."

Rachel laughed. "You spoil her."

Brodie leaned down again and whispered in his wife's ear.

"Get a room," Tuck said. Once again, his eyes returned to Ryn.

The quilters started scooting back their chairs and breaking up. Cait and Deydie were already at the counter, paying the bill.

Bethia patted Ryn's now relaxed hand. "I'll show ye where ye'll be staying—the room over the pub."

"No," Ryn said, glancing first at Tuck and then at her bag with her clothes in it by the door. "I'll be fine. Deydie pointed out the pub earlier. She said there's only the one bedroom at the top of the stairs. Besides, I'd like to finish my tea first." What she'd really like to do was to keep an eye on Tuck for a little while longer.

But then the man in question surprised her, as he hailed Bethia from two tables over. "I'll make sure the lass gets to the pub safely."

Bethia nodded as if *safely* was code for something more intimate. "Right. I'll let ye sort Ryn out."

Ryn's face felt as warm as her hot tea. She took a sip to hide her embarrassment. "Thanks for everything," she mumbled to Bethia.

"We'll see ye bright and early in the morn?" Bethia asked. *As if Ryn might find more interesting things to do between now and then.*

"Yes, first thing in the morning."

Bethia rose from her chair and met up with Deydie at the front door. The two of them spoke and then turned back to Ryn. Bethia was smiling, but Deydie wasn't. She looked as if she wanted to warn Ryn again about *shenanigans* and what that could lead to.

Unfortunately, Tuck scooted back his chair and stood. "Rachel, Brodie, if you don't mind, I'm going to join Ryn, so she won't have to sit alone."

The two turned to Ryn.

"She could come and join us," Rachel offered.

"Nay," Tuck said quickly. "We have Whussendale things to discuss." He left and took the seat across from Ryn.

She frowned at him. "What Whussendale things?"

Tuck cocked his head at the counter and whispered. "They're newlyweds. With Hannah, they don't get much alone time."

Ryn glanced over to see Hannah seated at the counter with a coloring book, crayons, and a chocolate milk. The restaurant owners and patrons seemed to work in unison to give Brodie and Rachel a few moments alone.

Ryn wondered what it would feel like to be part of a community who cared about her as much as Gandiegow cared for the newly-weds.

"That's very astute of you." Ryn took another sip of tea. "Are you staying in Gandiegow tonight? It's kind of late to be going back to Whussendale, isn't it?"

"Aye. I'm staying in town. Ross asked me to take over for him in the morning as his wife Sadie needs routine blood tests done first thing. She's waiting on a kidney transplant." Tuck filled Ryn in on Sadie's condition and how Sadie's brother Oliver was going to share a kidney with his sister.

"And you, Ryn? How are ye feeling?" Tuck asked. "I was worried about ye this morning."

Damn him for being a caring person, making her feel all soft and fluffy inside. "I'm fine. My stomach was a little messed up this morning. All is good now."

Tuck glanced down at her full plate of food. "Are ye sure you're okay?"

"Yes. I just want to go to bed."

Tuck stood. "I'll get yere bag."

But Ryn got that feeling everyone had eyes on them again. "No. You stay and eat. I can get it."

Apparently, though, Tuck was deaf. By the time she stood up, he was waiting for her at the door.

Once outside, she turned to him. "Aren't you a little concerned with how this looks?"

"How what looks?"

"Stop playing dumb."

Tuck came to a stop. "If I worried every time Gandiegow judged me, I'd never know a moment's peace." He gazed out at the sea. "I don't care what they think."

She knew he did care. As they walked through town, the noise from the pub got louder and louder. When Deydie had shown her

The Fisherman earlier, the place hadn't been open. And Ryn hadn't given a thought to staying above the bar. But the pub was definitely alive now. It wasn't just the noise that was getting to Ryn. She worried what everyone would think if Tuck took her inside, sporting her night bag over his arm. Would they think they were shacking up tonight?

She grabbed his sleeve, bringing them to a stop just outside the pub. "Let me go in alone."

But Tuck didn't act as if her words had registered. He was staring down at her hand on his arm. She read the emotion and wasn't surprised when he pulled her into the shadows, leaned her up against the wall, and kissed her. Hard.

It was surreal—the drums from inside reverberating against her back, the wail of the pipes, and the pounding of her heart.

She laid her hand against his chest and pushed. "What about keeping a distance?"

"Screw the distance." And he kissed her again. With more passion. Her breath caught as she could feel his heart beating against her palm.

She clutched his shirt and pulled him closer. He kissed her neck and moved lower. She adjusted so he could get to any part of her he wanted.

He had a way of making her forget everything, especially her resolve.

The pub door slammed and footsteps fell on the stone porch. Tuck grabbed her hand and they ran for the back of the pub, where he pinned her against the wall again. This time, though, he cupped her cheek gently. "New plan." He took a couple of deep breaths. "Forget everything I said before." He kissed her again, but when his hand slipped under her shirt and cupped her bra-covered breast, she pulled away.

"Too fast." She wiggled out of his arms, adjusting her shirt. She couldn't get perspective with Tuck so near. She still felt his handprint against her skin, how it had moved intimately up her back and then around to her front. "I better get inside and to bed."

Tuck gave her a teasing smile. "That's a hell of an invitation. Aye, I'll join you."

"Alone." But that one word was so hard to say. "We can't be lovers, Tuck." *Not now.* Her plans were revising quickly. What if she took the time for them to be friends first? Maybe then she wouldn't turn into a lovesick idiot!

The expression on Tuck's face transformed into hurt, and then anger. "Is there someone else?"

"Yes. *Me.*"

But that seemed to throw him off even further. "What does that mean?"

"I'm working through some things." She had no intention of explaining the truth—how she'd fallen many times for the wrong guy. She was afraid if she shared even a little part of her story, she'd end up embarrassing herself, and bearing too much of her soul in the process.

"What things?" He looked offended now, as if he'd been lead on, only to have his face slapped.

Ryn put out her hand. "I'll take my bag."

Without argument, he handed it over and stayed where he was while she walked to the front of the building. It was too soon to congratulate herself for being strong. For resisting him.

It took everything she had to pull open the pub door and go inside. She wanted nothing more than to run back out, throw herself at him, and be encircled within his strong arms again.

Instead, she ignored the crowd and marched up the steps behind the bar and made it to her bed alone.

෫෧෬

Tuck slumped against the stone building. He couldn't believe he'd been so weak. But the Almighty couldn't blame him for wanting to have Ryn look at him again with those soft eyes of hers. And the contentment he felt when he held her in his arms...

He sighed.

Besides, Ryn wasn't Elspeth. But the lass certainly had Elspeth's play book—driving him crazy.

"*Effing hell,*" he said on an exhale. Why couldn't he have kept his distance?

Though the pub was right here, it wouldn't do any good to try to drink his worries away. With Ryn above stairs, he wouldn't put it past himself to sneak up there, climb into bed, and kiss her until he felt whole...and contented again.

15

MAGGIE STEPPED THROUGH the entrance to the hospital, knowing her routine of seeing John should be old hat by now. But to her core, she felt like a rowboat without oars—adrift, directionless. She wasn't herself anymore. She always thought she was a strong woman, but now she was as sturdy and mighty as a squid splayed on the dance floor. Life had beaten her up and thrashed her about. She barely had the energy to take the elevator up to her husband's floor.

Aye, she shouldn't feel like she was treading water. There were plenty of things for her to do. Deydie certainly had high expectations, wanting her to get the next Whussendale Kilts and Quilts Retreat going. She didn't even have the wherewithal to give a proper thank you to her American cousin for taking over as she'd done. Maggie should invite her to dinner or bake her a cake.

But truthfully, Maggie had nothing left to offer. And the only person to blame for her life's upheaval was Tuck. His easy-go-lucky manner had left John hanging. Now her husband was a shell of the man he used to be.

If only John would get better. His injury was healing, but losing his hand had caused his spirit to fester, infecting and killing his good nature, and destroying the life they'd known together. *Damn Tuck for tearing my life apart.*

She reached John's floor and plastered on a smile. He couldn't see her dismay. Her biggest problem today was she had to tell him of her conversation with Mum last night. He wouldn't like it. Just more bad news for him.

She opened the door and walked in. Ross and Ramsay stood, both looking upset.

"We better head out," Ross said.

"Get well, brother." Ramsay was known far-and-wide for his laughing teasing manner. But there were no smiles and light-heartedness now.

John didn't even glance up as his brothers left.

Maggie knew her brothers-in-law wanted to speak to her in the hallway, but she couldn't discuss with anyone her worry—John was slipping away from them all and would never be the same again.

"Close the door," her husband said, as if the chill of death had passed through him.

Maggie did as he asked, but remained by the door.

"I'm not a wee babe," John said. "I don't need babysitters."

"They weren't here as sitters. Your brothers wanted to see you," Maggie defended.

"I'm capable of being alone. Ye shouldn't have asked them to come...to leave their boats, their wives. I won't be a burden."

Each encounter with her husband left Maggie more fearful. She couldn't go stand by him, else he would see how she trembled. And even scarier, the Almighty, whom she'd trusted in her whole life, had forsaken them all—Ross and Ramsay, she and the kids.

"I'll be right back." She escaped out into the hall, going in the opposite direction of her brothers-in-law, and headed for the restroom. She barely had the door closed behind her, when the tears began to come.

"Help me," she cried.

The path ahead was blurred and she didn't know what to do next. There was no way out of the despair that surrounded her. And even worse, there was no way to jar her husband back into being the man she'd known him to be.

※※※

Ryn was so exhausted that the noise downstairs didn't really register, as she pulled the brightly-colored sheep quilt over her bone-weary body. She didn't sleep well, though. She felt chilled and her stomach pained her all night.

In the morning, when she looked in the mirror, she was shocked to see how pale she was—the whitest of muslins. She put on extra blush, hoping no one would notice.

Though everyone at Quilting Central was doing a good job on their quilts, the morning crept toward the noon hour at a snail's pace. Ryn declined to have lunch with them.

Deydie stopped her at the door. "Where are ye going?"

It was raining too hard outside to say she was going for a stroll, so Ryn told the truth. "I'm headed back to the room over the pub to lie down for a few minutes."

"Good," Deydie said, surprising her. "Ye look like hell."

Ryn gave a half-hearted laugh. "I'll be back before one. Promise." But the truth was, she wasn't sure she could keep it.

※※※

At one o'clock, Tuck finished up on the boat, and without realizing it at first, he headed straight for Quilting Central. He should go to the parsonage to check in with his brother or to Pasta & Pastries to grab a bite to eat. Instead, he stupidly marched toward the one woman who wanted nothing to do with him.

He'd gone a bit mad. Shouldn't he want to be shot by a harpoon rather than to see Ryn again? Wouldn't it be better to have any sort of torture than to gaze upon the near identical face of his ex? God, he didn't want to stir up those old feelings and relive the pain of the past. But apparently, his rational brain and his blasted feet weren't on the same page. He halted under Quilting Central's metal sign which hung above the door.

After taking a deep breath, he went in. But as he scanned the room, he didn't see Ryn.

Deydie waddled to the front and stepped up on the low-rise stage. She frowned down at her men's wristwatch before looking up at the quilters and clapping her hands to get everyone's attention. "While we wait for the American lass to return, I need to let you know the hairdresser will be here next Thursday, if ye're in need. Stop by the General Store and pick yere time. Meagan'll not be back in Gandie-gow again until the end of May. And some of ye, I might add, are looking pretty rough."

Tuck thought that was the caldron calling the kettle black. The bun at the back of Deydie's head was half undone with her white tendrils escaping down her hunched back.

Deydie cleared her throat loudly over the whispering women. "In the last week, we had three more groups sign up for retreats. We're close to having the rest of the year booked out. Make sure to look at the schedule and sign up for the times that work for ye."

Deydie's worried gaze traveled to the door, but found him instead. She nodded in his direction, as if telling him to stay, but spoke to the room. "Git back to work on yere quilts now. I'll check where that lass is."

Too late for him. Deydie barreled in his direction as if she was a freighter and he was a dinghy in her path.

"Tuck, find that lassie and drag her back here by the hair, if need be. She promised to be back by one, but as ye can see, it's coming on half past."

Tuck could've begged off, if he'd been faster to come up with a reasonable excuse. But only the truth sat in his brain, flashing like a neon sign: *Being near the lass makes me feel things I shouldn't.* He couldn't say this aloud. And Deydie, the old bat, wouldn't she have a heyday with that information? Probably take her broom to his head and then blab the truth all over town.

"Where did she say she was going?" he asked.

"To lie down in the room over the pub." Deydie shook her head. "Aye, she didn't look well this morning." Her old face scrunched up like a prune. "But that's no excuse for missing a quilt retreat."

He nodded and quickly left for the pub. His hurried pace matched his level of concern. When he arrived, Ryn wasn't coming down the stairs, which was the scenario he'd played out in his mind on the trek over.

He crossed the room to the bar and took the wooden staircase leading up, two at a time. The upper level only had two rooms—the restroom and the bedroom, where sometimes out of town guests stayed.

He knocked on her door. "Lass, are ye all right?"

"No," she said with a groan.

"I'm coming in." He gave her a second to cover up, in case she was indecent. But when he went in, she was fully clothed with the sheep quilt twisted around her, her body curled up into a ball, and arms hugging her middle. She was as pale and white as the kirk's steeple.

He rushed to the side of her bed and squatted down. "What's wrong?" He brushed back the hair from her face, as the warmth of her cheeks registered. "Ye've got a fever."

"I don't feel good."

He pressed his hand against her forehead and took a moment to gently caress her hair before reaching for his phone. "Don't worry.

I'll call Doc MacGregor. He'll fix ye up."

Doc picked up on the second ring. "What's going on, Tuck?"

"I'm calling about Ryn Breckenridge, the lass from America. She's sick, Doc. Can ye come over right away to the pub?"

"Nay. I'm at the hospital. Give her the phone and let me speak with her?"

"Sure." Tuck put his phone in Ryn's hand. "Doc wants to talk to you." He didn't move away to give her privacy, because he couldn't stop stroking her hair, her arm, hoping to give her comfort.

Ryn brought the phone up to her ear. "Hello."

She listened and then answered Doc's questions. "I've felt kind of lousy for the last month or so. My stomach has been hurting. Sometimes it's worse than others." She paused. "Yes. I've had a little fever here and there. Nothing I couldn't handle."

Panicked, she looked up at Tuck. "Is that necessary?" Then she handed the phone back to him.

"What's going on, Doc?"

"Bring her to the hospital. I'll check her out here."

"We're on our way." Tuck hung up. She looked helpless, but he knew that was just the illness. He'd discovered a thing or two about Ryn—she was one tough and gutsy lass. Tough as any Scottish woman. For her to come all the way to Scotland alone…

"I know ye like to argue with me," he said. "But ye'll not argue with Doc MacGregor. Let me help ye up."

She nodded, looking like a whooped pup.

He knelt down and wrapped an arm around her waist. "Lean on me."

"What about the quilt retreat?" she asked as she wrapped an arm around his shoulder.

He paused, close to her. Even though she was sick, and he shouldn't, he drank her in as if she was whisky and he craved intoxication. "When we get to the car, use my phone to call Deydie.

She'll understand."

"She said I looked like hell," Ryn said wryly.

Together, they stood, but she winced as she tried to straighten up.

"I've got you," he assured her. "The car park isn't far." He grabbed her purse as he helped her out the door. "The stairs are too narrow for us to go side by side." He went first and she leaned on him while he slowly walked down. At the bottom, he quickly and easily scooped her into his arms.

She waggled her feet, but didn't seem to have the energy to give a full-fledge protest. "I can walk. Put me down."

"Be still." With long strides, he made it to the door. "I'm speeding up the process." He was careful as he crossed over the threshold—a reverse wedding night scenario. A memory flashed across his mind. He'd been ridiculous back then when he'd planned how he was going to carry Elspeth on their wedding night.

But this is a different lass.

Ryn laid her head on his shoulder, bringing him back to the present. He glanced down at her. *Aye, totally different.* She looked up at him with something close to gratitude and then she shut her eyes. From this angle, she didn't look a thing like Elspeth. Maybe he should hold Ryn close at all times.

As they got to the car park, an auto came down the hill with St. Andrew in the driver's seat. Tuck didn't stop. He went straight to Hugh's loaner and put Ryn to her feet, though he still supported her.

Andrew pulled up beside them and rolled down his window. He seemed judgmental until his eyes darted to Ryn. He softened with concern. "What's happening?"

"Ryn isn't well. Doc MacGregor wants to see her at the hospital as he can't get away. Will ye do me a favor and let Deydie know?"

"Aye."

"Thank you," Ryn said weakly as she slipped into the car.

Andrew addressed Tuck. "Call me from the hospital. Let me

know how she's doing."

"Will do." Tuck got behind the wheel and started the car. He glanced over to make sure Ryn was strapped in. "I'll get ye there safely."

He backed the car out and drove up the hill. As he hurried to the hospital, he couldn't help compare the last time he'd driven there. He wondered about Raymond, the one who'd had the heart attack, hoping it all turned out well for him.

Tuck glanced worriedly over at Ryn again. Doc didn't mention anything about her condition being life threatening, though it was disconcerting he needed to see her right away. Ryn didn't look good, so Tuck prayed like he hadn't since he was a lad, when he'd been a true believer. *Lord, please let her be okay. I really care for her!*

That thought was a heavy revelation. Tuck had made his decision to keep his distance, but he was close enough now to reach out and touch her. He hit a rough spot in the road, and as the car pitched forward, she winced. He took her hand and gently squeezed. "Sorry. I'll do better. Everything's going to be okay." He squeezed again to give his words credence, but also to reassure himself.

She gave him a weak smile, before laying her head back and closing her eyes.

"I'll warn you if there are any other rough patches." The words should've been benign, but the statement seemed to come from someplace deep within him. A scary place. A place full of meaning and compassion. A place he hadn't allowed another woman to occupy since he was seventeen. He pulled his hand away and tightly gripped the steering wheel, driving a bit faster.

An hour later, he pulled into the hospital. "Can you walk or do I need to get you a wheelchair?"

"I'll walk." She undid her seatbelt.

He disembarked and hurried to the other side, helping her out. Once inside the hospital, he put Ryn in a chair, grabbed her paperwork from the front desk, and then rang Doc.

"I'll be out in a few minutes to get her," Doc said.

"I'll let her know." Tuck turned back to Ryn to give her the news, but as weak as she was, she still had the wherewithal to slap a hand over her paperwork.

Was she hiding it from him? Tuck understood—some things were personal—but it still made him wonder. He took his eyes off her paperwork and brought them back up to her face. "Doc MacGregor is with a patient, but will come get ye in a minute." He gave her an encouraging smile.

But Doc didn't come. Instead, he sent a nurse. Before there could be any argument, Tuck made it clear he wasn't sending Ryn off into the belly of the hospital alone. "I'm her husband."

Ryn's look of shock was comical. He dared her to contradict him with a raised eyebrow, but the little minx opened her mouth anyway, and he knew she meant to set the nurse straight. He had no choice but to silence her with a quick kiss. While he was so close, he whispered into her ear. "They won't let me stay with you, if they think I'm anyone beside yere family. Roll with it, luv. I'm not letting ye go in alone." He glanced at the double doors to get his meaning across. "Okay?"

She nodded. "Okay."

Tuck supported Ryn as they followed the nurse to the triage room. The nurse retrieved a tourniquet and a syringe off a small stainless steel table. "I need to draw some blood."

Ryn shifted toward her, turned ghostly white, and then passed out.

Although he was shook up, Tuck caught her before she slipped out of her chair. "What's wrong with her?" he demanded from the nurse, his heart beating wildly. Then he gently shook Ryn. "Ryn? Ryn?"

Doc MacGregor walked in, seeming unfazed by her unconscious

condition. "Tuck, put her on the table."

"What happened to her?" Tuck's heart wouldn't go back to normal. But he did as he was told.

"It was the needle," the nurse explained, as she put a smelling capsule under Ryn's nose.

Doc picked up Ryn's limp wrist and patted it. "Ryn, wake up."

Ryn roused. "What happened?"

"Ye fainted," Tuck said, not feeling fully relieved.

"Relax. It's normal," Doc reassured. "It's completely harmless, as long as there's someone there to protect the patient if they fall. A certain percentage of the population has the same reaction as our new friend here."

Tuck rolled his eyes at Doc's chattering. *Why doesn't Gabe get on with it and find out what's wrong with her?*

Ryn nodded. "I should've warned you. I've had this problem my whole life."

"Ye scared the *shite* out of me," Tuck said.

Doc stuck his hand out to Ryn. "I'm Gabriel MacGregor. It's nice to meet the quilter who's caused quite a stir in Gandiegow with yere…what's it called?"

"Modern quilt," Tuck provided.

Doc frowned over at him. "Ye need to leave so I can examine my patient. I'll come find you when I'm done."

Tuck opened his mouth to argue, but Ryn stopped him.

"I'll be okay."

He took her hand and ran his thumb over it. "Are ye sure?"

"Yes."

Reluctantly, Tuck placed her hand back in her lap and let go. "I'll be right outside."

Gabriel raised an eyebrow at him. "Ye'll be in the waiting room."

"Aye." Tuck left and made his way back out. But once there, he couldn't sit or relax. Instead, he paced until Gabe appeared with a frown on his face.

Tuck rushed over to him. "What's wrong?"

"Ryn's being prepped for surgery. It's her appendix."

"Surgery?" Tuck's blood pressure rose. "Is she going to be okay?"

"I'll let you know how she's doing, once she's out." Gabriel nodded and then rushed off.

Tuck pulled out his mobile and called his brother. As the phone rang, he told himself he was only calling to give an update on Ryn, and not because he knew his brother's voice would calm him.

"What's going on?" Andrew asked. "Is Ryn all right?"

"Doc is taking her to surgery. Appendix."

Andrew didn't miss a beat. "I'll get Moira and then we'll be on our way."

"Ye don't—" Tuck tried, but Andrew had already hung up.

The next hour crept by. He couldn't stop thinking about how pale and weak Ryn had been, making every bad scenario surface in his mind. It didn't help that the hands on the clock were going in slow-motion.

It was nearly two hours before Doc came through the double doors and straight to him. "Sorry about the wait. I had to rush off to another emergency after Ryn's. She's in the recovery room and doing fine."

Tuck's chest opened up and he could finally draw a deep breath…something he hadn't been able to do since seeing Ryn lying in the room over the pub, curled up in a ball.

"She's going to be okay," Gabe said. "The question is, are you?"

"Can I see her?" Tuck asked eagerly. It was too late to be cool and calm. Doc had already seen him acting the fool, fawning all over Ryn.

"Nay. In a while. I'll let you know when you can come back. Go get some tea and biscuits." Doc laid a hand on his shoulder. "Relax.

Yere lass is going to recover just fine."

Tuck didn't correct him, but went to find something to drink. Just as he was ordering a cup of tea, his phone rang.

"Where are you?" Andrew asked.

"Café," Tuck said.

The next hour's wait wasn't nearly as stressful. Knowing Ryn was all right, and the fact that Andrew and Moira were there beside him, made his two cups of tea and three tea cakes go down better than if he'd been on his own. *Ryn is going to be okay,* Tuck kept telling himself.

When Doc texted him Ryn's room number, Tuck wanted to head out immediately, but shared the info with Andrew first. "She's in room 423."

Andrew stood, but Moira, still sitting, put a hand on his arm. "Tuck, ye go on. We'll visit with her when ye're done." Moira's voice was always soothing, but right now, her words had a gentle firmness that Tuck appreciated.

"Thanks." Tuck hurried to the elevators.

When he got to Ryn's room, he took a deep breath, before opening the door. He found her dozing.

She must've sensed he was there, because she opened her eyes. "Hey."

"Hey," he said back, stupidly, but he was so happy. "How are ye feeling?"

She smiled. "I'm not feeling a thing." She lifted her arm with the IV. "There must be some happy juice flowing in here."

"Aye. Painkillers. Doc said you're going to be fine." Tuck grinned at her as if he was a savant. He took her hand and squeezed. He never realized how good it felt to have someone special, and to be by her side when she needed him most.

"When do I get to go home?"

Tuck's stomach flinched at the thought. *I don't want ye to go home. I want ye here with me, here in Scotland.* But the statement would've been inappropriate and would've shocked her. Hell, he was shocked to have the notion even cross his mind.

Ryn studied his face. "Why the frown? Did Doc say when I can get out of here?"

"Oh. He didn't say." Tuck's pulse returned to normal and he relaxed. *So she didn't mean she wanted to go back to the States.*

He pulled up a chair and sat down. "Andrew and Moira are downstairs."

Ryn looked surprised. "They are? They didn't have to come." She paused as if selecting the right words. "Thank you for bringing me, but you don't have to stay, either."

He answered truthfully. "Yes, I do have to stay."

"Because the Laird said so?" She frowned, as if she already knew the answer to it.

"Nay. I'm staying because I want to be by your side."

"Oh." She seemed as if she'd been taken off-guard.

Well, hell, it was about time she had a clue of what he'd been going through. Since meeting Ryn, she'd kept him off-guard, too. How could this emotional teeter-totter, she'd caused within him, make him feel more right with the world than he'd ever been?

The door opened and a nurse walked in. "I need to check yere incisions."

Tuck nodded to Ryn. "I'll step out and tell Andrew and Moira how you're doing. If I know them, they'll want to pop up to see you. Is that okay?"

Ryn nodded and Tuck left.

His step felt lighter and his chest did, too. He turned the corner and nearly ran into a couple—a bathrobed man who was clutching a woman's arm.

Tuck was high, still feeling the effects of Ryn being okay. *And just being around her.* It took a moment for his brain to catch up with what he was seeing, and then another moment for it to fully register who it was in front of him. And who it was he nearly toppled!

John and Maggie. Oh, God!

Subconsciously, Tuck scanned John. Before he could stop himself, his eyes fell to where John's missing limb should be, but wasn't...and Tuck felt sick.

16

"JOHN?" TUCK WASN'T PREPARED to see him and didn't know what to say.

How're ye doing? seemed asinine, as his appearance and demeanor made it clear how John was doing: John looked like he'd been rolled under the boat.

And Tuck couldn't say, *I'm sorry for what I did to ye.* Much too late for that. *Sorry* certainly didn't come close to describing how tortured Tuck felt over his part in John getting hurt. They stared at each other for a long moment.

John glanced over at Maggie and growled, "Go."

At first, Tuck thought John was telling Maggie to leave them alone, but it took Maggie turning and pulling John away from him to understand.

John blamed him. Utterly. Completely.

And Tuck couldn't blame John for it.

Tuck blamed himself, too.

∞

When Tuck returned to Ryn's hospital room with Andrew and Moira, Tuck was as pale as her hospital gown, as if he'd seen a ghost. She wasn't the only one who was concerned about Tuck…the priest was worried about his brother, too. Andrew kept glancing over at him.

Moira came over shyly. "How are ye?"

"Better," Ryn said. "I feel bad about the retreat, though. I hope Deydie isn't too upset with me."

Moira's laugh sounded like soothing wind chimes. "Deydie's upset that you didn't tell her how bad ye were feeling. Ye'll probably get an earful when she arrives."

"Deydie's coming here?"

"Aye. She'll probably bring half the quilters with her."

Andrew stepped forward and smiled. "Be lucky the hospital has strict visiting hours or else they'd be camping out in yere room for the duration."

Tuck positioned himself at the foot of Ryn's bed and touched her blanket. "Ye should rest, lass."

"Aye," Andrew said. "We better go." He nodded toward Tuck. "We're going to step in and see John first. To see how he's feeling." Andrew acted as if Tuck's interior was made up of eggshells, especially where John was concerned.

"I'll stay here with the lass."

Andrew and Moira said goodbye and left.

Tuck sat in the chair next to Ryn's bed. "Rest. If Gandiegow is descending upon ye, then you'll need yere strength."

She reached out and took Tuck's hand. "Thank you for everything." She held onto him and closed her eyes. Holding his hand comforted her and she planned to milk being sick for all it was worth.

What felt like moments later, she woke, hearing whispers around her in the hospital room. She opened her eyes and couldn't believe the clock showed three hours had passed. Also, she couldn't believe the crowd in her room. She looked up at Tuck who stood near her head. Deydie, Bethia, Cait, Sophie, Rowena, and Sinnie were there. Surprisingly, Lara, the clerk from Ryn's first day in Whussendale, was there as well, standing toward the back.

Deydie waddled over to her. "Yere coloring looks better. When will ye be up and at it?"

"Gran," Cait said as if trying to curb Deydie.

"She doesn't know," Tuck answered. "Doc hasn't said." He looked as if he was contemplating leaving and Ryn wondered if he planned to get a nurse for riot control.

Bethia patted her hand. "Ye poor dear. Ye've had a rough day."

"She certainly looked *rough* this morn," Deydie jabbed.

"What my Gran's getting at is that you were missed this afternoon." Cait put her hand on her rounded stomach. "I took over for you. I hope that was okay."

But Ryn was fixated on Cait's baby bump. All the old memories of being pregnant and upset came back. The shock. The dread of telling her mother. Being conflicted about what to do. Then after the abortion, her feelings had congealed into a stew of emotions she was certain she'd never sort out.

Ryn glanced up at Tuck, but he didn't seem as if he'd read her mind just then. And hopefully he hadn't read the medical form she'd filled out either, where she'd written down *abortion* under previous medical procedures.

Tuck laid a hand on Ryn's shoulder, reminding her she hadn't answered Cait's question.

"Yes. Thank you for taking over and teaching the rest of my workshop." She cleared her throat, as it was still scratchy from surgery. "Thank you all for coming to visit."

Deydie pulled Rowena and Sinnie forward. "We have a gift for ye."

Sinnie handed her a tissue wrapped bundle. "I hope ye like it."

Ryn unwrapped the small lap quilt. Bright colors were mixed with earthy tones, which seemed to fit how she was feeling right now. The quilt was backed with Minky, the softest fabric ever.

"It's a comfort quilt," Deydie said. "The lassies were making it as a charity quilt, but we decided ye needed it more."

Ryn's heart swelled at their thoughtfulness. She held the fabric to her cheek. "I love it. Thank you." Never in her life did Ryn have this many people care about her at once. When she'd had her tonsils out at eight, her mother and Granny Kay were there for her. When she was recovering from her abortion, her mother gave her soup, but then mostly left her alone.

Rowena handed her a card. "Ye can look at it later. We all signed it—both the Gandiegow quilters and the Whussendale lassies, too."

Ryn scanned the room, feeling right and whole, despite having surgery only a few hours before. For the first time in her life, she felt like she belonged.

Bethia caressed her arm. "Are ye all right?"

Ryn blinked away the tears.

But before she could say anything, Deydie was at her side again, taking the Comfort quilt from Ryn and spreading it over her legs. "The lass is fine. Now, everyone get out. She needs her rest."

For the care Deydie was taking, as she made sure Ryn had her hand on the soft Minky, Ryn was softening toward the old woman pretty quickly. Which was a shock.

"Thank you." Ryn said.

Deydie smoothed out an edge. "'Tis nothing."

Ryn glanced up at Tuck to see if he'd seen how nice Deydie was being to her. Also, she wondered if he was going to leave, too, for surely *everyone get out*—which Deydie had said—included him, too. Ryn hoped he wouldn't go.

Deydie stared at Ryn shrewdly and then looked at Tuck with a hard gaze. "Ye, too, scoundrel. Out. We need to talk about the car. Some of the lassies want to do some shopping here in Inverness, while others of us need to get back to Gandiegow."

Tuck laid a hand on Ryn's shoulder, and she believed he would ignore Deydie's decree and stay.

She was also more awake and with it now. She wondered *where* she might go when discharged from the hospital. A hotel, until she was healed enough to make her next move?

"And Ryn," Deydie said. "It's all been decided. Ye'll not infirm in Gandiegow. Ye'll be headed off to Whussendale when Doc says ye can go home. 'Twas the steps to the room over the pub that made the decision."

Ryn was relieved she didn't have to stay in a hotel that she couldn't afford. "Thanks." She wouldn't let herself worry just yet over what the surgery would cost either.

Tuck squeezed her shoulder. "I'll not be long. Do as Deydie says and rest."

That earned him an appreciative nod from Deydie before she spun and left the room.

Surprisingly, Tuck leaned down and gently brushed his lips over her. When he walked away, he seemed reluctant to leave. Or it could've just been her overactive imagination.

She fell back to sleep and woke to see Tuck dozing in the chair beside her. The lights had been dimmed in the room and it was dark outside. Tuck must've sensed she was awake because he opened his eyes, too.

"Do ye need something to drink?" He leaned forward and grabbed her cup, holding it out to her.

"Thank you." She took it from him. "You didn't have to stay."

He shrugged. "I didn't *have to,* but I *wanted to.*" He sat back watching her.

"When do you have to head to Gandiegow? Soon?"

He shook his head. "Ross texted. I'm not working the boat today. Besides, I have no way of getting there. Deydie took the car and I chose to stay here instead of hitching a ride back to Whussendale with Sophie and the group."

"Sleeping in that chair can't be comfortable," she said.

"Aye. But my only alternative is to climb into bed with you." He scanned the length of the hospital bed. "There's not enough room."

She opened her mouth to tell him she'd make room, but clamped her lips together. She was too vulnerable right now, feeling way too close to him. Cuddling up against his warm body and leaning on him emotionally would be wonderful. But too intimate, in her state of mind.

He took her hand and kissed it. "Stop worrying, lass. I was only teasing ye about the bed. I'm fine right where I am."

The next time Ryn woke, the nurse was coming in to check her vitals and her incisions, and Tuck was gone. He returned with a cup of coffee and with Doc MacGregor right behind him.

Doc discreetly took a peek at her three incisions and declared, "Everything looks good. Ye're going home this afternoon. Does that work?"

"Aye," Tuck said, before taking a sip. "Sophie and Hugh said they'll come and pick us up when she's discharged."

"She's going back to Whussendale?" Doc asked.

"Maggie's in Whussendale and Ryn is Maggie's cousin," Tuck explained. "Also, the women of the villages got together and decided. Apparently, there was quite a tug-a-war over who would get to keep Ryn."

Doc nodded. "Ah, I see." He smiled down at her. "The nurse will go over your discharge instructions in detail with you later on." He looked from one to the other of them. "Ye can return to normal activities in two to four weeks. No heavy lifting. You may seem fine, but ye need to heal internally. Just use good judgement." He gave Tuck a pointed look. "I mean it. No strenuous activity for the first two to four weeks."

Ryn knew what Doc was referring to and her cheeks heated up, blazing, as if in front of a roaring campfire. "I-I...no-no..." she stuttered. She wanted to tell Doc he'd misunderstood. And the misunderstanding was all Tuck's fault. Her gorgeous bedside companion had been paying way too much attention to her. Not that she minded Tuck's company. *Hand-holding. And a few kisses.* Doc just seemed to think things between her and Tuck were more than they were.

Doc closed her chart. "I'll pop over to Whussendale in a week's time to see how ye're doing. Promise to call if you have any questions before then."

"I will."

After Doc left, she and Tuck chatted for a while and then she slept some more. She was beginning to wonder if she would ever be able to stay awake for more than an hour at a time.

After her lunch was delivered, the shift nurse explained how to care for her incisions and what to expect over the next week and beyond. The nurse shooed Tuck out of the room so Ryn could dress.

When he returned, he looked very unhappy.

"What?" Ryn said, while looking down at yesterday's outfit. It didn't fit so well, as her stomach was distended from the gas they'd pumped into her to do the surgery. She was grateful she'd worn a dress.

Tuck shook his head. "It's not you. There's been a change in plans."

⋙⋘

Dammit! Would his bad luck never end? Tuck took out his phone, bracing himself for the bad news he knew was already there, and read Ross's text message to Ryn. "I'm bringing the van from Gan-

196

diegow to pick up Ryn and John. Sophie agrees it's the best plan. Hold tight. Will text when I arrive."

Tuck kicked himself now for not accepting the ride back to Whussendale from Sophie yesterday, when he'd had the chance.

"Why are you upset?"

"Well, ye wanted to know more about Maggie. I guess ye'll be meeting John." Though he didn't want to, it was past time he confessed to Ryn what he'd done to Maggie's husband. "I have good reason for not wanting to share an automobile ride with John. And I'm sure he feels the same way."

"Why?"

"It's my fault he's maimed," Tuck admitted.

Ryn didn't look shocked, only circumspect. "How?"

Tuck told her the truth, everything—from leaving the pub in time, to taking a nap, to finding Raymond, clutching his chest in his stopped car in the middle the road. Tuck finished with how he'd heard the news about John and how everyone blamed him. And God help him, he even told her about why he'd taken on extra work, so he could funnel money to John and Maggie...something he hadn't shared with anyone but her.

Ryn listened and didn't seem horrified in the least of the terrible thing he'd done to John and his family. She took his hand and rubbed it, as if trying to bring the circulation back to his existence. "Tuck, the only thing you did wrong was to do the right thing. You didn't make it to the boat on time and you have a good excuse. From what you've said, it seems to me John's injury isn't your fault at all."

"But don't ye see? I'm known for cutting it close and being late. It's a horrible flaw to have. I even missed Andrew's wedding because I missed the ferry." He could've shared why he hated weddings, but he didn't.

She shrugged her shoulders. "Okay, so missing your brother's wedding isn't great. But the question is have you been late to anything since John's accident?"

"No." But he wasn't happy Ryn didn't see the truth about him. Everyone in Gandiegow did.

Ryn held his hand to her heart, which made his own heart skip a beat.

"I think you should forgive yourself. Otherwise, whenever you hear John's name, you're going to be miserable. And if he's going to live in Whussendale, and with you there, too, don't you think it's time to bury the hatchet?"

Tuck liked the earnestness in Ryn's blue-gray eyes. He liked how she held his hand against her chest. But he wasn't ready to let his sins go. Perhaps because John, Maggie, and Gandiegow would never let him forget the horrible thing he'd done.

She moved their clasped hands to her thigh. "You know, John has to take most of the responsibility in what happened. It sounds like he was messing around with a piece of equipment when he really should've had some backup there while he did it."

Tuck was frustrated with her, so he concentrated on her thigh. "I don't think ye have the right of it, but now, at least ye know."

She looked over at him with what looked like pity. "I think I'll take a nap until it's time to leave."

He let go of her hand and went to the window to look out. The sky was gray, which matched his mood. He imagined John's mood would be just as dark. At least Ross would be there. Not as a buffer, per say. In the past, Ross had a way of using his calm demeanor to smooth out John's tough captain's exterior. Maybe the ride to Whussendale wouldn't be so bad after all.

Later at the front entrance, while waiting for Ross to pull up, Tuck tamped down all his emotions and didn't even move an eyelash when John was wheeled up and parked right next to Ryn. They were quite the ill-matched bunch. And Tuck had to admit, *This is going to be the longest effing ride of my life!*

Ross hopped out and ran up to John as he was wheeled out. When he reached out to guide John into the front seat, John jerked away.

"I'm not an invalid," he snarled.

Tuck tried to put John out of his mind as he carefully helped Ryn in through the side door and settled her in her seat. He climbed in, too. "Lean on me, lass," he said quietly.

Once they were all buckled in, Ross did his damnedest to engage John, but his attempts only made John's mood darker and the ride more uncomfortable. After several more tries, Ross gave up and they made the rest of the trip in awkward silence.

Just as they were pulling down the lane to Kilheath Castle, Ross's phone rang. "Hallo." He paused. "We're almost there. We'll be out front in a few minutes."

Ryn was fast asleep, so Tuck gently woke her by whispering. "We're home."

Ryn opened her eyes and looked around sleepily.

They drove past the wool mill and made the trek down the hill, along the curve, and then up the hill again to the castle. When it came into view, Tuck saw a group standing outside.

"The welcoming committee," Ross said cheerfully.

John growled.

Ross looked over at his brother with concern, but didn't acknowledge John's feral mood. He pulled the van to a stop and Tuck counted off the assembly—Maggie, Dand, Hugh, Sophie holding Irene, and a few others from the wool mill, plus one person he didn't know.

"What's my mother-in-law doing here?" John barked.

"I'll let Maggie tell ye," Ross said.

"No. *You* tell me!" John said.

"From what I was told, Coira packed up and came to help Maggie with the bairns."

And to help with John, too, Tuck thought.

"Nay," John said. "Coira's come to torture me."

Ross tried to smooth things over. "I expect she's lonely with her husband gone." Ross's message was clear: *John have some compassion.*

"Why didn't Maggie tell me?"

"Probably afraid she'd upset ye," Ross said.

"You think!" John's mood from the hospital to here felt like a sunny picnic compared to his mood now.

Tuck took Ryn's hand and squeezed, hoping to protect her against the bad vibes John was putting off.

John glared at Ross. "And the rest of them? What are they doing outside?"

"Don't ruin it for them," Ross said quietly. "They care about you." He paused. "We all do."

Ross jumped out and ran around to John's side of the van, as if to open his door. But John managed on his own with only mild fumbling.

John was barely to his feet before Dand ran to him. "Da!" He hugged his legs.

John patted him, but the action seemed more like he was swatting him away. "Enough of that now."

Maggie walked to him, beaming. "We're glad ye're home."

John examined his surroundings and his expression was clear: *This isn't my home!*

Tuck had to hand it to Maggie, who was putting on a great act. She looped her arm through her husband's, pretending John was as happy to be there as she pretended she was. "We've planned a welcome home dinner. Dand even made party hats."

John's answer was a grunt.

Tuck got out and Sophie joined him at the side of the van. She leaned in. "Ryn, I've made up a room for ye, if you would like to stay here with us at Kilheath."

Ryn looked over at Tuck with semi-pleading eyes. He understood. The castle wasn't big enough to give her space from the Armstrongs's drama.

"Nay. Ryn would like to stay in the potter's cottage," Tuck said, as if the two of them had discussed it at great lengths. "She'll be more comfortable there, being it's cozy and all. A better place for her to heal." He paused, giving Sophie his attention. "If it's all right with you, I'll keep an eye on her in the evenings, if ye'll have someone check in on her during the day while I'm gone."

Ryn cleared her throat, as though making herself known. "Is that okay with you, Sophie?"

Sophie's gaze bounced from one to the other of them. "Certainly. That's fine. I'll be happy to get someone to check in on you." Her eyes lit with merriment and he knew her next words were meant to taunt him. "I'm sure Declan could spare an hour or so and would be happy to do it, while ye're away, Tuck."

Tuck had to work hard at not growling like John. Declan, according to Willoughby, was quite the lady's man. And Tuck's past sins came back and smacked him in the chest, making him feel awful. He was starting to have an inkling of what he'd put Brodie through, when Rachel and Brodie were in the thick of things and trying to work it out between them.

Sophie's eyes beamed. She'd baited the hook, and dammit, Tuck had snapped at it. But then her eyes fell on Ryn's worried face. "Nay. I believe Declan is too busy with repairing the cottages. No worries. I'll be happy to check in on you."

Immediately, Tuck's breathing calmed.

Ryn's features calmed, too. "Thank you. I'm really sorry for any trouble you went to, getting the room ready for me."

"No trouble at all for me," Sophie laughed. "I had Rowena do it. I quite enjoy being the Laird's wife."

"If it's okay, I'll drive Ryn to her cottage now," Tuck said to Sophie. "I'm sure she's anxious to lie down."

"I'll fix ye both plates and send them up for you." Sophie patted the van and shut the side door, leaving Ryn still sitting in the back. "Tuck?"

"Yes?"

"Let me know if she needs anything, will ye?"

"I will."

"And Tuck? I think ye're making a wise choice."

Shocked, Tuck didn't respond, but climbed into the vehicle. He should've disagreed. He knew exactly why Sophie had gotten the wrong idea about him and the American lass. He'd been too attentive, too possessive, acting too much like Ryn was his. He stared out at Sophie, who only waved back as if she'd nailed him with the truth. Which pissed him off! He put his hand on the door handle, ready to hop out and set her straight. *I haven't made any choice!* But like a quilt thrown over a fire, the truth blanketed him and extinguished his denial. *Aye. I guess I have.*

He put the vehicle in gear and drove away, feeling for the first time in a long time, safe with a woman.

"Tuck?" Ryn said.

"Yes, lass?"

"Thanks for taking me home."

శဝလ

John wanted to roar. Why couldn't they leave him the hell alone? He hated the people of Whussendale and his family making a fuss over him…making a fuss because he was an *effing* one-armed man.

Dand tugged on his sleeve as they walked across the driveway toward the castle. "Da, will ye take me fishing on the loch? The Laird took me and I caught a brown trout."

Maggie jumped in and saved him from answering. "Not now,

Dand. We have the party, remember?" She gave John a saccharine smile and he hated that, too. His accident had turned Maggie into a different person. She never would've put up with his shit moods before. She would've made him straighten up weeks ago.

"Party?" John would rather attend a funeral right now than a party.

Hugh put his hand on John's shoulder, the one that had a complete arm below it. "Aye, we set up the dining room."

"I made party hats!" Dand said excitedly.

"Let's head in." Hugh left him and joined Sophie at the bottom of the steps.

The crowd surrounded John as they made their way to the castle. It felt *effing* claustrophobic.

Coira, unfortunately, positioned herself next to him.

Oh gawd! What now? She'd never had a good word for him, since he'd set his eyes on Maggie when they were young.

"Ye look awful, John," she said, right on cue. "Do ye think it's the hospital food that did it to ye?"

Nay. More than likely it's the present company, but John kept the sentiment to himself.

"Mum, he looks fine," Maggie said, squeezing his arm.

But she wasn't fooling him. Maggie couldn't be taking it well that Coira had come to help. The old badger never had a good word for anyone, likely the reason Lyel up and died. She'd probably harped on him one too many times and he decided to end it all by running his auto into a tree. *Lucky Lyel.*

John wasn't proud of the mean thought, but it entertained him, and nothing had entertained him since his own accident.

But he did feel sorry for the lassies—Maggie, Rowena, and Sinnie. Their relationship with their parents had never been smooth sailing. Lyel was no prince—drank too much, caroused some, too—and the women knew it. Coira, included. Maybe that's why she was such a hard woman to deal with.

John followed the crowd into Kilheath Castle. What a behemoth! Ostentatious, too. A far cry from a fisherman's cottage.

Maggie leaned into him. "The Laird is in the process of having one of the larger cottages fixed up for us."

"I may be as weak as a babe," John said in a fierce whisper. "But I'll not take charity. Laird or no."

"Nay," Maggie said, but she seemed embarrassed. "It's a benefit of heading up the Whussendale Kilts and Quilts Retreat."

He didn't say more. He was afraid if he did, he'd yell at them all. He was sick to death of everyone making decisions for him as if he was an invalid, a powerless man. But the truth was, that was exactly the way they saw him. Exactly the man he'd become.

Hugh pointed up. "Maggie, why don't ye show John to your room? Mrs. McNabb said tea will be ready in fifteen minutes."

Reluctantly, John climbed the stairs behind Maggie.

Dand raced ahead. "My room is the best. 'Cept I have to share it with baby Irene."

Maggie looked at John over her shoulder. "Their room is right next to ours."

Was Maggie getting used to this high-living? John never imagined his wife being satisfied in a place like this. And yet, she seemed at home, chatting to him as if they owned the place. Hell, the best he'd ever done for them was to buy his mother and father's cottage for them. But now, with one arm and the promise he'd made Maggie, he couldn't fish, provide for them. Not even give his family something as nominal as their life back in Gandiegow in their own fisherman's cottage.

On the second floor, Dand ran down the hall and opened a door. "This is my room, Da. Come see."

John made his way down and peeked inside. The room was four times bigger than his bedroom at home.

"We're in here," Maggie said at the next opened door. "There's a washroom en suite for us."

John nodded and entered. The canopy bed was draped in some fancy red pattern. The windows were covered with the same fabric. The room was big and open, and John couldn't breathe.

"The toilet is through there," Maggie said, pointing at a door.

John headed for it and closed the door behind him. He looked in the mirror and hated who he saw. *How am I going to survive this?* The pain in the middle of the night from his phantom arm was nothing compared to this.

He lost track of time. Maggie knocking on the door, brought him back to the next torturous thing he had to do.

"It's time to go down for tea."

He opened the door to see her anxious face gazing back.

"Are ye going to be okay?"

"Aye." But it was a lie.

When they got downstairs and into the dining room, once again Dand ran toward him with Irene right behind. This time Dand held out a folded paper hat.

"Here, Da, I have yere hat." But Dand was coming in too fast, and the marble floor was too slick for his stockinged feet. He slid and stopped himself by reaching up and grabbing John's nub of an arm, protected only by the Ace bandage sleeve.

The pain was searing and John yelled, "Owwwh!" All of his emotions rose to the top and came tumbling out. "Dammit, Dand! What the hell is wrong with you?"

Irene came to a halt, her eyes wide. Then she burst into tears, wailing, as if John had spanked her.

Dand's eyes were swollen with tears, too. "I didn't mean—."

"Just stop it!" John yelled. "All of you! Just stop it!"

The words reverberated throughout and the room went silent. He absorbed their expression of horror in torturous slow-motion, knowing he could never come back from what he'd done. And, by God, he just wouldn't give a damn anymore!

Maggie stood gobsmacked, frozen, certainly unable to pretend now that everything was all right and things were going to be unicorns and rainbows from here on out.

Sophie and Hugh looked embarrassed and at a loss for words. Ross stared at the floor. The various townsfolk glanced at each other awkwardly.

Dand and Irene ran to Maggie, as if she was the shelter against the storm. She picked up the wailing Irene and Dand buried his face in her dress, while she wrapped comforting arms around them both.

But it was Coira who found her voice first and marched up to John, wagging her finger in his face. "John Armstrong, ye can't yell at my grandchildren like that."

Aye, even a father's right has been taken away from me now.

Sophie and Hugh ushered the others out of the room. Ross retrieved his niece and nephew, shushing them gently as they made their way across the room. He shut the door behind him. John was grateful to his brother to not be on display anymore—the one-armed man being taken down a peg by a four-eleven banshee.

Coira turned on Maggie then. "And you! Why are ye pussyfooting around yere own husband? He's not a simple-minded man. He's not an invalid."

For the first time, he had some respect for Coira. But then she carried on.

"He's a bully! That's what he is! And ye better take care of it! 'Tis not my job to show him the right of things. 'Tis yeres." Coira stopped then, her hard expression crumbling. Maybe she was thinking about how she couldn't change her own husband, Lyel.

Tears streamed down Maggie's ever-growing red face and she glared at her mother with the long practice of a journeyman. "Out, Mum!"

"Fine. I need my peace and quiet. My husband just died," Coira muttered as she left, too.

John was alone with his wife. Between fishing and the kids, they'd spent more time alone together since his accident, than in all the years of their marriage. But he had no intention of being alone with Maggie now. He put his hand up. "Don't say a word." He already despised himself as it was. He didn't need a lecture from her to drive the point home of how horrible he'd become.

Maggie shook her head. "I've something to say, and ye're not to silence me." She took a shaky deep breath, as if all the hurt was bubbling up inside her, a stew of pain and betrayal. He'd done this to her, but God, he didn't want to hear her put it into words.

She did anyway. "I've put up with ye, because ye're my husband and I love ye. But I've had enough. Ye'll not take yere black mood out on us anymore. This *thing*, John—." she waved her hands in the air to encompass him, "—just didn't happen to you. It happened to all of us. We've all been affected."

Her eyes dropped to the floor to the crumpled hat Dand had offered him. She leaned over and picked it up. "Dand wanted to do something special for ye. We all worked hard to make this a good welcome home just for you. But ye've spoiled it."

Maggie seemed more like herself than she had in weeks, her voice holding no room for compromise. He may now be dead inside, but at least the woman he'd married hadn't completely disappeared. He could see she was back and he was glad of it.

He stared at the floor, shaking his head. "I agree with ye. I have ruined everything. I've no excuse, except my heart has turned black. Stop wasting yere time on me, Maggie. I just want to be alone."

Maggie moved toward him. "Ye don't mean that."

He put his hand up once again. "I do." He looked her square in the eyes so she could see there was no room for concession in his words either.

As he left the dining room, he didn't look back. The guest of honor had wrecked the party, end of story. And John was completely to blame for ruining his own life. He knew Maggie blamed Tuck, but John had known better than to work the winch drum alone. He didn't know when he'd started taking responsibility for the accident, but at least now, he was man enough to admit it. He'd heard enough tragic stories over the years, about stubborn fisherman working alone, and now he was one of the cautionary tales.

He returned upstairs to the room Maggie had shown him. But he didn't find solace. He was imprisoned—an otter who'd gotten caught in a trap and there was no way out.

Maggie didn't come after him, either. He sat on the edge of the bed, staring at the wall. Later, he heard rustling in the room next to his, but there were no sounds of happy children, no playing, and no giggling as should be. Not long afterward, a tap sounded on the door.

"John?"

It was Sophie. He wasn't surprised when it wasn't his own wife.

"I've brought ye a tray. Can I bring it in?"

"No," he said firmly. "I'm not hungry." Hate had killed his appetite.

"All right."

He got up then and went into the bathroom and filled a cup with water. He drank it down, the cool liquid not washing away the bitterness which consumed his insides. Self-hate begat self-hate, and had him hating himself more.

Five minutes later, there was another knock.

"It's Hugh," came through the door. "Let me in."

John could ignore Sophie, but it was never wise to ignore the Laird. Especially now, that John was part of his community. He opened the door.

Hugh frowned at him. "I don't care if ye're not hungry. Ye have to eat." He walked across the room and set the tray on the small writing table by the window.

John wanted to ask after Maggie and the children, but didn't.

Hugh crossed his arms over his chest. "John, there's something ye need to know."

"What?"

"Maggie has packed up. She and the kids are gone."

17

TUCK QUIETLY SHUT THE DOOR behind him as Ryn slept. He was concerned about leaving her alone, but he wanted to gather food for her from the castle, and he'd agreed to help Declan for a bit with the new plumbing for John and Maggie's cottage. All this had to be completed in the next couple of hours before Ryn woke and needed him.

Any other day, he would've walked to Kilheath, but Ross would need the van to get back to Gandiegow. Also, driving to the castle made his errand go faster. When he arrived outside the kitchen doors, Maggie was exiting with her subdued children in tow.

She stopped short, staring at him as if weighing her options. And everything felt wrong about the scene. Her face was drained and her upper lip trembled, as if she'd met with yet another tragedy. Her eyes were red and nearly swollen shut from crying. Dand usually had the energy of a hundred lads, but he held his mother's hand as if he was a quiet, demure boy. Baby Irene sucked her thumb, lying against her mother's chest…she'd been crying, too.

What had happened while I was at Ryn's cottage?

Maggie walked toward Tuck with her brow furrowed. She acted as if she'd have to endure another lump. "Take me to Gandiegow," she ordered.

Tuck opened his mouth to say *I can't,* but a completely different statement tumbled out. "Are you all right? What's happened?"

"I need to get to Gandiegow. Now." She glared at him as if to say, *You owe me this much!*

And she was right. Tuck did owe her.

"Give me a second to tell Sophie where I've gone." He would also text Declan that the plumbing would have to wait.

Tuck ran inside and found Sophie in the parlor, sitting in front of her therapy light, looking upset, too. Either too much company or the overcast day had gotten to her.

"Why does Maggie want me to take her to Gandiegow?" he asked.

Sophie's eyebrows pinched together. "All hell broke loose. John blew up in front of us. Then Maggie and John had a terrible row."

"Where's Ross?" Tuck asked. "He could take Maggie and the kids, couldn't he?"

Sophie's eyes shot him the you're-out-of-luck expression. "Ross and Hugh ran off to Here Again Farm, leaving the children with me. Hugh said something about being needed for the *lambing.* I'm pretty sure those two fabricated an excuse so they could escape what was going on here."

"Are you okay?" Tuck asked.

"I'll be fine." She glanced at her therapy lamp as if it was all she needed. "Ye'll take Maggie, then?"

"Aye. But what about Maggie's things? Surely, that one suitcase she has isn't all her possessions."

"She didn't want to go back into the room with John in it."

"I see." The Armstrongs were a mess and Tuck felt more guilty than he had before.

"Their arguing is not yere fault," Sophie said. "It's none of our faults. It's just the way of things."

"I know," he said, but he still felt responsible. "I better go. Can you do me a favor? Or get someone to do it for me?"

"Anything," Sophie said.

"Please deliver food to Ryn's cottage for me? She's asleep at the moment, but I wanted to make sure she wants for nothing when she wakes."

"Of course, I'll look after Ryn until ye get back."

"Thank you." Tuck saw a pen and paper lying on the side table. He grabbed it and scratched out a note. "Can ye also give this to Ryn?"

"Sure," Sophie said with a knowing smile.

Tuck wound his way back through the castle, worrying about the drive to Gandiegow. This would be his second trip today wrought with awkwardness because of an Armstrong. *More trials. More penance for me to pay.* But he owed Maggie and John.

The thought of Ryn traipsed through Tuck's mind and he felt better. At least things seemed to be good between them. He'd keep the American lass present in his thoughts to get him through the van ride ahead. Also, going to Gandiegow would give him a chance to pick up Ryn's overnight bag from the room over the pub. That was a consolation.

When he walked into the kitchen to leave, Maggie's mother Coira was trying unsuccessfully to push a large trunk through the doorway to the outside.

Tuck rushed to her. "Here, let me help ye with that."

Coira looked up in surprise. "Good. Finally, a strong man to come to the rescue." She stood back and held the door open for him.

The trunk weighed a ton. He wielded it through the doorway, trying not to tear up the woodwork in the process. "Where are ye taking this?"

Coira huffed as if she was the one hefting the monstrous trunk. "I just got here, but now, I'm going away with Maggie. She needs me, ye see. I hated it when we moved from Gandiegow five years ago for Lyel's job. Dand wasn't quite three." She paused. "But now, my husband's gone. My girls and the grandbairns are all I have left."

Tuck could see her grief and felt bad for the woman. He knew a little of Maggie's family. Sinnie and Rowena still lived in the cottage that belonged to their parents. "Will ye stay with Maggie or with Rowena and Sinnie?"

"Maggie, of course."

From John's comments earlier, Tuck knew how the eldest Armstrong would feel about his mother-in-law setting up shop in his house. Tuck wondered how Maggie would feel about her mother staying with her, too. When he got the trunk through the door and carried it to the van with Coira following him, Maggie's expression was clear—she wasn't keen on Coira tagging along.

Maggie glared at Tuck, but what was he supposed to do?

The side door was already open and Tuck could see Dand sitting in the back. Maggie hoisted Irene inside. "Dand, will ye buckle her?" Maggie didn't get in, but closed the side door. She turned to her mother. "Mum, there's something I need to say, right here, right now."

"What?" Coira's formidable gaze would've brought many a men to their knees, but Maggie held strong.

She planted a hand on the van—either for support or maybe to provide more protection to the bairns inside. "I'm not in the mood for any lectures from ye. I've enough to worry about at the moment. And if I don't get some peace, this splitting headache will be the end of me. So I'm asking ye please to give me a break."

Coira scanned Maggie's disheveled appearance. "Ye look as if ye're at the end of a short rope."

Maggie rolled her eyes and opened the side door again. "Mum, ye can sit in front with *him*." She pointed to Tuck as if he had a communicable disease.

Coira got in the passenger side and Tuck took his spot in the driver's seat. He glanced in the rearview mirror at Maggie, who sat between her children. Maggie was gazing out the window. But she had a caring arm around Dand, and with her other hand, she stroked Irene's hair.

As soon as he started the engine, Coira turned on the radio to BBC Scotland. As he wended his way along the backroads of the Highlands, Tuck decided listening to the news was better than the uncomfortable silence of a van-full of unhappy passengers.

When Tuck got them to Gandiegow, his job of transporting wasn't over. He unloaded Coira's trunk, but left it by the van. "Maggie, I'll carry yere things." He didn't give her a chance to argue, but took off for her cottage with her and her children's luggage. She didn't look grateful or say thank you. She had other things on her mind.

Like a strange funeral procession, they walked to John and Maggie's cottage in silence. Dand wasn't talking a mile a second and Irene was fast asleep on Maggie's shoulder. Along the pathway, several people peeked out their windows, but no one left their houses to come out and greet them. Aye, the news had already traveled from Whussendale to Gandiegow about the troubles in the Armstrong family.

As soon as he dropped off Maggie's things, he went back for Coira's trunk. Andrew met him at the van and took the other side.

"How is she?" Andrew asked.

"Coira or Maggie?" Tuck asked, but he knew. "I've never seen Maggie so upset." And he wondered what in hell was John going to do?

"Let's get this delivered and then stop by and have tea with us," Andrew said.

"Nay. I need to get back." Tuck didn't go into the details of how he planned to care for Ryn. Hold her close. Give her comfort.

But Andrew was no dummy. "Where is Ryn staying?" His look asked a more direct question: *Is Ryn staying with you?*

"She's settled into her cottage. I'll look in on her from time to time." Tuck didn't mention their cottages shared a wall. And he also didn't mention that *looking in on her from time to time* meant he was going to camp right beside Ryn's bed—day and night.

"Just look in on her?" Andrew's question was a warning. "I don't want to tell you how to live yere life, but—"

Tuck cut him off. "Ha! Ye enjoy telling me how to live my life." But he should cut Andrew some slack. St. Andrew couldn't help himself. It was the priest's business to tell people how they should live.

Andrew, ever patient, waited, making sure Tuck was finished with his thought before pressing on. "As I was saying, ye should be careful around the American lass." Andrew laid a hand on Tuck's shoulder. "I just don't want ye to get hurt again."

"I know ye don't." Tuck knew Andrew's heart was in the right place, as he was the only one who really knew what Tuck had gone through when Elspeth had broken his heart. Andrew also was the only one who really saw Tuck for who he was. Except...

Well, that had changed, hadn't it? Sometimes, when Ryn looked at Tuck just so, he felt as if she understood him like no other woman had. *Not even Elspeth.*

When they delivered the trunk, Coira thanked them. Maggie was nowhere in sight.

Outside, Tuck told Andrew goodbye and then drove the Gandiegow's Range Rover back for Ross to use later. When he arrived, he left the car at Kilheath and hurried to see Ryn.

As he approached her cottage, he heard female voices floating through Ryn's opened window. It sounded as if Ryn was speaking with Cait Buchanan.

Tuck didn't mean to eavesdrop, but he did.

"Ryn, the baby's kicking. Do ye want to feel?" Cait asked.

"No," Ryn said, which surprised Tuck.

"What's wrong?" Cait said. "Don't you want to have children?"

"I can't have children," Ryn answered, her voice sounding sad.

Tuck stopped short. *Ryn can't have children?*

Quietly, he crept the extra steps to his cottage and slipped inside. He needed a moment to regroup and process Ryn's statement. And to figure out why the news bothered him so. Had he, on a subconscious level, been thinking about him and Ryn long-term? That they would be together and have a family one day?

Nay. That's crazy. But was it?

But she can't have children, the voice in his head reminded him. And though he had known he'd never have a family of his own, after Elspeth's betrayal, Tuck suddenly wanted all the same things he thought he was getting when he was seventeen. Love. Companionship. Kids. Family.

All the things that Andrew had...but Tuck didn't.

❧

Ryn, lying in bed, stared at her cottage door, anything not to see the pity in Cait's eyes. Ryn should've been clearer with her new friend.

"I'm sorry ye can't have children." Cait laid a hand on her belly. "That has to be tough. I've had two miscarriages and they tore me apart."

Ryn would have to tell her the truth, but the question was *How much to share*? "It's not that I can't have children, it's more like I won't. Or shouldn't."

Cait leaned closer. "I don't understand."

"It's complicated." Ryn never talked about the abortion she'd had at fifteen. Not with another living soul. The healthy thing she

216

should've done was to discuss it with her mother, when she was alive. But from day one, her mother acted like it was best to pretend as if the abortion had never happened.

Cait squeezed her hand. "No pressure. Just know I'm good at keeping secrets." She laughed. "Not something everyone in Gandiegow can claim. Whatever ye have to say will go no further than me. Promise."

Ryn felt it was the truth.

Suddenly, the urge to talk about children, the abortion, and the turmoil she'd gone through, bubbled up and overpowered Ryn's long silence on the subject.

"I had an abortion when I was fifteen. Since then, it's been clear I shouldn't have children. It's not guilt that plagues me. I know I had no real choice in the matter. My mother insisted. It's just this sense that I shouldn't. I can't explain it."

Cait took her hand and squeezed. "Ye poor hen. And rest assured, mum's the word." She gave Ryn a hug. "From a friend, I know how ye're feeling. My college roommate experienced the same thing when she had an abortion our freshman year." Cait paused, as if she didn't know if she should say the rest.

"What?" Ryn prompted.

"My roommate and I had a lot of late-night talks about it. She finally admitted that *not having children* should be her punishment for what she did."

Ryn sucked in a breath.

"I know, crazy, huh?" Cait smiled soothingly. "I told her I didn't think it worked that way. The guy my roommate was dating was a total dirtbag, and my friend was only waking up to just how awful he was when she found out she was pregnant." Cait's eyebrows pinched together with the memory. "He hit her, Ryn. And she had no options. No money, and no support from her family."

"What did you say to her to make her feel better?"

"I just told her what I hoped was true." Cait paused, gazing at Ryn for a moment. "I don't know where you stand on the subject of God and redemption, but I told her what I believe: She shouldn't punish herself for her decision, because God loves us no matter what."

Ryn let that soak in for a moment. All this time, had she believed she shouldn't have children because she was punishing herself, too?

"What happened to your friend?" Ryn said. "Tell me there's a happy ending."

Cait brightened. "Yes, the best kind. She's so happy now. Finding real love changed those feelings for her. Love is truly amazing. My friend is married now and has three children. She lives in Chicago with her husband." Cait gazed off in the distance, as if trying to see what was going on in Illinois, thousands of miles away. "I really need to drop her a line."

"Do you really believe love changed everything? Can it really be that easy?" Ryn asked. She guessed it didn't matter anyway, as she'd vowed to remain single. *No true love for me.* Surprisingly, Tuck popped up in her mind. Like unexpectedly receiving a bouquet of roses on a *blah* kind of day.

Cait laughed. "Anything that involves *love* is never easy. Finding true love is never going to be a piece of cake." She smiled, placing her hand on her belly again. "But definitely worth it. How about I tell you how Graham and I met, and you decide if choosing love is such an easy path."

Ryn nodded.

"It all started when I returned to Gandiegow…" Cait proceeded to tell Ryn about how she and her famous husband found each other, and how true love blossomed, healing them both. Yes, Cait was right. It wasn't easy, but very interesting.

When Cait was done, she stood. "I think it's time for ye to rest now." She went to the window. "How about I shut this? It's cooled off, don't ye think?"

"Yes. Thanks."

Cait gave her a final hug. "I'll give you a call tomorrow to see how ye're doing." And she left.

When she was gone, Ryn was able to think on what Cait had said. One day, would she really be able to get over her mental block against having children? She thought about her gorgeous next door neighbor, Tuck. Her feelings for him had shifted from *I-have-to-stay-away-from-him* to *I-can't-get-enough*.

She pulled his note out, which she'd stored under her pillow.

Dear Ryn,

I'm sorry I had to leave you for a while. As soon as I get back, I'll be at your beck and call.

Truly,

Tuck

Her stomach squeezed deliciously, just reading it again. Tuck had been so attentive, so caring. He wasn't like the other jerks she'd dated. He'd treated her well. And he could kiss like no tomorrow. The decision was made. She would give him a chance to be her one true love. As scary as that was to her.

She picked up her phone from the side table and texted him:

Where are you?

She held her phone—and her breath—and waited for him to reply back. But instead, she heard rustling on the other side of their shared wall. Then she heard his door open and close. Anticipation whirled through her, as he knocked on her door.

"Come in," she said throatily, though she didn't know where that had come from.

Tuck opened the door and walked in, beaming at her. Her vision was even clearer and it felt good to have settled on what she wanted. *Yes! Tuck is the one!*

He came straight to her, carrying a red rose. "For you."

It felt like a date, as long as she forgot about her incisions, and the fact she was on painkillers.

"Thank you, kind sir," she replied. She patted the area beside her on the bed. "Sit." She was being quite the brazened hussy. But truthfully, how much trouble could they get into with the condition she was in?

His smile grew at the invitation. "Let me find something to put the rose in first." He looked under the counter and came out with a jar. After taking care of the rose, he climbed in bed beside her and slipped an arm around her shoulders. "Better?"

"Much."

They were acting as if they'd done this hundreds of times, and it felt wonderful.

"I want to talk to you," he started, but then he kissed her hair.

"What about?" she asked.

"There's just something I want to tell ye," he said.

"Oh?" For a second, she worried if he'd heard through the window, while she and Cait talked. But wouldn't he be acting strange if he'd heard about the abortion? Surely, he hadn't, or else he wouldn't be holding her like he was.

He shifted so he was looking into her eyes. "I want to tell you something. And I don't know why I want to." He sat back, looking straight ahead, as if speaking face to face was too much. "I think it's because of how easy it is to talk to you. To confide in you," he added.

She gazed up at him. "What is it you want to tell me?"

"It's just, well, something bad happened when I was seventeen."

She rested her head against his chest again. "Tell me."

"Remember my ex?"

"The ballbuster?"

"Aye, Elspeth," he said on a heavy sigh. "I was crazy about her back then. We were stupid and in love. Well, she got pregnant."

Ryn waited, but he paused so long, she thought that might be the end of the story and her mind started to fill in the blanks.

He has a child.

Or what if he wants to get back together with Elspeth for the child's sake?

He began again. "I was going to marry her. I told my parents, arranged the church for a Friday morning ceremony with the pastor, even bought her a corsage."

"What happened?" Ryn asked. The tone of his voice suggested tragedy. *Had Elspeth and the baby died in a car accident?* Ryn felt bad for calling her a *ballbuster* now.

"Elspeth didn't show." Tuck laugh wryly. "She left me at the altar." He stopped talking for a long moment and she knew he was reliving it. "Instead of getting married that day, she got an abortion."

Oh, crap! Oh, crap! He did hear Cait and me talking! But there was no condemnation in his tone, no pulling away.

He continued on, "I never saw it coming. Aye, Elspeth was tearful about the pregnancy, worried about telling her family, but she seemed happy I was going to fix everything by marrying her."

"I'm so sorry, Tuck." But Ryn's mind was spinning over how he was feeling now and what this meant for them.

"I hate Elspeth for it," he said vehemently. "Before that day, I wasn't capable of hate. I was young and naïve, so certain people were genuinely good and that things always worked out. We were *in love.* Isn't everything supposed to work out when two people are *in love?*" He spat the words *in love* out as if they were a bitter fruit.

Ryn had nothing to say. She closed her eyes, trying not to cry. Her new hope of finding true love with Tuck had been instantly dashed with his story.

And yet, Tuck went on, "There's more. I was such an idiot. I found her that night, lying in her bed at her parents' home, crying, and she told me the truth. The baby wasn't even mine, but a bloke's from the university, she'd been stepping out with. She said she was sorry for what she'd put me through, but she just wanted to be with him." He sighed again. "I heard it didn't work out between them." Vindication should've been sweet, but he didn't sound happy about Elspeth not getting her happy ending.

"I don't know what to say," Ryn said honestly.

"There's nothing to say." He kissed her hair again, as if bookending the story. "I just wanted ye to know, that's all."

It seemed a stretch and it begged the question: *Do you want true love now?* But Ryn couldn't ask it.

He tilted his head down to see her face. "How are ye feeling?"

Like I want to cry. "Tired," Ryn said. *And disappointed.*

"Why don't ye rest." Tuck was being so considerate it made Ryn want to sob. "I'll stay with you, in case you need anything."

But the one thing Ryn wanted, she couldn't have. She couldn't have Tuck as her true love, and now everything seemed up in the air. A half hour ago, she'd thought the proverbial search for true love was over. But nothing but a question mark loomed before her now.

Tuck gently took her into his arms and kissed her. The sorrow she felt was trying to ruin the kiss, but Ryn fought back, pushing her lost hope aside and just letting herself feel the wonderfulness of his lips on hers. Oh, how good and safe she felt while in his arms.

When the kiss was over, he pulled away, laying his forehead against hers. "Rest now, luv." He stood, staring down at her for a moment, then he pulled a kitchen chair beside her bed and sat.

She closed her eyes, hoping the tears didn't leak out. Maybe she could keep him for a while. While she recovered. While she was in Scotland. *Maybe.*

The only thing she was sure about was that she could *never* tell him about her own abortion. *Not ever!* It was bad enough that Ryn looked like Elspeth-the-ex, but to have had an abortion like her…would make Tuck hate Ryn, too.

18

J OHN LEFT THE CASTLE and walked to Hugh's office, but only after questioning the cook as to where to find him. The wool mill was a succession of buildings, some shiplap, some stone. A few were prettily painted with stripes, but mostly they were a creamy yellow. John found the building which had Office written on the outside door. But when he tapped, no one answered. He checked the door and it was unlocked. He entered to find there were several doors with names and titles below them. He found Manager and knocked again.

"Come in," Hugh said.

John entered and the young Laird looked surprised.

He recovered quickly, "What can I do for you?"

"The cottage. The one ye were fixing up. Is it good enough for me to move there today?"

Hugh's eyebrow rose. "Aye. If that's what ye want. I'll get Declan to take yere things there straightaway."

"No!" But then John cursed his blasted temper. He tamped down his emotions. "I mean, I'll do it myself. 'Tis not much that I have."

Hugh opened one of the desk drawers and pulled out an old-fashioned key. "Your cottage has the green door in the middle of the horseshoe of homes. I know you have physical therapy most days, but when ye're up to it, I could really use some help."

John suspected the truth. The Laird was fabricating a job to give him something to do. Or to keep him out of everyone's way.

"It's not what ye think," Hugh said. "I really do need help here in the office. Tally, my bookkeeper, is taking some time off to be with her mum who is gravely ill and living in St. Andrews. I have a hard enough time juggling the wool mill business without having to figure out her job as well. I reckon since ye own a successful boating business, you'd know yere way around accounting software."

John looked at him circumspect. "Aye. I'm decent with numbers."

"The software update arrived. It'd be a great help if ye could get that installed, too."

John glanced down at his right hand that was no longer there. Then he stared at the bookcase behind Hugh. The physical therapist said John would have to retrain his brain to write and work with his left hand.

"Then ye'll do it?" Hugh asked expectantly.

"Yes." John felt defeated.

"After ye get the accounting caught up, I hope ye can help me with another matter. As it's the month of May, this is the beginning of shearing season and the wool mill is ramping up to handle the new wool. Tuck, I'm sure, would appreciate all the help he can get with the machines, as the process will go to sixteen hours a day. He's had his hands full since he got here—one breakdown after another. Not to mention how he's taking care of Ryn...you know, Maggie's cousin."

John knew. He'd ridden in the van with her. "Aye."

"What time is your PT appointment?" Hugh glanced at the schedule on his desk. "I could possibly take ye."

"Nay. Ross is planning to." John wasn't looking forward to seeing him either. Ross would more than likely berate him for his outburst with Maggie, but his brother wouldn't do it with yelling. No, Ross would handle it with calm logic that would piss the hell out of John.

"Good. All right, then." Hugh looked at him as if he was worried, but the Laird had a good head on his shoulders and kept his sentiments to himself.

"I'll be fine to get things moved in on my own," John reassured, and then he left.

An hour later, John hauled his second bag to the cottage with the green door. He was winded, exhausted, and disgusted with himself for not being able to get everything in one load. But that was the outcome of having only one arm. He didn't unpack. He sat on the edge of the bed, bone-tired. Finally, he gave into how weak he felt and laid back. He woke to knocking at his door.

"John? Are ye in there?" The door opened and Ross and Ramsay came in.

"What the devil?" John said, trying to sit up quickly, but he fell over, forgetting he only had one arm for which to push himself up.

"We went to the castle and Sophie said ye were here," Ross explained.

"She's not happy about it," Ramsay added.

"Yeah." She'd given John hell earlier for leaving Kilheath.

"Yere appointment," Ross reminded him. "We better get going."

John stood. "Ye both didn't need to come. Ramsay, don't ye have a touristing boat to attend to?"

Ramsay shrugged. "Tuck is taking the visiting gents out today for me. We have four from Glasgow who want to experience a bit of our North Sea fishing."

"Ye should be doing it, not Tuck. 'Tis yere business, not his," John argued.

Ramsay gave him a look that said John wasn't the captain of the boat and couldn't push him around. "I had more important things to tend to today."

John knew what that meant, and as soon as he slipped into the front passenger's side of the vehicle, Ross started in on him.

"Tell us what's going on. Why is Maggie back in Gandiegow with the bairns, and ye are here?"

John answered to no one, except maybe the Almighty, and right now, they weren't exactly on speaking terms. "It's none of yere affair."

"Aye, it is," Ramsay piped in from the backseat. "Ye're family. Maggie is, too. Ye need to apologize to her for whatever jackass thing ye did."

John clammed up. He didn't have to explain himself to his brothers. Besides, he didn't do anything. Maggie agreed to move them to Whussendale without really discussing it with him first. It was she who needed to apologize to him!

Even-tempered Ross glanced over and then back at the road. "Brother, there are worse things than losing an arm." John knew he was speaking of Sadie, who was preparing for her kidney transplant.

But Ramsay filled in the blanks another way. "How about like losing yere family. That's worse than losing an arm, isn't it?"

At any other time, John would've agreed, but things had changed. His whole world had flipped upside down and the same rules didn't apply anymore. His brothers couldn't understand.

The rest of the trip was in complete silence. The three of them were used to not talking on the boat, but usually on car rides, Ramsay entertained them with stories of his antics. The quiet was maddening. When they pulled into the parking lot, John was never happier to see the hospital in his life.

Therapy was hard. Just trying to strengthen his left arm wore him out. Baby Irene could've wrestled him to the ground, for the shape he was in.

"Ye're healing," the petite blond physical therapist assured him. "Give yourself a break. It takes time to come back from this kind of injury. Ye'll be yourself again before ye know it."

"Not soon enough," John growled as he lifted the weight again. Every exercise gave him the chance to take his frustrations out on the equipment, and he welcomed the opportunity. He wouldn't think about Maggie and the kids. He wouldn't think about how the doctor advised him against returning to fishing. Or the fact that Maggie told him he couldn't. And he wouldn't think about his damned brothers who waited in the outer room as if he was a child having a tooth pulled by the dentist.

"Last one," the therapist said. "You can do it."

"I don't need a damn cheerleader," he muttered.

"Aye, that's were ye're wrong," she said, as if she'd encountered every type of out-of-sort grizzly bear. "Now, let's get some ice on yere shoulder for ten minutes. I noticed ye were favoring it."

When he was finished, he met up with his brothers.

"How about we head to Gandiegow?" Ross asked.

John was exhausted, but not so much that he couldn't set his brothers straight. "Whussendale. I promised the Laird I'd help to work on the machines."

Ross gave him a shocked look. "What?"

Ramsay leaned up to the front seat. "I told ye to just drive him to see Maggie and not give him the choice."

John cranked his head around and glared at his youngest brother. "I can still kick both of yere arses."

Ramsay gave John his cocky smile. "Ye'd have to catch me first, old man."

"Sod off," John said. "I'm not that much older." Only nine years.

227

Ross grinned but said nothing. John knew what he was thinking—at least things were a little back to normal between the three of them.

John laid his head back against the headrest, knowing he was going to sleep all the way back to Whussendale. The physical therapist had been the one to kick his arse today. Ross may think things were better, but the reality was that the rest of John's life was shite. *Complete shite*. And there wasn't a damn thing he could do about it.

ↅↄ✕ↄↄ

Ryn carefully rolled to her side, away from Tuck, and stared into the dark. The moonlight crept through the window, which would make it easier to see her bedmate. If she turned around to look. He was close enough for her to reach out and touch him. Instead, she stuck a pillow between them, to keep her hands from exploring the planes of his body.

Her first night out of the hospital, Tuck had slept in a kitchen chair next to her bed, reminiscent of when she'd slept in his bed in his cottage. The next night, though, he wore her down with reasons why he needed a good night's sleep and why it would be beneficial to her.

Ye want yere manservant wide awake to wait on ye hand and foot, don't ye?

He made her laugh with all his arguments, and she finally acquiesced, allowing him to slip into the large bed and lay beside her.

Though he'd promised to be a perfect gentleman—not make any moves whatsoever and keep his hands to himself—he couldn't seem to stop touching her. While they lay in bed, he soothed her with light touches here and there—rubbing her back or caressing her arm. Always there, comforting her.

It was wonderful!

But she was miserable!

Even with both of them fully clothed in modest pajamas, he was driving her hormones toward doing something she would regret. Thank goodness she had three new incisions and doctor's orders standing guard to keep them apart. At least for the time being.

Being so sleepy helped, too. She'd slept a lot over the last four days, dozing in and out, with Tuck at her side as much as he could be. Whenever she woke, he was there, getting her food, drinks, and an ibuprophen, if she needed it. But she was regaining her strength and awake more and more. Every time he did something nice for her, she had to remind herself she was supposed to be letting go. *Practice makes perfect.* But being weak in body, she was weak in spirit, and soaked up his goodness, instead of pushing him away.

"Are ye awake?" Tuck asked.

"Yes." She gingerly rolled over to face him.

He removed her barrier pillow, propping it under his head. "Can I get ye anything?" He started to sit.

When she grabbed his arm to stop him, it hurt, and she groaned. "Ow. No, I don't need anything." An idea came to her. One of self-preservation. "Actually, if I'm being honest—" which she wasn't, "—I think I would rest better if you slept back in your cottage."

"Nay. I don't want to leave ye. What can I do to help you sleep better?"

"Stop breathing?" she suggested, trying to make a joke. "It's just...I'm used to sleeping alone."

"Good," he said.

"What I mean is, that I'm a light sleeper. Every time you move, I wake up." *Liar-liar-pants-on-fire* skipped through her brain.

He gently pushed her hair away from her face. "But what if you need something in the night?"

"I'll call," she said. "Or throw a book at the wall. You're close by. Besides, Doc MacGregor said it's important for me to get my rest."

Tuck didn't look happy that he'd have to leave her bed. Truth be told, she wasn't singing Dixie about it, either. She liked having him here. Liked hearing him breathe beside her. Liked playing house with him. But this wasn't real. She had to do something, anything, to not fall for him.

"Okay." He tried to sit again, as if he meant to leave now.

She reached out again, being careful this time, and touched his arm. "Stay here with me tonight, though."

"Are you sure?"

She nodded. "Yes. Stay."

He lay back beside her. She didn't tell him he was making it hard for her to follow through. Her heart, after all, was on the line and in danger of succumbing to the crush she had on him.

Her hand was still on his arm. She should've pulled it away, but instead, she left it there and scooted closer to him. He seemed rigid to her, as if he might be angry she was kicking him out of her bed.

Guilt had her running her hand up to his shoulder, trying to lessen the blow of his banishment. Yes, she was giving him mixed signals, and yes, she enjoyed how solid his muscles felt. But she was only trying to soothe his bruised feelings. *Really*.

She laid a palm on his chest and felt his heartbeat for a moment or two. Her hand then skimmed his six-pack. She blamed Tuck for what she was doing. It was totally and completely his fault. If he hadn't been the nicest man she'd ever met, and if he hadn't been sleeping next to her, *driving her crazy*, she never would've sought him out and been so bold.

"Ye're making this hard on me, lass." His voice sounded jagged and out of breath. He was a man trying to speak while climbing a mountain through rough terrain. "You need yere rest, don't ye?"

She should stop, but now that she'd started...well, she wasn't a quitter. She shifted again, this time to nibble at his neck, rolling carefully so as not to agitate her incisions.

He groaned and then clutched her hand, halting it. "Lass, no. Ye just had surgery."

She kissed his shoulder lovingly. "I'm not doing anything. Just messing around." She leaned over to get access to his lips, but winced, when the action pulled at her stitches.

He gently gathered her to him. "Are you all right?"

"I need you to kiss me."

He didn't need to be told twice. He leaned over, propping himself high enough so he didn't touch her abdomen, and kissed her tenderly at first. Mr. Considerate was a great kisser, but Ryn liked it more when Mr. Plunder took over and kissed the socks off of her. The man was a wonder with his mouth and she decided his current position left her hands plenty of room to roam freely up his back and down again.

He growled, "Ye're a tricky one." He captured her hands and gently moved each of them to her sides to shackle her wrists under his hands. He kissed her again, bringing her into submission.

"Oh, Tuck," she said, when he moved to her neck and kissed her there. "What are we going to do?"

"We're going to wait until ye're up for more strenuous activity," he said, misinterpreting her dilemma. "And then we're going to see it through to the end."

Ryn was so conflicted. He was looking at the immediate and she was looking at the big picture. She needed space. From him! And from her growing affection for this amazing man.

But hell, she'd have to admit the truth. Not even a million miles would be enough distance to keep her for wanting him...for always.

He kissed her once more and lay back beside her, replacing the pillow between them like before. "Go to sleep. Ye need yere rest. Especially since I need you in tip-top shape. *Soon.*"

Ryn rolled away, staring at the opposite wall. *I really must be feeling better.* Which meant it was time to come up with a new plan.

She sighed. After surgery, she should've gone to Gandiegow to recover, instead of Whussendale. Being here had only drawn her and Tuck closer.

Tuck laid a hand on her back. "Ryn, there's something ye need to know." He paused long enough, she felt certain he must be searching the night for the right words. "I don't normally say things like this, but well…I like ye a lot."

She didn't move. Not even her lungs. For she couldn't breathe. If only she'd met Tuck before. Back when she had hope. Back before her outlook on having a good relationship was favorable. Back before she knew he'd hate her, if he found out she had an abortion, too.

"Lass?"

She didn't say anything back. She couldn't. Pretending to be asleep would save her from telling him that she liked him, too. *Loved him.*

When the sun rose, she came wide awake, keenly aware Tuck was beside her.

She opened her eyes and he gave her a slow, heart-melting smile.

"'Morning, lass."

"Morning," she mumbled. She felt awkward and shy around him in the light of day. Maybe it was because her hands had taken a little advantage of him, not too many hours of ago. More than likely, her shyness was brought on by what he'd said to her in the dark of night.

"I'll fix ye a cup of tea." He gave her a quick kiss before getting out of bed.

She allowed the affection, but decided then and there, she couldn't abide his lingering kisses anymore. If she let her heart get anymore tangled up with him, she might not be able to see her way back to the inevitable reality—a future without him.

A knock sounded at the door, then voices.

"Wait!" It was Sophie.

"Why are ye yelling?" Deydie said.

"Ryn might not be decent," Sophie said, clearly trying to alert her.

"Deydie!" Tuck whispered. "I'll duck into the bathroom."

The knocking reverberated again. "I'm coming in," Deydie said, and the door opened.

Sophie looked around wildly and seemed surprised and relieved to only see Ryn.

Deydie waddled over to the bed. "How are ye feeling, lass? All better?"

"I'm getting there," Ryn said, trying not to look at Tuck, who was peeking through the crack in the bathroom door.

"Good, good," Deydie said.

Sophie stepped farther into the room and glanced toward the bathroom. "Oh." She shot Ryn an *are-you-crazy* look.

Deydie spun around and frowned at Sophie. "I've never seen ye so jumpy. What's wrong?"

"Nothing. It's just Ryn is still abed and needs her rest. How about we call on her later?"

Deydie rested her hands on her substantial hips. "We're already here. So let me talk to the lass."

Deydie took the nearby kitchen chair and plopped down in it. "Ye did a nice job with the quilt retreat here, and not a half-bad job in Gandiegow—though ye were in terrible straights and didn't finish." She turned to Sophie. "Make us some tea."

Deydie shifted around to see Sophie, and Ryn took the opportunity to glance at the crack in the bathroom door. She was grateful Tuck's face had disappeared. She wondered how long he could hide out, especially since Deydie seemed to be settling in.

"What's there to eat for breakfast?" Deydie asked.

"Toast?" Sophie offered, still looking panicked.

"Make some eggs, too. Scrambled. Doc says protein is important, especially first thing in the morning."

Ryn carefully scooted to the edge of the bed and slipped on her robe, which had been lying at the end. "If you'll excuse me." She put her feet over the side and her toes began searching for her house shoes. She was stiff and any movement hurt, but she had to warn Tuck it was going to be a while. She didn't want to think what would happen if Deydie had to pee!

That thought, and Sophie running the water, was a horrible combination, reminding Ryn she hadn't gone this morning.

"Where are ye off to?" Deydie said. "I'm not done talking to you."

"Sorry. Bathroom break," Ryn said.

Sophie's eyes grew, which would've been amusing if the situation wasn't dire.

Ryn supported her aching abdomen and hurried to the bathroom, trying not to open the door too wide to show Deydie who lurked inside.

At first glance, Ryn didn't see Tuck. She pulled back the shower curtain and didn't see him on second glance either. *Where is he?* The opened window gave her a clue and she let out her held breath. She leaned out and Tuck was nowhere in sight. She closed the window, made use of the restroom, washed hands, looked in the mirror, and wondered how she'd gotten herself into such a mess. She dawdled a bit more and finally was ready to join Sophie and Deydie for tea.

When she stepped out, she had a fright. Tuck—*no-pajamas-but-completely-dressed-for-the-day-in-his-kilt*—was sipping a cup of tea.

"Good morning, lass."

"Morning," Ryn mumbled, as her cheeks heated up. *Didn't they do this already?*

Sophie seemed to be staring awfully hard at the eggs she was cracking. Apparently, the eggs were funny, because she was smiling at them, too.

Tuck turned to Deydie, acting natural and comfortable around her, except the throbbing vein at his temple gave him away. "So what brings ye here today?"

"We've schedule a new quilt retreat for Whussendale. We got a call this morning from the quilters in Dumfries, but Gandiegow is already booked for that weekend." Deydie's cheeks squished up into a smile. "Ryn did such a fine job before, I wanted to let her take care of this retreat, too."

"Nay," Tuck said calmly. "The lass needs to heal. Doc MacGregor said so. Running another retreat would be too much for her."

Deydie shook her head. "Bah. She'll be grand. It's nearly a month away. Besides, the Whussendale quilters will help. Right, Sophie?"

"Sure, but..." The toast popped up and she busied herself with grabbing the butter, while Tuck took over again.

"Ryn will sit this one out." His voice was strong and firm.

Ryn felt a little like a rag doll, being pulled this way and that. At the same time, by the way they were talking around her, she was pretty sure they'd forgotten she was in the room.

Deydie stood and glared up at Tuck. "What business is it of yours, Tuck MacBride?" Her head bounced with authority as she spoke.

Sophie jumped into the fray, defending the big Scot, as if he was helpless to do so. "Tuck has been helping us take care of Ryn."

Ryn was tired of being a bystander in this conversation. "Hold on a second." To start, she nodded to Tuck. "Thank you for your concern, but I've got this." Then she addressed Deydie. "Tell me what you're talking about specifically. What would be my duties? Planning? Setting up? Teaching?"

Deydie gave her that scary grin. "Ye're a spunky lass, though, ye still look like hell. Lay back down. We'll talk while ye keep yere feet up."

Ryn's brain was spinning. *This is perfect!* Running another retreat would keep her busy. She wouldn't have time to pine over Tuck, dream about their unrealistic future together, and while away the hours fantasizing over the intimate things she and Tuck could get up to together.

"I'll do it," Ryn said, sincerely glad Deydie had dropped in unexpectedly.

"Lass," Tuck started.

Ryn put her hand up. "It'll be fine. I have almost a month. I can start today. I'll make notes from my bed."

Tuck didn't look happy.

But tough. Ryn had her heart to protect and her sanity to maintain.

"We'll all be here to help ye," Sophie said, bringing four plates to the small table.

"Nay," Deydie said. "Ye're the Laird's wife and the kiltmaker's apprentice. We won't take any more of yere time. Ye have plenty to do already." Her eyes went to the ceiling, as if an idea had just popped into her head. "I'll send ye someone from Gandiegow to help." She acted as if she had the perfect person in mind.

Tuck downed his tea and then frowned at the room, before zeroing in on Ryn. "I see ye have everything under control here. I've things to do."

"What about breakfast?" Sophie asked.

"I'm going to have coffee with Willoughby." Tuck left.

Ridiculously, Ryn wished he'd kissed her goodbye, something he'd done every time he'd left the cottage in the last four days.

But today is a new beginning, she reminded herself.

Sophie shot her a worried expression. "The eggs are done, Ryn.

I'll fix ye a tray."

"No." Ryn slid out of bed. "It's time I get back to normal."

Over the next week and a half, Ryn got better. Not only physically, but she'd gotten more rational, too. Yes, she'd gone temporarily boy-crazy over Tuck MacBride, but she was recovering, keeping her emotions in check. *Most of the time anyway.*

And she wasn't doing a half-bad job of keeping Tuck at a distance, too. Every day before she saw him, she deliberately turned her emotions from *hot-for-him* to cold and chilly. His warmth was so enticing and she needed her cool composure for protection against his amazing kisses, loving arms, and his generous nature.

By the sideway glances Tuck was giving her, he'd noticed the change. She expected him to take the hint, but instead, he only tried harder to make her happy. Which only made her more melancholy. She successfully dodged his every question of *Is everything all right?* She responded with her version of the truth, *I'm fine, just busy.*

She was busy with the upcoming retreat, but she wasn't fine. She was wretched and depressed. She missed the wonderfulness of her budding relationship with Tuck. She missed him sleeping beside her at night. She missed how happy she felt, before she figured out they didn't have a shot of being together in the future.

She tried to hold the truth close so she wouldn't be pulled back in again. They couldn't be a couple, now that she understood his deepest disappointment. Sure, he'd gotten over the fact she and Elspeth resembled each other. But it was so much more than that. Ryn could never let on how deep their similarities ran. What else they had in common. For if Tuck knew the truth, Ryn couldn't bear for him to look at her with the same loathing he clearly *held on to for dear life* for his ex.

19

TUCK WALKED INTO the weaving building, wearing his kilt and his tool belt, but had more on his mind than fixing machinery. He needed to fix whatever had gone wrong between him and Ryn.

It had been a little over two weeks since Ryn had come home from the hospital. Things had turned weird between them, and had become more awkward with each passing day. He had no idea what had happened to make things turn bad between them. The more he tried to make things right, the more she withdrew. It was starting to feel like the Elspeth fiasco all over again. Except without the pregnancy.

Tuck put in earplugs and walked through the facility to find the machine which was down. As he walked through the mill, he waved to a couple of workers who looked up and nodded to him. Whussendale was beginning to feel like home.

Tuck found machine three, assessed the situation, and clamped a pair of vice grips on to loosen a bolt. He blindly reached for the rubber mallet on the floor behind him and was surprised when it was placed into his hand. He spun around to find John with a frown on his face.

Tuck was utterly speechless, which was fine. He couldn't be heard above the machinery anyway. He took the mallet and pounded on the handle of the vice grips, trying to loosen the bolt, but really he was trying to get a grip on the situation. Why was John here?

Tuck had seen John around the village the last couple of weeks, wearing the mandatory Whussendale wool mill tartan and logoed shirt. Tuck knew John was working for Hugh in the office, and Tuck had steered clear of him. But why in the hell was he here now?

John pointed and yelled above the noise, "Did you check the cam?"

Indeed, there was a chunk of fluff caught in the cam. "Thanks." John just saved him from taking the blasted machine apart.

For the next half hour they worked in tandem to get the next problem machine back in perfect working order. And they did it with as little communication as humanly possible.

John checked his watch. "I have to go." And he walked away.

"That was strange," Tuck muttered under his breath. He still couldn't believe John would help him...of all people. And then to leave so abruptly. But his leaving could be more easily explained. Tuck figured he was off to physical therapy or some other kind of doctor's appointment. Tuck worked the rest of the day alone.

For the next two weeks, he kept his head down, pulling nets for part of the day and working at the wool mill for the other part. Every day, John would join him to help fix the machinery, somedays leaving early for an appointment, other days, staying until the evening meal. They never spoke much, except about the task at hand, which reminded him of working on the boat with John. With each passing day, Tuck was getting more comfortable with John, and he definitely wasn't going to complain. Having another soul to help troubleshoot the equipment was priceless.

All the while, Tuck couldn't keep his mind off of Ryn. Things still weren't back to where they were. When he'd tried to kiss her an hour ago, she'd turned her head away so fast from him, that he missed her lips and grazed her shoulder. He wanted to say *What the hell!* But he headed over to Hugh's office instead to pick up today's work orders.

Outside the weaving building, Tuck opened the door but stopped when he heard his name called.

It was Lara. "Tuck, wait up. I've something to ask ye."

Lara had been nice to him from the start, but she wanted more from him than he was prepared to give. Not now. Not ever.

"What's going on?" he asked. "Is the dishwasher broke again at the café? Or is there something wrong at the dye shack?"

She gave him a shy smile. "No, not that." She chewed her lip for a moment. "It's just there's a céilidh[2] in Lasswool, Friday night. I wondered if you wanted to go. With me." She looked as if she was holding her breath.

The first thing that popped into his mind was *I'm off the market.* But he couldn't say that. And by the way Ryn was acting, he was definitely still on the market, because she'd put him back on the shelf. Lara was a kind girl with a pretty smile. What would be the harm in doing something nice for her? By her anxious and expectant face, it would certainly make her happy for him to say *yes.* "Okay. Why not?" Out of the corner of his eye, he saw Sophie come to a stop at the bottom of the hill.

With excitement, Lara grabbed his arm, leaned up, and kissed his cheek. "We're going to have a great time. Ye'll see."

"Okay," he said again, worried by the frown Sophie was giving him. "I better get inside and get to work."

Lara smiled widely and swayed side to side as if her hips couldn't help it. "See ye later."

---

[2] Pronounced (KAY-lee)

He ducked into the building, afraid Lara might throw air kisses to him next.

Immediately regret settled in. He'd just given hope to a lass who'd made moon-eyes at him from the beginning. He should go find her now and bow out. Quickly. Before he did any more damage.

It hit him then, the number of women he'd toyed with since he was seventeen, given hope to when he'd had no intention of committing to any of them. It didn't matter he'd made it clear with each one from the start, how he wasn't the marrying kind. They'd all thought they could change him.

Magnus, the head weaver, joined him and laid a hand on his shoulder. "I'm glad ye're here. We need that machine up and going now. We've orders to fill."

"Aye," Tuck replied. He couldn't go find Lara now, but as soon as the day was over, he'd break the date. Maybe by then, he'd know just the right words to let her down gently.

John joined him and they worked on the loom for the next two hours. When it was running again, Tuck checked his watch and then put his tools away. If he was going to make the afternoon tide, he'd have to leave now. His other chores would have to wait until later.

"Heading to Gandiegow?" John asked. Apparently, he knew the tide schedule for today, too.

Tuck nodded.

"Are ye coming back to Whussendale afterward?" John seemed pretty chatty for him.

"Aye. I'm coming back to Whussendale." Tuck had to check in on Ryn and see if she needed anything from him. But recent history showed she wouldn't. He was in unchartered waters with her. She needed nothing from him, but he needed everything from her.

"I'll go with ye." John walked away, leaving Tuck to grab his tools and to wonder what was going to happen next.

They met up at the car a short while later, as Tuck had to change into his dungarees first. John had his rain jacket in his sole hand—the same jacket Tuck had seen him wear a hundred times on the boat. *John means to go fishing.* Tuck wanted to ask him if that was a wise idea. And dammit, it was too late to slip away and text Ross or Ramsay to tell them what John planned to do.

Well, Ross would know soon enough, as he and Tuck were to pull the nets together this afternoon. *But not if I don't get a move on.*

As soon as they got in the car, Tuck turned on the radio to help with the silence. It didn't matter though. John seemed to have slipped inside himself as he stared out the front window.

When they arrived in Gandiegow, John exited the car and started walking into the village. Tuck quickly pulled out his phone on his way to the boot of the car to retrieve his Wellies. Before he could dial though, Andrew hailed him from the edge of the car park.

"Can I talk to ye a second?" Andrew asked, coming toward him.

"A second is all I have. I don't want to be late." Tuck pointed to John's back.

Andrew nodded with understanding. "I'll walk with you to the boat."

They took off at a quick pace.

"I was going to ask after Ryn, but first, I have to know what John is up to. Is he here to make up with Maggie?"

"Nay. I believe he's going fishing," Tuck said wryly.

"Fishing? Did his doctor approve it?"

Tuck stared over at his brother with a look of disbelief. "As if John would confide in me? I still can't believe he wanted to catch a ride with me to Gandiegow! I have no idea what the hell he's up to."

Tuck saw John was almost to the boat and it was too late to call his brothers.

"And Ryn is fine. She is working on the next retreat with Sophie and Lara. How are Maggie and the kids doing?"

"She's keeping to her cottage. Moira and Amy delivered groceries to her, but Maggie wouldn't visit, saying she had a headache and had to lie down. Everyone is taking turns watching Irene. And Ross and Ramsay are taking Dand off Maggie's hands to give the lad some exercise."

Tuck motioned to the boat. "We'll talk later. I'm going to run ahead."

"Go on," Andrew said. "It's good to see you."

"Aye." Tuck hurried the last few steps to the dock, watching as John held on tightly while stepping aboard.

Tuck made it to the boat a moment later, just as Ross came out of the wheelhouse.

"John?" Ross said, clearly confused. He looked over at Tuck questioningly.

"He hitched a ride with me," Tuck answered.

Noise down below rose up as Ramsay and Dand made their way up on deck.

"Da!" Dand ran toward him, but stopped short from hugging him, as if remembering their last encounter.

John clutched the mast, steadying himself as he went down on one knee, opening his arms in invitation.

Dand carefully stepped into the embrace.

John balanced Dand on his knee. "Listen, son. I'm sorry about before. I never should've yelled at ye as I did. For a while, ye'll have to be careful around yere ole da. Just until my arm heals."

Dand nodded and slowly reached a hand out, hovering over the Ace bandage sleeve. "Does it hurt all the time?"

"Not so much," John said.

Dand's eyes looked earnestly into his father's. "Are ye here to go fishing?"

"Aye," John said, seeming surprised by his own answer.

Dand looked up at his uncle. "Can I go fishing, too, Uncle Ramsay? Pleeease!"

Tuck saw the look of hurt on John's face. It had to sting that his son had deferred to his brother, instead of getting permission from him, his father. But what could John expect?

Ramsay tousled his hair. "I'll text yere mum that ye'll be with us."

John looked up a Ramsay with a slight shake of his head. The meaning was clear: *Don't tell Maggie I'm here.*

Brodie stepped onto the boat. "Ye have a boatload today, Ross." He scanned the deck. "Anyone want to help me this afternoon instead?"

Tuck was the odd man out, being the only non-Armstrong present for the all Armstrong men's family reunion. "Sure. I'm happy to help ye, Brodie."

John cleared his throat, the action clearly directed at Tuck. "I'll meet ye at the car afterward."

"Aye." Tuck nodded and left to join Brodie on his fishing boat.

As soon as they were underway, Brodie summoned him to the wheelhouse. "What's going on with you and John?"

"Hell if I know."

"Best buddies now?"

"Nay. Not even close."

Brodie nodded in comprehension. "And Ryn? Rachel was asking after her. How is she feeling? All healed up?"

"She's doing well." Tuck wished he had someone to talk to about her, but he didn't. He kept his mouth shut about his concerns.

"Ye should stop by and see Rachel. She's been quizzing me and I know nothing. She thinks something is going on between you and the American lass."

Tuck tapped the door jamb. "Yeah, well, I'm going to check on the bait."

Tuck and Brodie made it through the afternoon run in record time...and with no more uncomfortable questions. As they were heading back, the Indwaller—the Armstrongs's boat—had just pulled into the harbor, too.

Tuck helped Brodie secure the lines and unload the catch, before making his way over to see if John had changed his mind and would indeed stay in Gandiegow with his wife after all. But that hope was dashed when Tuck stepped on the boat.

Dand tugged on his father's hand. "Are ye going to see Mum now? And Irene? They miss ye." With a pleading smile, the boy's question lay expectantly on his young windblown face.

"Nay. Not today," John said. "Tuck has to get back to Whussendale. He's my ride."

Dand's shoulders sagged. "I miss ye, too."

John looked helpless. Ross and Ramsay took their spot on either side of their nephew, each placing a hand on his shoulder in comfort. And solidarity.

Ramsay broke the silence first. "I'll walk ye home. Yere mum probably has yere tea ready."

Dand shook his head. "Nay. She's probably in bed, sleeping. That's all she does anymore."

Ramsay ruffled his hair. "Then ye'll come home and eat dinner with Kit and me. My little matchmaker is a darn good cook."

Tuck glanced over at John, who looked defeated. But he rallied for a moment.

"We better get going," John said awkwardly. "See you soon, son."

There was no hug, no tearful goodbye, just Dand straightening his shoulders. "See you." He walked off the boat and down the dock by himself.

Ross shot his older brother a look of disappointment before ducking back into the wheelhouse.

Ramsay nodded his head in the direction of Dand. "Get yere shit together, John."

John's face grew red, but as he opened his mouth, Ramsay's hand shot up like a flag, as if it was too little, too late.

Ramsay stepped off the boat then and took long strides, slowing only when he caught up with his nephew.

Tuck wished he was anywhere except for here. *Lucky me. I get to be the one to ride back with John!*

"Let's go." John's voice was laced with anger. But as he went to step off, John lost his footing from the waves rocking the boat. Tuck reached out and steadied him, keeping him from falling into the drink.

John jerked away. "Off me!" He stomped from the boat and down the deck.

Tuck held back, giving John his space. *Aye, the ride back will be crap!*

But he couldn't wait to get home to Whussendale. Ryn was in the wool village. Ryn made him smile. Ryn made him feel calm. Except she hadn't really, lately. Not in the last two weeks. Being with her only brought on more questions than it did answers.

Tuck followed, but didn't catch up to John. The man needed time alone, and well, Tuck needed time away from the man.

Tuck had only stepped off the dock, when Deydie came out of Quilting Central with Coira following with a large floral duffel bag in hand.

"Tuck!" Deydie said. "I want a word."

Reluctantly, Tuck dragged himself to where she stood with Coira by her side. Dread washed over him as he sensed something unpleasant was coming.

"Ye need to take Coira with ye to Whussendale."

Tuck glanced at her duffel again and saw it was jam-packed.

Deydie didn't keep him in suspense, but patted Coira on the back. "For now, Coira is going to take over the Whussendale Kilts and Quilts Retreat." Deydie seemed pretty chummy with Maggie's mum. "Coira will do a great job. I called Sophie and she said they'll fix up a place for her at the castle."

Tuck wondered what had gone on here in Gandiegow to have Coira leaving so quickly. Did she and Maggie have a row?

Ice ran through his veins at the reality of Deydie's declaration. "What about Ryn?" Was she leaving? Going back to the States?

"I think it's best. Give Ryn time to rest more. Gabriel mentioned she shouldn't push herself just yet. The American lass will teach, of course, but Coira here will do the rest. It's a big job, running a retreat." Deydie glared at him. "Go on now. Coira has a lot to do to get ready."

Tuck nodded, feeling somewhat appeased and relieved.

It was obvious Deydie and Coira didn't see John when he walked by Quilting Central a few minutes ago, because neither one said a word about it. Aye, the ride back to Whussendale would be a long one, as no love was lost between John and Maggie's mum.

"Let me take that," Tuck said, relieving Coira of her bag.

"Thank you." Coira smiled and he could make out some of Maggie's features—her piercing blue eyes, her height, and the seriousness toward life etched on her face. Coira's long braid down her back was completely gray, whereas Maggie's bound locks were as black as midnight. But the nice thing about Coira, as far as Tuck was concerned, she at least smiled at him, when others here in Gandiegow didn't. But he guessed she could be frightening. A severity to her lay just below the surface. No wonder Coira and Deydie got along...*kindred spirits no doubt.*

They walked along companionably, but when the parking lot came into view, Coira stopped. "Who's that?"

"John." Tuck knew it was coming, but wouldn't it have been nice if John had disappeared before she'd seen him?

"What's he doing here in Gandiegow?"

"Ye'll have to ask him," Tuck said, passing the buck.

Coira marched the rest of the way to the car, looking as if she was going to give him an earful. Which meant Tuck would be subjected to that earful, too. *Can't I catch a break?*

The moment John saw his mother-in-law was apparent. He went from leaning casually against the vehicle, to attention, and then a wary expression crossed his face...and stayed there! In the next second, he got into the backseat of the car, as if he couldn't stand to look at his mother-in-law for another moment.

Great! Now the earful would happen within a closed area.

Tuck stowed Coira's duffel in the boot and then opened the car door for her.

He was barely inside—not even having a chance to turn on the radio for tuning them out—when Coira lit into John.

"Were ye here to see yere wife?"

"No," John answered in a monotone.

"Then why were ye here?"

"To check on the boat."

"Couldn't ye have had the decency to see Maggie, too?"

John pursed his lips. "Ye know, she wouldn't approve of me being out on the water."

Tuck knew it was more than that. Something much deeper was at play. *John's not ready yet to resume his old life.* But it wasn't Tuck's place to get involved so he kept his damn mouth shut. He was just the reluctant chauffeur.

He managed to turn the radio on then. He glanced at John in the rearview mirror and the beat up fisherman shot Tuck a grateful nod back for the noise.

But John didn't realize it was self-serving. Tuck needed time to think. He had his own problems waiting for him back in Whussendale.

Machinery to fix.

A date he needed to break.

248

And Ryn...the woman he cared about, who was giving him the cold shoulder. *Literally*, he thought, remembering the missed kiss this morning.

∞∞

Maggie put the pillow over her head, trying to block out the knocking at her front door. She'd done well ignoring everyone since she'd arrived home in Gandiegow. On other days, there'd been knocking, too, but she hadn't answered, and eventually, whomever it was had finally gone away.

But this person was persistent. *Too persistent*. If it'd been family, they would've come on in—Ross and Ramsay to get Dand, and Rowena and Sinnie to get Irene. Mum had only stayed an hour in her cottage with her, before Rowena and Sinnie convinced their mother she needed to give Maggie space. *Thank the Almighty for that*.

Maggie rolled out of bed and trudged down the hallway toward the knocking. When she opened the door, Emma, the town's therapist, stood there, prim and proper as any Englishwoman...and very determined.

"Good. I see you are up." Emma plowed her way in. "My knuckles were beginning to bruise. Tea?" She walked straight to the kitchen, grabbed the kettle, and filled it. "I hope you have biscuits. The news I bring requires the chocolate ones."

"What are ye talking about?" Maggie just wanted to crawl back into bed. "Can't we do this later?"

"No. It has to happen now. We have all given you space. Though your family asked me to speak with you earlier, I respected that you wanted to be left alone."

Maggie rubbed her eyes. "Then why are ye here now?"

Emma gave her a wry look. "Because I drew the *short straw* at Quilting Central."

"Ye're not making sense," Maggie said.

"Sit. We'll talk after the water boils and while the tea steeps." Emma dug around in the cabinets. "Ah, here we go—Tunnock's Tea Cakes." She made a tray with two teacups, the tea cakes, and napkins. The kettle whistled and she poured the water into the prepared teapot. She brought it all in on the tray and set it on the coffee table.

"Say what ye came to say so I can go back to bed." Maggie didn't mean to be rude, but her patience was worn thin from all the trials in the last couple of months. She took a deep breath and tried again. "Tell me what's going on."

Emma took her hand. "John was in Gandiegow today."

"What?" Maggie looked around as if he was going to pop out from behind the couch. "Where?"

Emma looked at her with a sad expression. "He's already gone back to Whussendale."

"I can't believe he was here and didn't come to see me. To see us!" Maggie's soul ached. What happened to her warrior husband, who had her believing in love, when she'd seen nothing but arguments between her own parents growing up?

"He saw Dand," Emma said.

"How did he see Dand? Dand was with Ramsay. Ramsay would've let me know if John was in town." Maggie, still in shock, couldn't believe the news. She wanted to ask how John was doing. And part of her wanted him to be suffering as much as she was.

"Yes, Ramsay and Dand were together." Emma paused and Maggie knew she wasn't going to like what came next. "On the boat. John, Ross, Ramsay, and Dand all went out on the boat together."

"No!" Maggie said. "The doctor agreed with me that John shouldn't fish anymore. It's too dangerous."

"And yet, John was out on the boat this afternoon."

Maggie stood and paced across the floor. "How did John get to Gandiegow?"

Emma sighed. "You are not going to like this either. It was Tuck."

"Tuck?" Maggie was sick and tired of Tuck MacBride meddling in her life...*ruining it.*

Emma guided her back to the sofa. "Here. Have some tea." She poured both of them a cup and then unwrapped two tea cakes.

"Why?" Maggie repeated, more to herself than Emma. "Why didn't he come to see me?"

"I have a theory," Emma said. She took a sip of tea and a nibble of the tea cake. "Take a bite. It really will cheer you up."

"What's your theory?" Maggie drank a little tea and the warm liquid felt good to her dry throat.

"John views himself as a different person now," Emma started.

"He's still the same man," Maggie argued. "He's just had an accident, is all."

"You and I know that, but John has to figure it out for himself. Not to be too *new age*, but your husband will have to find himself, find his place in this new world of limited possibilities first, before he can go back to being part of his relationship with you. He's looking for his *worth.*"

"But he can do that with his loving family around him," Maggie reasoned.

"Apparently, he wants to do it on his own. And no matter how much you want to rush him and how much it's going to hurt, you're going to have to let him. For now, he's decided this is a journey he has to take alone."

Maggie put her head in her hands, wanting to hide from the truth. She was surprised her hands were wet from tears. "And what if he doesn't *find himself?*"

Emma laid her hand on Maggie's back, rubbing circles into it.

"Do you really want to be with a man who isn't who he ought to be?"

"I don't know," Maggie said.

"I think the answer will come to you. You are a strong woman, Maggie. Stronger than most. You are going to have to find a way to work through this. For your children's sake. I'll be here every step of the way. The whole village will be. You know that."

Maggie heard the underlying message and she couldn't imagine it. Would it be better to raise the kids on her own, than for John to be with them, and for him to not be the man that they all knew him to be?

The front door swung open and Dand ran in, but he stopped short. "Mum, ye're up?"

Maggie straightened. "Aye. My nap is over with."

Ramsay entered the cottage and shut the door. He looked surprised to see Maggie, too, and he stared at her as if she was a complete mess. Which she was.

Dand came over and leaned against her. "Ye've been crying again."

That tore her up inside.

Dand turned her cheek so she could look at him. "The greatest thing happened today. Da came to Gandiegow."

"That's what Emma was telling me," Maggie said bravely. It was hard to keep her heartache to herself—John ignoring her felt like a betrayal. *But I have to be strong for my children.*

"He went on the boat with me. I caught a fish, Mum," Dand said excitedly. She could see he was pouring his heart into every word, trying to get her excited, too.

"Ross and I were there," Ramsay said. As if that would lessen the blow.

"Well, I think this is great news," Emma piped in, smiling at Dand. "You should go write your father a letter and tell him how much it meant to you to see him today."

"That's a good idea." Ramsay shot Emma a grateful look and steered Dand down the hall to his room.

Emma gazed steadily at Maggie. "I could be wrong, but I think John coming to town today was progress."

"Aye. At least he spent time with his son." But Maggie worried. She might never get back the man she married. The strongest man she'd ever known.

20

R YN SAT IN THE BALLROOM, putting fabric kits together for the upcoming retreat on Friday. Though Ryn was teaching her True Colors quilt again—to a group of out-of-town quilters—the pressure was off. Coira had taken over the administrative duties of the retreat, becoming Whussendale's *Deydie*. Bossy, but tolerable.

Ryn was getting hungry and told herself as soon as she was done with the next kit, she'd wander into the kitchen to see what Mrs. McNabb was whipping up for lunch.

She glanced up to see Sophie.

Sophie peered around cautiously before stepping in, and pulling the pocket doors closed behind her. "Good. Ye're here. And alone." She acted weird, which was out of character for her.

"What's up?" Ryn said. "Did the red fabric arrive?" But clearly it hadn't, because Sophie held nothing. The only thing she had was the worried expression on her face.

"No fabric yet." Sophie quickly walked over and sat down.

Ryn was starting to get nervous. "What's wrong? Is Tuck okay?"

Sophie shook her head. "He's fine." She paused. "He's well, for now."

"Tell me."

"I saw something, and then I've heard several accounts of the same story. I don't want to gossip, but I care about ye."

Ryn braced herself, feeling whatever it was, it had to do with Tuck.

"Pence and Pound Everpenny—sister and brother twins who work at the wool mill—said Lara told them she's going on a date with Tuck on Friday night." Sophie's pitch rose higher with every word. "Is it true?"

Ryn's world tilted and she couldn't speak.

Sophie wrung her hands. "I saw Lara and Tuck together and wondered what was up. Lara's body language spoke volumes, if ye know what I mean."

Ryn had a hard time pulling herself together, but she finally did, at least enough to say something. Though it was a lie. "Well, good for them. I hope they have a lovely time."

Sophie frowned, clearly not getting the response she expected. "Don't you care that Mrs. McNabb saw Lara leave just now for Inverness to buy a new dress?"

Ryn turned away from Sophie's intense gaze. "It's their business. I don't have a say in what goes on in Tuck's life, one way or another."

"But you and Tuck? I thought you had an understanding."

Ryn examined her nails, focusing on how they needed filing. What she wanted was to find Lara and tell her to stay away from her man. "Tuck and I don't have anything." But it wasn't true. They'd shared so much. "We're just friends."

Sophie scooted her chair back, looking ready to argue, but the pocket door slid open.

And the devil himself walked in!

Tuck nodded to them both. "Have ye seen Lara? I stopped by the dye shack, the café, and her place. I can't find her. And I need to speak with her now."

Sophie peered at Ryn and raised an eyebrow, giving her an *I-told-you-so* look. Her eyes conveyed another message: *You better lock him down tight quickly, or you're going to regret it.* But maybe that was just Ryn's imagination.

Ryn felt stupid, as if she'd shrunk to two-inches tall. How could Tuck come in here and confirm so boldly his budding relationship with Lara? Especially, after what he and Ryn had shared! Even though the fault lay with her—for she had pushed him away—anger rose up inside.

Ryn lashed out, wanting to show Tuck she didn't give two pennies about his new affair. "We heard Lara is off to Inverness, buying a new dress for her date *with you*. You really need to keep track of your women. Perhaps a spreadsheet of their comings and goings would help."

"What?" Tuck looked stricken. "Shite." He shook his head. "Listen, Ryn—"

But Ryn had picked up her glass of water and was marching for the door. "Sophie, I'll see you later. I'm hungry. I'll be back in a bit."

Her appetite had disappeared, soured by bad news. She stomped off toward the kitchen.

Two seconds later, Tuck caught up to her, gently taking her arm and bringing her to a stop. "Hold up."

Ryn pulled away, pretty sure she was going to blubber if he spoke to her. "Not now, Tuck. I'm not in the mood." She went into the kitchen, but was afraid he might come after her, so she ran straight out the back door.

She needed a few moments alone to pull herself together. Sophie had mentioned a cabin in the woods and had even pointed out the direction. Ryn wasn't sure she could find it, but anything was better than standing around here, waiting for Tuck to see her cry.

She walked across the driveway toward what looked like a path and slipped in between the trees. The act of walking with a purpose—being intent on finding this cabin—brought Ryn's thoughts into line. *Physical therapy for the broken hearted,* she thought ruefully. The farther she went, the clearer the path seemed—on both how to get to the cabin, and how she would spend the rest of her time in Scotland.

Ryn wouldn't take this *Lara-Tuck* thing lying down. She wasn't a wimp. She had to do something. It might not be right, but Lara couldn't have Tuck. At least not now, while Ryn was alive and breathing in Scotland.

The forest opened into a clearing and on the other side sat the rustic, but quaint cabin. She slowed her pace and walked toward it, thinking about her plan.

Though she couldn't have a future with Tuck, she could have him for the meantime. He could be part of her life...until she left.

She wanted his companionship. She wanted him in her bed. And for once in her life, she wouldn't be some dreamy-eyed woman who fantasized about finding her one true love. Or have them nestled into a four bedroom house and growing old together, before dessert had been served on their first official date. She was going into this brief torrid affair with her eyes wide open.

Of course, someone would have to tell Lara to lay off Tuck. Ryn appointed herself to deliver the news!

She made her way across the field and knocked on the cabin door. When no one answered, she looked around first before going in. But she wasn't alone. Tuck stood on the other side of the field, gazing at her with his hands on his hips.

She stood her ground, staring back...*eyes wide open*. He strode toward her and didn't slow down when he got near. When he stepped onto the cabin's porch, he gently gathered her into his arms and kissed her…the first real kiss they'd had since they'd made out in her cottage many nights ago. She didn't push him away and he certainly didn't seem as if he was letting go anytime soon.

The kiss went on and on, becoming more passionate with each second. Ryn felt good about her decision to be with Tuck…for now. Of course, the kiss might've had something to do with sealing her resolve.

Finally, Tuck eased back a little, cupping her neck. "Why did ye leave so quickly, luv? It used to be I didn't mind a little cat and mouse." He brushed back her hair. "But I don't want games between us, Ryn." He paused as if he wanted her to absorb that truth. "You have it all wrong why I need to speak with Lara."

Anger at hearing Lara's name made Ryn pull away. At the same time, her phone dinged that a text had come in. She ignored it. She and Tuck had business to discuss. "You have to tell Lara that the date is off."

He grinned at Ryn. "Aye."

"I mean it. I don't want to play games either," she said.

Tuck smoothed her hair, as if he was trying to ease away her ruffled feathers. "Don't worry. That's the reason I was looking for Lara. I needed to cancel." He took a deep breath, as if an explanation was coming. "Immediately after agreeing to go with her to the céilidh, I knew I couldn't do it. *Because of you.* Because of me and you together." He paused, giving Ryn plenty of eye contact. "But, luv, ye have to understand why I considered Lara's offer. Ye haven't exactly been the most welcoming of lasses in the last several weeks."

Ryn nodded. "Yes. I know. I'm sorry."

This time Ryn's phone jangled with a call. Once again, she ignored it.

Tuck pointed to her ringing pocket. "Do ye need to take it?"

"This isn't the time," Ryn said.

"Ye have more important things to do?" He took her into his arms again.

"*Aye.*" She leaned in, pressed herself against him, and wrapped her arms around his neck. "Kiss me, Tuck."

He laughed as he bent down to oblige. "I like a woman who knows what she wants."

And yes, Ryn wanted him.

The kiss was full of promise. A kiss like theirs could only lead to one thing—*making love.*

As Tuck's lips moved to her neck, planting a row of kisses there, Ryn issued out another order. "Inside the cabin. Now." She hoped there was a bed where they could consummate their torrid affair. And wouldn't it be romantic if he carried her over the threshold?

But that kind of thinking was what had gotten her into trouble from the moment she first noticed boys…beyond them pulling her pigtails and her stealing their GI Joes. Ken had nothing on those soldiers.

Tuck shook his head and seemed reluctant to stop kissing her, but he did. "Nay. We can't be together. Not yet. I have to speak with Lara first to make things clear."

Ryn looked at him, hoping he would be specific on how he meant to make things *clear*. In her experience, most men didn't understand the concept of the word.

"I'm taken," he said, pinning a bow on Ryn's hope. They were on the same page.

Ryn's phone rang again.

"Answer it," he said. "It must be important for them to keep calling and texting.

Caller ID showed it was Sophie and Ryn answered.

Sophie jumped right in. "Are ye okay? Where are you? I went to your cottage, but ye're not there."

Ryn glanced up at Tuck. "I'm standing outside the cabin. I hope it's okay that I came here."

"Of course, it's okay. You can use the cabin anytime. Are ye alone?"

"No," Ryn said truthfully.

Sophie's smile could be heard through the phone. "Good. But let Tuck know Lara just arrived back in town."

ಐಐಂ

Tuck watched as Ryn's frown grew. What had Sophie just said? Ryn hung up and didn't keep him waiting.

"I have a message for you," she said. "Lara's back in Whussendale."

Tuck pulled Ryn into his arms and hugged her. "There's no reason to feel jealous. I told ye where I stand. Lara is a nice lass and she's owed an explanation from me, that's all."

"I know." Ryn pouted.

"Come on. Head back to the castle with me."

"No. Not right now. While I'm here, I want to go in and check out the cabin."

"Are ye sure you're okay?"

"I'll return to Kilheath soon. Coira will be looking for me. And I still have a lot to do to get ready for the retreat."

"Tonight then?" he sounded eager to his own ears.

She smiled at him. "Yes. Tonight."

He kissed her goodbye and left her standing outside the cabin as he walked back across the field.

He pulled out his phone and texted Lara: Can you meet me at the café in 15 minutes?

Tuck really wasn't looking forward to this conversation. But he'd been rash and now he had to let Lara down as gently as he could. An idea floated down from heaven, as if the Almighty had taken mercy on him.

Tuck rang up Declan.

"Do you have plans this Friday night?" Tuck asked.

"I don't know. Why?" Declan said suspiciously.

"Ye know Lara?"

"Aye," Declan said.

"Can ye take her to the céilidh in Lasswool on Friday?"

"That's a strange question coming from ye, as word around the wool mill is that ye're taking Lara yereself." Declan could be such a smartass.

Tuck sighed. "Do me a favor, mate. Ye take Lara and I'll owe you one. She's a nice lass."

"Tell me why ye're not taking her yereself." Declan seemed to want to dig in and annoy Tuck more.

"I realized I wasn't free," Tuck said honestly.

"The American lass?" Declan replied. "Gossip is ye're quite the stud for having two women on the ropes."

"Just one," Tuck said. "Just Ryn." *I'm off the market.* And the thought made Tuck smile. "I'm on my way to speak to Lara now. Can I tell her ye'll take my place? That's, of course, if she'll have ye."

"Sure, I'll take her," Declan said. "As ye said, she's a nice lass."

"Good man," Tuck said. "We'll talk later." He rung off and made his way out of the woods.

The wool mill's café only had five small round tables in the cramped dining area. Lara sat at the back. Two teacups and two biscuits waited along with her. She gave him a wide smile and held up a shopping bag.

Tuck felt awful she'd bought a new dress for their date. He'd have to find a way to pay her back. He took his seat.

Lara grabbed his arm. "I can't wait until Friday so ye can see my new outfit." She beamed. "On sale, only twenty pounds!"

Tuck leaned forward. "I'm really sorry, Lara, but I'm going to have to break our date."

"But only this morning…" Lara looked so disappointed.

"Aye. This morning. I misspoke."

"It's Ryn, isn't it?" Lara sat back and used her thumb to point out the window, as if an apparition of Ryn stood there watching in. "She's to blame."

What could Tuck say that didn't sound foolish—like *my heart belongs to the American lass*—or anything else that might hurt Lara more?

He told her the truth. "I'm to blame for not being clear within myself as to where I stood. But now I am. If ye're willing, Declan would like to take my place at the céilidh. I spoke with him already about it."

Lara crumbled her biscuit, bit by bit. "I guess I could go with Declan." She glanced down at the shopping bag beside her.

"He's a good man," Tuck reminded her. "Definitely an upgrade from me, I'd say."

He watched as she mulled over the idea of Declan. Reluctantly, she nodded.

"Am I forgiven?" Tuck asked.

"Aye, forgiven. But only if Declan is a good dancer, doesn't step on my toes, and I have a good time." She gave Tuck a small smile.

Tuck stood. "I'll tell him to brush up on his dance moves before Friday. Okay?"

"Okay."

He said goodbye and went to the counter to pay for their tea and biscuits. He added an extra twenty. "Can ye give this to Lara after I leave? Tell her the dress is on me. She'll know what it means."

As he walked outside, he stared in the direction of the castle, thinking of Ryn. Thinking of tonight. Thinking he really couldn't wait!

He texted her: Tonight feels like an eternity away. Meet me at my cottage now?

He watched his screen for her reply, willing her answer to be positive. Within seconds, a message came in. His heart soared momentarily, but his good mood was dashed when he saw the text wasn't from Ryn, but from John.

Can you take me to my appointment at the hospital?

When? Tuck asked.

Now.

Dammit! But he owed John.

Tuck texted Ryn back first. Sorry. John needs a ride to his appointment. I'll see you tonight.

Ryn replied with both a sad face and a smiley face.

Tuck answered John. I'll meet you at the car.

Minutes later, Tuck found John leaning against his vehicle. He seemed to be scrolling through the pictures on his phone. Tuck wanted to tell him to go home to see his wife and children in person…instead of on his phone.

"What's wrong with you?" John asked.

Besides you cramping my love life? "Nothing," Tuck said. "Ready?"

"Aye." John pocketed his phone and got in the car.

Tuck felt a little guilty for having an attitude. "Physical therapy today?"

"Aye."

Tuck turned on the radio, but John turned it off.

"How is the American lass feeling? Back to normal after her surgery?"

To Tuck, the question felt as if it had come from nowhere. "Ryn? She's feeling much better."

"I saw her a while ago, as she stormed out of the castle. She definitely had more fire in her than when we rode back from the hospital together." He didn't even pause. "Ye fancy her?"

Shocked, Tuck glanced John's way and John stared back. The man's eyes had mischief in them. Tuck hadn't seen that much life in John since before the accident.

"Have ye gotten bored with helping around the wool mill and decided to start playing matchmaker now?" Immediately, Tuck wondered if the sarcastic response would hit John the wrong way. But dammit, everyone should quit pussy-footing around the man.

John's grunt was part laugh. "Aye. Ye're sweet on her. My brothers are quite happy with their American wives. I suppose ye will be, too."

"What?" Tuck sputtered.

"Never mind." John turned back on the radio, acting pleased with himself for rattling him. But then he turned the radio off, looking serious, all playfulness gone. "Don't wait too long to tell her how ye feel. Do ye hear?"

"Really?" Tuck shook his head. "Ye've got a lot of advice for me about my relationship, when ye're a man living apart from yere own wife?"

He expected John to take his head off, but instead he exhaled deeply.

"Touché," John said.

"How about we make a pact?" Tuck suggested.

"What kind of pact?" John asked skeptically.

"We should both work on winning over our prospective women."

"I don't know," John said, sounding a bit defeated.

"What do you have to lose?" Tuck waited a moment, but John didn't answer him. "Think about it, okay?"

John didn't reply and was quiet for a while, which was fine with Tuck. He was consumed with what John had said. He cared about Ryn a lot. *But marriage?* He wasn't that kind of bloke anymore. He wasn't Andrew. Or John. Or any of the other happily married men in

Gandiegow or Whussendale.

Tuck looked over at his companion and saw John's melancholy draped over him like a veil. "Hey, on machine two, I noticed a couple of the headles need to be adjusted," Tuck said. "Any suggestions on the best way to go about it, so the machine isn't down too long?"

John's blank stare turned to interest. "We could have a replacement shaft ready. Pop the old one out, put the new one in."

The two of them discussed the upcoming maintenance for the rest of the trip, and Tuck couldn't help but be amazed at how comfortable they'd become with each other.

When they reached the hospital, Tuck dropped off John and parked. Once inside, he bought a newspaper, which he carried to the lobby and read. Much later, John came through the double doors, looking worn and drawn. A jab of guilt hit Tuck, but it was nothing compared to the guilt he'd felt immediately after the accident. It occurred to him his guilt was waning. He wondered what that could mean.

Without speaking, Tuck folded his newspaper and followed John out to the car. For the first half of the trip back, the car was silent, except the sounds of the engine and the wheels on the road.

Tuck was so wrapped up in his own thoughts—Ryn, John's trials, and what needed to be done at the wool mill—that when John spoke, his meaning didn't register.

"What?" Tuck asked, glancing at him.

"I don't blame ye," John said quietly.

Tuck's mind whirled. *Surely, he isn't talking about his injury.* Tuck peeked at John out of his peripheral vision.

"The accident." John stared straight ahead, as if seeing a different view out the front window than was actually there. "I know I aimed my anger at you, but I blame myself."

Tuck didn't know what to say.

John continued on, as if he had replied. "Aye, ye should've been there on time, but the truth is, I had a lot on my mind with Maggie being so upset over losing her da the night before. I was reckless and careless. And carelessness and fishing don't mix." John held out his amputated arm. "The fault is not yeres, 'tis mine."

Tuck felt confused and oddly vulnerable. *If I'm not to blame, then where does that leave me?*

21

RYN SAT IN THE BALLROOM with Coira, Sophie, and someone new to her, Pence Everpenny. The four of them were working hard on the retreat for tomorrow. Well, at least three of them were. Ryn had a hard time focusing on the fabric lying in front of her. Like a boomerang, her thoughts kept returning to Tuck, instead of the looming quilt retreat ahead. Coira had to keep her on task, or else Ryn would still be sitting in the kitchen, staring off into space, dreaming about the evening activities planned with Tuck.

"Come now," Coira chided, and not very kindly. She must've gone to the Deydie school of management. "Ye have to get those kits done or else the lassies from Dumfries will have nothing to work with when they get here in the morn."

"Yes. I know," Ryn said, sorting the fabric.

"'Tis a nice design ye made," Coira said. The turnabout seemed as if she was trying to coax Ryn into keeping her mind here, instead of elsewhere.

Sophie's phone rang. When she answered it, she turned and smiled at Ryn. "All right." She paused. "Okay. I'll let her know."

She hung up and grinned widely. "That was Tuck. He and John are back."

"And?" Ryn said, knowing there was more.

"He wants to know if we need him for anything." Sophie looked ready to bust out laughing. "Ryn, do you?"

Yes, Ryn needed Tuck, but she certainly wasn't going to say so.

Coira tilted her head to the side. "Are ye sweet on Tuck?"

Ryn started to deny it, but Sophie jumped in first.

"Coira, we have this, don't we? Ryn should head back to her cottage and rest. It takes a long time to heal from surgery." Sophie was laying it on thick.

Coira squinted at her as if her glasses couldn't examine the situation close enough. Finally, she answered. "Aye. But don't be late in the morn."

Ryn didn't hang around, in case she changed her mind. She said goodnight and hurried home, anticipation quickening her pace. From her spot in the road, Ryn could see the lights on in Tuck's cottage.

"I guess that's where we're going to meet," she said to the wind.

She knocked on his door, and when he answered, she had to laugh. His sleeves were pushed up to his elbows and his masculine hands wore yellow rubber gloves. "Suzy Homemaker?"

But then she noticed his face—full of emotion. Yes, he was happy to see her, but there was something more there. Vulnerability?

He pulled her in, closed the door, and then hauled her in for a kiss. Once again, it was full of emotion.

"Are you all right?" she asked.

"Just a trying day."

"Maybe I can make it better."

"Ye have already."

His words made her insides go all gooey and warm. He'd done so much for her—making her feel welcome in Scotland, his friendship, and taking care of her. It thrilled her she could do the same for him. Not to repay him, but just to be there for him, like he was for her. She whispered in his ear, "Make love to me, Tuck."

Her words turned him feverish and he kissed her hard, only to pull away quickly. He searched her eyes. "Can we? But aren't you still recovering?"

She nodded. "I'm fine. I *Googled* it. As long as we're careful, it'll be okay." She wanted him so badly that even if every website doctor in the world said she had to wait another week, she was going to be with Tuck tonight anyway! But everywhere she checked online, the news was good. She slipped her hands inside his clothing and pushed his jacket from his shoulders.

He looked conflicted. "Gawd, Ryn, I know I should be strong and insist we wait—"

"It's okay. I promise to tell you if something starts to hurt." She wrapped her arms around his neck and pulled him down. "Now kiss me."

He surprised her by gently scooping her off her feet and into his arms, and then carrying her to his bed.

She laid her head on his shoulder. "Tell me you have some protection?"

"Always," he said. And then as if realizing how that might sound, he sputtered, "I mean, it's best to—"

She put a finger to his lips. "Don't worry about it." She knew his heart.

"No other woman has ever looked at me the way ye do. As if you see who I really am."

"You're a good man, Tuck MacBride." The best man she'd ever known. "Do me a favor, though. Lose the rubber gloves."

He laid her on the bed and as he rid himself of the gloves, she felt compelled to warn him.

"My incisions…are ugly," she said, hugging her stomach.

"Nay, they couldn't be ugly if they're yeres. Everything about you is beautiful." He seemed so sincere she couldn't help but believe he spoke from his heart.

He leaned over to kiss her as he got in the bed with her. "Ryn, I care for you so much. I think I—,"

She silenced him by putting her finger to his lips again. "No talking." If he was going to announce his feelings, and later, it turned out to be bullshit, she didn't want to hear it. For this moment, she wanted to believe he cared for her...*deeply*. She needed rose-colored glasses now. She needed him.

Tuck made love to her like no one ever had. His bed became a world unto its own, where her past and his past didn't exist. When they were done, they held each other and dozed. Somewhere in the night, they made love again, and she knew she'd fallen in love with him. All would've been right with the world, except the reality was this magical time couldn't last.

Deep in her heart, she couldn't pull off being a *torrid affair type of woman*. She'd never been the kind to even have a one-night-stand. Also, if they kept making love like this, sooner or later, she would start planning a future for him and her, which wasn't going to happen. Because Tuck wouldn't want her, if he knew the truth. She couldn't have him for always. *Only for now.* What a lie she told herself that she could have an affair, a fling, and walk away unscathed. She fell back to sleep and woke with a start.

"'Tis yere phone," Tuck said, groggily. He reached over the side of the bed and then handed her phone to her.

"Hello," Ryn said, her morning voice sounding more like Kermit the Frog's than her own.

"Where are ye?" Deydie hollered. "I'm here. Ye're not."

Ryn sat up. "What time is it?"

"Ye're late! Get yere arse to the castle. The retreat is set to start in eighteen minutes."

270

"Oh crap," Ryn said. "I'll be right there."

All her doubt came back. Her love for Tuck was for naught. She'd been warm and cozy in his arms through the night, but the cold hard truth of the morning smacked her, surely as if Deydie had whacked her with her broom. Ryn pulled the quilt up, covering her nakedness.

Tuck stood, grabbing his boxers. "Let me make ye some tea before ye go."

"No. I have to get over to my cottage." Ryn felt awkward, their dreamy bubble ruptured with a single phone call. "I need a quick shower. Deydie sounds like she's going to skin me alive."

Ryn cringed at Tuck's frown. He knew she was pulling away. But he just didn't understand.

"I'll see you tonight?" he asked.

When she hesitated, his frown grew.

"I don't know." She slipped on her shirt and snatched up her bra, clutching it in her hand. "So much to do."

Tuck turned his back on her and Ryn wondered if that was an omen of things to come.

৪৩৫৫

Maggie pulled up to Kilheath Castle, her nerves threatening to overtake her as she turned off the car. "I shouldn't be here." No matter how many times she said she wasn't going to check up on John, she couldn't help herself. She ached for him.

She looked around the grounds of the castle, but saw no one. She could've saved on petrol by riding along with Deydie an hour earlier, but that would've required dodging Deydie's questions as to why Maggie had wanted to come to Whussendale.

"I have every right to be here. I'm here to help with the retreat, is all." That would be her excuse when she was asked. And she would be asked. The truth was Maggie couldn't stand it anymore. She had to get a glimpse of her husband.

She pulled out her phone and texted her mother: I've come to help. Meet me outside.

Sure, Maggie could walk in alone, but she'd feel better if her mum was beside her. She and Coira didn't always get along, but that didn't mean she didn't love her. *And need her.* The one thing she did know was she and her mum got along much better when they weren't living in the same village. *Mother-daughter relationships are complicated,* Maggie thought.

She got out of the car as Coira came through the kitchen door.

"Get in here," her mother said, with a confused expression on her face. "I didn't know ye were coming. We better hurry. We're set to start any minute."

At that moment, John and Tuck came from around the other side of the castle and halted as soon as they saw her. What seemed weird to Maggie was how the two of them looked like a couple of chums. But how could John and Tuck be friends? Especially after what Tuck had done.

Maggie couldn't hear what Tuck said to her husband, but his words looked in earnest. At first John shook his head *no,* and Tuck's response was to shove John in *her direction*!

What in hell is going on here? She felt like she'd stepped into an alternate universe, as John walked toward her and with Tuck grinning in the background.

"What are ye waiting for?" Coira said.

Maggie didn't know.

John stopped in front of her, looking as if this was his first time he'd been this close to her. "Do ye want to go on a walk with me?"

The question took her off-guard. "When?"

"Now." He cranked his head around and glanced at Coira, then back at Maggie. "If ye can get away."

Giddiness built inside her, the same way it had the first time John had asked her out when they were teens.

"Okay," Maggie said.

"This way." John led her toward the loch behind the castle.

Maggie hadn't felt this happy in a long time. And she wondered then, if she'd dropped the ball. Had she let the weight of parenting, housekeeping, and life in general, keep her from putting her relationship with John first? For being with John made her feel as if she was her best self. And she loved her husband more than anything in the world.

"Maggie," her mum hollered. "I thought ye were going to help with the retreat."

Maggie smiled at John and then at her mother. "I got a better offer."

John took her hand and Maggie leaned into him.

She didn't want to ruin what was happening, but she had to know. "Tell me. What's going on with you and Tuck?"

৪০03

Tuck watched as Maggie and John walked away, hand in hand, and he felt pretty great about himself. He'd forced John to talk to his wife and it looked as if things were going well. But now Tuck was stuck fixing the carding machine on his own.

He resisted every temptation to go inside and check in on Ryn. *Just to see her.* He didn't understand why or how things had become awkward between them this morning. Everything had been spot-on. More than spot-on. It had been perfect! He'd never felt like this about a woman. Not even Elspeth. And he was beginning to see just how much of a boy he'd been back then. A strange thought crossed his mind. *I should forgive Elspeth.* He looked up at heaven. That was the one thing he'd sworn he would never do. But now, his feelings for Elspeth seemed inconsequential when compared with how he felt about Ryn in the here and now.

"I wish you well, Elspeth. Wherever you may be," he said, as he walked down the road, though only the trees on either side heard him. He meant it, really meant it, and his step became lighter.

When he arrived at the wool mill, Lara bounded out of the dye shack. "Hold up."

Tuck stopped and waited for her to join him. "How was the date with Declan?"

"Good. And I wanted to tell you that you were right."

"I like the sound of that. It's not something I hear very often. But what am I right about?"

Lara flipped her hair at Tuck. "Declan was a much better choice for me." She laughed, nearly skipping as she made her way to the office.

When Tuck arrived at the carding area, he got right to work on the scribbler machine. The problem wasn't an easy one, which was great for him. He needed something to distract himself from the problem with Ryn. Two hours passed before the scribbler was working again. Moments later, John arrived.

"Where's Maggie?" Tuck asked.

"She went home to the kids." John knelt down to inspect Tuck's work.

"I thought you might go home with her."

"Not today." John patted Tuck on the back. "You and I are heading back into the city to pick up my prosthetic."

"Now?"

"Aye."

Tuck looked at his greasy hands. "Let me clean up first."

Fifteen minutes later, they were on the road.

Tuck glanced over at John, who was grinning. "I take it things went well on yere walk?"

"I think she's forgiven me for being a horse's arse."

"That's good," Tuck said, feeling his world tilt a little bit back into place.

"And you? How has it worked out with Maggie's cousin?" John asked.

Tuck didn't know what to say. "I think I messed it up. And I'm not sure what I did."

"Aye," John said, as if he'd experienced the same phenomenon in his own relationship.

"Everything was fine. Wonderful even. And then things changed."

"They always do," John said. *"Take heart.* That's my only advice."

"Ryn can't have kids," Tuck blurted out, though he had no idea why. But maybe it'd been weighing on his mind. "I'll kick yere arse if ye tell anyone. I'm not supposed to know."

John stared at him, circumspect. "First, of course, ye can trust me not to tell anyone. And secondly, how do you know Ryn can't have kids?"

"I overheard her tell Cait."

"Oh?" John said. "Overheard?"

"The window was open. It's not like I had my ear pressed to the wall or anything."

John nodded, seeming satisfied. "I can tell ye have feelings for the lass. Is this a game-changer?"

"It's not like we're getting married or anything. It's just…I want her to know I'm okay with it." Tuck felt super awkward, wishing he hadn't brought up the subject. "In case, you know, things do go further."

"Are things going to go further?" John said.

"I don't know," Tuck said, feeling more than a little annoyed. And pressured. The truth was, he'd liked to see if he and Ryn could go the distance.

"How do ye feel about children? Would ye be okay not having

any bairns of yere own?"

"I've always liked kids. Hannah is great. So are Dand and Mattie. But I haven't been able to visualize having any of my own." Not since Elspeth. In the next second, Tuck had to acknowledge that wasn't true. Ryn had him thinking about having a family again. *With her!* And all the time, too. "We could adopt. Look at little Glenna and sixteen-year-old Harry. There are kids out there that need parents."

John nodded. "Then I think ye should talk to Ryn. Tell her ye're okay with adoption."

"We're not exactly to that point." Though Tuck had gotten there awfully fast himself. He was ready to have a serious conversation with her about the future. "Besides, it would be awkward. I'd have to admit to eavesdropping. And that would make me look like a bastard." He glanced at John. "I didn't do it on purpose. It was an accident."

"Let me think for a minute." John paused and stared out the front window as if pondering where he might set his fishing nets next. Finally he spoke, "If I were you, I'd drop hints here and there, to let her know where you stand. You know, say things like *I don't need children to be happy*. That way, it'll force her to bring up the subject, give her a chance to tell you that she can't have kids."

"I don't know," Tuck said honestly. "What if she doesn't take the bait?"

"Trust me, mate. It's the best way. Ryn will take the hint and understand. That way ye need not mention that ye eavesdropped. Women are so intuitive that it's scary." Once again, John acted as if he'd had firsthand experience. "Dangle the idea in front of her and she'll run with it. And all will be well."

"Okay," Tuck said. "But if this doesn't work, what am I going to do then?"

"We'll cross that bridge when we come to it." John smiled at him as if he had Tuck's back.

And Tuck realized that perhaps he had more than just Andrew for a brother. John had become a brother, too. How could they have gotten to this place? Especially after the journey they'd been on and the circumstances they'd been through.

Tuck waited in the lobby for John while he received his prosthetic. When he came out, John looked more than a little sheepish.

He lifted up his metal tonged hand. "It'll take some getting used to. But I'm determined."

On the way back, the two talked of everything and nothing, but along the way, they made some critical decisions about the maintenance schedule for the wool mill.

Tuck glanced over at John. "What are your plans in the upcoming days? I think ye should ask your wife to go on a picnic with you."

"That's actually not a bad idea. I know just the place to take her, too," John said. "And you? What's your next step with Ryn?"

"I'm going to ask her out."

John nodded. "It's about damn time."

The second Tuck arrived home in Whussendale, he texted Ryn: Let's go out tonight on a proper date.

Moments later, Ryn replied: I can't. Coira and I are hosting the quilters for dinner and then evening entertainment. I'm staying at the castle until the retreat is over. Deydie insists.

Desperation crowded in and Tuck couldn't ignore the truth any longer. Ryn was slipping away. And there wasn't a damn thing he could do about it.

Unless…he decided to sign up for the retreat, too.

ৡৎ

John walked swiftly from the car to his cottage, wanting to be alone for this phone conversation with Maggie. Helping Tuck with his love life had energized him into working on his own. The walk with Maggie this morning was a good start, but he needed to do more.

As soon as the door was closed behind him, he rang up his wife.

When she answered, John felt as if he could fly. Sail over Whussendale and straight into the harbor of Gandiegow.

"Would ye and the children like to go on a picnic with me today?"

"Where?" Maggie's voice sounded as light as a feather.

"'Tis a surprise." He held his breath, hoping she wanted to see him again as badly as he wanted to see her.

"I'd love to."

He'd have to call Ross and Ramsay to help out. And this would be John's first time driving since the accident. But nothing would keep him from his family now. "I'll pick you and the children up at three. Dress warm."

୨୦୧୧

Tuck knocked on Hugh's office door. "Can I speak with you for a minute?"

Hugh glanced up from his paperwork and motioned him in. "Have a seat."

Tuck paced instead. "I need to take some time off. Starting now." He watched Hugh's reaction and was relieved when the Laird didn't grimace.

"It's personal," Tuck added.

"Are ye needed in Gandiegow?" the Laird asked.

"Nay. I'll be here in Whussendale."

"So if we need ye, can we call?"

"Of course," Tuck said. "One more favor. May I use a computer?"

Hugh pointed toward his opened door. "Use the one in Tally's

278

office. I just turned it on for Lara. She'll be stopping by to order supplies for the dye shack."

"Thanks." Tuck headed across to the other office. He quickly searched online for the Whussendale Kilts and Quilts Retreat website, found it, and filled out the registration form. After paying, he printed out the receipt.

"If ye can't beat 'em, join 'em," Tuck said aloud as he snatched up the receipt and headed out the door, smiling. Once outside, he jogged to the castle.

He barely stopped when he reached the side door to the kitchen. He waved to Mrs. McNabb as he passed through. Tuck found Ryn exactly where he expected her—leading the class.

He knew he was smiling goofily at her, but dammit, he couldn't help himself. She looked up and saw him, and he tried not to be discouraged when her surprise turned into a frown.

Something poked him in the chest. He looked down to see Deydie glaring up.

"What are ye doing here?" She poked him again. "Ye've done enough, don't ye think, by making the lass late for the retreat."

Tuck opened his mouth to deny it.

"I know ye took advantage of Ryn. All of Whussendale has been buzzing about it. Leave now, before I find me a broom."

"Here." Tuck thrust the registration receipt at her.

"What's this?" She peered at it with her rheumy eyes.

He'd bested Deydie and couldn't help but smile. "I signed up for the quilt retreat. Where do ye want to put me?" He glanced around at the available spots.

Deydie's angry gaze flew back to him. "What are ye up to?"

"Learning how to quilt," he said, without missing a beat.

Sophie joined them with an index finger to her lips. "*Shhh.* Ye're disturbing the class."

Deydie shoved the registration slip under Sophie's nose. "How was he able to do this?"

Sophie took it and blushed. "I guess we should've closed registration when the class started."

"As ye can see, I paid for the retreat." He wasn't backing down. He was staying, with or without their permission. "Sophie, where would ye like for me to sit?"

By this time, Ryn's mouth was gaping open, as enough of their conversation had drifted to the front. Coira must've heard, too, because she was hustling her way through the tables to be part of the action.

"There's an extra spot at the first table," Sophie said.

"He can't stay," Deydie huffed.

Coira took the sheet from Sophie. "Aye. He can stay. Pick up yere kit over there and I'll get a sewing machine set up for ye."

Deydie opened her mouth, but Coira calmed her by laying a hand on the older woman's arm. "Ye wanted me to handle things here. And I will. Go on, Tuck."

As he walked to the side table, where the fabric kits sat, he couldn't help but thank his lucky stars that Coira had taken a liking to him from the beginning. If not for her, Deydie would've bounced him from the room.

Just as he was taking his seat upfront, Ryn called for a break.

"Be back in fifteen minutes."

All eyes were on her as she made a beeline for him.

She pulled him through the French door to the balcony. "What are you doing here?" Ryn's whispered hiss repeated Deydie's sentiments, word for word.

"The *quilting teacher* couldn't take time off to see me, so I decided to join the retreat."

She pinned him with an incredulous stare.

He continued on. "Men get a bad rap for not following up after a date."

"Last night was hardly a date," she argued.

"Still, ye know what I mean. If this was the only way to show you that I wanted to see you again, then so be it."

"Well, okay, so you showed me. I appreciate the gesture, but now go."

He shook his head. "Nope. I'm here for the long haul." His words took on new meanings, as they swirled around in his brain. The thought was frightening and he blurted out, "I don't want a family." That's what John had told him to say, wasn't it?

Immediately her eyes widened, and she looked vulnerable and hurt. "That's fine. I don't want one either." Her words were clipped as if she'd sheared them, especially close, for his ears only.

He tried again. "I'm happy with the way things are. Between us," he clarified. But her look said he'd only poured mud into the clear water. "What I mean is I'm not looking to have children and a family."

"Fine." She left the balcony, returning to the ballroom.

Tuck stared over the edge and considered jumping! How could he have screwed things up, making them worse? John's advice was probably sound for anyone else but him. Tuck had the unsettling feeling Ryn had just taken a step toward leaving his life forever.

Coira peeked her head outside. "All clear?"

Tuck didn't know who she was looking out for—Ryn, Sophie, or Deydie?

Coira hustled onto the balcony with him, bringing a small stack of fabric. "This is for you. I've already cut everything out so you can get to sewing right away. Do ye know how to use a sewing machine?"

Tuck hadn't met a machine he couldn't fix or run. "I'm a fast learner."

"Come inside and I'll get ye started."

Tuck followed her in, but didn't see Ryn anywhere.

"Over here," Coira said. At a sewing machine, up front, she positioned a red circle of fabric on top of a white square. After adjusting the machine in front of him, she stood back. "We're just going to rough edge this appliqué. Keep the edge of the presser foot right at the edge of the circle. Now, put yere foot on the pedal and press slowly."

Tuck did as she said, but apparently he was heavy-footed, because the machine raced ahead and his stitch ran off the circle. He quickly lifted his foot and the needle stopped plunging into the fabric.

"That's my fault," Coira said. "Let me get ye some practice fabric. I'll slow down the machine, too." She leaned over, clipped threads, and adjusted the controls.

He took the fabric from her and positioned it as she'd done before.

"Easy this time," Coira said.

Tuck had seen his mother sew...she'd made it look simple. But like with anything, he knew it would take practice. Gently he pressed the pedal with his foot and the needle eased into the fabric, slowly, consistently. He carefully shifted the fabric as he stitched around the circle.

Coira clapped her hands excitedly. "Ye weren't lying. Ye are a fast learner."

When he was done with the practice circle, she laid another on the throat of the machine. "Now, let's do one for real."

Tuck repeated the process and was able to handle the machine a little faster than a turtle's pace this time. By the time the retreat goers meandered back into the room, he was on his third circle block. The women crowded around and watched, as if he was a rare piece of china on display.

A heavy-set woman leaned close to him. "There's nothing sexier than a man who knows his way around a sewing machine." She had the gravelly voice of a two-pack a day sailor.

"Aye," said a tall woman, who winked at him.

"Lordy, the way ye handle that fabric and machine, why is it that ye aren't married?"

How did this woman from Dumfries know he wasn't married? He shouldn't be too surprised. The grapevine moved faster than the speed of light in Whussendale.

Just then, Ryn trudged into the room and her eyes found him. If he was reading her right, she didn't like that there were women gathered around him, drooling... as if he was a Cadbury Bar and they were hankering for chocolate. Tuck hoped Ryn understood he wasn't enjoying the attention either.

He stared back at Ryn, needing to get her alone so he could tell her again he didn't need bairns to be happy.

"I'll tell ye why I'm not married," he said to the crowd. "It takes a while to find the *right one*."

The women *oohed* and clucked as if he was Graham Buchanan, the movie star. Ryn looked away, and he was afraid his declaration hadn't been understood.

A large, buxom woman squeezed in between the women standing directly behind him. As she walked by, she ran her hand along his shoulder. Her strong perfume and overt gesture were overpowering and Tuck felt caged in.

Coira saved him. "Break it up." She waved her arms, as she barreled over and dispersed the crowd. "Ye've seen enough. Now back to yere seats so our American friend can show us the next step in making yere own Modern quilt."

Tuck's mobile dinged. When he looked down and saw the text from Hugh, he blessed the Laird for his timing. The weaving machine has seized up. Cut your vacation short.

It was just as well. Ryn wasn't responding as she should. She should be thrilled he cared enough to be there. Tuck turned off his sewing machine and stood.

"Where are ye going?" said Two-Pack-a-Day. "Ye only just got here."

He lifted his phone as evidence. "Duty calls." He stared at Ryn to get her reaction, but she was fussing with the fabric on her table, seemingly working hard not to meet his eyes.

Coira tugged on his sleeve. "Come by this evening and I'll help get ye caught up. I can't believe I'm going to say this to a man, but Tuck, I believe ye might be a gifted quilter."

"Thanks." But learning to stitch wasn't the reason he was here. "I'll see ye this evening."

Wouldn't it be grand if he could fix Ryn's feelings toward him as easily as he could fix the equipment at the wool mill?

He liked her. *Really liked her!* Now, he needed to convince Ryn that she should like him, too.

22

M AGGIE GRABBED HER children's coats hanging on the hook by the cottage door, and snatched up Irene as she toddled by. "Let's get bundled up."

Dand bounced up and down. "Where is Da taking us? To Spalding Farm? To the cliffs?"

"I don't know," Maggie said, for the umpteenth time. "Yere father said it's a surprise. He's on his way. Now put on yere hat."

The door opened and Irene squealed, trying to wiggle away from Maggie. John stood in the entryway, smiling and windblown. Maggie had missed her man looking this way.

"All ready?" With a mischievous grin, John set down the basket that smelled of fresh garlic bread from Gandiegow's restaurant, Pastas & Pastries. "Does anyone here want to go on a picnic?"

"I do!" Dand yelled.

Irene stumbled over to her father and into his opened arms. Dand was right behind her.

That's when Maggie noticed John's prosthetic. It all became real...what John had gone through. And she understood. How hard it must have been for a strong Scot to believe he was less! To her, John would always be the same. Her rock. The love of her life.

"Aye. I'm ready to go, too." Maggie felt such love for the man before her. "Are ye going to tell us yet where we're headed?"

John smiled. "Be patient."

He carried Irene and Dand gently grabbed a hold of the shiny tonged hook which replaced John's hand. Maggie stopped and held her breath, wondering if John would blow up again at their boy.

He smiled down at Dand. "I'm still learning how to use it. But I believe it'll be handy, don't ye?"

"Ye could make Uncle Ross and Uncle Ramsay call ye Captain Hook now, Da."

"Aye. I could," John answered, his voice a little strangled. *The nickname hurt.* Maggie saw the sting flash in her husband's eyes. Things weren't exactly perfect, but at least he was trying and they seemed to be on the right track now.

Since John had the kids under control, she grabbed the picnic basket and held the door open for them. "It smells great."

"Dominic fixed it up for us. Claire threw in a couple of chocolate chip scones for dessert."

Outside, it only took a few moments of heading in the direction of the docked boats to know what John was all about. The other two Armstrong brothers waited on Ramsay's tourist boat, holding children's life vests.

Maggie looked over at John. "A picnic on Ramsay's boat?"

John shrugged. "I thought it would be better suited for the family. The Indwaller is for business, not pleasure."

Maggie nodded. "Okay then." She put aside her trepidation, telling herself she was just happy her husband wanted to be with them, again.

Ross nodded to her. "It's a calm day for a cruise."

She looked out and it was indeed a calm day.

As John stepped aboard, he reached up and touched the cross which hung on the side of the wheelhouse. It warmed her that John still knew who was in charge of the boat, and she wondered if he had requested this calm day from the Almighty for their picnic.

Ross and Ramsay each took a child and dressed them in their life vests with Dand only mildly complaining. She was glad for the extra sets of eyes to watch the children. Dand wasn't so much of a problem. Irene, though, didn't know her limitations when it came to tumbling over the side of the boat.

Once they were underway, Maggie saw John's joy—*pure, unobliterated joy!* He'd been wrong about the Indwaller—his statement about their fishing boat being *business only*. It didn't matter whether a boat was for business or pleasure, her husband loved being on the water, plain and simple.

Suddenly, Maggie knew she'd been wrong, too. She should've stayed out of it. She never should've induced the doctor to tell John he couldn't fish anymore.

"Come sit with me, wife." John picked up Irene and settled her on his knee.

Maggie joined him and leaned into him. "Are ye ready to return to fishing full time?"

He pulled back, as if taken off-guard, but settled back against her. "Aye. Ye understand, don't ye, that a man needs his work to feel whole?"

"I know." But it'd taken her a while to get there. "Ye'll be safe?"

"I'll be careful." John leaned over and kissed her, but Irene pushed her mother away.

"She's a daddy's girl," Maggie said, laughing. "I don't know what I'm going to do with her."

John kissed his daughter's head. "Don't change a thing. I love her to pieces. Because she's just like her mother."

∽◌∾

Ryn didn't see Tuck for the rest of the day while she and the retreat goers were in the ballroom. When they all gathered for dinner, she hoped Tuck would join them, but he didn't show. At the evening gathering, her anticipation grew, but once again, he didn't make an appearance. *What point was it for him to sign up, if he never attended?* Alone, Ryn toddled off to her bed in the castle, feeling disappointed and frustrated.

Unfortunately, Deydie was settled in the bedroom next to hers. The old woman had made it clear she'd be listening. "No shenanigans!" Deydie had repeated at least three times to Ryn tonight.

Ryn's double bed felt lonely. Repeatedly, she gave herself a talking to: *You can't go to Tuck's cottage. It would only undo all the work you've done.* She had trouble falling asleep, as her mind kept mulling over ways to sneak out and find him. She had to know what he meant: *It takes a while to find the right one.*

After a restless night, she climbed out of bed in the morning and quickly readied for the day. As she slid back the pocket doors to the ballroom, she half-expected to find Tuck waiting there for her, but the room was empty. *Too early. He'll be here later,* she assured herself. She glanced at his machine and beheld a curious sight. Overnight, his stack of quilt blocks had grown.

Have the other women contributed their blocks to his pile, trying to gain his favor? But Ryn didn't see a single love note with a phone number on it slipped among the blocks.

Ryn picked up the top block and examined it. The stitches were nearly perfect—close to the edge like an experienced appliquér.

Coira walked in then and caught Ryn fondling Tuck's quilt pieces.

"I worked with him late last night," Coira said. "He's a whiz when it comes to sewing. He can make them faster than me now."

Ryn couldn't believe he'd been down here...with her upstairs! If only she'd come down for a glass of milk!

A group of quilters walked into the ballroom, chatting, and settled themselves behind their machines.

Because they were here now, Ryn couldn't find out more about Tuck. Also, she couldn't probe Coira too much, without giving her a clue as to how she felt.

Ryn walked to the front with purpose and positioned two of the full length vertical pieces on the design wall. Her emotions were a shambles. She wanted Tuck, but she couldn't have him. While she messed with her quilt pieces, her eyes kept a lookout for the first sign of Tuck's arrival.

As the minutes ticked away, Ryn's hopes fell. Finally, Deydie waddled in with a steaming mug in her beefy hand. She cleared her throat and tapped the men's watch she wore on her thick wrist. Ryn took the hint and got on with the class.

The morning dragged on and she had to keep reminding herself to be pleasant, though she desperately wanted Tuck to join the retreat again.

At eleven, Coira came to the front and announced the retreat was over. She stood by Ryn as the quilters packed up their things.

"Let's leave Tuck's machine up in case he wants to come back again tonight," Coira said. "I'll text him and let him know."

And while you're at it, could you ask him where in the hell he was today? But Ryn stopped herself from saying it, hoping her expression was as neutral as the background fabric in a quilt.

Deydie and Coira guided the quilters to their bus, which would take them back to Dumfries. Ryn and Sophie stayed behind to put the room back as it was.

Sophie looked ready to ask her a million questions. "That was something, wasn't it?"

At first Ryn thought she was speaking about the retreat, but she couldn't be so lucky.

"Tuck, I mean. I can't believe he stood up to Deydie like he did yesterday. He must care for you an awful lot."

He probably just wanted to get into my pants again, like all the others. By now though, Ryn knew that wasn't true. *Tuck is different.* He wasn't a bastard at all. He was a caring and decent guy.

"I don't know," Ryn said honestly to Sophie's statement. "I have no idea why he joined the retreat."

Sophie picked up his machine and put it on the smaller table Coira had brought in. "I know why. He couldn't stand to be away from ye."

"I doubt that."

Even if that was true, it didn't do Ryn any good. Tuck was a wonderful man, but he couldn't be part of her future. He'd made it clear he didn't want any kids. Which might have been fine before...

Since speaking with Cait about her college roommate, Ryn's mindset had changed, and hope had taken root. Maybe she could have children, a husband, and a loving family. She deserved to have those things, didn't she?

But the insurmountable wall stood high between her and Tuck, and made more complicated, because she knew how Tuck felt about abortion. If they were together, *really together*, she wouldn't keep that kind of secret from him. Those kinds of omissions had a tendency to fester and kill a relationship.

No. They were better off not together. She and Tuck could never be a real couple.

Ryn didn't leave the castle until four, carrying her dinner in a sack Mrs. McNabb handed to her as she left. She began walking down the road back to the cottage she'd been borrowing from Hugh and Sophie. With the retreat over, she had a lot to think about.

What was she going to do next? A big blank stared back at her. Maybe it was time to go home. Pick back up where she'd left off.

She was surprised when she'd made it all the way down the hill and up again without noticing a single tree or rock along the way. It was as if she'd been transported there, twenty feet away from her cottage. She was even more surprised to see Tuck on his small porch, sitting on a kitchen chair, staring at his phone. He looked up just as her eyes landed on him. He stood.

"I've been waiting for you," he said. "We should talk. Come inside."

The last time they'd been in his cottage, she'd ended up in his bed. "No." She couldn't afford to spend time with him and break her heart further when she left. Which would be soon. Very soon. Tomorrow maybe. She pulled out the key to open her door.

He was there and took the key from her, giving her a bit of *déjà vu.* He unlocked the door and pushed it open. "There are things I need to say."

"Fine. But I'm tired and I want to go to bed."

He gave her a hopeful smile. "Sounds good to me."

"That's not what I meant. I'm tired and need sleep. But first, I have to know. Tell me why you didn't come back to the retreat."

"A big problem at the mill with a big order that needed to be filled. It took until an hour ago to get it fixed." He shut the door and stood before her, a serious man. "Ryn, I don't know what happened between us. We were getting along so well."

We were naked, was the reason.

He took a step closer. "Why did you shut me out?"

She dropped her things on the table, frustrated with him. "What we have, Tuck, is just a fling. Nothing more."

He hung his thumbs on his jean pockets. "What if I want it to be more?"

Why couldn't he just leave her in peace? "It can't be more."

"Why can't it?" he said, glaring at her now, the tough man wanting his way.

She let the silence speak for her.

"Talk to me, Ryn." He shook his head as his eyes glanced heavenward, as if God would have to intercede to help him control his temper. "Whatever it is, we'll work through it. Together. Now tell me."

"It's not something we can work out. We're temporary." *I knew it from the moment you told me about Elspeth and the abortion.*

"Is this about me saying I didn't want a family?" Tuck said. "I told John it was a stupid idea."

"What are you talking about?" Ryn said.

Tuck's cheeks grew crimson and he turned away. "I asked John's advice about something."

"About what?"

"Listen," Tuck started. "John said I should drop hints and let you know that I don't need a big family."

"John? I don't understand." What had Tuck been telling people?

"Forget John," Tuck said, looking frustrated. "I've been trying to tell you I don't need a cottage full of bairns to be happy." He paused, giving her a sad, pitying look. "I know ye can't have kids."

"Where did you get that idea?" Ryn said, incredulous.

"I didn't mean to, but I overhead ye talking to Cait."

"Cait?" But in the next second, she remembered. *Oh, God, did Tuck hear the rest?*

He took her hand. "Ye see, I made my peace with it."

Ryn jerked her hand away. She grabbed for the kitchen chair to steady herself.

Tuck wasn't done punishing her. "Luv, kids aren't a deal breaker for me."

This is so frustrating! She was tired of tiptoeing around Tuck. Tired of keeping the truth from him. Something inside her snapped. "Kids aren't a deal breaker, but I'm sure abortion is!" It was better to put their relationship out of its misery now, with one fell swoop, than let it drag out until her broken heart couldn't be repaired. Too late, though. Her heart was a goner.

Momentarily Tuck looked confused. "Abortion?"

Ryn threw her bag at him, and she wasn't even the *throwing-stuff-at-people* type of girl. Then he pissed her off more when he caught it, instead of letting it knock him upside the head.

"Yeah, abortion," she said ruefully. "You made it abundantly clear how you feel about women who have had them."

"What are you talking about?" Tuck said. "You can't know if ye're pregnant. We only just had sex."

It was her turn to roll her eyes now. "Listen closely, dude. This has nothing to do with you or us *getting it on*. Apparently, when you were eavesdropping, you didn't stick around for the juicy part of the conversation."

"I'd heard more than I should've." At least he looked contrite for listening in.

She shook her head, knowing how this would drive a stake through the heart of whatever good feelings he had for her. But she had to push on. "It's not that I can't get pregnant—" she started "—I just believed I didn't deserve to have children." Her hand went to her chest...to calm her pounding heart.

"That's ridiculous, Ryn. How could you feel like ye don't deserve children? Ye're the best person I know. You'd make a wonderful mother."

"You don't get it!" Her patience was gone and she barreled ahead recklessly. "I've had an abortion! I was fifteen when I got knocked up, and my mother took me to the clinic to take care of it!" If she wasn't so tired, she might've told him the whole horrid tale with candor and calm dignity. But as it was, she was yelling. She glared at him, needing him to despise her as much as he despised his ex. If he walked out now, hating her, that might be the only way she'd survive loving Tuck.

You'll never stop loving him, that damn little voice taunted.

But she hadn't told him the crux of the story. And part of her wanted to save-face. It would only take four words, too. "Essentially, I was raped."

Ryn watched as her news covered Tuck, as if it was sticky tar. He seemed to have trouble breathing, but he recovered quickly. His brows crashed together, his face turned an angry red, and he looked as though he might explode.

She hoped he would say something. *Anything.* But he was no longer acting like *Chatty Cathy.* She should've been prepared, because sure enough, he marched out the door without so much as an *adios* or a wave goodbye.

Tears sprang to her eyes and she didn't stop them. She might as well cry. There would be tears for a long time to come for this one. For this was the first man who was worth keeping.

Tuck was the love of her life.

But now he was the one who got away.

23

T UCK STARTED THE CAR and headed for Gandiegow. He needed the long drive to process what Ryn had just told him. *Abortion! Rape! What the hell!*

He used to have a clue as to what was coming around the bend, but that was before he met Ryn. The only thing he knew for sure was that he had to get away. He needed time to think, alone.

Thank God, Andrew had texted him, not a half hour ago, asking for a favor. His brother wanted him to watch Glenna overnight so he and Moira could go into Inverness for an impromptu getaway. What's weird was that Andrew could've gotten any number of Gandiegowans to watch Glenna, but Tuck wasn't going to argue with the legitimate excuse to flee.

The road stretched out before him, his thoughts all consuming. He was so conflicted.

Ryn and Elspeth had more in common than their appearances. They shared an experience, too. But with some vast differences.

Elspeth was seventeen and had finished secondary school when she turned up pregnant.

Elspeth chose to have her abortion with her *baby-daddy* driving her to the clinic, not being forced there by her mother.

And Elspeth hadn't been raped. Ryn had! She'd been the victim. And Tuck wanted to punch the son-of-a-bitch who had hurt her! He saw red and drove faster.

He couldn't believe all the other feelings he was having. Like being pissed at Elspeth again! But he'd only just forgiven her!

One of Andrew's old sermons came back to Tuck. *Forgiveness isn't a one shot and done deal. It's an ongoing process, which has to be repeated again and again. But take heart! Once you've forgiven once, forgiving again, becomes easier and easier.*

And hell, another sermon hit him over the head, too. *Not forgiving someone is like drinking poison and expecting the other person to die.*

Tuck sucked in a deep breath and lifted his foot off the gas pedal, not wanting to put off what needed to be done for another fifteen years. "I forgive you, Elspeth." Moments later, he felt less angry. But forgiving Elspeth only left more room for him to dwell on Ryn.

Maybe he should've said something before he stomped out on her. But he probably would've only made things worse. How could he explain that he'd loved Elspeth, but only in the way of a teenager—fueled by hormones with no real understanding of the depths of a man's commitment. Loving Elspeth didn't come close to how he felt about Ryn!

Tuck laughed. "Oh, shite. I love Ryn." He felt elated, relieved, and was absolutely certain everything was going to be all right with them.

He wanted nothing more than to turn the car around, but he was almost to Gandiegow by now and he'd promised Andrew he would come.

Tuck drove down the hill and parked in the lot. The second he was out of the car, he pulled out his phone. He had to tell Ryn he loved her. But his phone wasn't working—not a single bar. Maybe he'd have better service when he got to Andrew's.

As he headed into town, there was an extra bounce to his step.

"Hey, Tuck," Ross called from the deck of the Indwaller. "Can ye stop by for a second?"

Tuck glanced at his watch, then hollered back to Ross, "For a minute." He jogged over to him.

As he headed down the dock, Ramsay and John appeared from the Indwaller's wheelhouse, and all looked right with the Armstrong brothers. Tuck couldn't help but smile...John had worked things out. As Tuck boarded, he touched the wooden cross.

"I'm glad I saw you," Ross said. "We wanted to call and talk to you, but Gandiegow doesn't have any mobile services until Wednesday."

"Or so they say," Ramsay said. "I expect it will take a mite longer. Our cell tower and internet are being upgraded."

A flash of panic hit Tuck. How was he going to let Ryn know everything was okay between them? This was something that couldn't wait.

John stepped forward, looking every bit the captain again. "Listen, the lads and I have talked. We appreciate all you've done, picking up the slack, while I was away."

Tuck felt a *but* coming on.

"*But* ye've worn yourself ragged and ye don't need to do it any longer. I think ye're needed more in Whussendale than here now." John's voice was strong, confident, sounding more like himself than ever.

Ramsay pounded Tuck on the back. "Aye. From what I hear, there's a certain American lass there that *needs* ye more than us."

Tuck glared at John, hoping he hadn't told his brothers everything, especially about Ryn not being able to have children. John seemed to understand his concern and shook his head no, which put Tuck at ease.

"Leave the man alone, Ramsay," Ross said. "Have some compassion. You of all people should remember what you went through to get yere wife, Kit. We certainly do."

"And with yereself and Sadie," Ramsay volleyed back.

Tuck hadn't been there for any of it, but he'd heard the stories. "All right. This is actually good timing. Only yesterday, Hugh asked me when I could go fulltime at the wool mill." And with Ryn in Whussendale with him, he wouldn't regret leaving Andrew in Gandiegow.

John held out his left hand. "Thank you for everything."

Tuck took it and shook. The moment felt pivotal, as if his world was shifting back into place.

"Aye, thanks," both Ross and Ramsay said, thumping Tuck on the back.

And wasn't it just like the Universe, to have him feel welcomed here in Gandiegow just as he realized his future lay in Whussendale?

Tuck nodded to the Armstrong brothers. "Andrew is expecting me." He stepped off the boat and left them to it.

When he arrived at the parsonage, Andrew opened the door. Tuck walked into the quiet house and looked around. It seemed neither Moira or Glenna was there.

"Where are the lassies?" Tuck asked.

Andrew followed him into the parlor. "Sit down, Tuck."

Panic washed over Tuck. Andrew's tone was the same as when he'd told him about John's accident.

"Is everyone okay? Moira? Glenna?"

Andrew sat across from him. "Everyone's fine. You and I need to talk."

"What's with all the gloom and doom?" Tuck asked. "I'm in no mood for an intervention, or whatever it is ye have going on here."

"It's not an intervention. It's something that needs to be said from one brother to another." Andrew had always been so serious, and now wasn't any different. "Ye work too hard, Tuck. And I think it's time for ye to move home, here to the parsonage."

"What are you talking about?" Tuck's new life was all set to begin in Whussendale. And for the first time in his life, he wanted to put down roots. *Deep ones.*

"Ye can't run away from yere problems anymore." Andrew gave him a concerned look. "It's time for ye to forgive yereself, and stop working yereself to death. John has forgiven ye. Now do yereself a favor and forgive yereself, too."

Tuck finally put a name to the feeling he had when John shook his hand. It wasn't just the guilt lifting. It must've been the start of forgiving himself for what he'd done to John.

"I'm okay," Tuck said. "John and I talked about it some. And I'm starting to realize it wasn't completely my fault."

Andrew nodded. "It was only an accident."

"Aye," Tuck said.

"Then move home. We miss ye."

"You don't understand," Tuck said. "I can't. I'm going to live in Whussendale."

"If ye're worried about the villagers of Gandiegow, they will accept ye eventually. I promise ye, all will right itself."

"That's not it. Whussendale is my home now. It's where I want to live. With Ryn."

"Ryn?" Andrew said, looking shocked.

"I love her." It felt good to tell his brother. "And if ye had any phone service in this blasted town right now, I'd call and tell her myself. This very minute."

"You haven't said anything to her yet?"

Tuck shook his head. "I only just figured it out on the drive here."

A knock sounded at the door. Andrew stood to get it. "Don't go anywhere. We're not done talking about this."

A moment later, Andrew led Brodie into the parlor.

"Brodie's here to see ye."

Brodie nodded. "I heard ye were in town. I could use some help on the morning run. What do you say?"

Brodie wouldn't ask unless he really needed someone. But Tuck also knew every fisherman in town was being more cautious, safer, since John's accident.

"Sure. I can help in the morn." Tuck glanced at his watch. It was six already. He was anxious to get back to Ryn and tell her how he felt. He turned back to his brother. "Do you and Moira really have a date, or was it just a ploy to get me here to have a talk?"

Andrew nodded, smiling. "We have a date. Moira and Glenna are waiting for us at Quilting Central. They were giving us some privacy."

Andrew, Brodie, and Tuck left the parsonage together, heading to Quilting Central. Tuck took a deep breath and reminded himself of what Andrew had said: *All will be right*.

He took comfort in his brother's words. Ryn wasn't going anywhere. He would see her when he got back.

ᏮᎧᏟᎧ

The morn was bright and full of promise. With pastry box in hand, Maggie rushed back to Quilting Central, knowing Sinnie and Rowena couldn't watch Irene for too long. Deydie had chores for them to do. But the perfect day and calm sea called to Maggie to take a moment to glance out at the water. Off in the distance, she could see the Indwaller sitting on the North Sea's horizon, the vessel sunning herself in the morning sun. She knew John was there—captain of the boat, content, at home on the water—and she wondered how she could have ever asked him to give up what he loved most, besides God and his family.

When she turned back to run her errand, a stranger strode toward her, a fortyish man with an expectant look on his face.

Maggie slowed. "Are ye looking for something?"

Forty smiled, his expression appreciative. "Aye. *Looking for someone.* I'm looking for Tuck MacBride. The hospital said he hailed from here."

Hailed wasn't the correct word, for Tuck had only squatted in Gandiegow. He was only in the village today temporarily. John told her Tuck planned to live in Whussendale permanently.

Just thinking about Tuck, brought vinegar to her mouth, ruining her lovely morning. John may have forgiven Tuck, but she never would. Aye, she'd figured out it was Tuck who'd been funneling money to her family. When she saw him next, she was going to tell him to knock it off. She and John were going to be okay and she'd been making plans—planning to take odd jobs, to be better set up for the future. But Tuck doing something decent for them didn't make up for what he'd done.

Maggie put her thoughts aside and answered *Forty*. "I was told Tuck's fishing today with Brodie." She glanced out at the water, but didn't see Brodie's vessel. "I'm sure he'll be back soon from the morning run. Is there something I can help ye with?" That's when she remembered *Forty* had said something about the hospital. "Hospital? What hospital?"

Forty smiled. "In Inverness. I'm here to thank Mr. MacBride for saving my life."

"What?" Maggie couldn't wrap her brain around it.

"Aye. My name is Raymond Martin. Tuck stopped to help me on the road. He put me in his car and drove me to the hospital. I was on my way to my sister's house, but then I had a heart attack."

Maggie couldn't believe it. Why didn't she know this? Why didn't they all know? "Tuck never said a word. When did this happen?"

"April 14th, in the wee hours of the morning."

Maggie knew the date. It had been seared in her mind. *The day of John's accident.*

Maggie pointed to Quilting Central. "Come with me. The others need to hear yere story." For she was having a hard time processing the news and needed support.

Not two paces later, Dougal the postie, came out of the General Store with his mailbag over his shoulder, heading toward the car park.

Maggie hollered, "Dougal, wait up a second." She dug in her pocket and pulled out the pad and pencil she'd placed there for calculating the yardage for a quilt. "Can ye put a note on Tuck's car for me?"

"Certainly," Dougal said.

She wrote out the note: Come to Quilting Central. You have a visitor.

⁞⁞⁞

From the edge of the car park, Tuck saw the flapping, white piece of paper under his windshield wiper and felt exasperated. "What now?" He felt good about helping Brodie this morning, but now he needed to get home to Ryn.

He read the note, but didn't recognize the handwriting. His first inclination was to ignore it, and if questioned later, he'd say it must've blown away in the wind. But maybe the visitor at Quilting Central was Ryn! Besides, he knew better than to *not go to* Quilting Central when summoned. Deydie probably wanted him to move something that weighed enough to give him a hernia. *More payback.*

He left the car park and headed back into the village, wishing like crazy for cell service. When he got to Quilting Central, he slipped inside, hoping not to interrupt the class. But the way the whole room turned in his direction, it was as if they were waiting on him!

Tuck's eyes fell on the outsider, who seemed familiar. Then he recognized the man—*Raymond!*—now looking healthier than the last time he'd seen him.

"Tuck, get up here," Deydie hollered. "Why didn't ye say anything to us, ye bampot?"

He trudged to the front.

A smiling Raymond broke away from Deydie, and with hand extended, met Tuck halfway.

"I'll never be able to repay ye." Raymond turned the handshake into a *bro* hug.

"I just did what anyone would've done," Tuck said.

"Ye saved my life!"

"Nay. The doctors did that." Tuck wanted to disappear. Or just to get out of here. But more importantly, he wanted to be on his way to Whussendale.

Bethia patted a chair. "Both of ye come sit. I'll get you some tea and biscuits."

The group squeezed in, effectively ushering the two of them in Bethia's direction. But Tuck stopped short when Maggie stepped in his path. Her lips were pressed together in more of a contemplative expression than a frown.

She put her hand out to keep him from going farther. "Wait. I'll say something first."

The room went silent and she turned all her attention on Tuck. "I've made it clear how I've felt about ye. I've berated ye and treated ye badly." Deydie moved next to her and held her arm, as if supporting her through her confession. "I was wrong, Tuck. I'm ashamed of myself for how I acted. I ask ye to forgive me."

With Maggie's last words, the room collectively exhaled.

Tuck was in shock, but Maggie's piercing blue eyes implored him to answer. "Of course, ye're forgiven. It's completely forgotten."

Bethia flanked Maggie's other side, patting her back. "That's a good lass."

Maggie turned to speak to the rest of them. "This is what I have to say to ye. If John can forgive Tuck, and if I can forgive him, then ye should, too!"

Deydie cleared her throat. "I'm sorry, too." She peered around the group. "We all are. Ye're not the bad egg, Tuck, that we thought ye were. Now, go sit down and have some refreshments."

Tuck did what he was told, but begrudgingly. *This is all well and good, but I need to get home to talk to Ryn.*

୫୦୧୫

Ryn spent the morning in Whussendale, closing down her life in Scotland. First, she used the internet to track down the shuttle company and then she called Peter, who'd brought her to the wool village in the first place. She made arrangements for him to pick her up later. Next, she found Coira and turned over her notes of what she'd learned about running a retreat. Before leaving Kilheath Castle for the last time, she said goodbye to Mrs. McNabb and then gave big hugs to both the Wallace and the Bruce.

Last night, using the money Deydie paid her for teaching the retreat, Ryn bought a cheap one-way ticket to Minneapolis. What she would do after she arrived in Minnesota was anyone's guess. Finally, she'd spoken with Sophie about giving her a ride to Gandiegow so she could wish her cousin Maggie well, and deliver the Goodbye quilt in person.

The only thing left for Ryn to do was to pack her completed True Colors quilt in her bag. She spread it out on the bed to fold it, but had a better idea instead. She slipped off her shoes, climbed up on the mattress, and hung the True Colors quilt where the Goodbye quilt had been over her bed. "I hope you'll be a useful warning to the next woman who comes to Whussendale. That a man's *true colors* always reveal themselves."

She stepped off the bed and returned her shoes to her feet. She spied her Featherweight sewing machine sitting beside her luggage at the door. "You're going to stay behind, too. Back in Minnesota, I wouldn't be able to use you anyway." She hoped the next occupant of the cottage liked to quilt, too.

As she slipped on her jacket, she took one last look about her cozy, temporary home. She'd loved it here, but now it was time to move on. She opened the door, rolled her bag out, and locked the door behind her, just as Sophie pulled up with the car.

Ryn put her baggage in the back and then climbed into the passenger's seat, holding out the cottage's key to return it. "I think this is the last thing to do."

Sophie slipped the key into her pocket, before putting the car in gear. "I thought about it overnight. Ye have to stay. Coira needs you to help get the Whussendale Retreat Center up and running."

"Coira will be fine," Ryn assured her.

Sophie gave her a meaningful glance. "Work things out with Tuck."

"There's nothing to work out."

Because Ryn didn't want to discuss it, she pulled out the *my-mom-died* card again. "Don't you think I've been through enough lately?" She didn't have the energy to feel guilty about using it either.

Sophie reached across the seat and grabbed Ryn's hand. "Aye. Ye've been through plenty."

The rest of the ride was quiet, but Ryn was feeling far from peaceful. What made matters worse was to see Tuck's car as they made their way down the hill to Gandiegow's parking lot. She told herself she didn't care he was here in the village. Or on the boat. Her mission was the same as it was on her first day in Scotland. See Maggie and give her the Goodbye quilt.

Sophie parked the car, but turned to Ryn first, before getting out. "Do ye want me to go with you to Maggie's cottage? I'm happy to keep you company."

"No. I'll go alone. I need to call the shuttle first and make sure Peter will be here on time. I'm going to go to the airport soon. Can I leave my bags here in the car?"

"Sure. I'll leave it unlocked."

Sophie leaned over and hugged Ryn fiercely. "I'm going to miss ye. I loved having you in Whussendale."

"I'll miss you, too," Ryn said back.

Sophie hopped out and hurried away from the car, saying she was off to visit with her mother.

Ryn pulled out her phone, but didn't have any service. *Oh, well.* She wouldn't worry as the shuttle should be here soon. Her flight wasn't leaving until much later in the day, but it was better to hang around at the airport than chance running into Tuck here in Gandiegow.

Clean breaks hurt like hell, but in the long run pulling the bandage off quickly should help her to heal faster. Deep down, though, she knew she would never recover from this one.

Ryn picked up the Goodbye quilt from the seat and headed into the village. She was grateful Deydie had pointed out Maggie's cottage on her first day here. She really didn't want to stop at Quilting Central to ask where it was.

Gandiegow was small and it only took her a few minutes to get to Maggie's door and knock.

John answered with wet hair and seemed surprised to see her. "'Morning, Ryn. Tuck's not here."

Hearing Tuck's name didn't help Ryn's nerves. "I'm looking for Maggie. Is she at home?"

"Nay. She's at Quilting Central. There's a stitch-in today. I was just heading there myself to pick up Irene. Should we walk there together then?"

"Sure." Ryn hoped they wouldn't run into Tuck.

John grabbed a jacket and shut the door behind him. "So what are ye doing in Gandiegow?"

Ryn held up the quilt. "I brought this for Maggie."

"Ye didn't have to do that. She and the bairns are off to Whussendale to see Coira in the morn."

"I won't be there," Ryn said honestly. "I'm headed home today."

John stopped walking. "Home? Is Tuck going with ye?"

Why did everyone assume they were together? "No."

"Does he know that ye're leaving?" John reached for his phone, as if he already knew the answer. "Dammit. No service." He looked over at the dock where the boats were tied. "And he and Brodie are already back to town."

Ryn touched his arm. "It's okay. We're not together."

"Does he know that?"

"Of course." Though she hadn't exactly said goodbye to him. Which wasn't completely her fault. She really didn't have the chance as he'd stomped out the door and away from her.

John looked worried. "I'll take ye to Maggie."

When they walked into Quilting Central, Maggie was standing near the door, holding Irene. The child squealed and put out her arms when she saw her father.

Maggie seemed surprised to see Ryn, as she transferred Irene over to John. During the shift, Ryn caught sight of Tuck, being pleasantly mobbed by the people of Gandiegow—everyone talking to him and patting him on the back.

"What's going on here?" Ryn asked Maggie. "I thought Gandiegow didn't like Tuck."

Maggie laughed. "It doesn't happen often, but Gandiegow has changed its mind."

"Tell me what's happened." Ryn couldn't believe how everyone smiled at him.

Maggie pointed to the man sitting beside Tuck at the small café table. "Do you see him? That's Raymond Martin. Tuck saved his life. He found him in his car along the road and took him to the hospital."

"Yes, he told me about that," Ryn said.

Maggie looked incredulous. "Really? Well, he never told any of us. Not even a hint of what he'd done."

Ryn hated to cut this short, but she had to go. Though she tried, she couldn't stop her eyes from volleying over to Tuck. Finally, she held out the quilt to her cousin. "I wanted to make sure you had this before I leave."

"Leave?" Reluctantly, Maggie took the quilt. "But ye only just got here."

"I'm headed home today." Sadness engulfed Ryn that she and Maggie never got to connect. Not really.

"You can't leave," Maggie gently touched her arm. "There's so much we need to talk about...like yere mother."

Ryn shook her head, feeling doubly sad. "My ride to the airport is on its way." She put her hand on the doorknob. "Goodbye."

Ryn caught the moment Tuck saw her standing there. He was up and out of his chair in a flash, taking long strides toward her. Maggie gripped her arm tighter, as if making sure Ryn couldn't bolt.

Tuck stopped inches away. "Ryn? What are ye doing here? Why aren't ye home in Whussendale?"

"Ryn's leaving." Maggie raised an eyebrow as if she'd tossed the ball in Tuck's court.

Tuck nodded to Maggie. "Don't worry. She's not going anywhere. I've got this." He took a hold of Ryn's arm. "We need to talk. Outside. Now."

♋

Tuck gazed down at the woman he loved. Ryn laid her hand over his and his heart thundered with happiness. But he and his heart had

308

it wrong. She used that hand to unhinge him from her.

"Fine," she clipped. "I'll talk to you outside, but only if we walk toward the parking lot. The shuttle will be here soon to take me to the airport." She stepped out and he followed.

Airport? "Ye can't be serious."

"Yes, I'm serious." She put her hands on her hips. "You made it abundantly clear how you feel about me, when I last saw you, stomping from the cottage." With the sea as her backdrop and with her cinnamon-colored hair swirling around her, she looked like a warrioress—on fire, determined, and strong.

Tuck reached for her again, but stopped. "Ye're right. I did a horrible job of it, didn't I?"

"Not my problem." She glared at him. "I can't change the past. I know how you feel. You can't get beyond what I did."

"That's not true. I am past it." He touched her arm for a brief second. "I reacted like an idiot and left because I was in shock. Plain and simple. I had one thing in my head—*that you couldn't have children*—and I was thrown off balance when ye were speaking of something completely different." He reached for her again, but she stepped back. "Ryn, I'd talked myself into never having a family, because I want to be with you. I don't care if we have kids of our own or not. The important thing is that I wake up every morning next to you."

She cocked her head to the side as if she hadn't heard him correctly and her mouth opened slightly. She was the one looking shocked now.

"Aye. Ye heard me right." He took advantage of her state and gathered her into his arms. "I love ye dearly, Ryn. You gotta know my heart and soul belong to you. From almost the beginning, I knew the truth, though I had a rough time admitting I could love again."

Bringing up Elspeth might've been the wrong thing to say, because Ryn pulled away.

"I don't know, Tuck. I'm afraid you think you love me, because you once loved her. Remember, I look like your Elspeth."

He shook his head and smiled. "Nay. No resemblance, a'tall. You, Kathryn Iona Breckenridge, are unique in every way. It's you I love. My one and only."

Ryn's eyes softened and he felt free to go on.

"Knowing you has made me want to be a better man. Before I met you, I never saw beyond the next day. But now, I see tomorrow, next year, and the years beyond. With you by my side, anything and everything is possible." He pulled her into his arms again. "I love you so very much. Please tell me that you love me, too."

She relaxed against him. "Oh, Tuck. Of course, I love you, too. From the first moment I saw your gorgeous face."

Tuck held her close for a long time. When he looked over, he saw the curtain pulled back at Quilting Central with the occupants gathered around the picture window. Every one of them had smiles on their faces. The sight of Gandiegow showing how they approved of him and Ryn together made Tuck smile back, too.

EPILOGUE

R YN HELPED MAGGIE lay out her quilting supplies in Kilheath Castle's ballroom. It paid to have Maggie's mother running the retreats in Whussendale, as they were able to secure the room for the weekend to work on a project together...just the two of them.

Maggie glanced up at Ryn and grinned. "So it's true?"

"Yes," Ryn said. "I'm due in July." It felt surreal. Her fairytale wedding to Tuck at the castle had been less than three months ago and now she was pregnant. Oh, how things had changed.

"Ye seem happy, really happy," Maggie said.

"I am."

Maggie laughed. "After we finish our Hello quilts, we better get started on a couple of baby quilts. One Modern and one traditional."

"I'm not having twins."

Maggie laughed. "Aye, but we don't yet know which the bairn will prefer—modern or traditional."

"You have a point." Ryn organized the fabrics into their prospective blocks.

"So tell me, Ryn. Cousin Kathy told me about yere family and the long line of Kathryn Ionas. If you have a girl, and name her Kathryn Iona, what are you and Tuck going to call her?"

"We're going to call her Ki, you know, using her initials."

"Awww, that's pretty. And if it's a boy?" Maggie prodded.

Ryn smiled at her. "Tuck came up with the name. He'll be John Andrew MacBride."

"Oh, Ryn," Maggie hugged her. "The name is lovely and John will be so pleased."

"A boy would be nice, but I'd really like to have a girl," Ryn said. "I'd love to see her and Irene playing dolls together. I'd like to teach her how to sew. There's so much I want to share with a girl…besides my same name." She wanted to teach her how to trust men. For her daddy had taught Ryn how to trust again.

Thinking of Tuck, reminded Ryn to pull out the wall-hanging he'd made, using the circle on a square blocks, he'd completed at the retreat. "It's finally finished. I quilted it for him."

Maggie examined the wall-hanging closely and then beamed at Ryn. "Who would've thought he would be so good at stitching."

"Never in a million years," Ryn said. "When I met him, I thought he was only good at being *gorgeous.*" She'd learned a lot since then. "He's such a good man."

"I know," Maggie agreed.

Coira leaned her head in. "You two better quit nattering on, or ye'll waste this time and space. Come Monday morning, I have a group of knitters coming to Whussendale, so ye're going to be ousted out of here on Sunday afternoon, no matter what."

"Hi, Mum," Maggie said. "Come sit with us later. If ye can."

"We'll see," Coira said. "I've a lot to do. Make sure you show Ryn yere Gandiegow Crossing Paths quilt." And she left.

Maggie laughed. "I'm glad she said something." She bent down and pulled a quilt from her bag. "I just took it off the frame." She spread it out.

"It's beautiful," Ryn said, remembering how she'd pieced the top together for her cousin.

Maggie beamed at her. "This quilt is extra special to me, because you helped me with it. We better do as Mum says and get to work, before the weekend is gone."

"Yes." Ryn retrieved the quilt design she'd drawn and laid it on the table. "What do you think?"

"I love how you used the Goodbye Quilt as your inspiration."

Instead of a tree sprouting up through the Sampler quilt, Ryn had decided on a swan. Tuck had traced one for her on a piece of paper. "Did I tell you that on my first day in Whussendale, I saw a swan on the loch?"

Maggie wrapped an arm around her waist and squeezed. "I'd forgotten about how much your mother loved swans. How about you add a cygnet—a baby swan to go with its mother?"

Ryn nodded. "I like it. It would fill the space better."

"You know, lately, all kinds of memories have been coming back to me about yere mum. Kathy and I used to get up to all kinds of trouble. I went along with her because she was older…and because I loved her so much." Maggie chuckled, as if remembering. "Would you like to hear some stories about me and her?"

"Yes." Tears came to Ryn's eyes.

Maggie dug in her pocket and pulled out a hankie. "Don't cry."

"It's probably the hormones making me mist up." But Ryn knew the truth. More than likely it was because all of her dreams had come true. A good man to love. A village to call home. And an honest-to-goodness family—Tuck's family and her own. She never imagined she could be this happy, and the best part was, this was only the beginning.

⊱⊰

KILTS & QUILTS™ POPPY SEED BREAD
COPYRIGHT©2018 BY LOUISE SITTON

Thank you, Louise, for sharing your recipe with Deydie and all of Gandiegow. (And us, too!)

3 cups flour
2 ½ cups sugar
1 ½ tsp baking powder
3 eggs
1 ½ cups milk
1 1/8 cups oil
1 ½ Tbsp poppy seed
1 ½ tsp vanilla
1 ½ tsp butter flavoring
1 ½ tsp almond extract

Preheat oven to 350°
Grease 2- 9X7 loaf pans.
Mix all ingredients in a large bowl. Beat for 2 minutes.
Bake for 45-60 minutes until center is done.
Pour glaze over loaves, while still hot.
Turn loaves out of pans while still warm.

Glaze:
¾ c sugar
¼ c orange juice
½ tsp vanilla
½ tsp almond extract
½ tsp butter flavoring

Mix all ingredients together until smooth, and then pour over bread.

If you enjoyed reading this book, please *recommend* it to your friends or your book club. And please *write a review*. Readers love them and authors depend on them. If you write a review for *Blame It on Scotland,* please let me know. I would like to **thank you** personally.

Email: patience@patiencegriffin.com

For Signed copies, visit:

www.PatienceGriffin.com

JOIN Patience's Newsletter!
...to find out about events, contests, and more!

www.PatienceGriffin.com

BOOKS by
PATIENCE GRIFFIN

—ഇര—

KILTS AND QUILTS SERIES:
ROMANTIC WOMEN'S FICTION

#1   *TO SCOTLAND WITH LOVE*

#2   *MEET ME IN SCOTLAND*

#2.5 *THE LAIRD AND I*

#3   *SOME LIKE IT SCOTTISH*

#4   *THE ACCIDENTAL SCOT*

#5   *THE TROUBLE WITH SCOTLAND*

#6   *IT HAPPENED IN SCOTLAND*

#7   *BLAME IT ON SCOTLAND*

—ഇര—

HAVE YOU BEEN TO WHUSSENDALE YET?

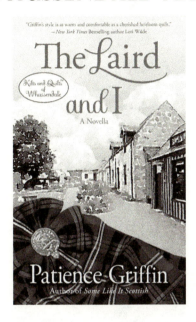

Last summer, Sophie Munro met Hugh McGillivray for the first time and she liked him instantly. But the dashing young Laird behaved as if she didn't exist…even though she was *Summer Sophie*—sunny and cheerful. Now in the dead of winter, *Winter Sophie* has arrived, and she's one despondent lass without her therapy light!

When Sophie receives a cryptic email from Hugh—*Can you housesit for me while I'm away?*—she's surprised, but agrees on one condition. While she's there, she wants to learn the ancient art of kiltmaking at his woolen mill. But mischief is afoot. The quilters of Gandiegow and Whussendale have plotted to bring the pair together, thinking they would make the perfect match. Hugh isn't so sure. Sophie has become indispensable as the kiltmaker's apprentice. And even the dogs like her best!

The Laird starts to realize Sophie's presence is healing his grieving heart, and he's doing his best to bring sunshine into her dark winter days. Will the Laird allow Sophie to leave when her time at Kilheath Castle is up? Or will he take a risk and keep her there forever?

FIRST IN THE
KILTS AND QUILTS SERIES

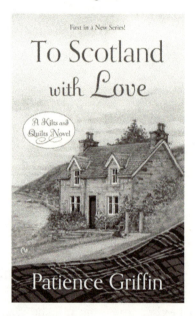

To Scotland with Love
Book 1, Kilts and Quilts

Amazon #1 Best Seller
Publishers Weekly starred review*
Double RITA® Finalist
New England Readers' Choice Best First Book
Golden Quill Best First Book

WELCOME TO THE CHARMING SCOTTISH

seaside town of Gandiegow—where two people have returned home for different reasons, but to find the same thing....

Caitriona Macleod gave up her career as an investigative reporter for the role of perfect wife. But after her husband is found dead in his mistress's bed, a devastated Cait leaves Chicago for the birthplace she hasn't seen since she was a child. She's hoping to heal and to reconnect with her gran. The last thing she expects to find in Gandiegow is the Sexiest Man Alive! She just may have stumbled on the ticket to reigniting her career—if her heart doesn't get in the way.

Graham Buchanan is a movie star with many secrets. A Gandiegow native, he frequently hides out in his hometown between films. He also has a son he'll do anything to protect. But Cait Macleod is too damn appealing—even if she is a journalist.

Quilting with her gran and the other women of the village brings Cait a peace she hasn't known in years. But if she turns in the story about Graham, Gandiegow will never forgive her for betraying one of its own. Should she suffer the consequences to resurrect her career? Or listen to her battered and bruised heart and give love another chance?

"Griffin's lyrical and moving debut marks her as a most talented new-comer to the romance genre."
-Publishers Weekly starred review

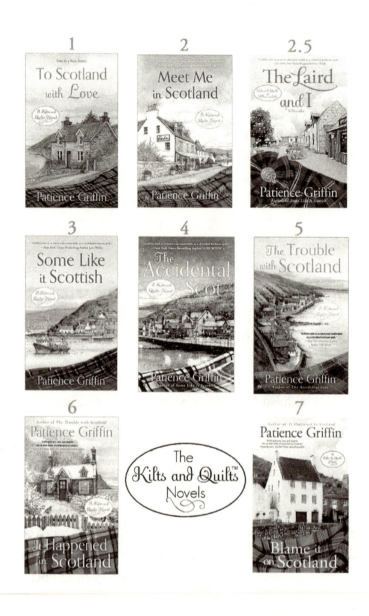

The Kilts and Quilts™ Novels

All materials herewith are protected under U.S. copyright laws.
Copyright © 2018 by Patience Griffin

Patience Griffin grew up in a small town along the Mississippi River. She has a master's degree in nuclear engineering but spends her days writing stories about hearth and home in the small towns of Gandiegow and Whussendale, Scotland.

Connect online at www.PatienceGriffin.com

CPSIA information can be obtained
at www.ICGtesting.com
Printed in the USA
LVHW04s1436060818
586123LV00005B/954/P